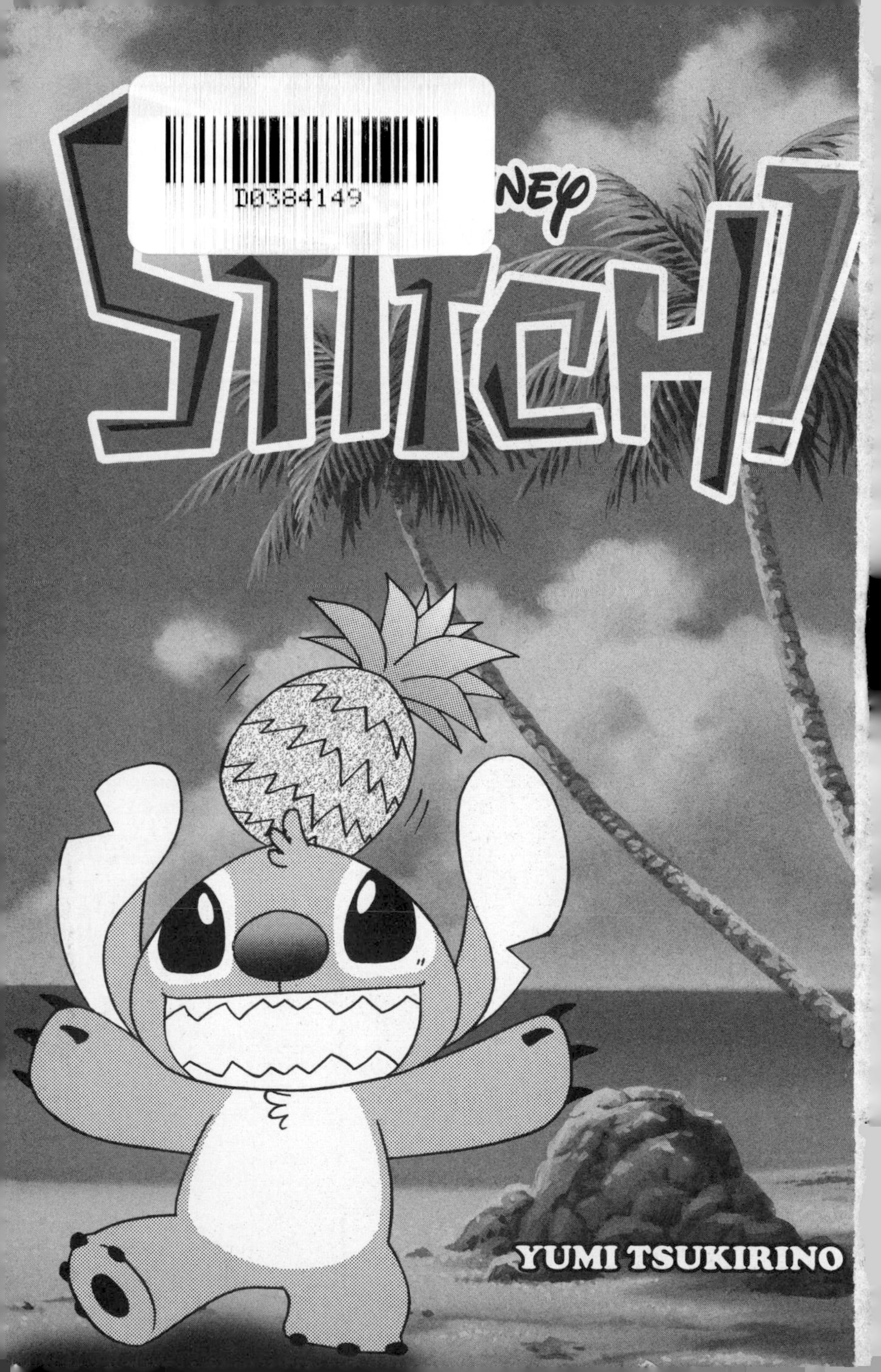
STITCH!
YUMI TSUKIRINO

CHARACTERS

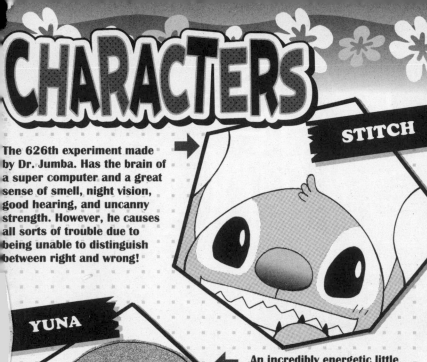

STITCH

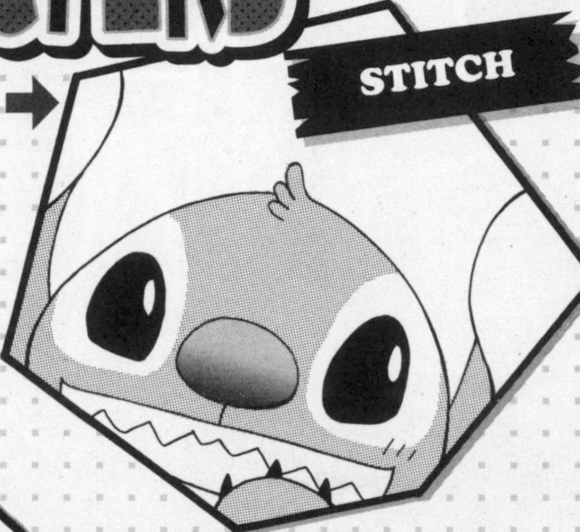

The 626th experiment made by Dr. Jumba. Has the brain of a super computer and a great sense of smell, night vision, good hearing, and uncanny strength. However, he causes all sorts of trouble due to being unable to distinguish between right and wrong!

YUNA

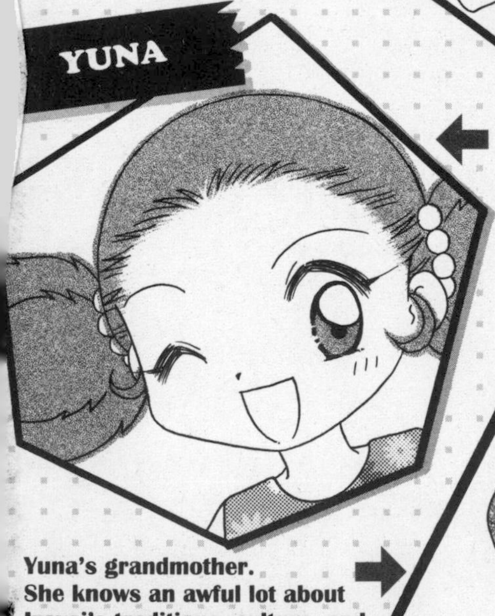

An incredibly energetic little girl living with Grandma on the Okinawan island of Izayoi. She is especially good at karate. As the next in line of the "Chitama-style Karate Dojo," she teaches karate to the students.

GRANDMA

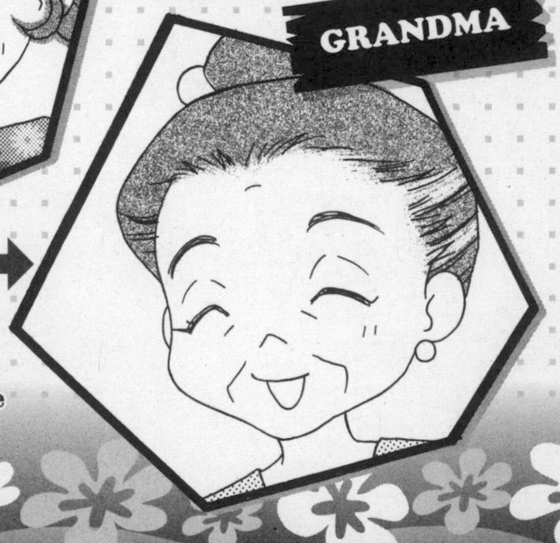

Yuna's grandmother.
She knows an awful lot about Izayoi's traditions, culture, and nature. In addition to those on Izayoi, she's also friends with yokai and spirits throughout the world.

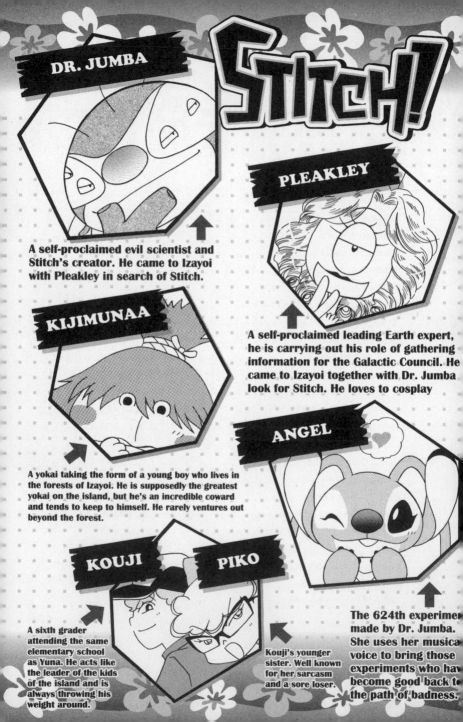

STITCH!

DR. JUMBA

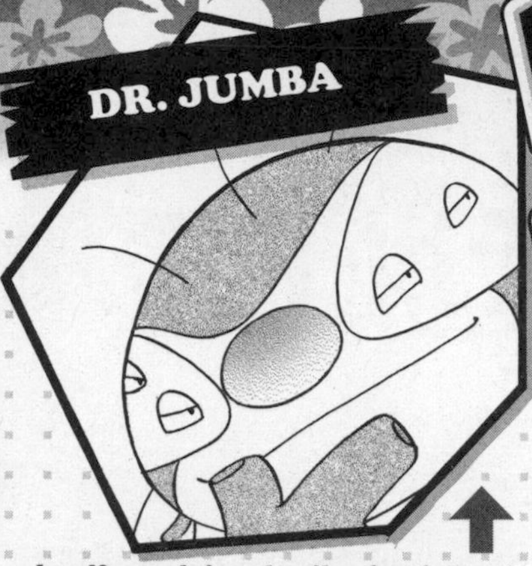

A self-proclaimed evil scientist and Stitch's creator. He came to Izayoi with Pleakley in search of Stitch.

PLEAKLEY

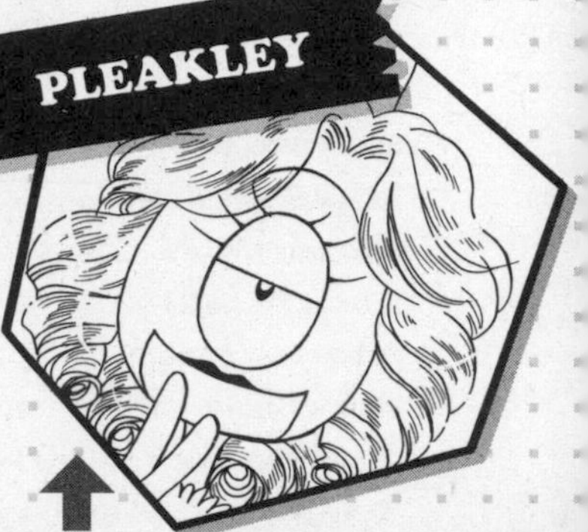

A self-proclaimed leading Earth expert, he is carrying out his role of gathering information for the Galactic Council. He came to Izayoi together with Dr. Jumba look for Stitch. He loves to cosplay

KIJIMUNAA

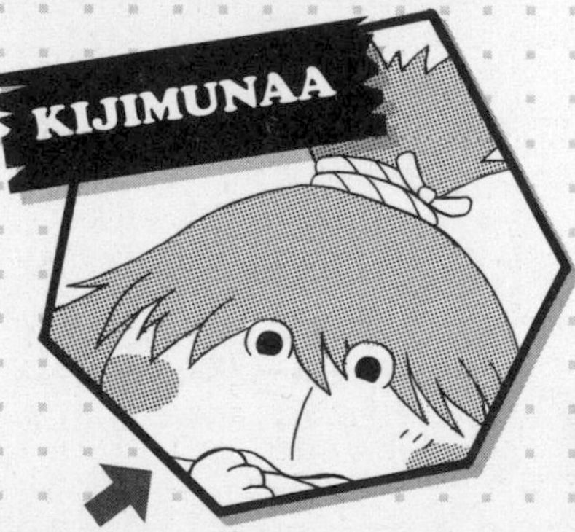

A yokai taking the form of a young boy who lives in the forests of Izayoi. He is supposedly the greatest yokai on the island, but he's an incredible coward and tends to keep to himself. He rarely ventures out beyond the forest.

ANGEL

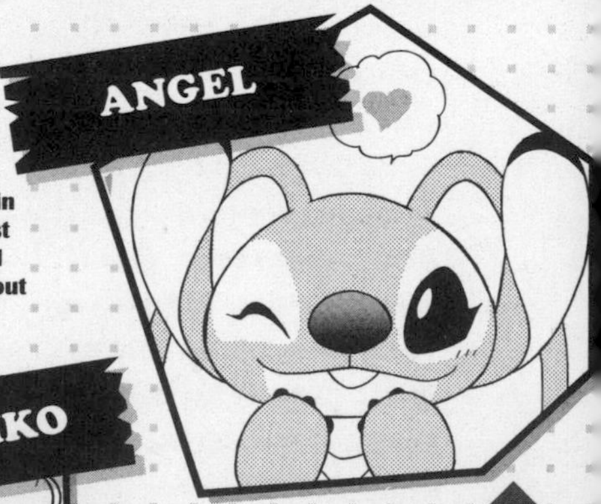

The 624th experimen made by Dr. Jumba. She uses her musica voice to bring those experiments who hav become good back t the path of badness.

KOUJI

PIKO

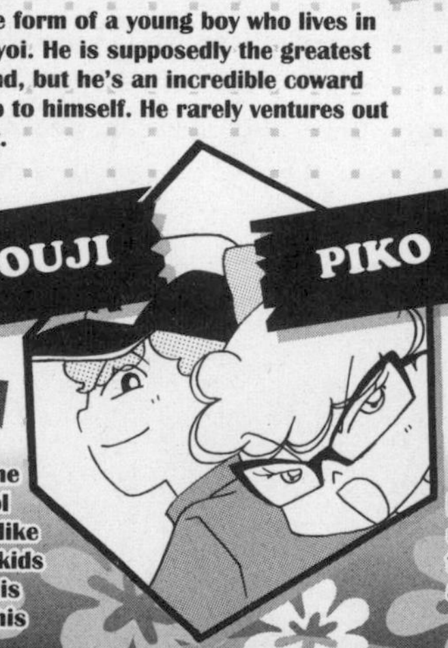

A sixth grader attending the same elementary school as Yuna. He acts like the leader of the kids of the island and is always throwing his weight around.

Kouji's younger sister. Well known for her sarcasm and a sore loser.

CONTENTS

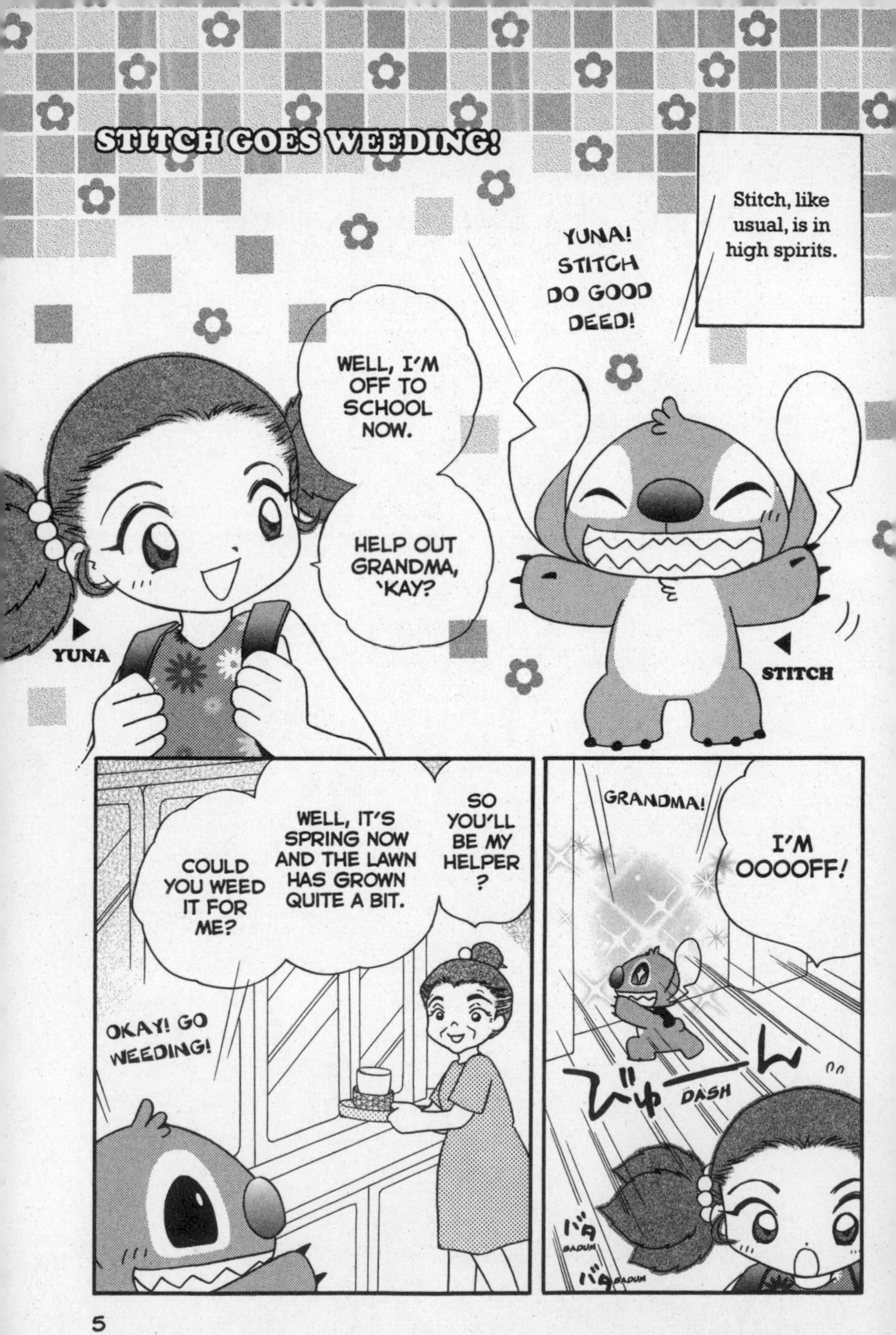
STITCH GOES WEEDING!
Stitch, like usual, is in high spirits.
YUNA! STITCH DO GOOD DEED!
WELL, I'M OFF TO SCHOOL NOW.
HELP OUT GRANDMA, 'KAY?
STITCH
YUNA
GRANDMA!
I'M OOOOFF!
びゅーん
DASH
バタ
BADUM
バタ
BADUM
SO YOU'LL BE MY HELPER?
WELL, IT'S SPRING NOW AND THE LAWN HAS GROWN QUITE A BIT.
COULD YOU WEED IT FOR ME?
OKAY! GO WEEDING!

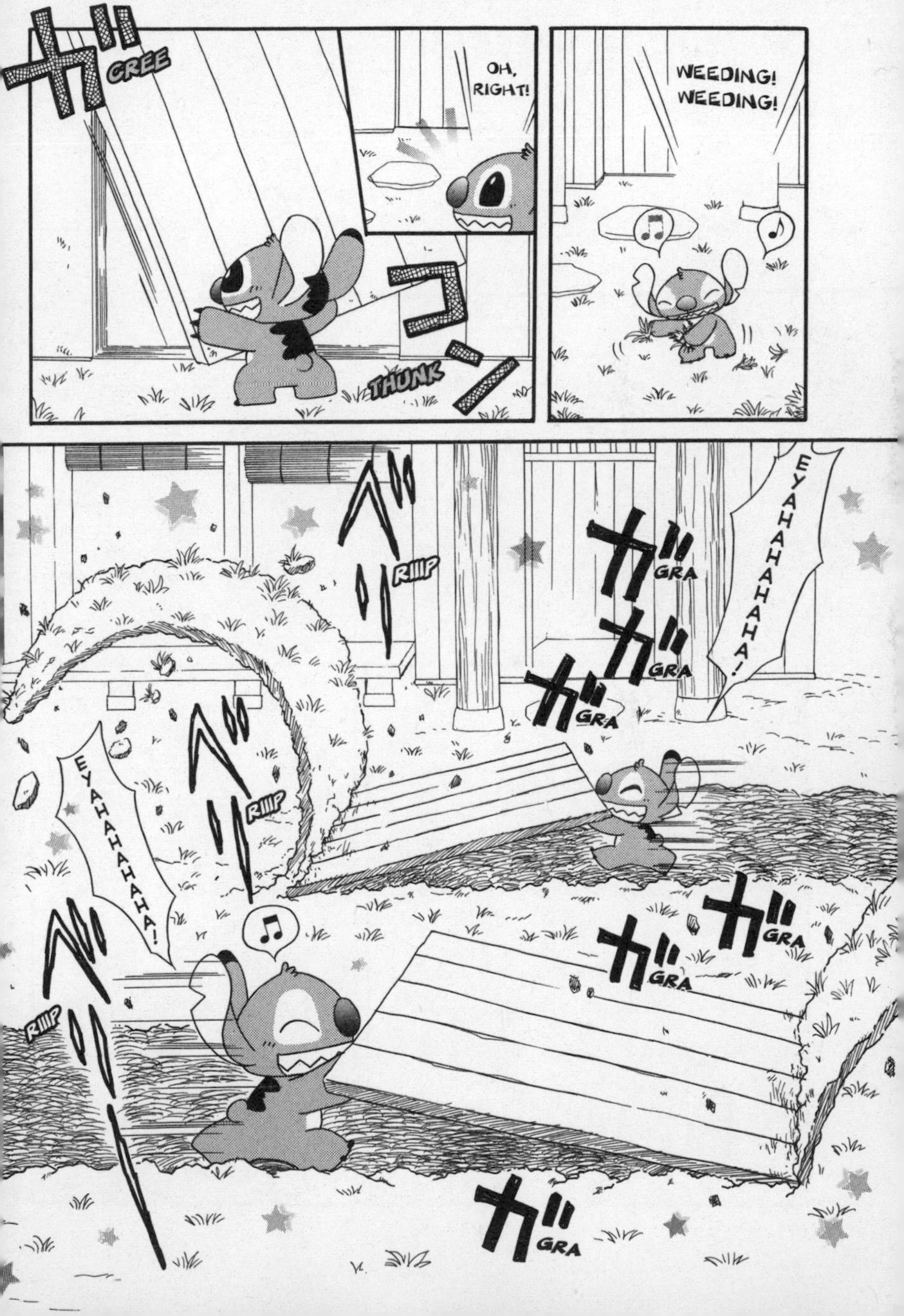
WEEDING! WEEDING!
OH, RIGHT!
CREE
THUNK
EYAHAHAHAHA!
GRA
GRA
GRA
RIIIP
RIIIP
EYAHAHAHAHA!
GRA
GRA
RIIIP
GRA

READ THIS WAY

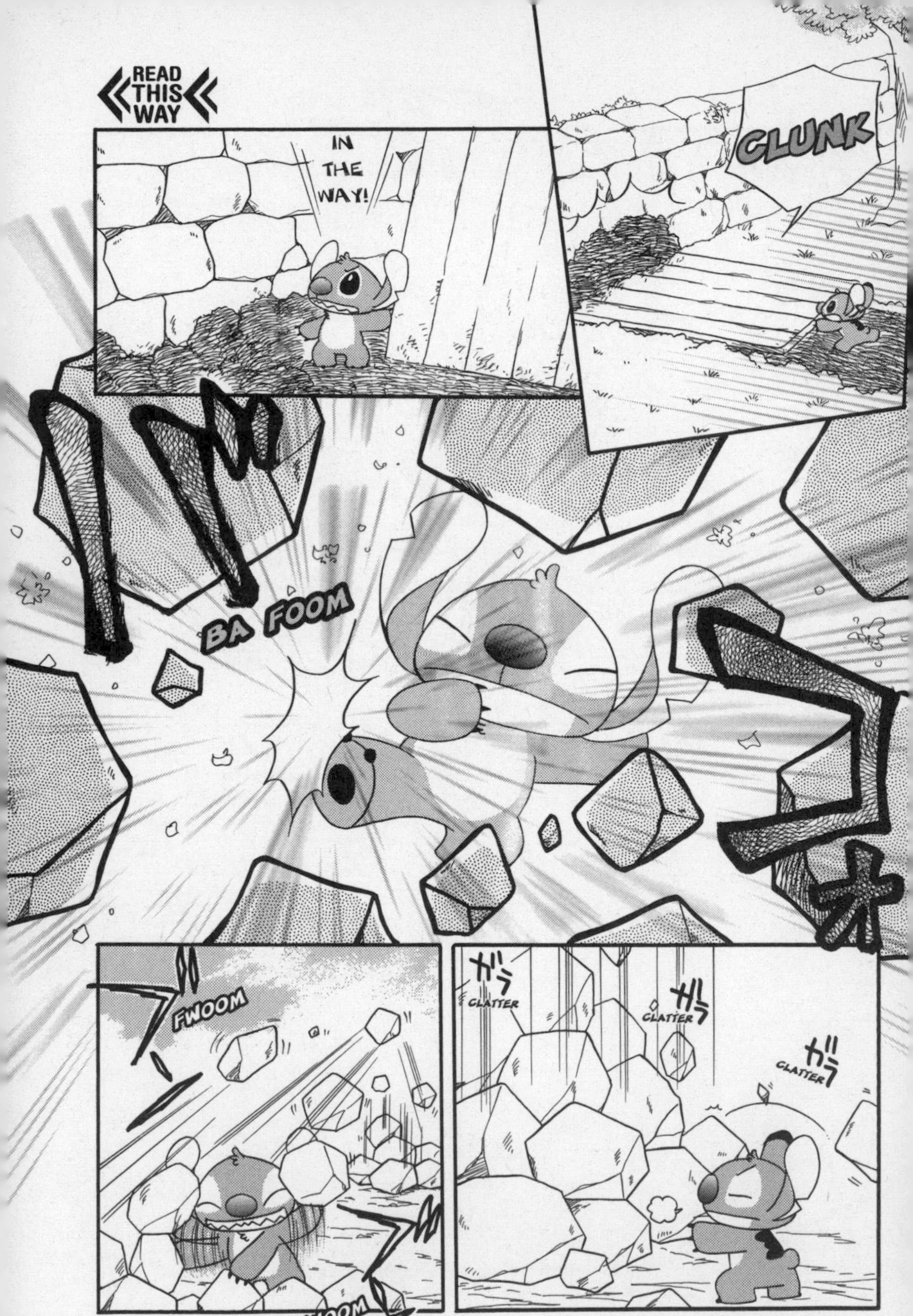

CLUNK
IN THE WAY!
BA FOOM
ガラ
CLATTER
ガラ
CLATTER
ガラ
CLATTER
FWOOM
FWOOM

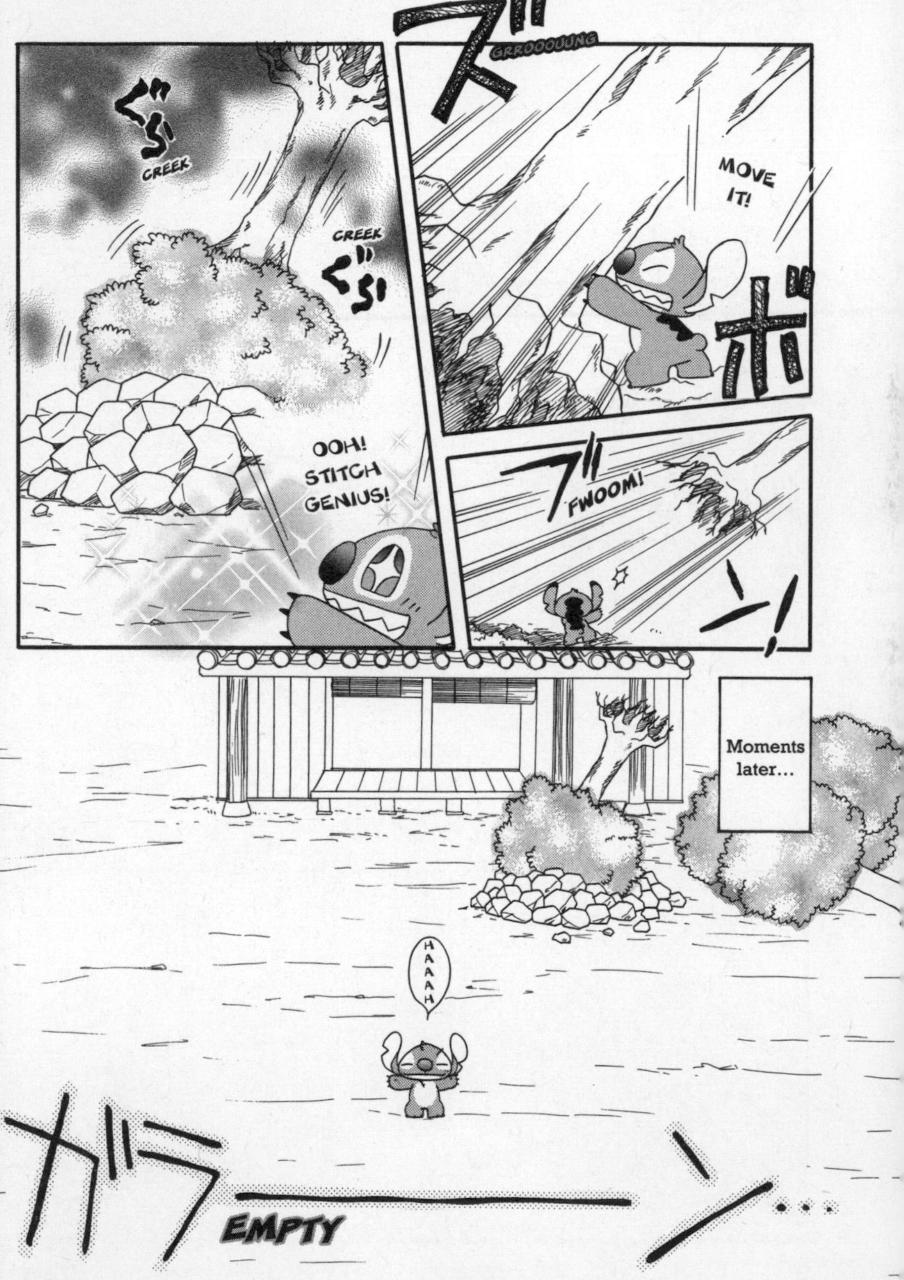
ズ
GRROOOUUNG
MOVE IT!
ボ
ブ
FWOOM!
!
ぐら
CREEK
CREEK
ぐら
OOH! STITCH GENIUS!
Moments later...
HAAAH
ガラーン...
EMPTY

READ THIS WAY

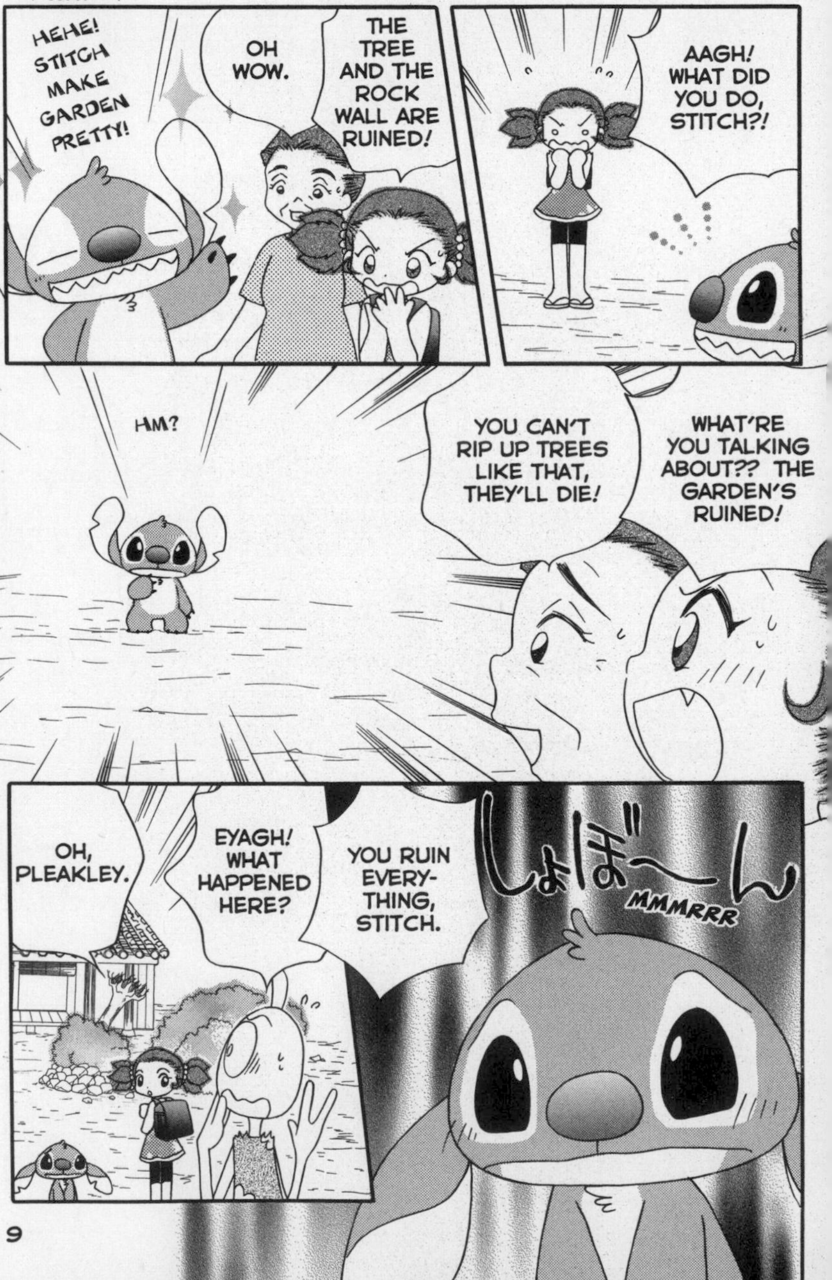
AAGH! WHAT DID YOU DO, STITCH?!
THE TREE AND THE ROCK WALL ARE RUINED!
OH WOW.
HEHE! STITCH MAKE GARDEN PRETTY!
WHAT'RE YOU TALKING ABOUT?? THE GARDEN'S RUINED!
YOU CAN'T RIP UP TREES LIKE THAT, THEY'LL DIE!
HM?
しょぼ〜ん
MMMRRR
YOU RUIN EVERY-THING, STITCH.
EYAGH! WHAT HAPPENED HERE?
OH, PLEAKLEY.

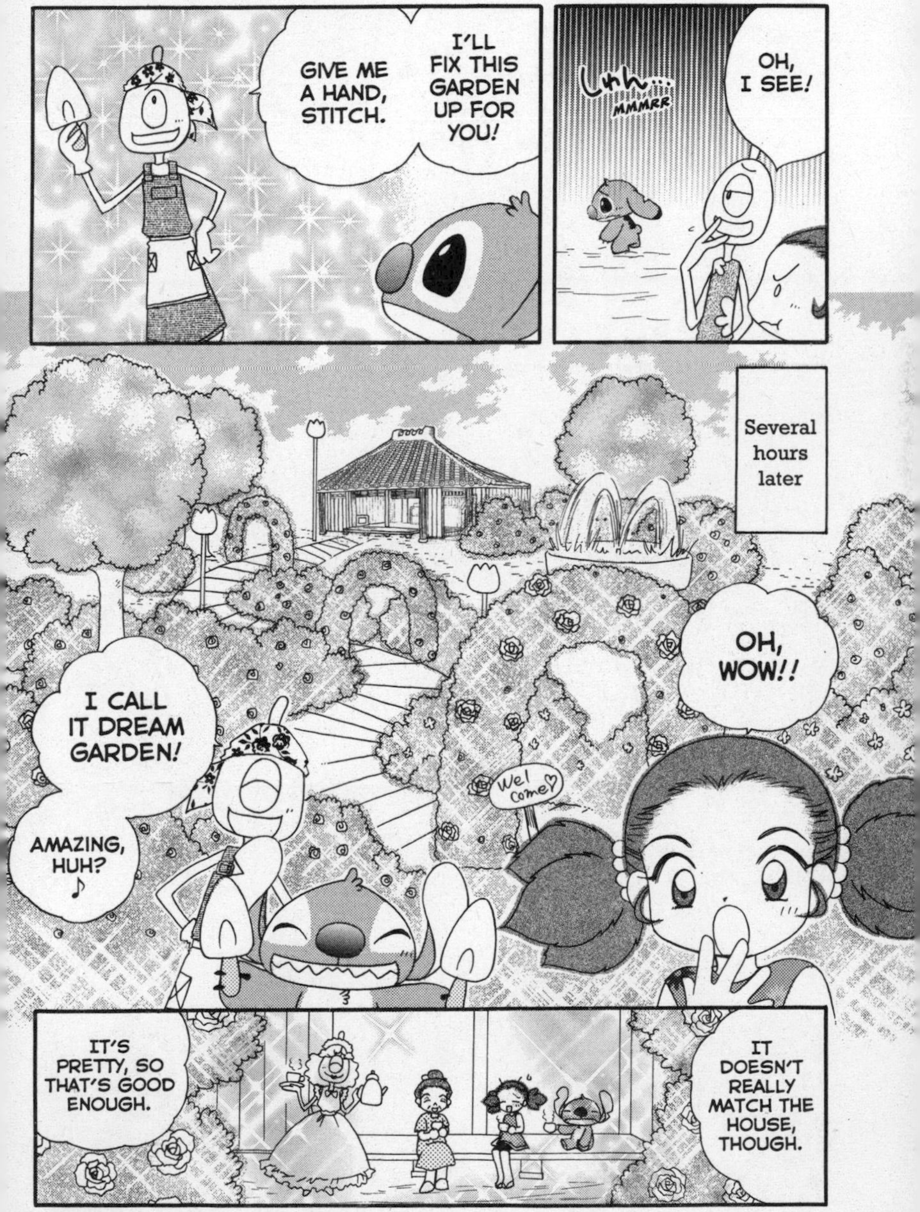
OH, I SEE!
しゅん…
MMMRR
I'LL FIX THIS GARDEN UP FOR YOU!
GIVE ME A HAND, STITCH.
Several hours later
OH, WOW!!
I CALL IT DREAM GARDEN!
Wel come♥
AMAZING, HUH? ♪
IT DOESN'T REALLY MATCH THE HOUSE, THOUGH.
IT'S PRETTY, SO THAT'S GOOD ENOUGH.

READ THIS WAY

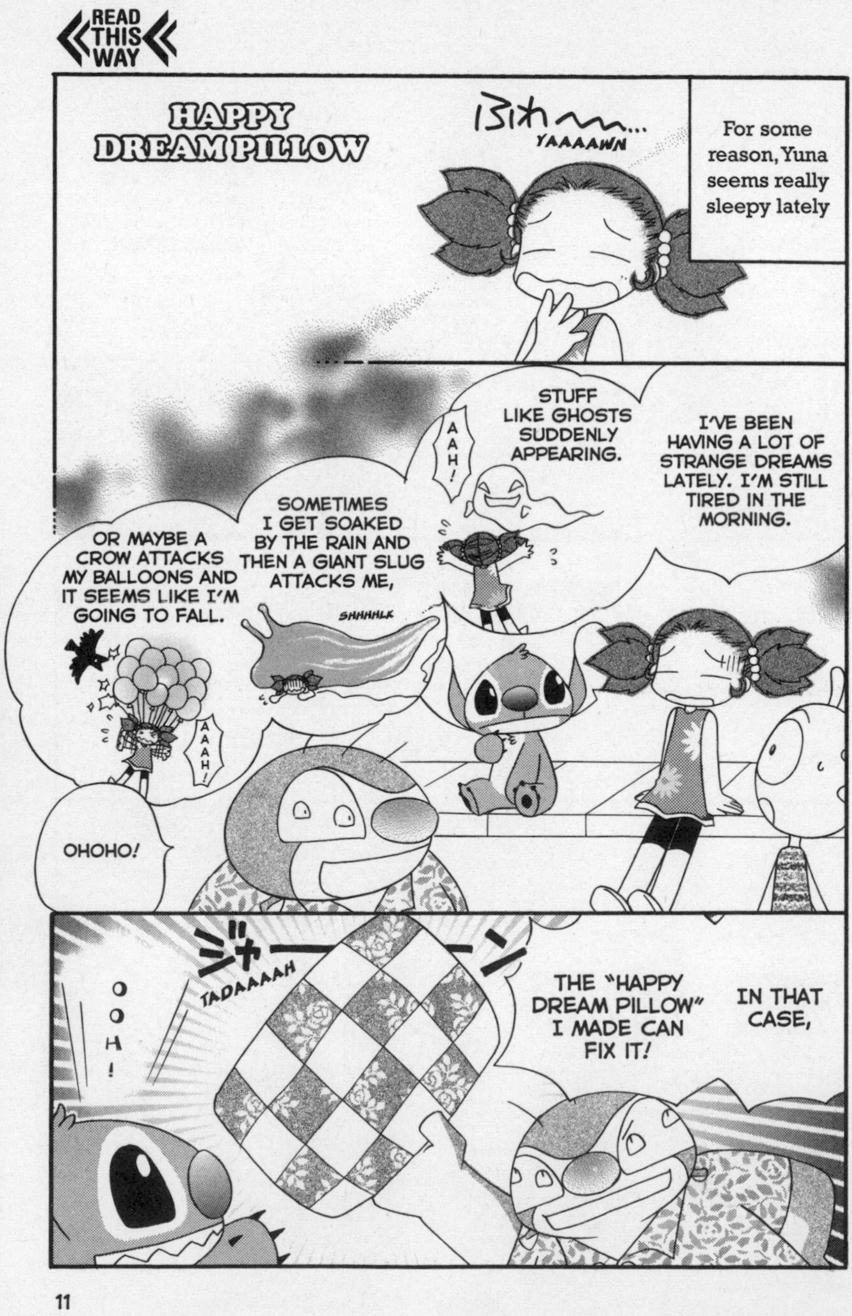

For some reason, Yuna seems really sleepy lately
YAAAAWN
HAPPY DREAM PILLOW
I'VE BEEN HAVING A LOT OF STRANGE DREAMS LATELY. I'M STILL TIRED IN THE MORNING.
STUFF LIKE GHOSTS SUDDENLY APPEARING.
AAH!
SOMETIMES I GET SOAKED BY THE RAIN AND THEN A GIANT SLUG ATTACKS ME,
SHHHHLK
OR MAYBE A CROW ATTACKS MY BALLOONS AND IT SEEMS LIKE I'M GOING TO FALL.
AAAH!
OHOHO!
IN THAT CASE,
THE "HAPPY DREAM PILLOW" I MADE CAN FIX IT!
TADAAAAH
OOH!

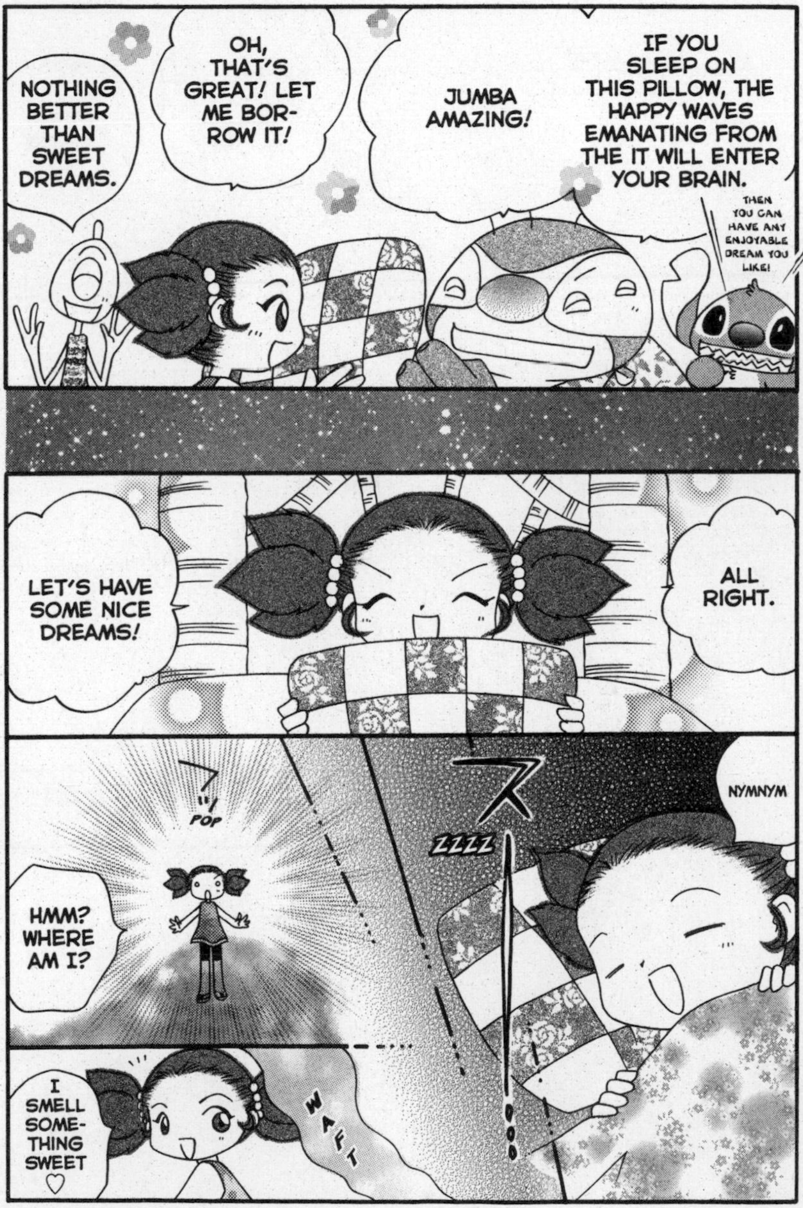
IF YOU SLEEP ON THIS PILLOW, THE HAPPY WAVES EMANATING FROM THE IT WILL ENTER YOUR BRAIN.
THEN YOU CAN HAVE ANY ENJOYABLE DREAM YOU LIKE!
JUMBA AMAZING!
OH, THAT'S GREAT! LET ME BOR-ROW IT!
NOTHING BETTER THAN SWEET DREAMS.
ALL RIGHT.
LET'S HAVE SOME NICE DREAMS!
NYMNYM
ZZZZ
POP
HMM? WHERE AM I?
WAFT
I SMELL SOME-THING SWEET ♡

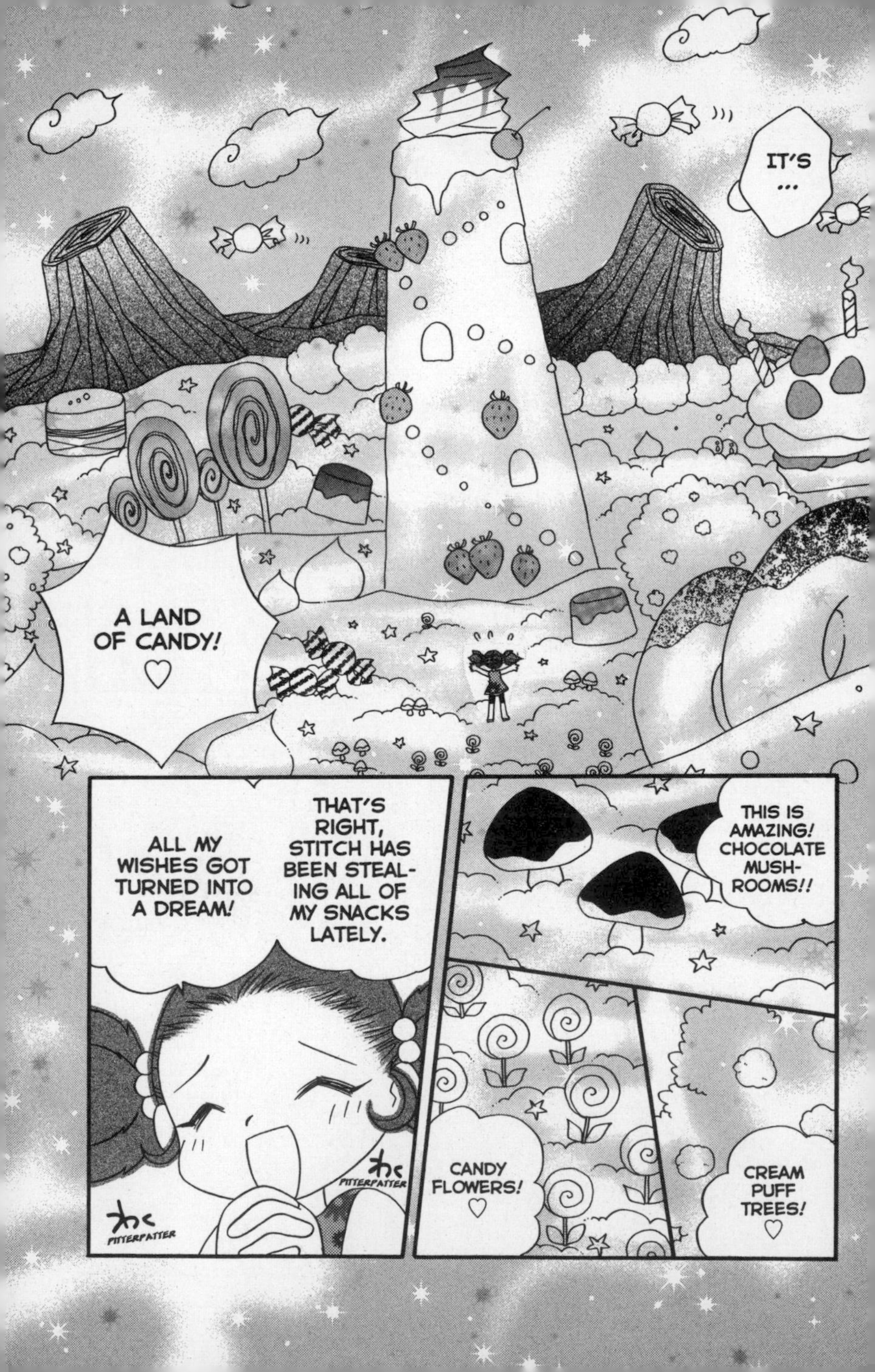
IT'S ...
A LAND OF CANDY! ♡
THIS IS AMAZING! CHOCOLATE MUSH-ROOMS!!
CREAM PUFF TREES! ♡
CANDY FLOWERS! ♡
THAT'S RIGHT, STITCH HAS BEEN STEAL-ING ALL OF MY SNACKS LATELY.
ALL MY WISHES GOT TURNED INTO A DREAM!
わく PITTERPATTER
わく PITTERPATTER

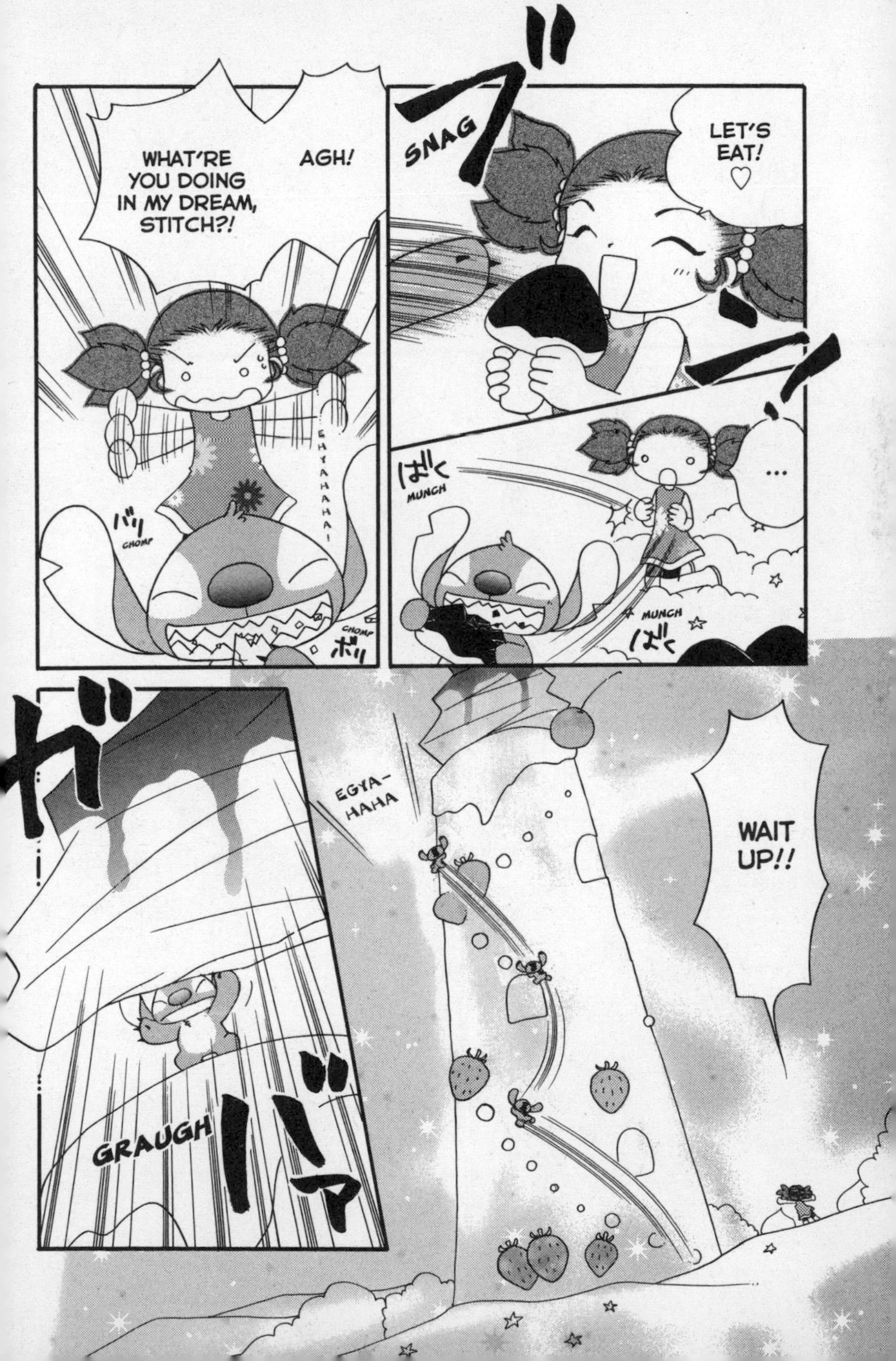
SNAG
LET'S EAT! ♡
ばく MUNCH
...
MUNCH ばく
AGH!
WHAT'RE YOU DOING IN MY DREAM, STITCH?!
EHYAHAHAHA!
バリ CHOMP
CHOMP ボリ
WAIT UP!!
EGYA-HAHA
GRAUGH

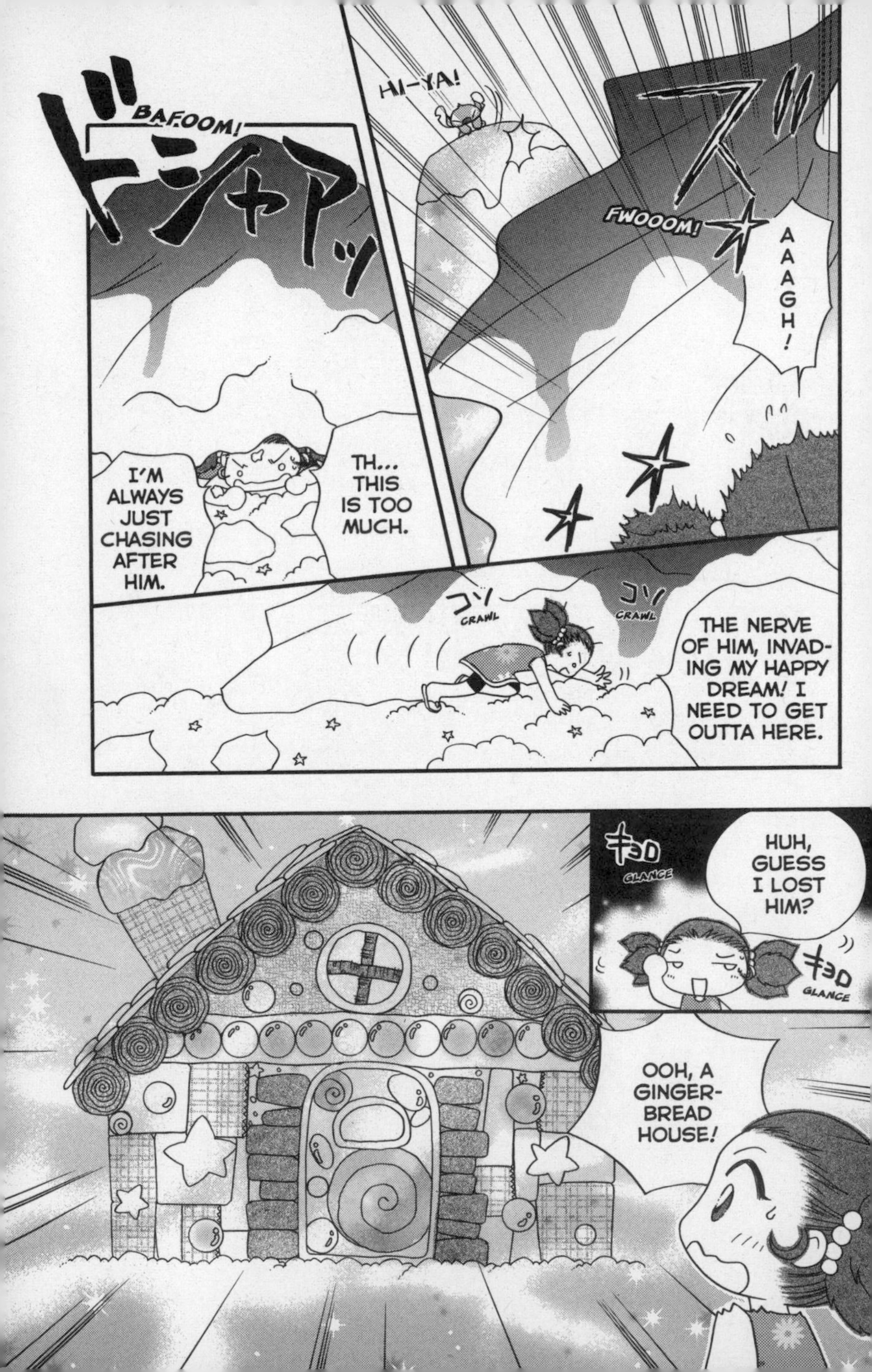
HI-YA!
FWOOOM!
AAAGH!
ドシャアッ
BAFOOM!
TH... THIS IS TOO MUCH.
I'M ALWAYS JUST CHASING AFTER HIM.
CRAWL
CRAWL
THE NERVE OF HIM, INVAD-ING MY HAPPY DREAM! I NEED TO GET OUTTA HERE.
キョロ
GLANCE
HUH, GUESS I LOST HIM?
キョロ
GLANCE
OOH, A GINGER-BREAD HOUSE!

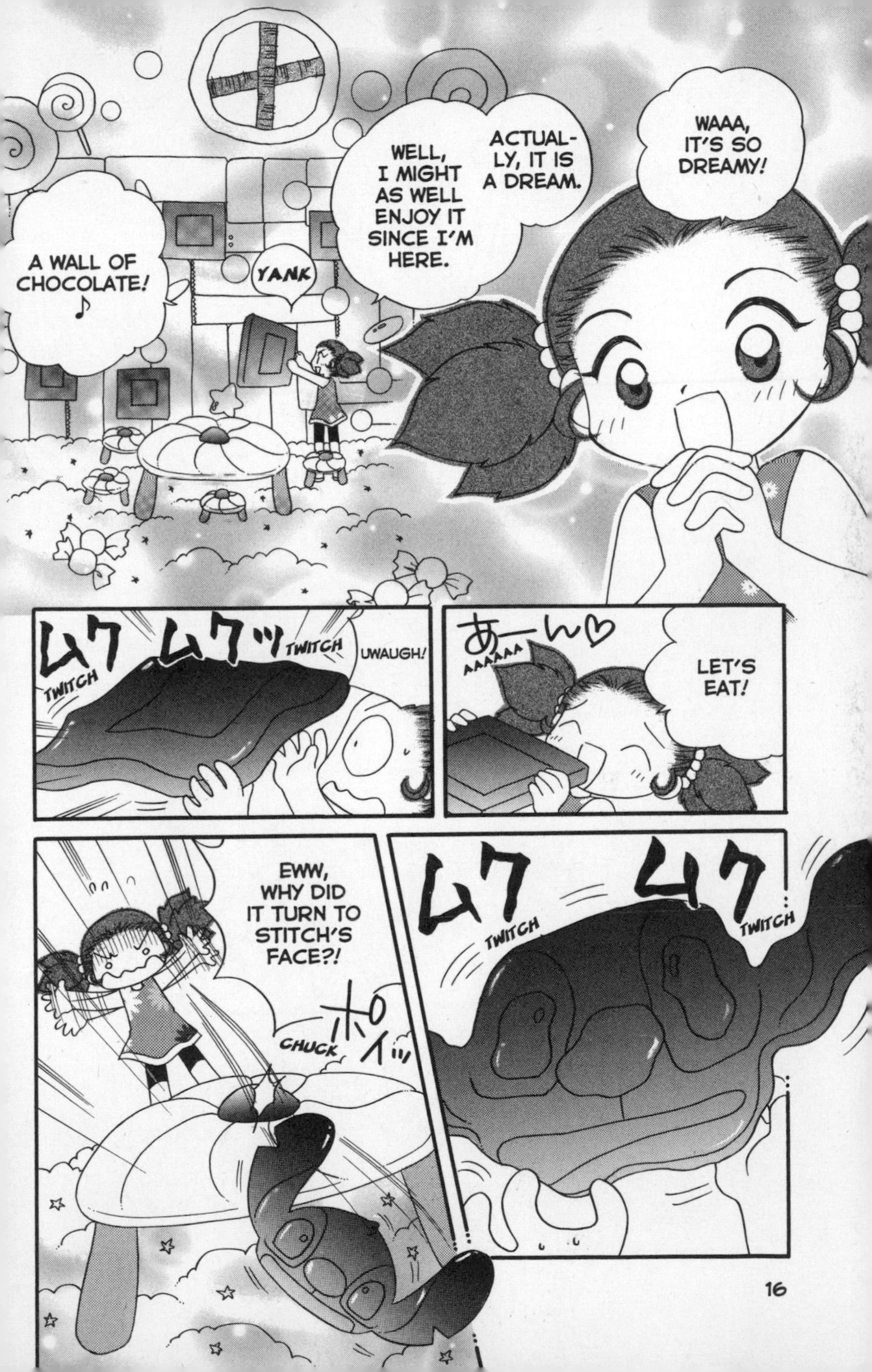
WAAA, IT'S SO DREAMY!
ACTUAL-LY, IT IS A DREAM.
WELL, I MIGHT AS WELL ENJOY IT SINCE I'M HERE.
YANK
A WALL OF CHOCOLATE! ♪
あーん♡
AAAAAA
LET'S EAT!
ムク ムクッ
TWITCH
TWITCH
UWAUGH!
ムク ムク
TWITCH
TWITCH
EWW, WHY DID IT TURN TO STITCH'S FACE?!
ポイッ
CHUCK

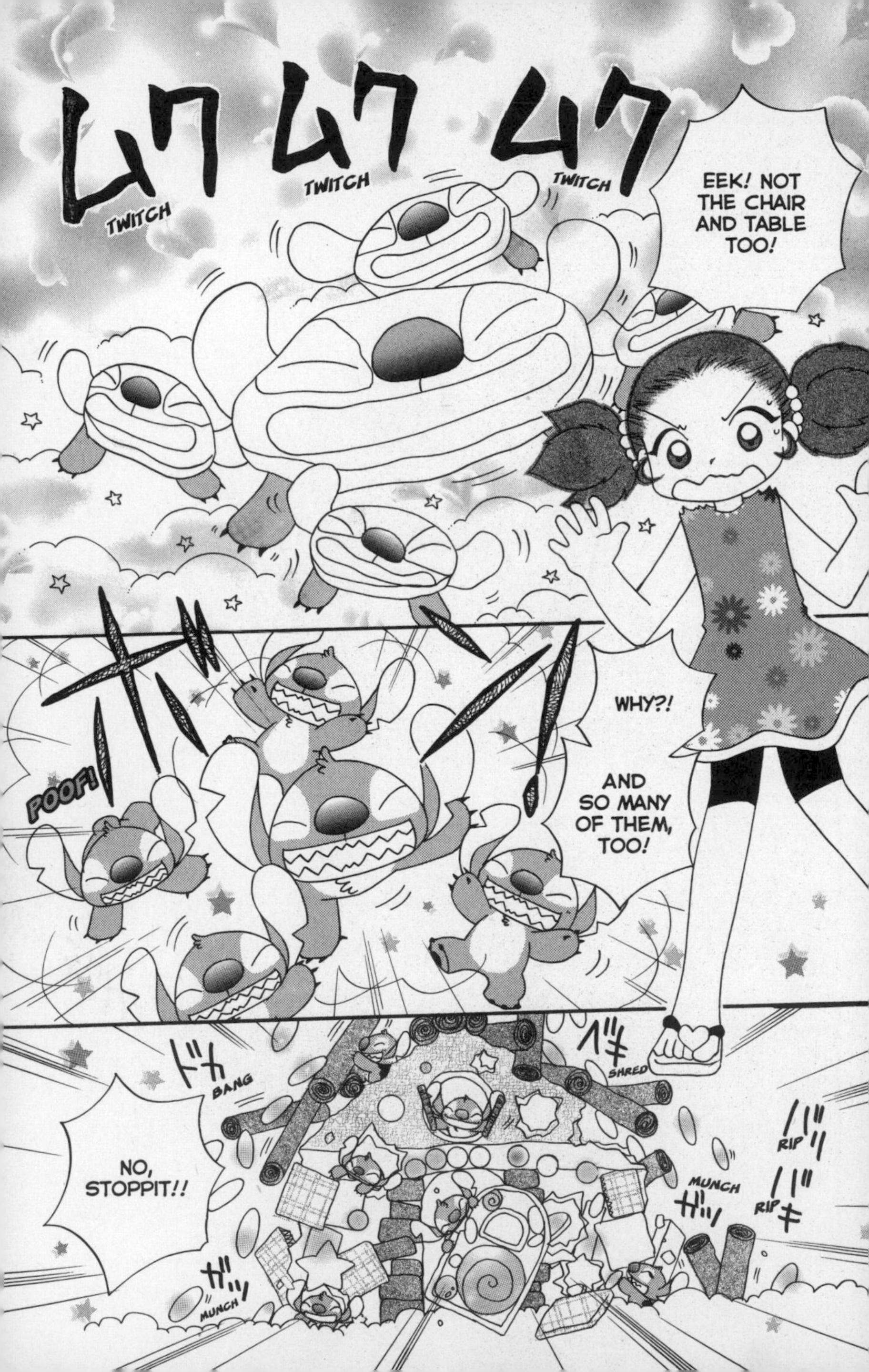
EEK! NOT THE CHAIR AND TABLE TOO!
ムクムクムク
TWITCH
TWITCH
TWITCH
WHY?!
AND SO MANY OF THEM, TOO!
POOF!
ベキ
SHRED
バリ
RIP
バキ
RIP
ガツ
MUNCH
ドカ
BANG
NO, STOPPIT!!
ガツ
MUNCH

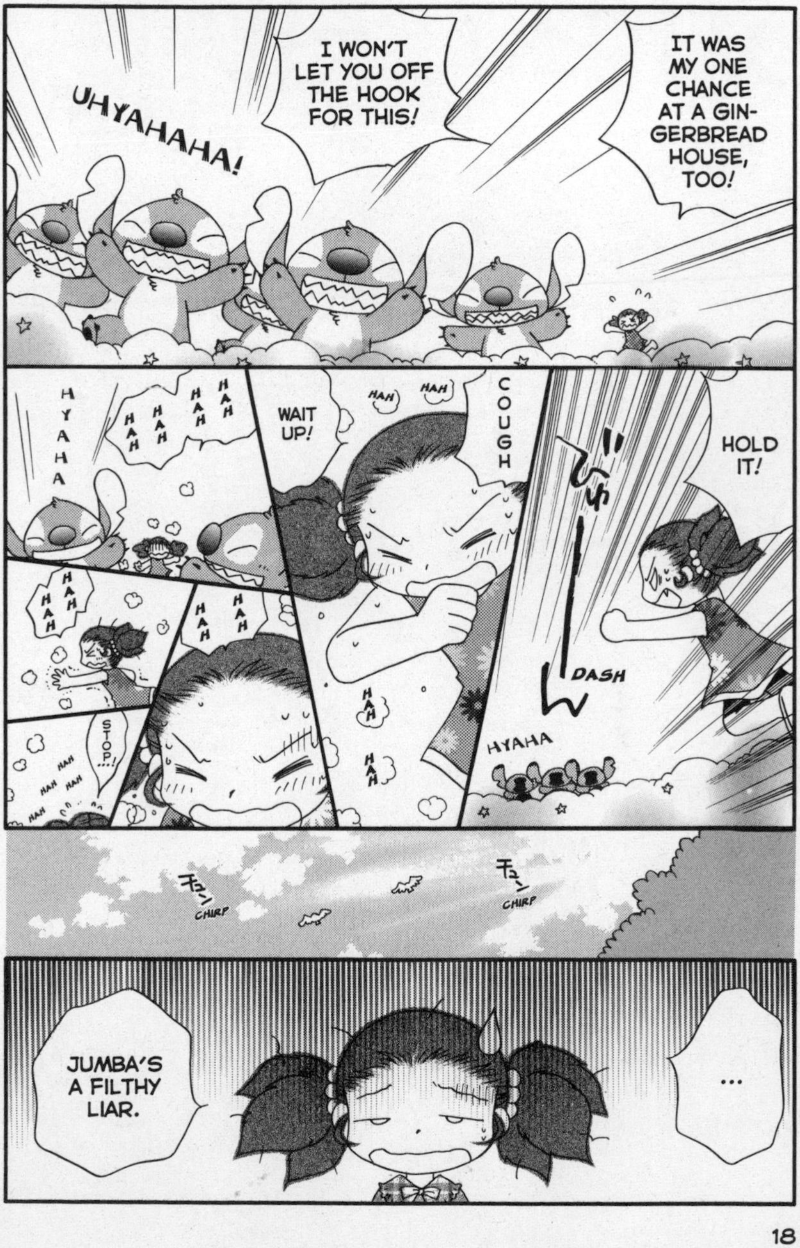
IT WAS MY ONE CHANCE AT A GINGERBREAD HOUSE, TOO!
I WON'T LET YOU OFF THE HOOK FOR THIS!
UHYAHAHA!
HOLD IT!
DASH
COUGH
HAH HAH
WAIT UP!
HAH
HAH
HYAHA
HYAHAHA
HAH HAH HAH HAH HAH HAH HAH HAH
HAH HAH HAH HAH
HAH HAH HAH HAH
STOP...!
HAH HAH HAH HAH HAH
CHIRP
CHIRP
...
JUMBA'S A FILTHY LIAR.

READ THIS WAY

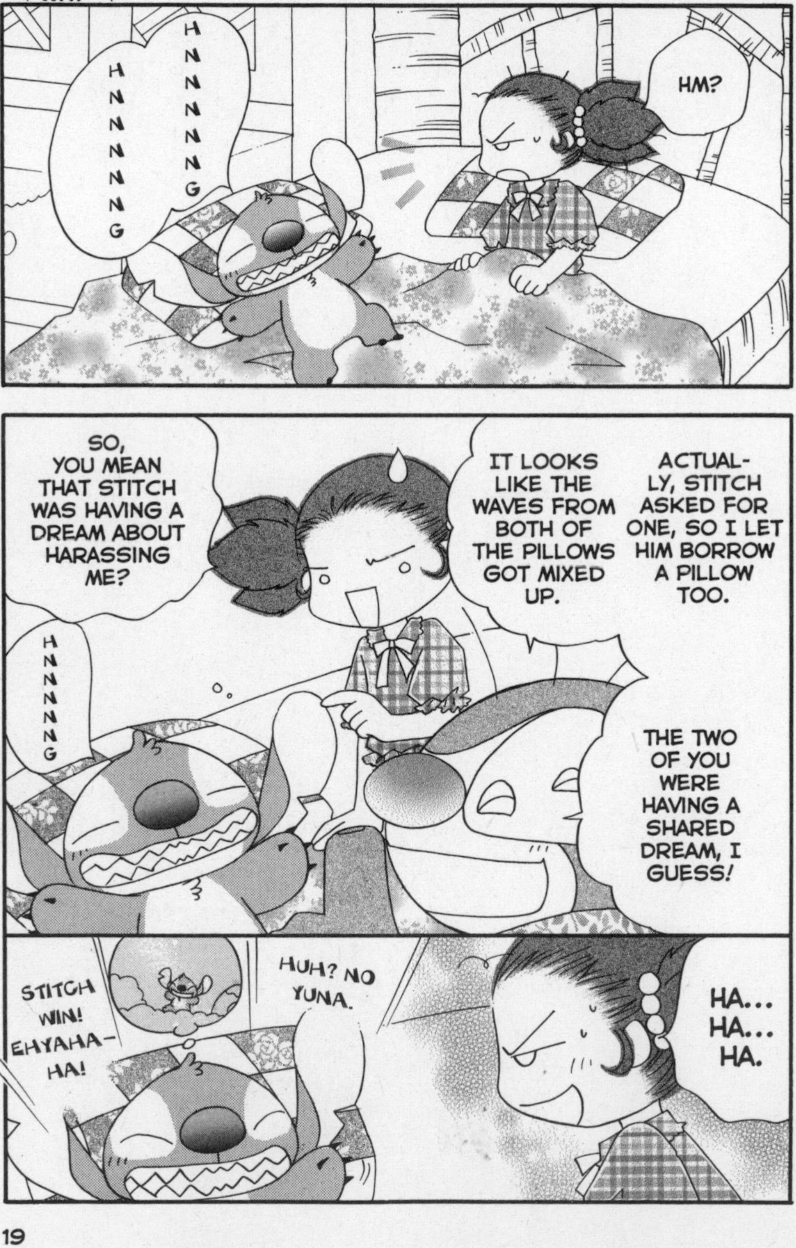
HM?
HNNNNNG
HNNNNNG
ACTUAL-LY, STITCH ASKED FOR ONE, SO I LET HIM BORROW A PILLOW TOO.
IT LOOKS LIKE THE WAVES FROM BOTH OF THE PILLOWS GOT MIXED UP.
SO, YOU MEAN THAT STITCH WAS HAVING A DREAM ABOUT HARASSING ME?
THE TWO OF YOU WERE HAVING A SHARED DREAM, I GUESS!
HNNNNNNG
HA... HA... HA.
HUH? NO YUNA.
STITCH WIN! EHYAHA-HA!

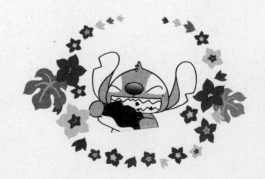

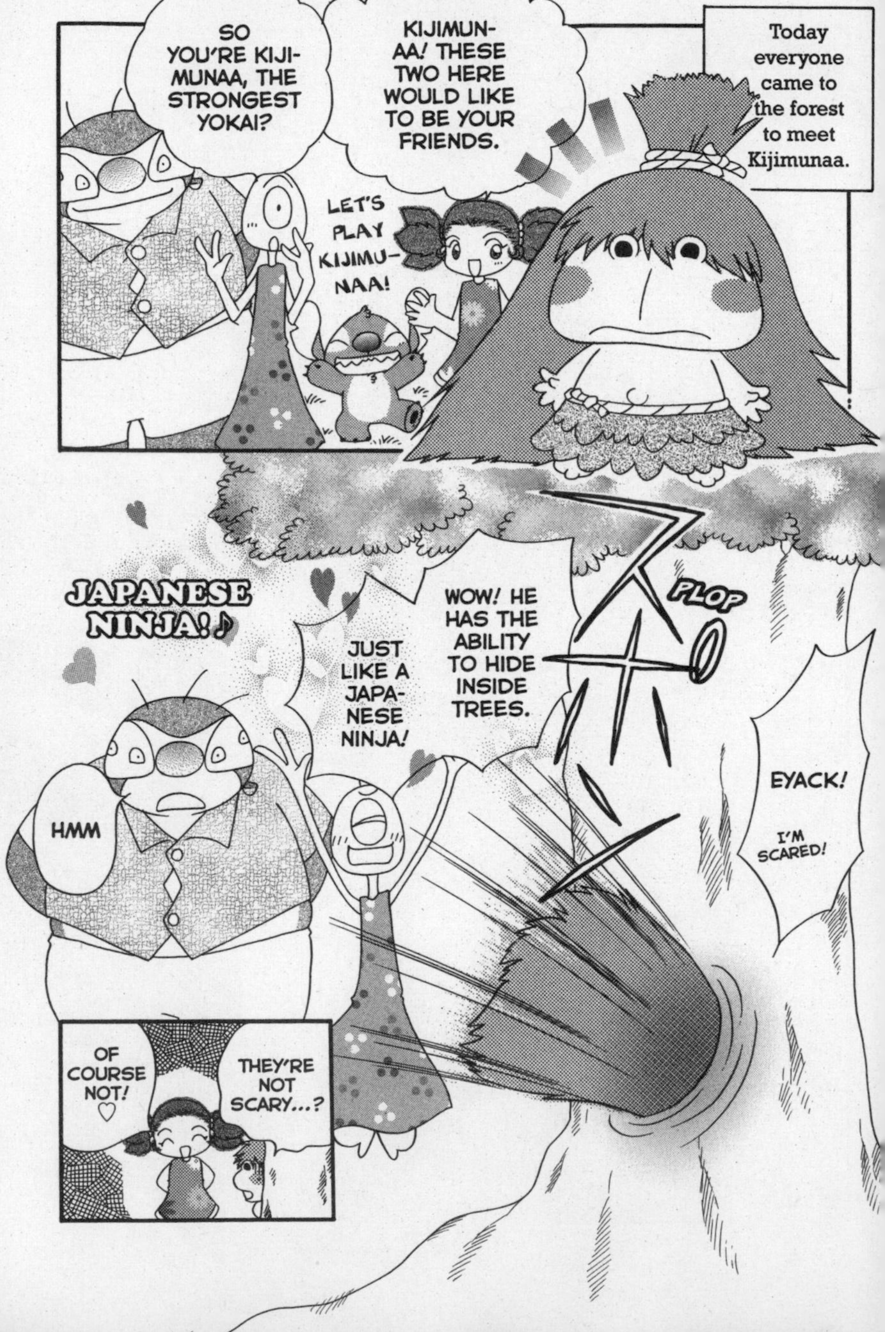
Today everyone came to the forest to meet Kijimunaa.
KIJIMUNAA! THESE TWO HERE WOULD LIKE TO BE YOUR FRIENDS.
SO YOU'RE KIJIMUNAA, THE STRONGEST YOKAI?
LET'S PLAY KIJIMUNAA!
PLOP
EYACK!
I'M SCARED!
WOW! HE HAS THE ABILITY TO HIDE INSIDE TREES.
JUST LIKE A JAPANESE NINJA!
JAPANESE NINJA!♪
HMM
THEY'RE NOT SCARY...?
OF COURSE NOT! ♡

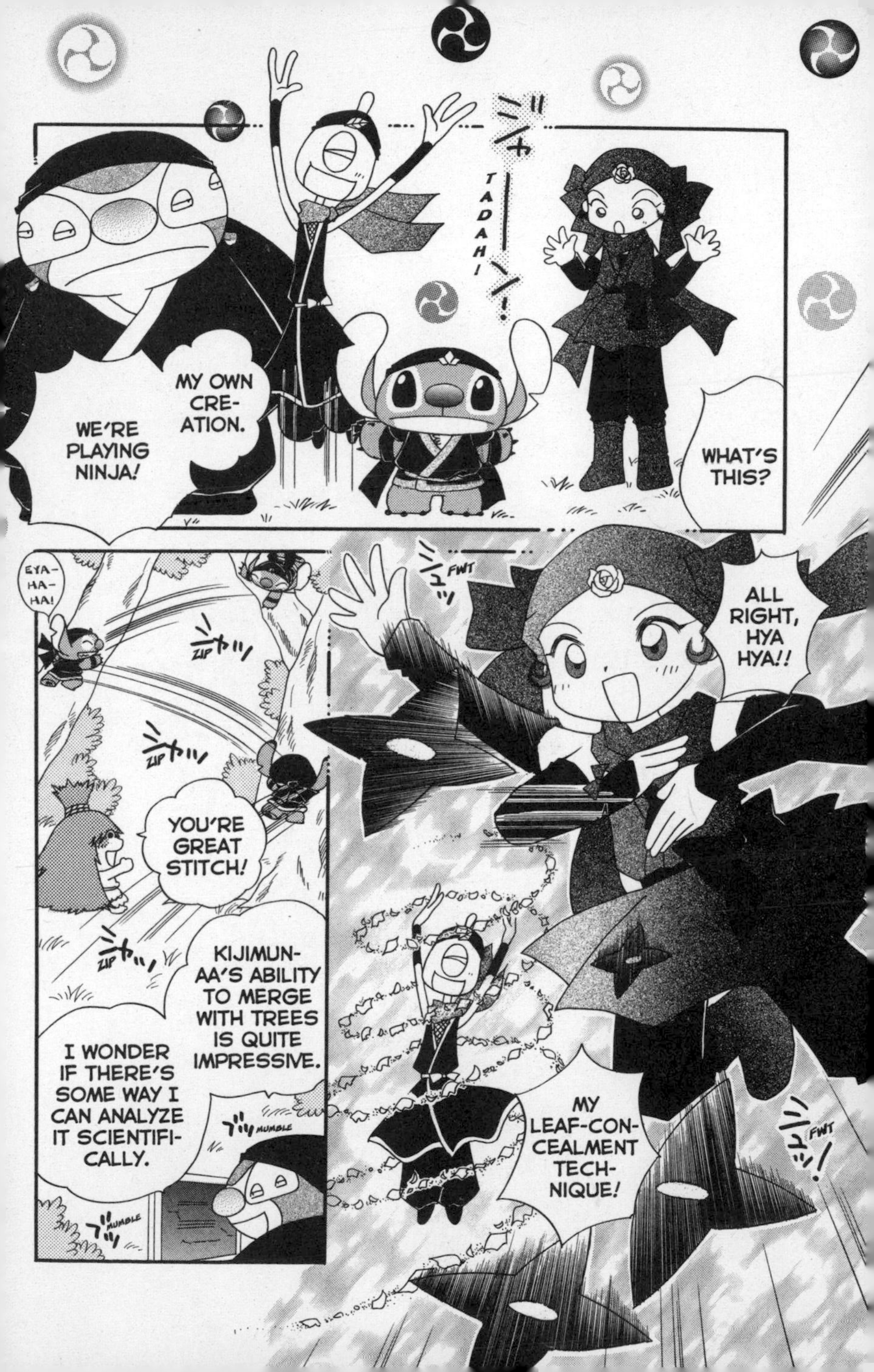
WHAT'S THIS?
TADAH!
MY OWN CRE-ATION.
WE'RE PLAYING NINJA!
FWT
ALL RIGHT, HYA HYA!!
MY LEAF-CON-CEALMENT TECH-NIQUE!
FWT
EYA-HA-HA!
ZIP
ZIP
YOU'RE GREAT STITCH!
ZIP
KIJIMUN-AA'S ABILITY TO MERGE WITH TREES IS QUITE IMPRESSIVE.
I WONDER IF THERE'S SOME WAY I CAN ANALYZE IT SCIENTIFI-CALLY.
MUMBLE
MUMBLE

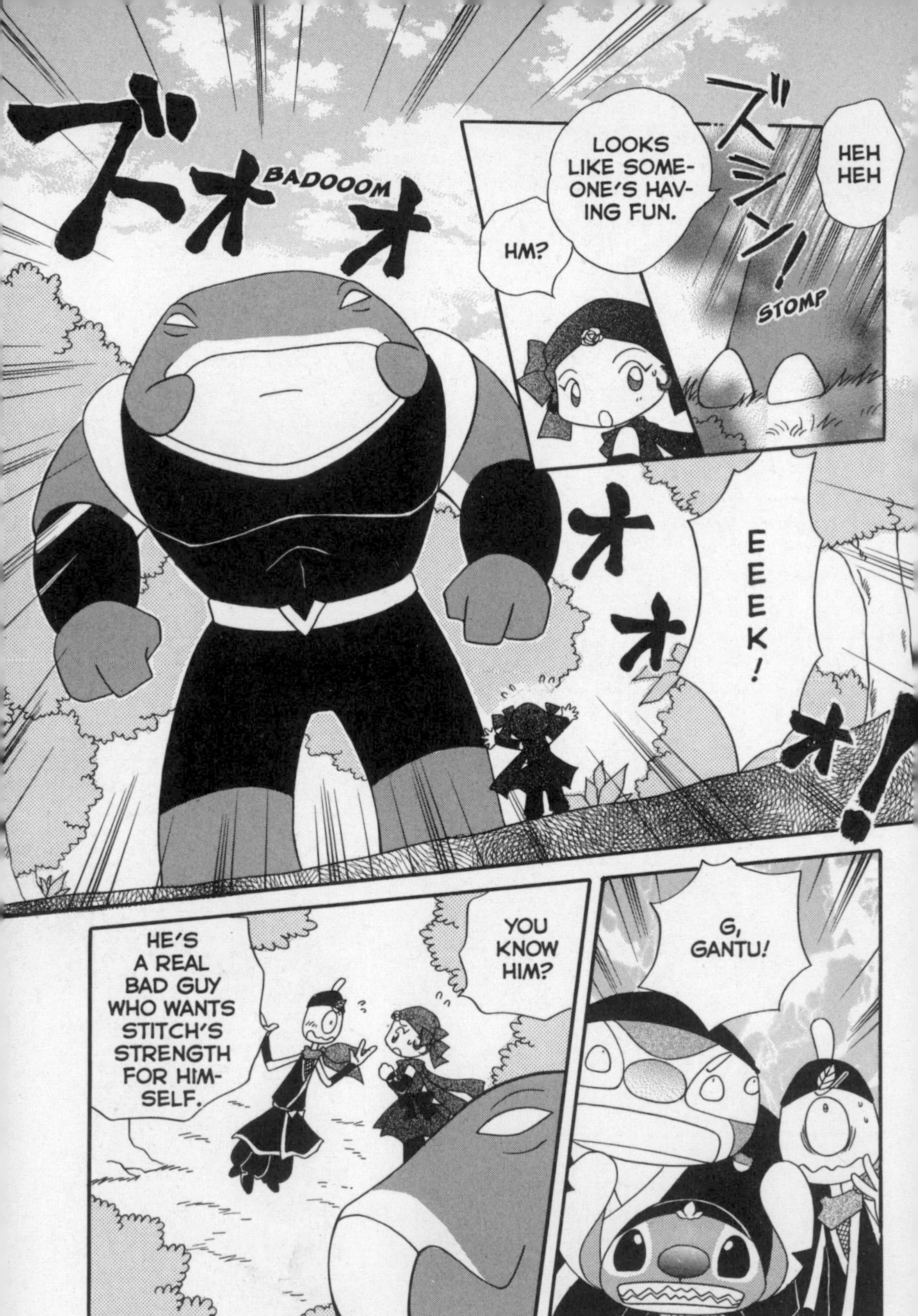
HEH HEH
ズシン!
STOMP
LOOKS LIKE SOME-ONE'S HAV-ING FUN.
HM?
オオオ!
EEEK!
ブオオ
BADOOOM
G, GANTU!
YOU KNOW HIM?
HE'S A REAL BAD GUY WHO WANTS STITCH'S STRENGTH FOR HIM-SELF.

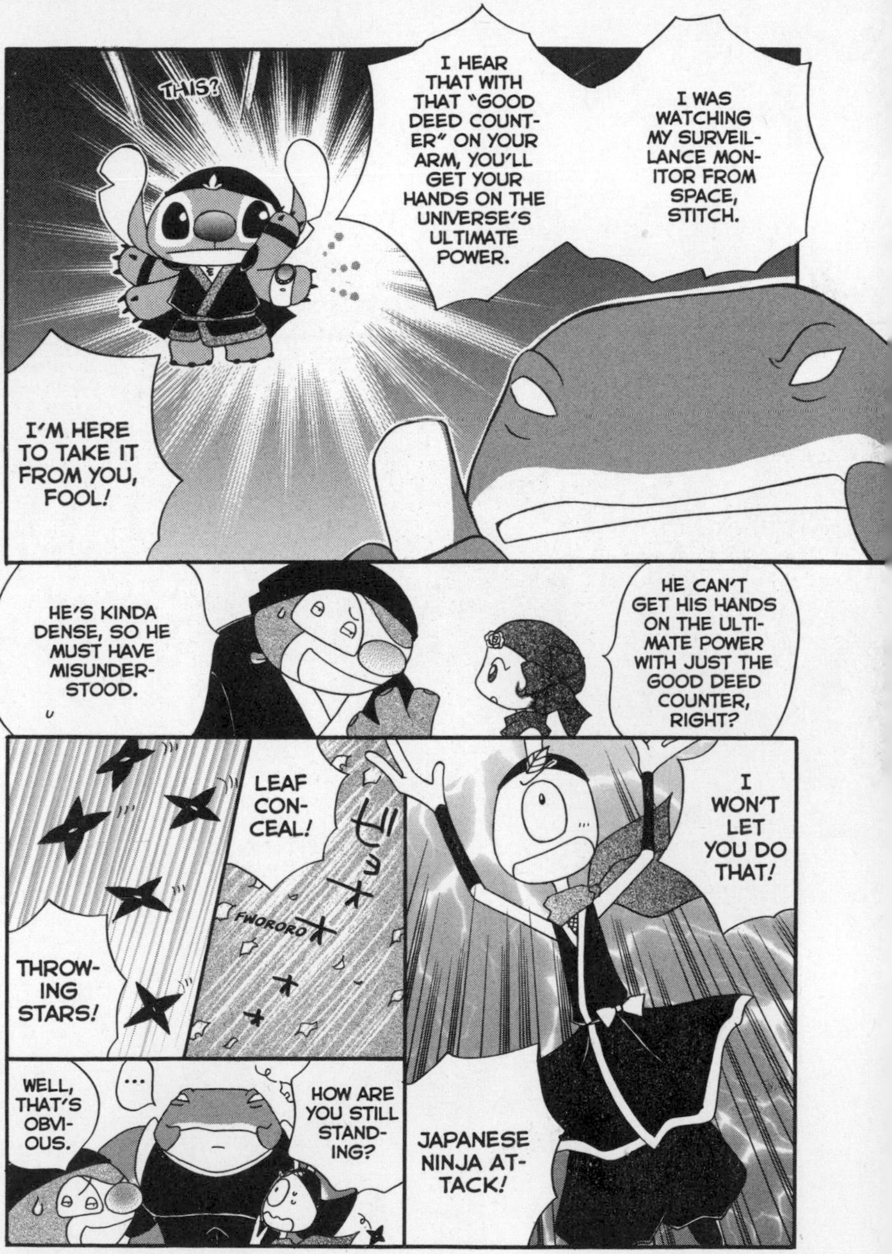
I WAS WATCHING MY SURVEIL-LANCE MON-ITOR FROM SPACE, STITCH.
I HEAR THAT WITH THAT "GOOD DEED COUNT-ER" ON YOUR ARM, YOU'LL GET YOUR HANDS ON THE UNIVERSE'S ULTIMATE POWER.
THIS?
I'M HERE TO TAKE IT FROM YOU, FOOL!
HE CAN'T GET HIS HANDS ON THE ULTI-MATE POWER WITH JUST THE GOOD DEED COUNTER, RIGHT?
HE'S KINDA DENSE, SO HE MUST HAVE MISUNDER-STOOD.
I WON'T LET YOU DO THAT!
JAPANESE NINJA AT-TACK!
LEAF CON-CEAL!
FWORORO
THROW-ING STARS!
HOW ARE YOU STILL STAND-ING?
...
WELL, THAT'S OBVI-OUS.

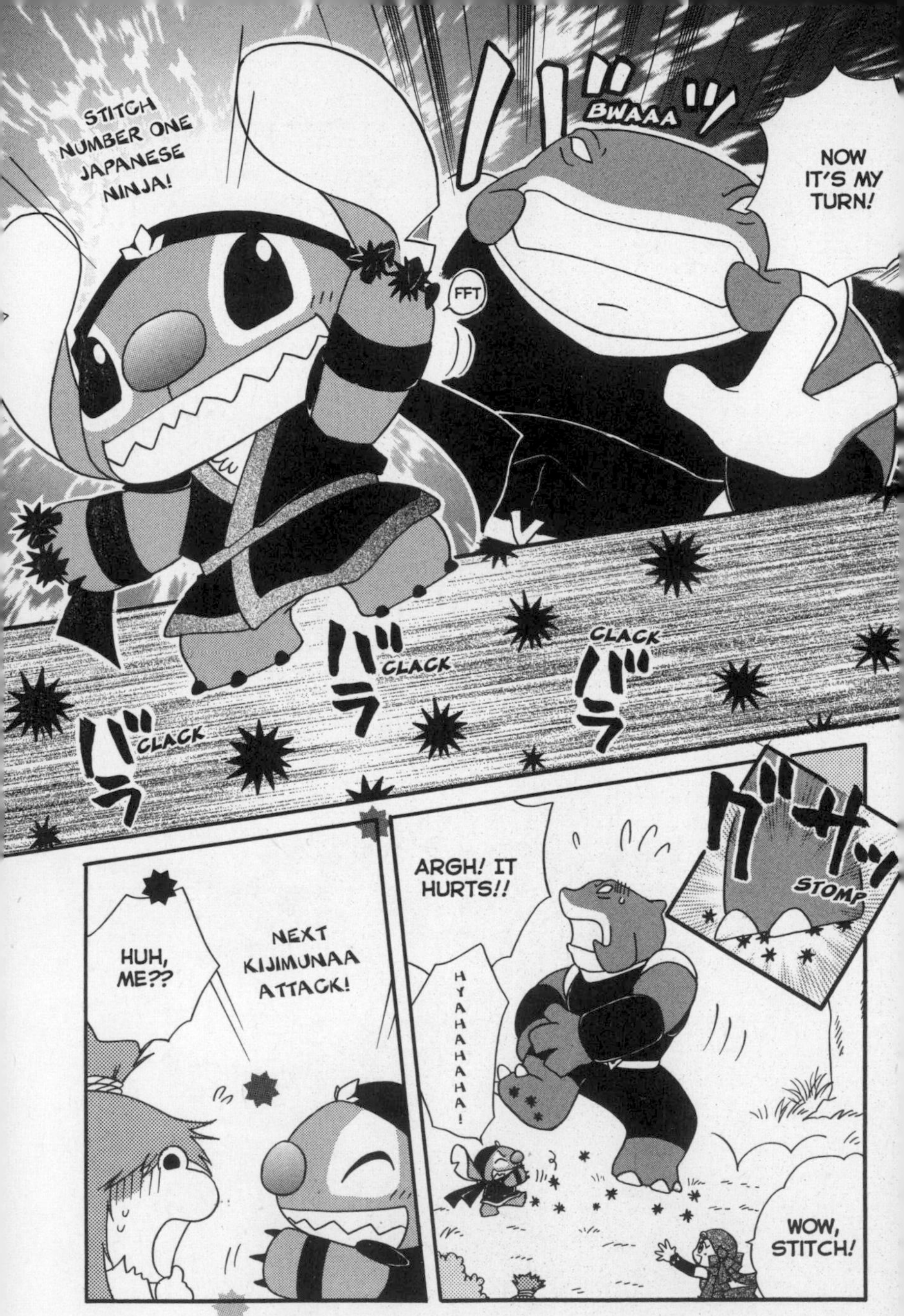
NOW IT'S MY TURN!
BWAAA
FFT
STITCH NUMBER ONE JAPANESE NINJA!
CLACK
バラ
CLACK
バラ
CLACK
バラ
STOMP
ARGH! IT HURTS!!
HYAHAHAHAHA!
WOW, STITCH!
NEXT KIJIMUNAA ATTACK!
HUH, ME??

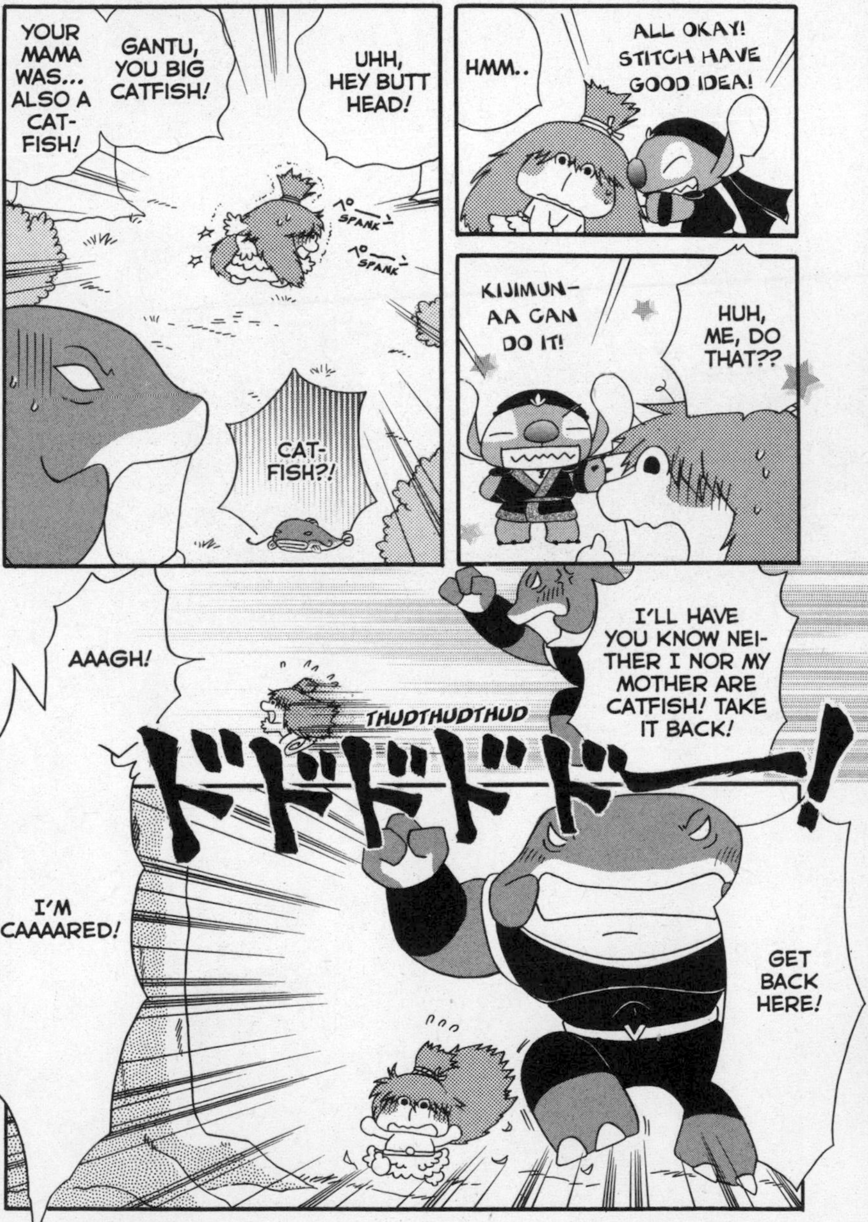
ALL OKAY! STITCH HAVE GOOD IDEA!
HMM..
HUH, ME, DO THAT??
KIJIMUN-AA CAN DO IT!
UHH, HEY BUTT HEAD!
GANTU, YOU BIG CATFISH!
YOUR MAMA WAS... ALSO A CAT-FISH!
SPANK
SPANK
CAT-FISH?!
I'LL HAVE YOU KNOW NEI-THER I NOR MY MOTHER ARE CATFISH! TAKE IT BACK!
AAAGH!
THUDTHUDTHUD
ドドドドドー!
GET BACK HERE!
I'M SCAAAARED!

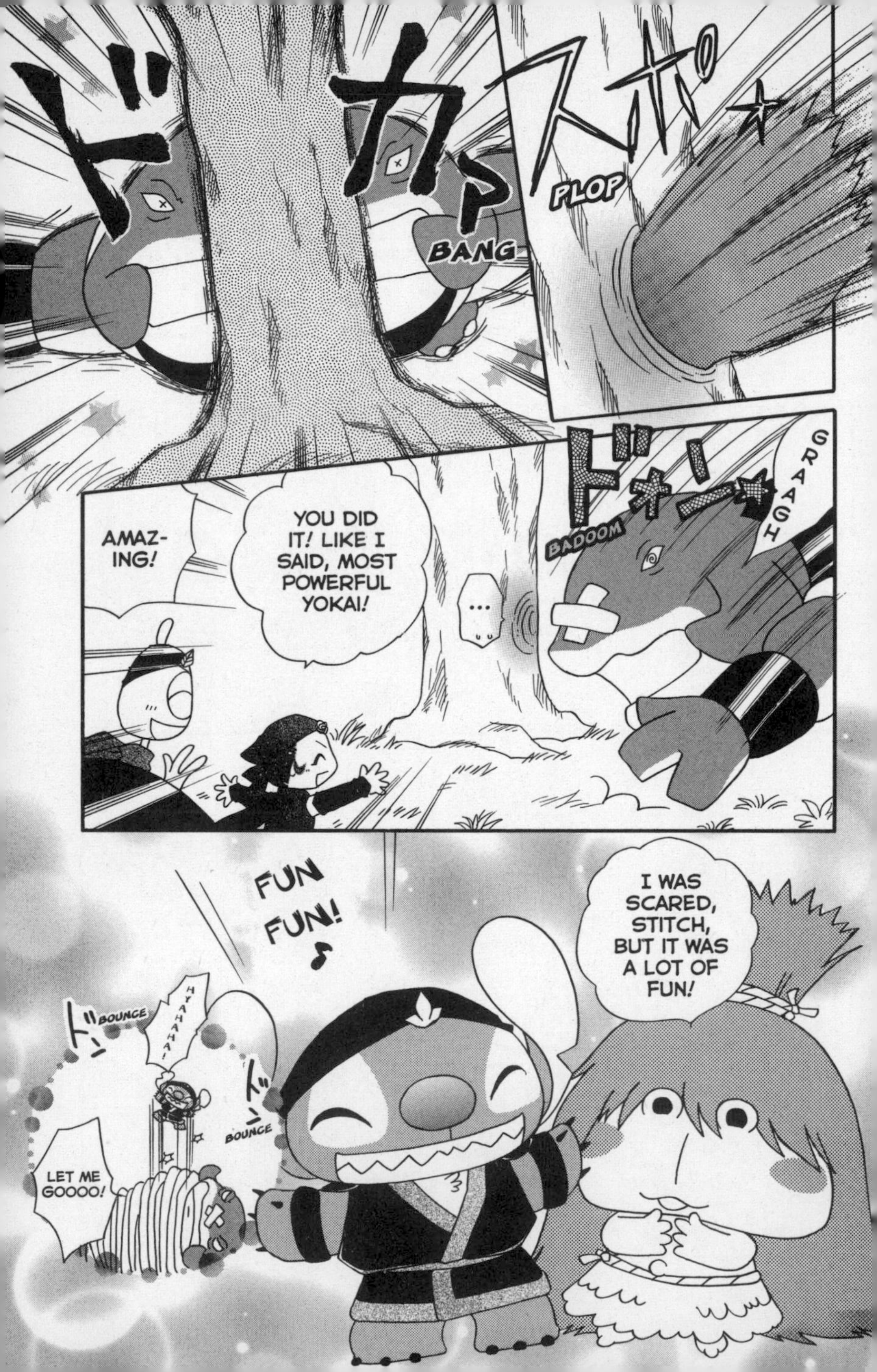
スポッ
PLOP
ドカッ
BANG
ドォーン
BADOOM
GRAAGH
...
YOU DID IT! LIKE I SAID, MOST POWERFUL YOKAI!
AMAZ-ING!
I WAS SCARED, STITCH, BUT IT WAS A LOT OF FUN!
FUN FUN!
ドッ
BOUNCE
HYAHAHA!
ドッ
BOUNCE
LET ME GOOOO!

A TREAT FOR ANGEL★

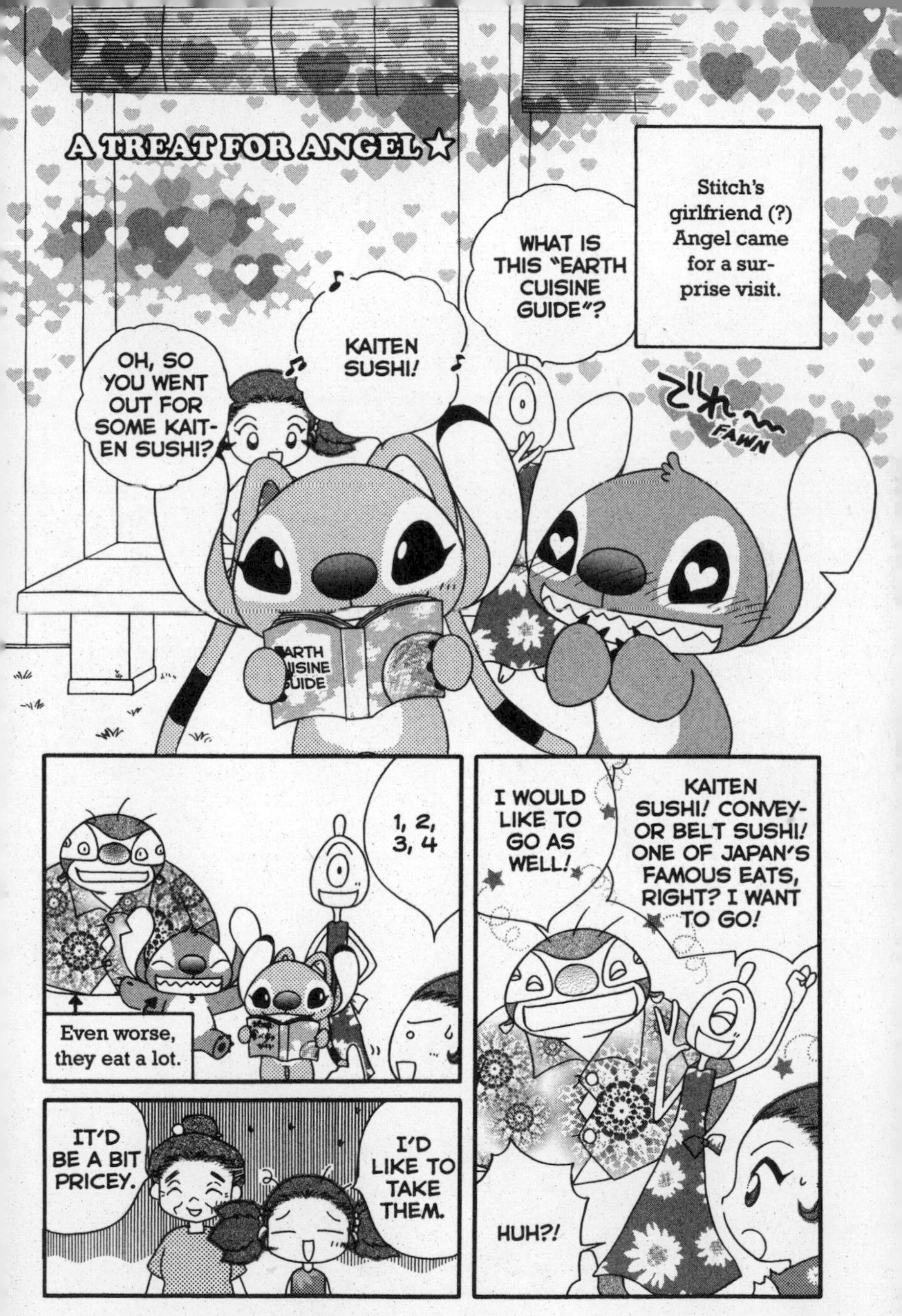
Stitch's girlfriend (?) Angel came for a surprise visit.
WHAT IS THIS "EARTH CUISINE GUIDE"?
FAWN
KAITEN SUSHI!
OH, SO YOU WENT OUT FOR SOME KAITEN SUSHI?
EARTH CUISINE GUIDE
KAITEN SUSHI! CONVEYOR BELT SUSHI! ONE OF JAPAN'S FAMOUS EATS, RIGHT? I WANT TO GO!
I WOULD LIKE TO GO AS WELL!
HUH?!
1, 2, 3, 4
Even worse, they eat a lot.
I'D LIKE TO TAKE THEM.
IT'D BE A BIT PRICEY.

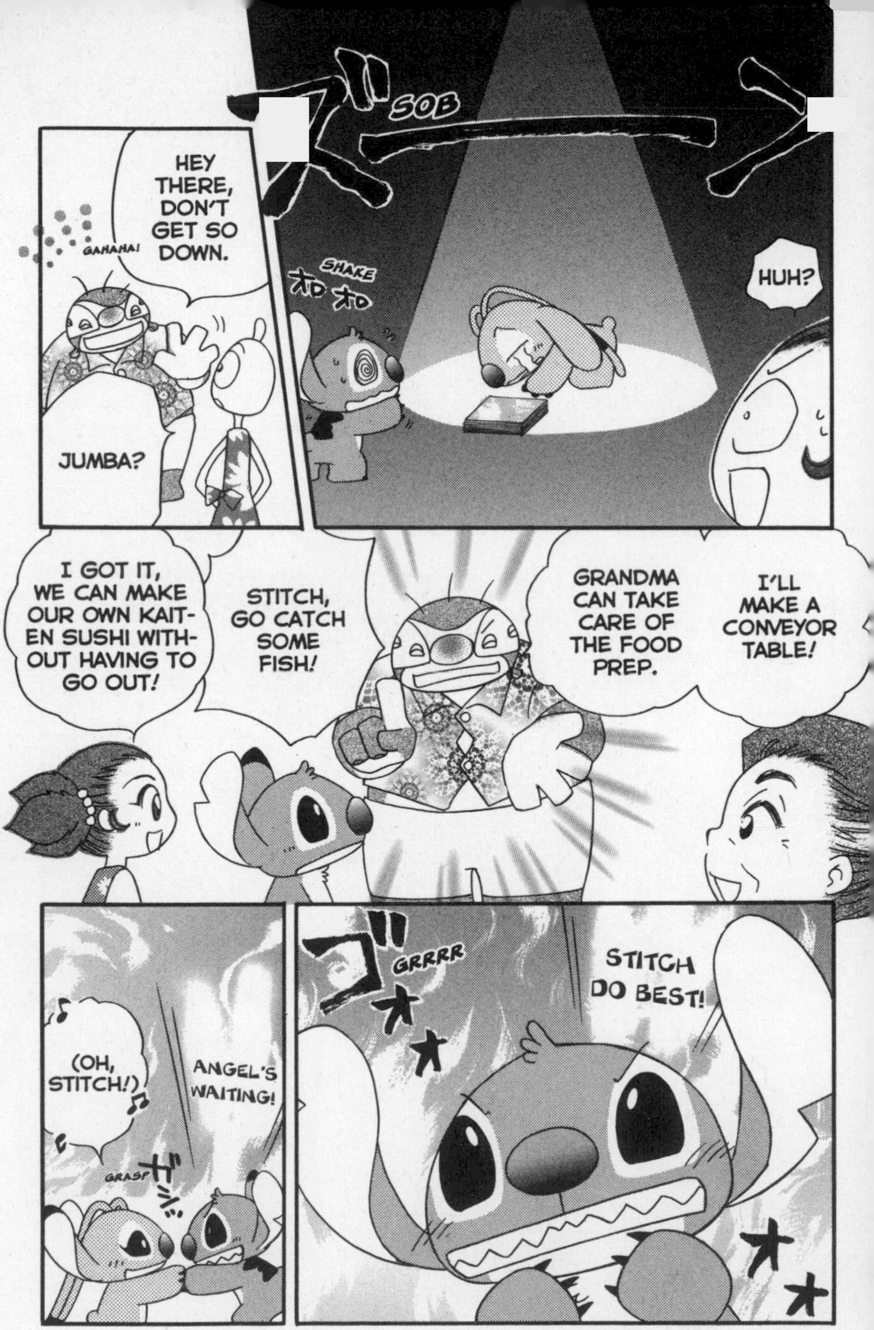
SOB
SHAKE
HUH?
HEY THERE, DON'T GET SO DOWN.
GAHAHA!
JUMBA?
I'LL MAKE A CONVEYOR TABLE!
GRANDMA CAN TAKE CARE OF THE FOOD PREP.
STITCH, GO CATCH SOME FISH!
I GOT IT, WE CAN MAKE OUR OWN KAIT-EN SUSHI WITH-OUT HAVING TO GO OUT!
GRRRR
STITCH DO BEST!
ANGEL'S WAITING!
(OH, STITCH!)
GRASP

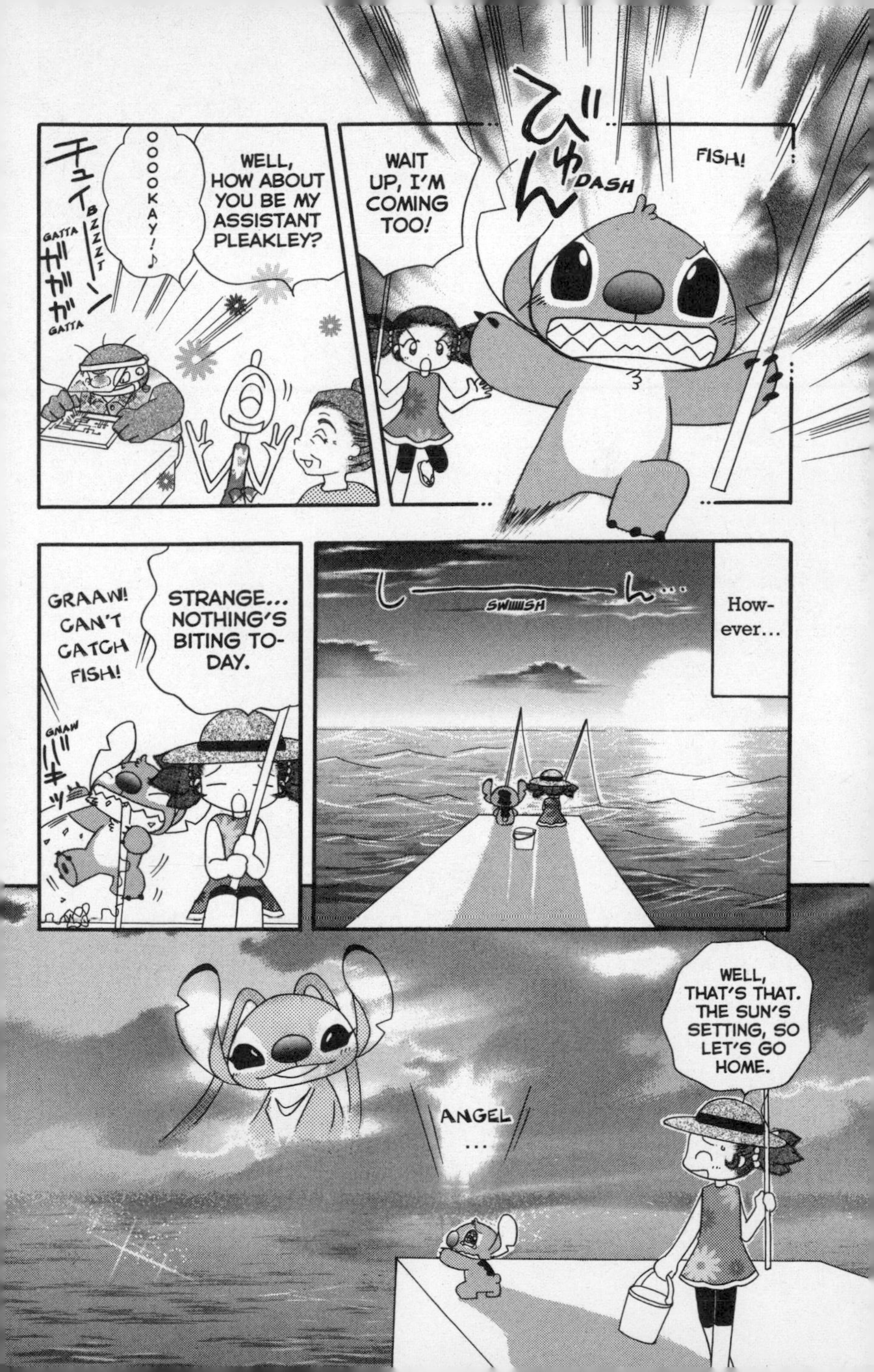
FISH!
びゅん
DASH
WAIT UP, I'M COMING TOO!
WELL, HOW ABOUT YOU BE MY ASSISTANT PLEAKLEY?
OOOOKAY!♪
チュイーン
BZZZT
ガガガ
GATTA GATTA
How-ever...
しーーーーん…
SWIIIISH
STRANGE... NOTHING'S BITING TO-DAY.
GRAAW! CAN'T CATCH FISH!
バキッ
GNAW
WELL, THAT'S THAT. THE SUN'S SETTING, SO LET'S GO HOME.
ANGEL ...

READ THIS WAY

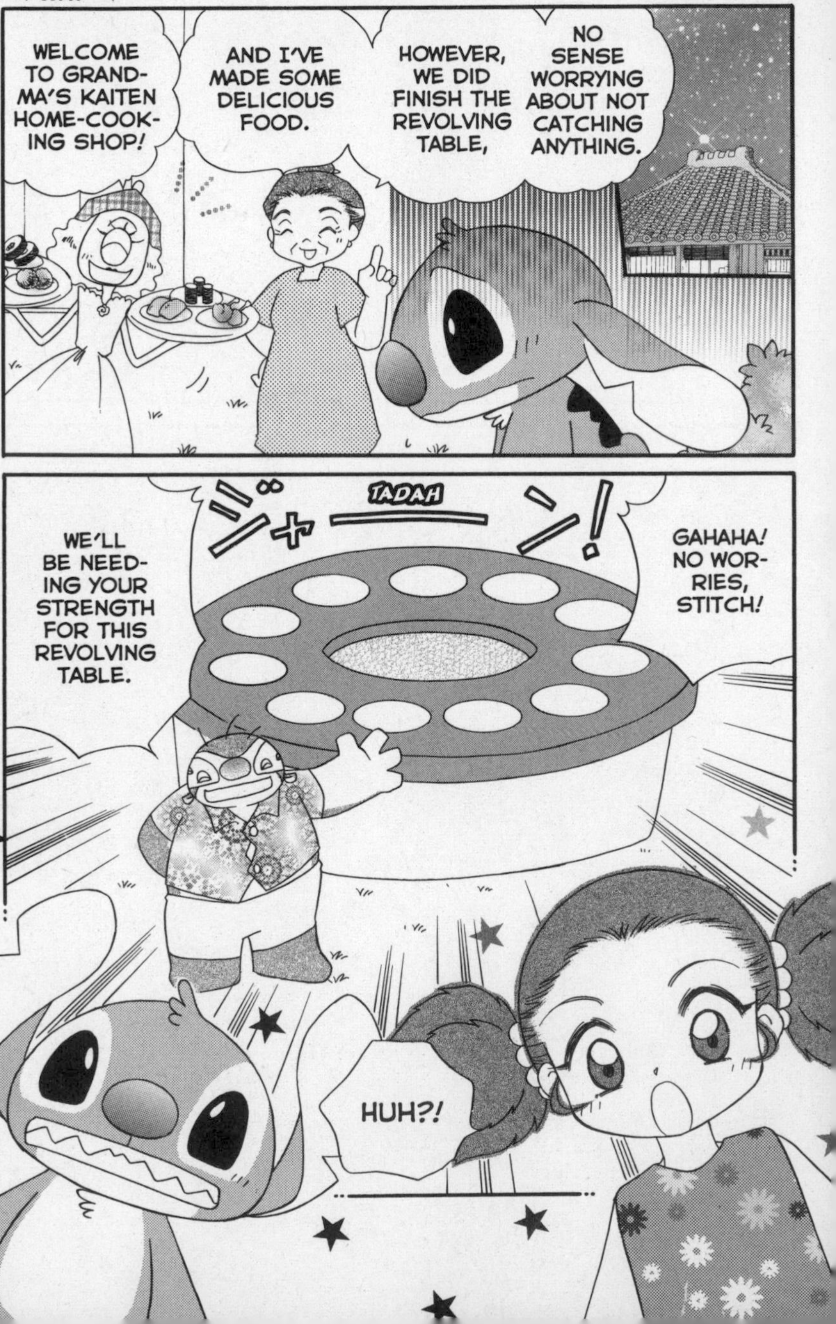
NO SENSE WORRYING ABOUT NOT CATCHING ANYTHING.
HOWEVER, WE DID FINISH THE REVOLVING TABLE,
AND I'VE MADE SOME DELICIOUS FOOD.
WELCOME TO GRAND-MA'S KAITEN HOME-COOK-ING SHOP!
GAHAHA! NO WOR-RIES, STITCH!
ジャーーン!
TADAH
WE'LL BE NEED-ING YOUR STRENGTH FOR THIS REVOLVING TABLE.
HUH?!

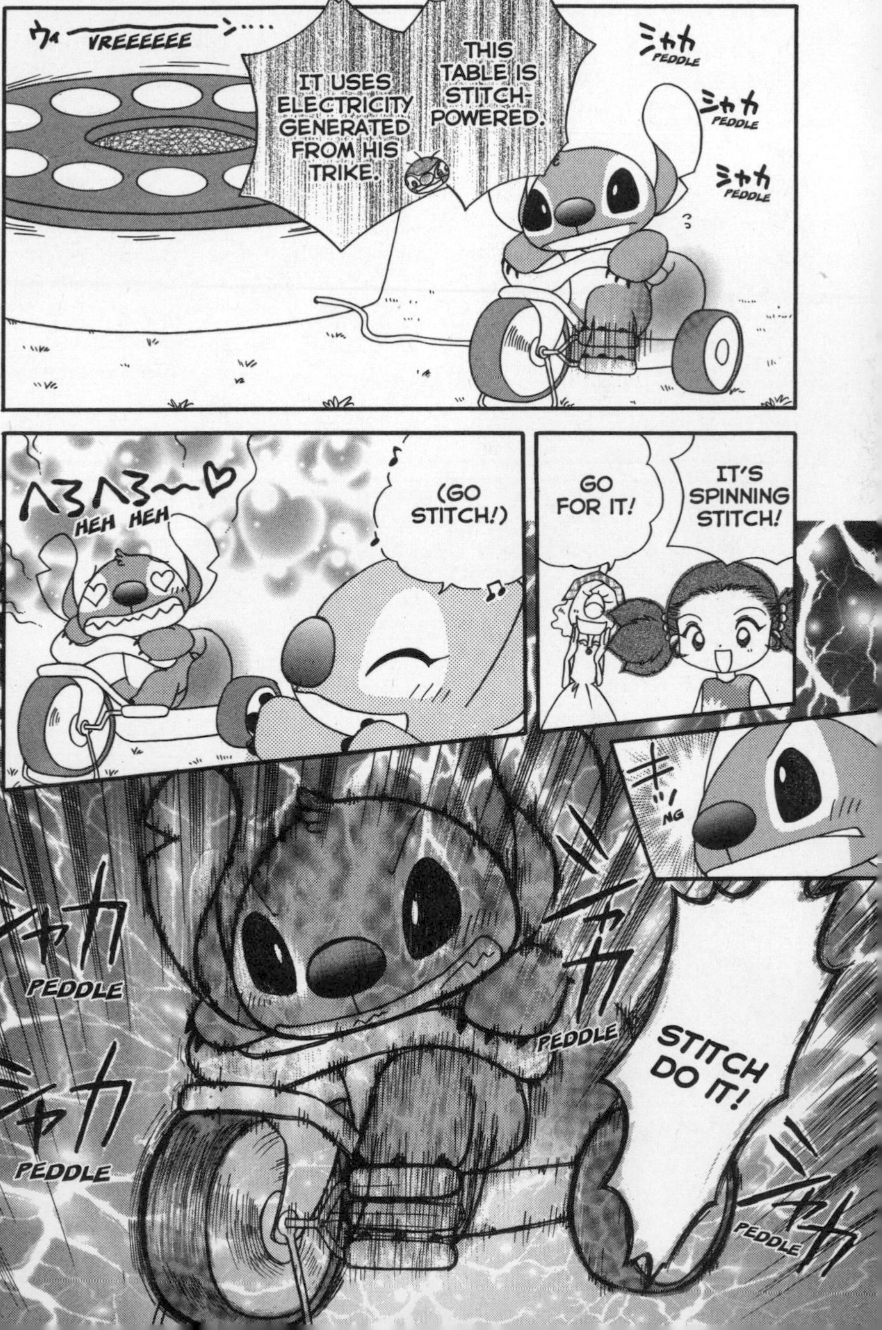
シャカ PEDDLE
シャカ PEDDLE
シャカ PEDDLE
THIS TABLE IS STITCH-POWERED.
IT USES ELECTRICITY GENERATED FROM HIS TRIKE.
ウィーーン.... VREEEEEE
IT'S SPINNING STITCH!
GO FOR IT!
(GO STITCH!)
へろへろ~♡ HEH HEH
キッ NG
STITCH DO IT!
シャカ PEDDLE
シャカ PEDDLE
シャカ PEDDLE
シャカ PEDDLE

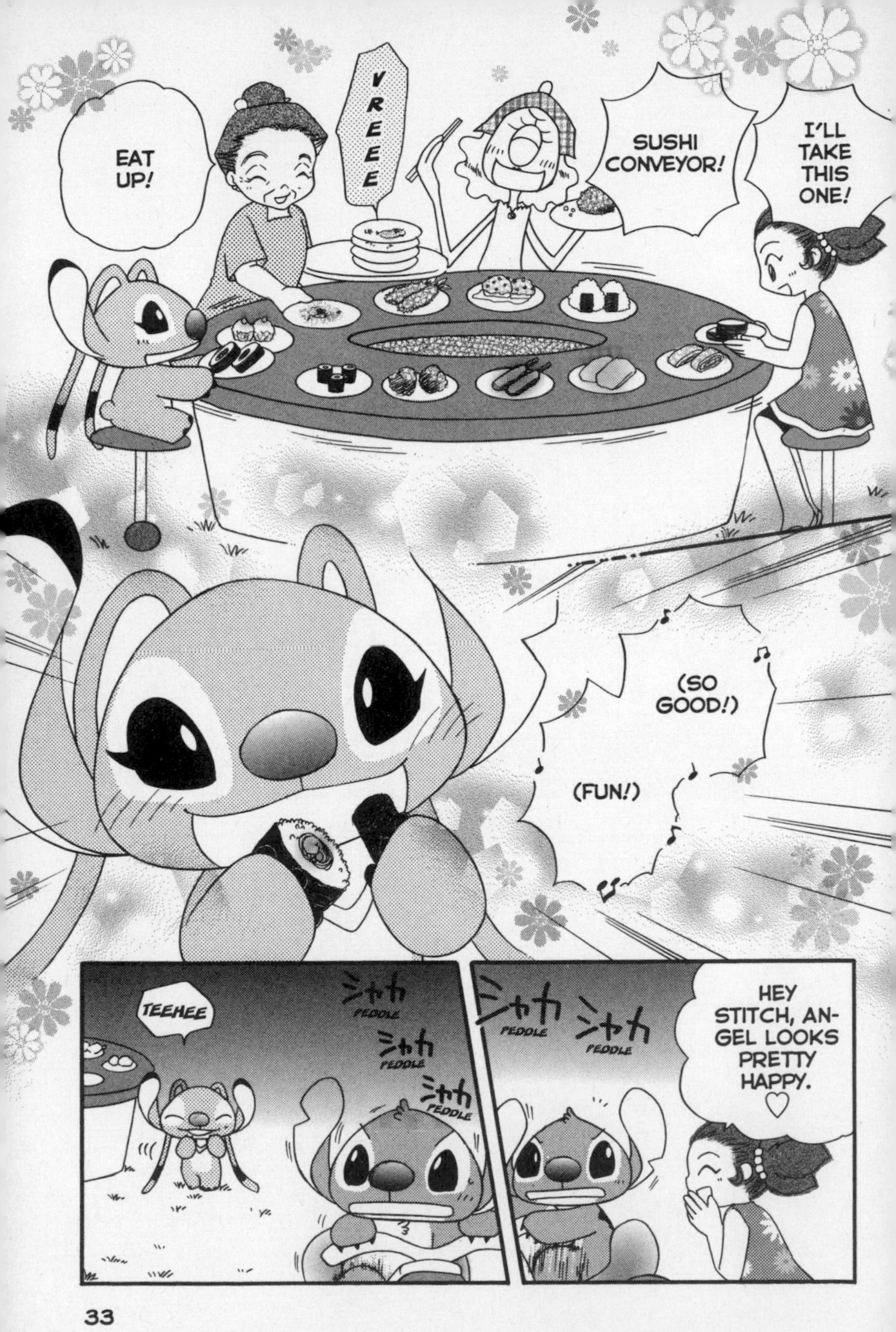
I'LL TAKE THIS ONE!
SUSHI CONVEYOR!
VREEEE
EAT UP!
(SO GOOD!)
(FUN!)
HEY STITCH, ANGEL LOOKS PRETTY HAPPY. ♡
シャカ PEDDLE
シャカ PEDDLE
シャカ PEDDLE
シャカ PEDDLE
シャカ PEDDLE
TEEHEE

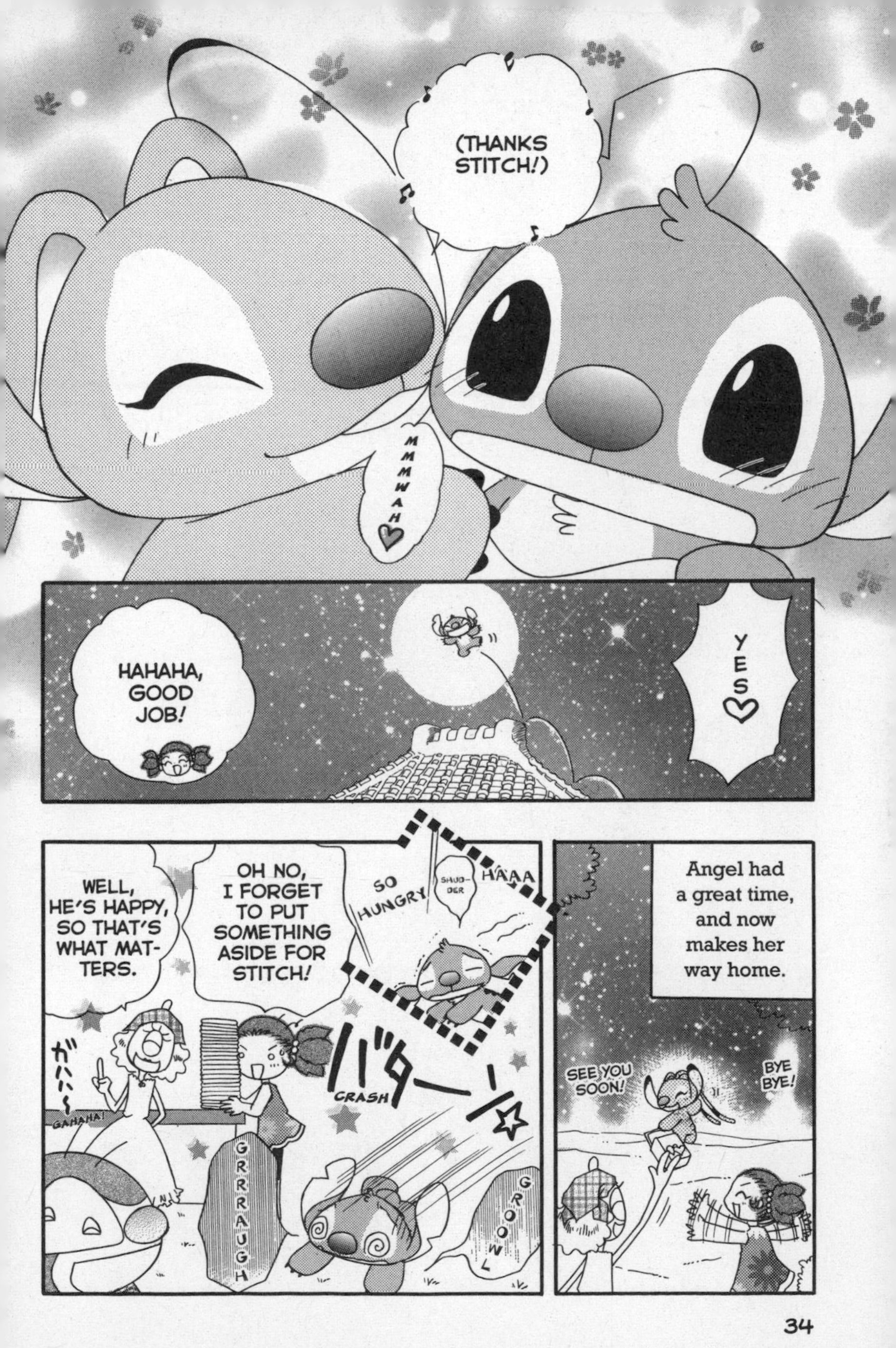
(THANKS STITCH!)
MMMWAH♥
YES♥
HAHAHA, GOOD JOB!
Angel had a great time, and now makes her way home.
BYE BYE!
SEE YOU SOON!
HÄAA
SHUD-DER
SO HUNGRY
OH NO, I FORGET TO PUT SOMETHING ASIDE FOR STITCH!
WELL, HE'S HAPPY, SO THAT'S WHAT MAT-TERS.
バターン
CRASH
GROOOWL
GRRRAUGH
ガハハ~
GAHAHA!

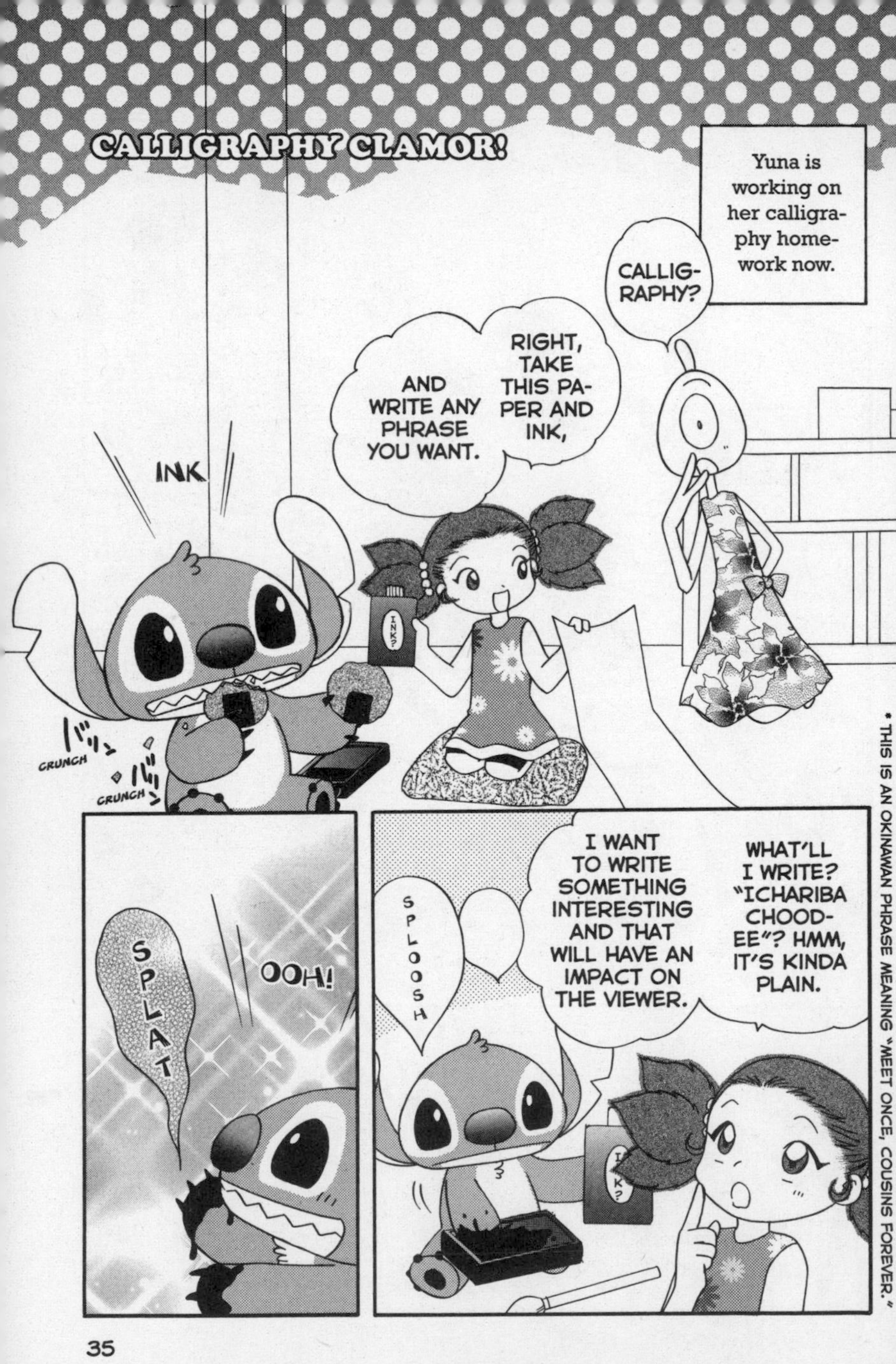
CALLIGRAPHY CLAMOR!
Yuna is working on her calligraphy homework now.
CALLIG-RAPHY?
RIGHT, TAKE THIS PAPER AND INK,
AND WRITE ANY PHRASE YOU WANT.
INK?
INK
CRUNCH
CRUNCH
WHAT'LL I WRITE? "ICHARIBA CHOODEE"? HMM, IT'S KINDA PLAIN.
I WANT TO WRITE SOMETHING INTERESTING AND THAT WILL HAVE AN IMPACT ON THE VIEWER.
SPLOOSH
INK?
OOH!
SPLAT

* THIS IS AN OKINAWAN PHRASE MEANING "MEET ONCE, COUSINS FOREVER."

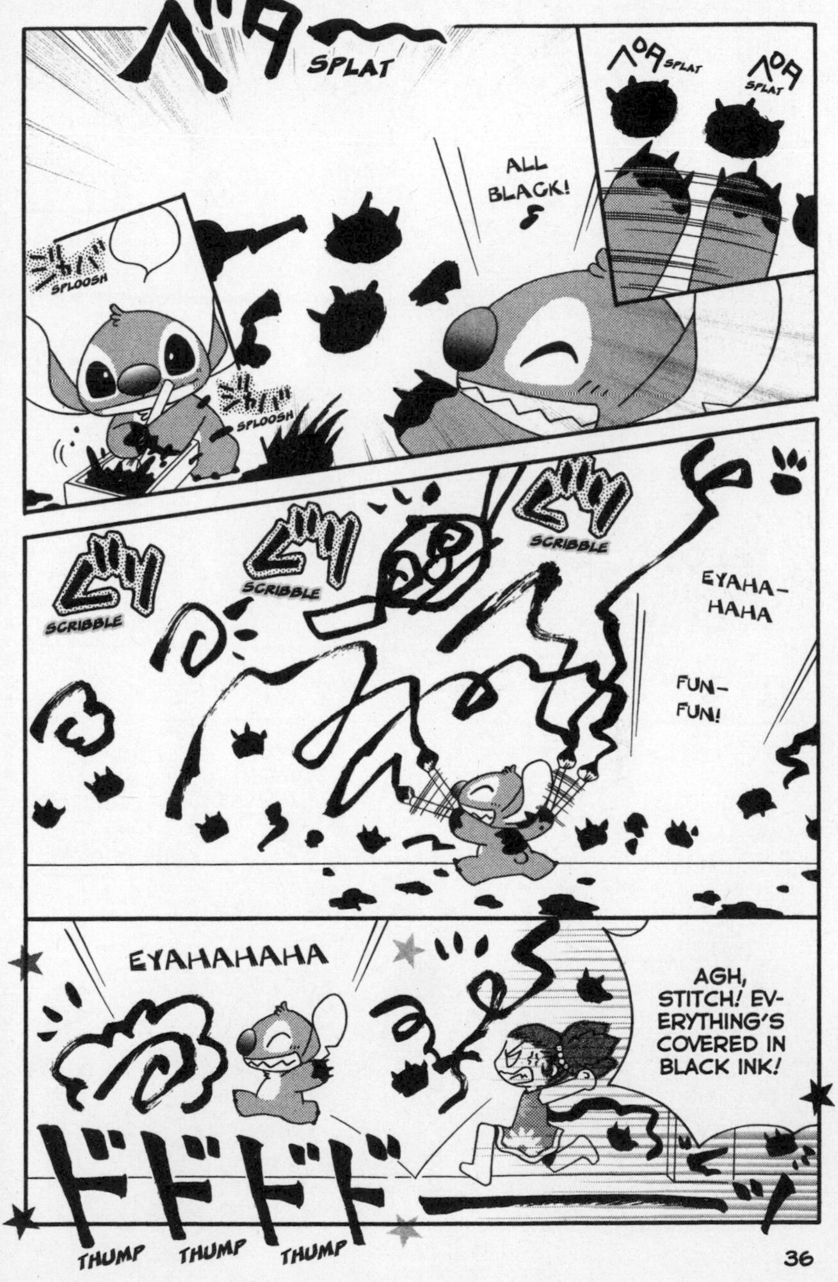
SPLAT
SPLAT
SPLAT
ALL BLACK!
SPLOOSH
SPLOOSH
EYAHA-HAHA
FUN-FUN!
SCRIBBLE
SCRIBBLE
SCRIBBLE
AGH, STITCH! EV-ERYTHING'S COVERED IN BLACK INK!
EYAHAHAHA
THUMP
THUMP
THUMP

READ THIS WAY

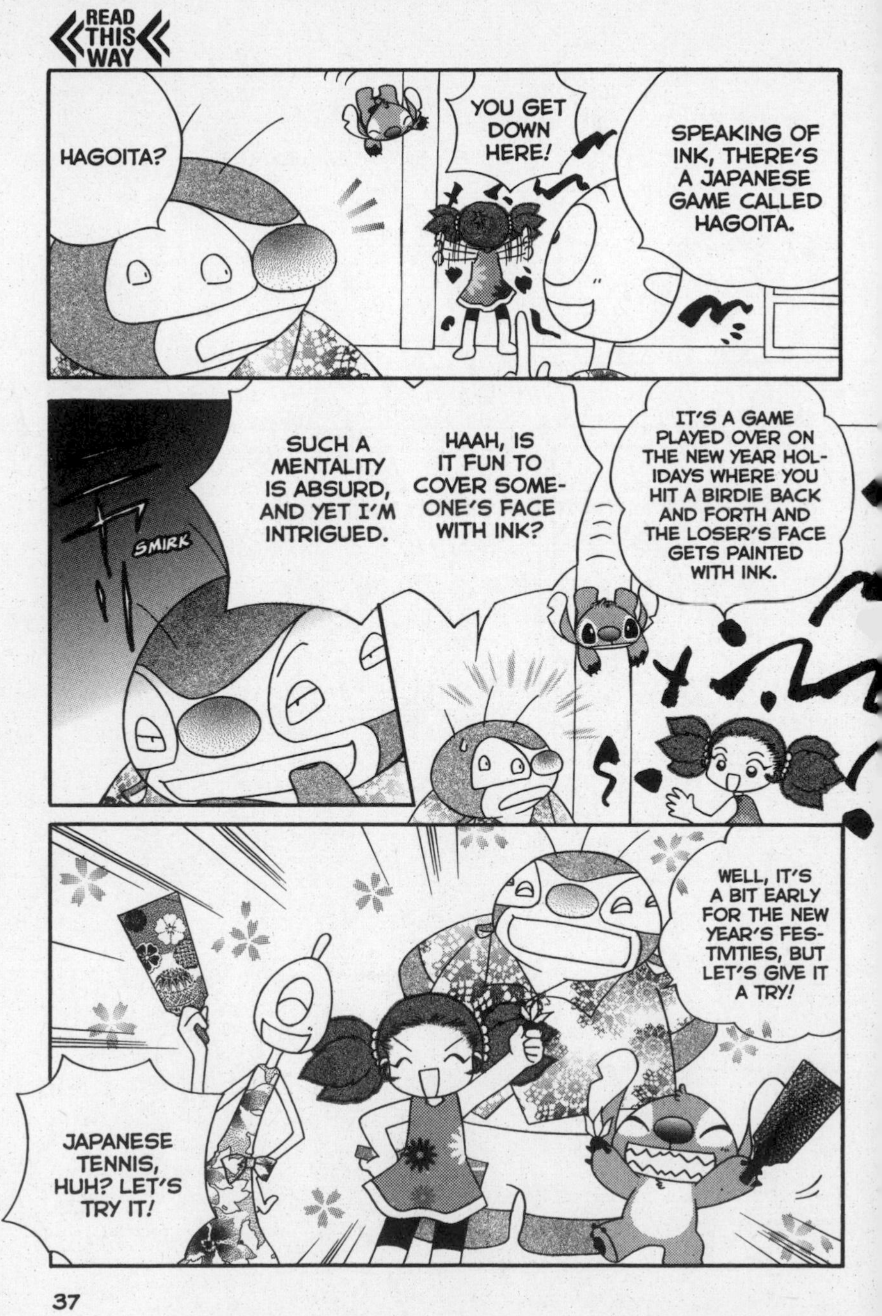

SPEAKING OF INK, THERE'S A JAPANESE GAME CALLED HAGOITA.
YOU GET DOWN HERE!
HAGOITA?
IT'S A GAME PLAYED OVER ON THE NEW YEAR HOLIDAYS WHERE YOU HIT A BIRDIE BACK AND FORTH AND THE LOSER'S FACE GETS PAINTED WITH INK.
HAAH, IS IT FUN TO COVER SOMEONE'S FACE WITH INK?
SUCH A MENTALITY IS ABSURD, AND YET I'M INTRIGUED.
SMIRK
WELL, IT'S A BIT EARLY FOR THE NEW YEAR'S FESTIVITIES, BUT LET'S GIVE IT A TRY!
JAPANESE TENNIS, HUH? LET'S TRY IT!

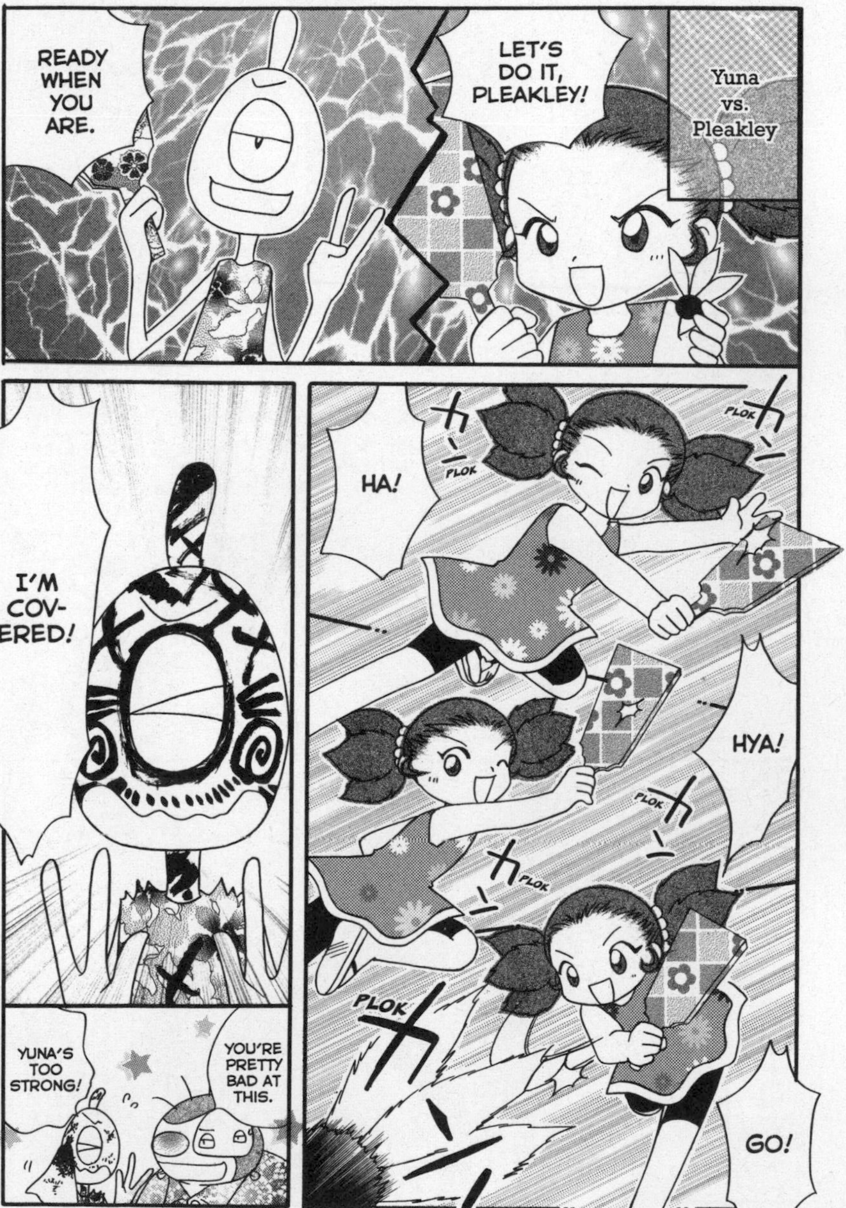
Yuna vs. Pleakley
LET'S DO IT, PLEAKLEY!
READY WHEN YOU ARE.
PLOK
HA!
PLOK
HYA!
PLOK
PLOK
GO!
PLOK
I'M COV-ERED!
YOU'RE PRETTY BAD AT THIS.
YUNA'S TOO STRONG!

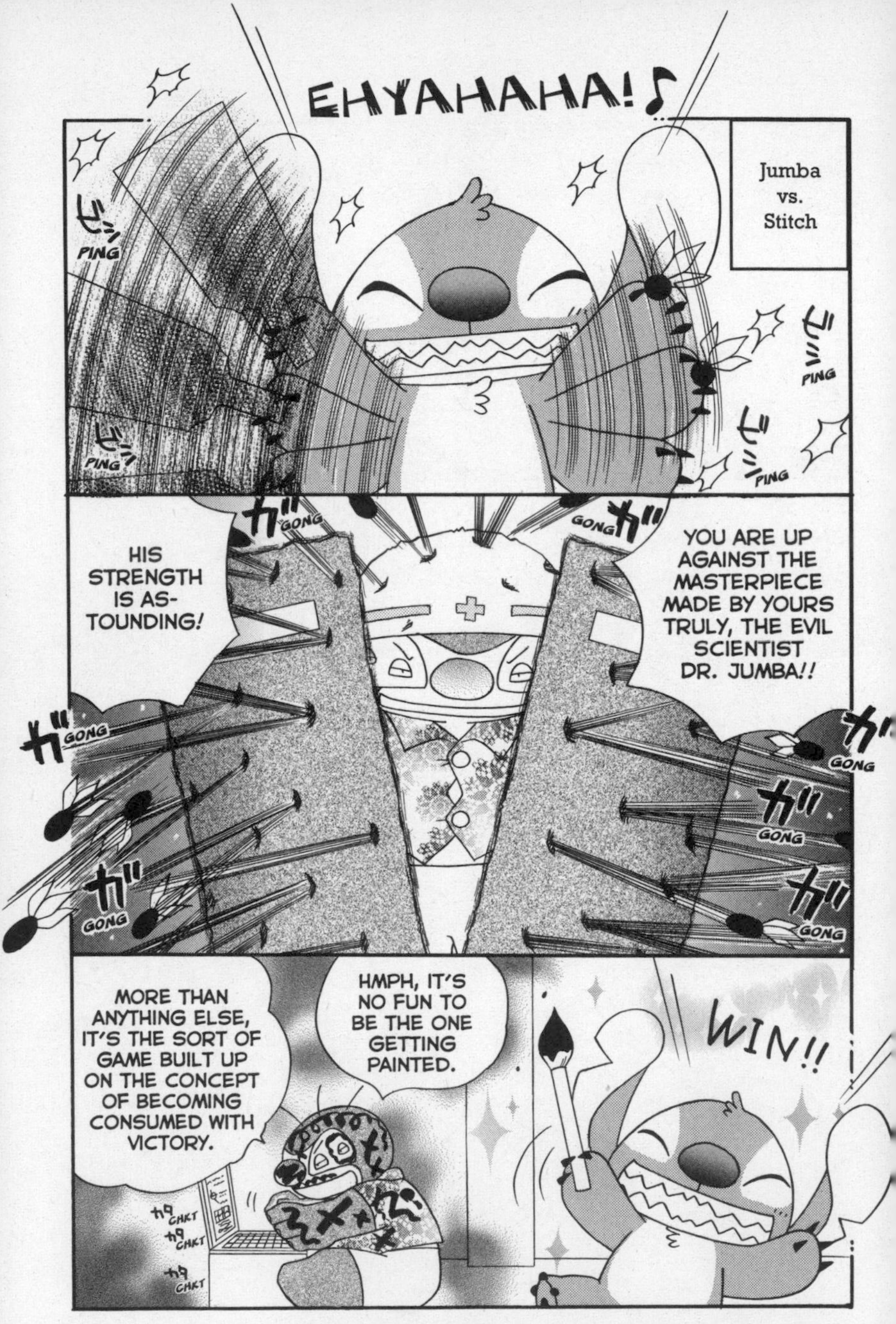
EHYAHAHA!♪
Jumba vs. Stitch
PING
PING
PING
PING
YOU ARE UP AGAINST THE MASTERPIECE MADE BY YOURS TRULY, THE EVIL SCIENTIST DR. JUMBA!!
GONG
GONG
HIS STRENGTH IS AS-TOUNDING!
GONG
GONG
GONG
GONG
GONG
WIN!!
HMPH, IT'S NO FUN TO BE THE ONE GETTING PAINTED.
MORE THAN ANYTHING ELSE, IT'S THE SORT OF GAME BUILT UP ON THE CONCEPT OF BECOMING CONSUMED WITH VICTORY.
CHKT
CHKT
CHKT

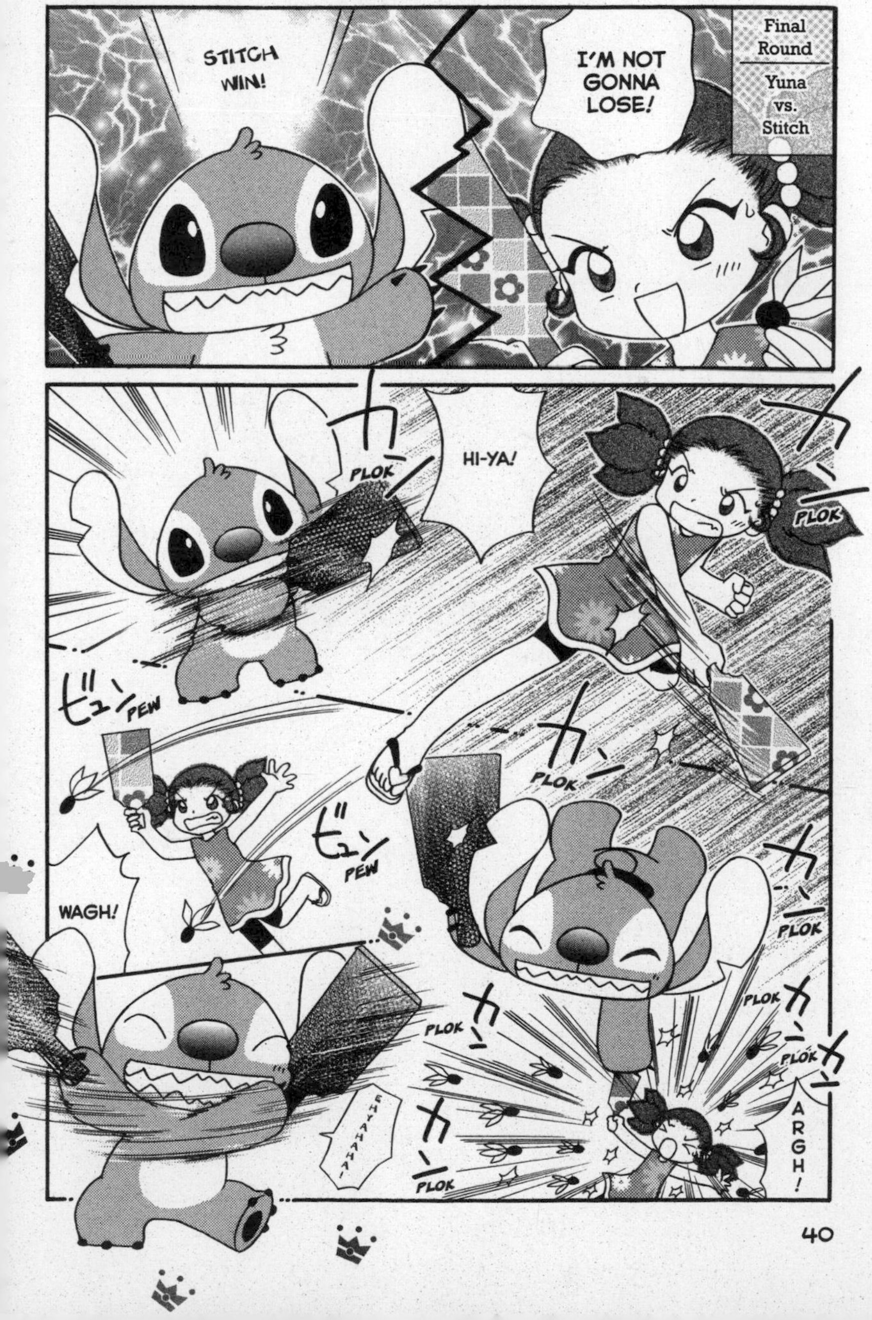
Final Round
Yuna vs. Stitch
I'M NOT GONNA LOSE!
STITCH WIN!
PLOK
HI-YA!
PLOK
PLOK
PEW
PEW
PLOK
WAGH!
PLOK
PLOK
PLOK
ARGH!
EHYAHAHA!
PLOK

READ THIS WAY

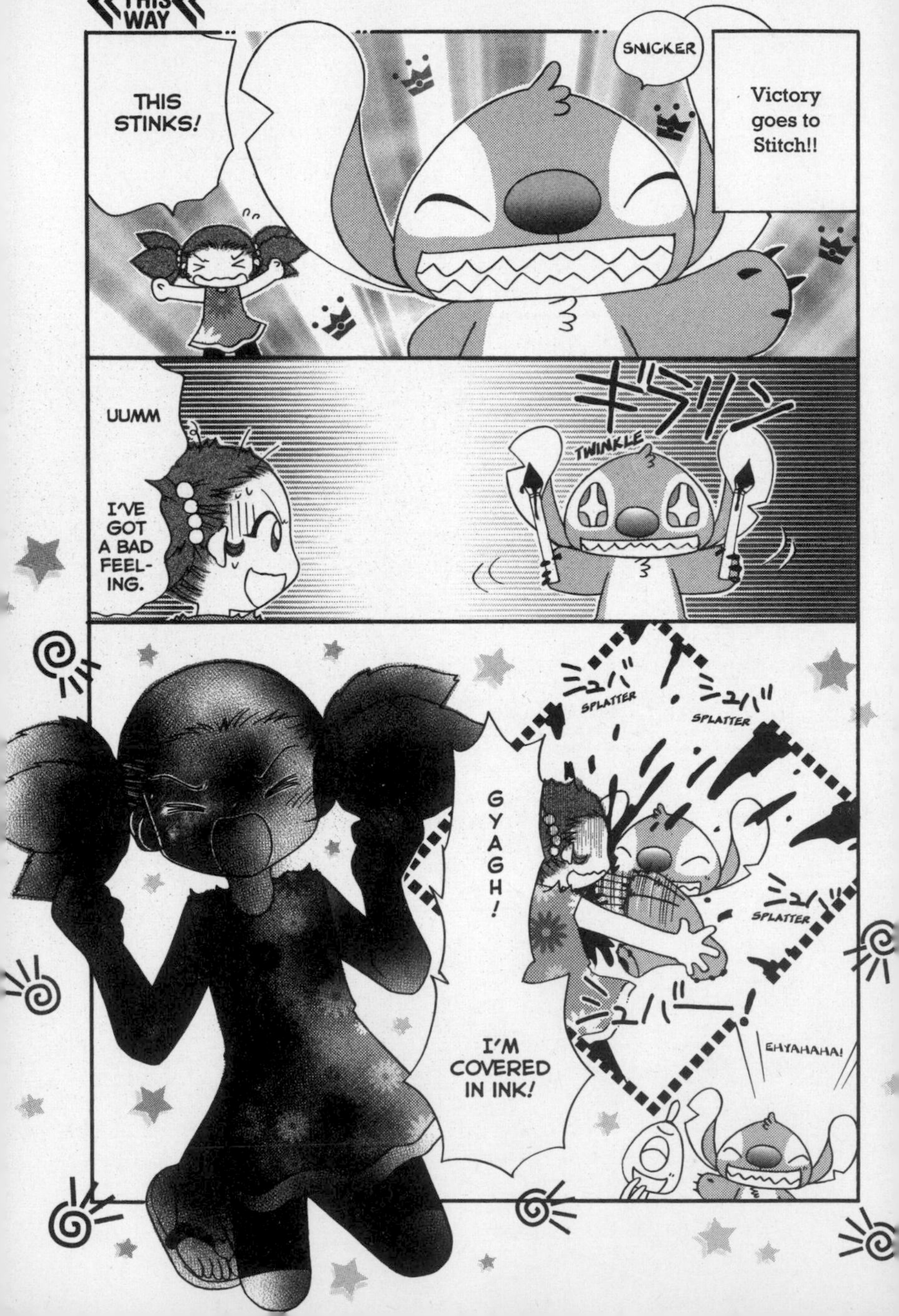

Victory goes to Stitch!!
SNICKER
THIS STINKS!
ギラリン
TWINKLE
UUMM
I'VE GOT A BAD FEEL-ING.
シュバ
SPLATTER
シュバ
SPLATTER
GYAGH!
シュバ
SPLATTER
シュバー!
EHYAHAHA!
I'M COVERED IN INK!

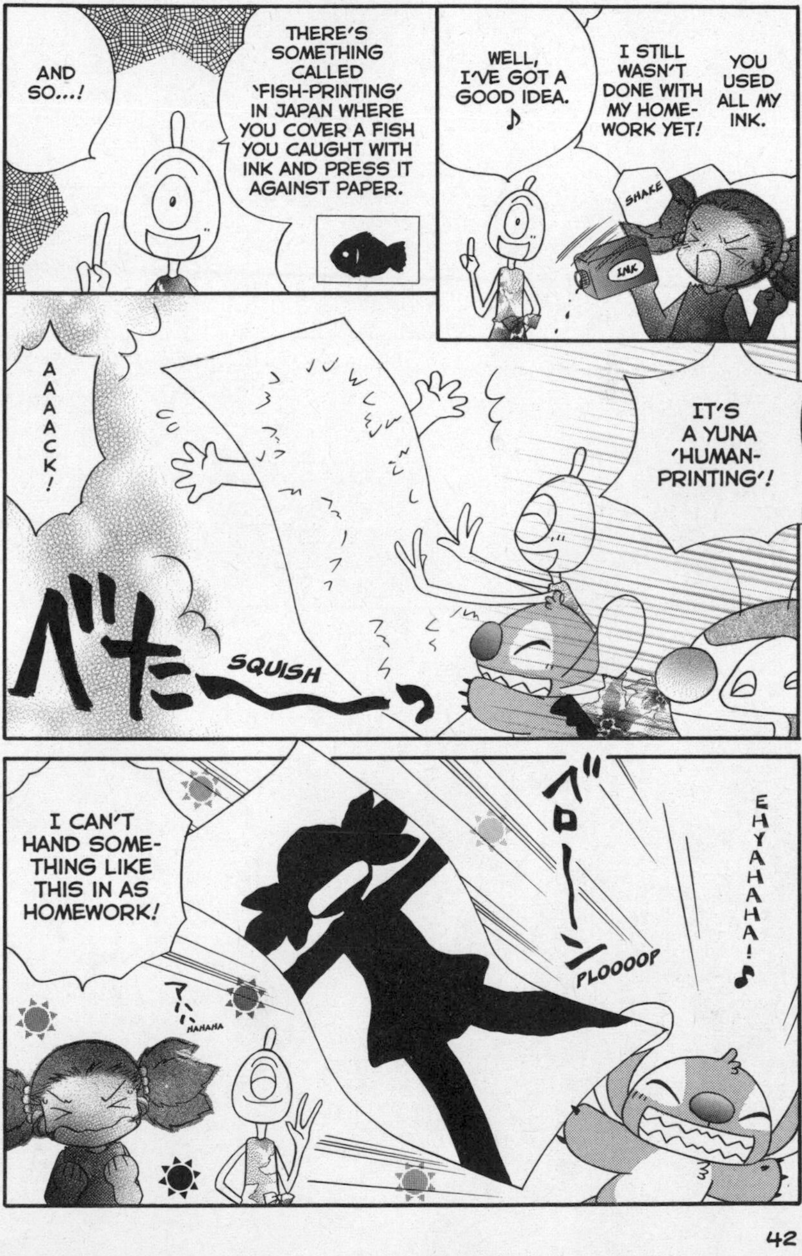
YOU USED ALL MY INK.
I STILL WASN'T DONE WITH MY HOME-WORK YET!
WELL, I'VE GOT A GOOD IDEA. ♪
SHAKE
INK
THERE'S SOMETHING CALLED 'FISH-PRINTING' IN JAPAN WHERE YOU COVER A FISH YOU CAUGHT WITH INK AND PRESS IT AGAINST PAPER.
AND SO...!
IT'S A YUNA 'HUMAN-PRINTING'!
AAAACK!
べた〜っ
SQUISH
ベロ〜ン
PLOOOOP
EHYAHAHAHA!♪
I CAN'T HAND SOME-THING LIKE THIS IN AS HOMEWORK!
アハハ
HAHAHA

YUNA'S HAND-KNITTED PRESENT!

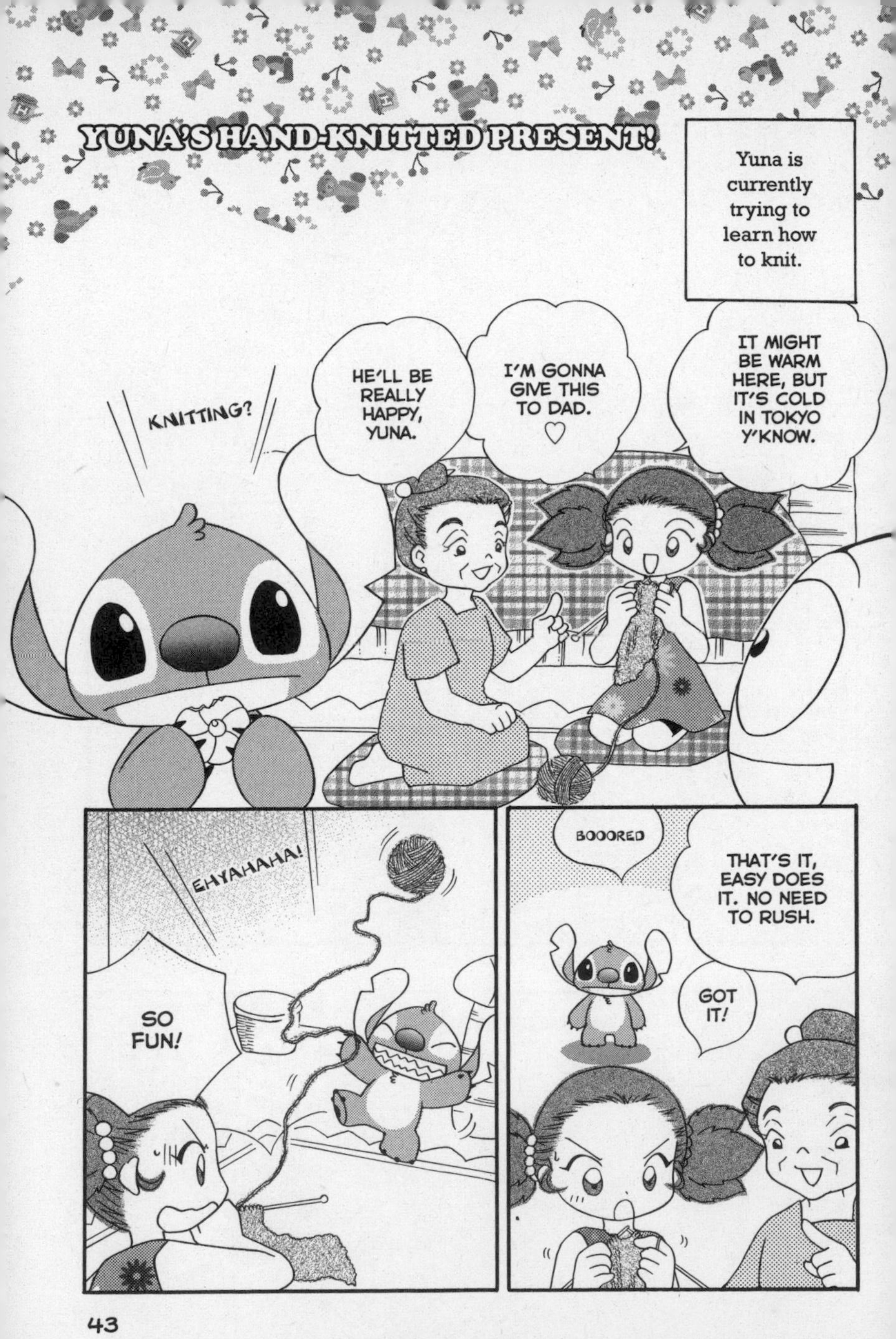
Yuna is currently trying to learn how to knit.
IT MIGHT BE WARM HERE, BUT IT'S COLD IN TOKYO Y'KNOW.
I'M GONNA GIVE THIS TO DAD. ♡
HE'LL BE REALLY HAPPY, YUNA.
KNITTING?
THAT'S IT, EASY DOES IT. NO NEED TO RUSH.
BOOORED
GOT IT!
EHYAHAHA!
SO FUN!

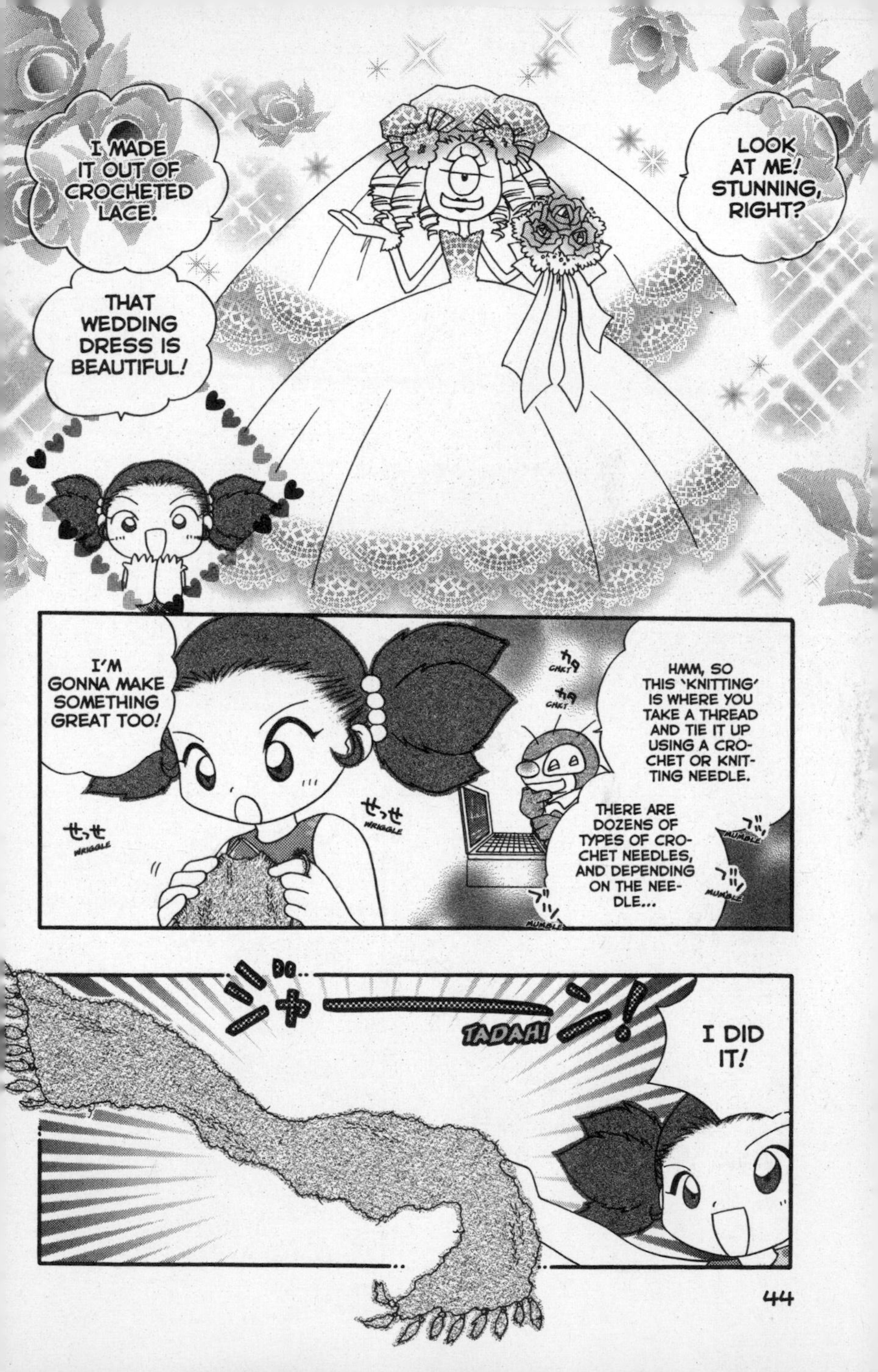
LOOK AT ME! STUNNING, RIGHT?
I MADE IT OUT OF CROCHETED LACE.
THAT WEDDING DRESS IS BEAUTIFUL!
カタ CHKT
カタ CHKT
HMM, SO THIS 'KNITTING' IS WHERE YOU TAKE A THREAD AND TIE IT UP USING A CROCHET OR KNITTING NEEDLE.
THERE ARE DOZENS OF TYPES OF CROCHET NEEDLES, AND DEPENDING ON THE NEEDLE...
ブツ MUMBLE
ブツ MUMBLE
ブツ MUMBLE
I'M GONNA MAKE SOMETHING GREAT TOO!
せっせ WRIGGLE
せっせ WRIGGLE
I DID IT!
ジャーン DO...
TADAH!

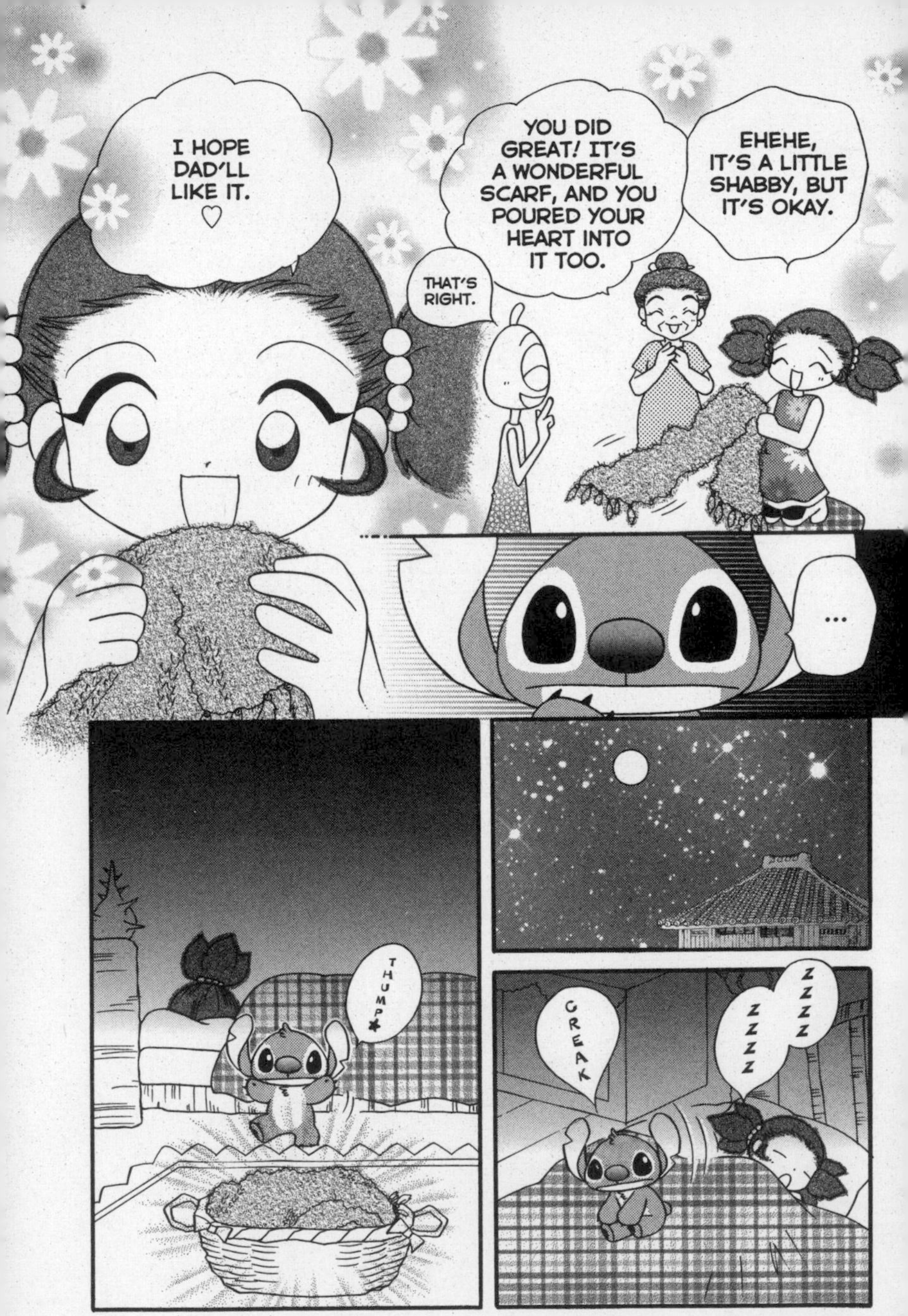
EHEHE, IT'S A LITTLE SHABBY, BUT IT'S OKAY.
YOU DID GREAT! IT'S A WONDERFUL SCARF, AND YOU POURED YOUR HEART INTO IT TOO.
THAT'S RIGHT.
...
I HOPE DAD'LL LIKE IT. ♡
ZZZZ
ZZZZ
CREAK
THUMP

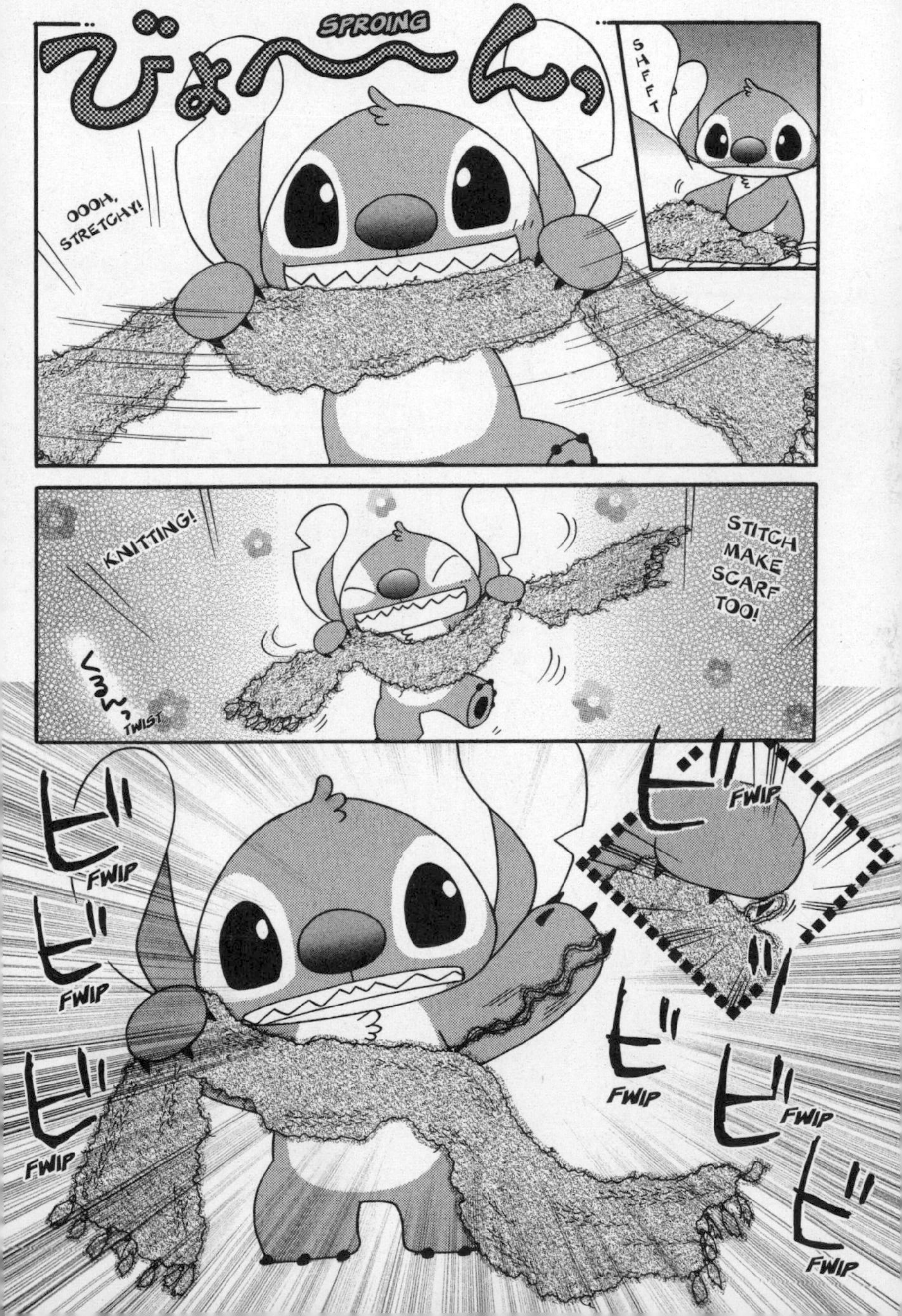
SHFFT
びょ〜〜ん
SPROING
OOOH, STRETCHY!
STITCH MAKE SCARF TOO!
KNITTING!
くるん〜
TWIST
FWIP
FWIP
FWIP
FWIP
FWIP
FWIP
FWIP

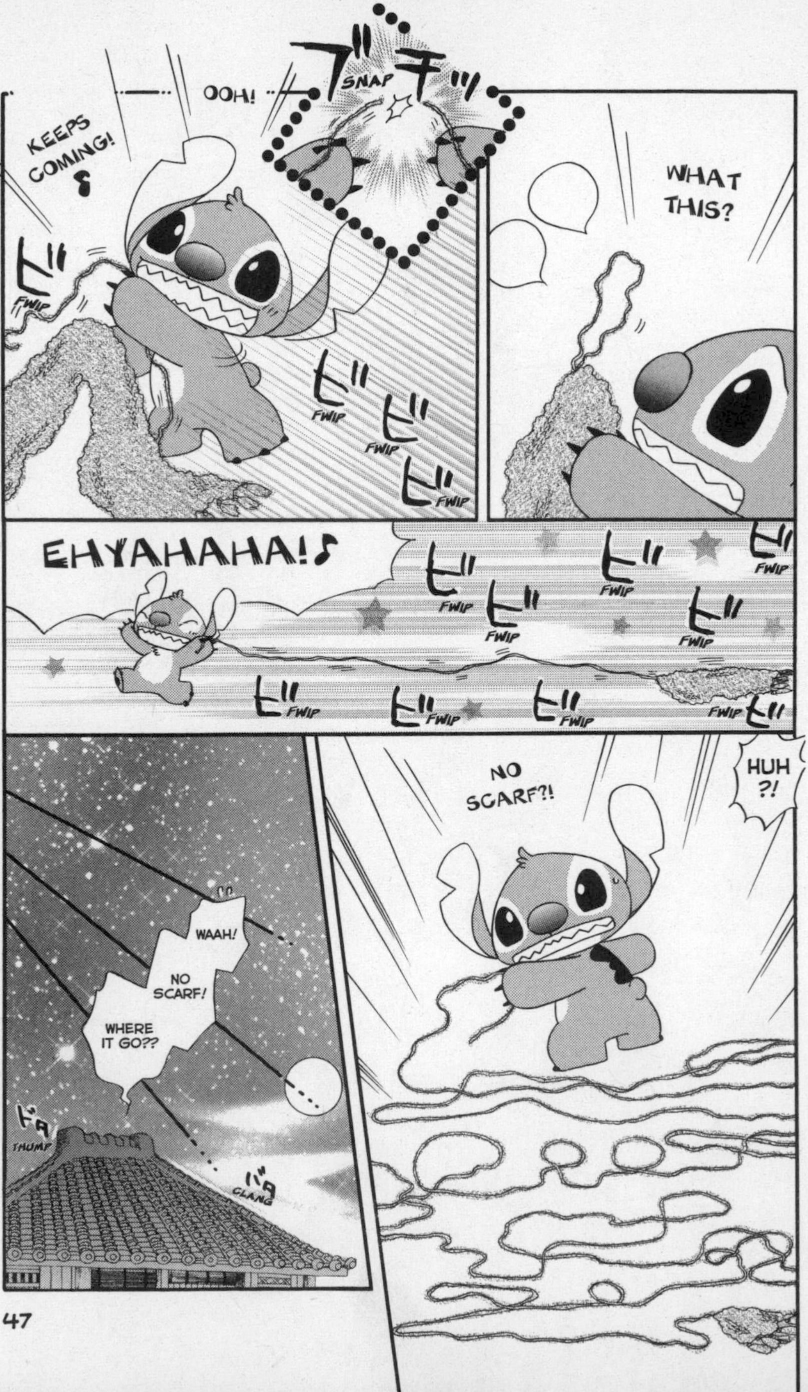
WHAT THIS?
ブチッ SNAP
OOH!
KEEPS COMING!
ビ FWIP
ビ FWIP
ビ FWIP
ビ FWIP
ビ FWIP
ビ FWIP
ビ FWIP
ビ FWIP
ビ FWIP
EHYAHAHA!♪
ビ FWIP
ビ FWIP
ビ FWIP
ビ FWIP
HUH?!
NO SCARF?!
WAAH!
NO SCARF!
WHERE IT GO??
ドタ THUMP
バタ CLANG

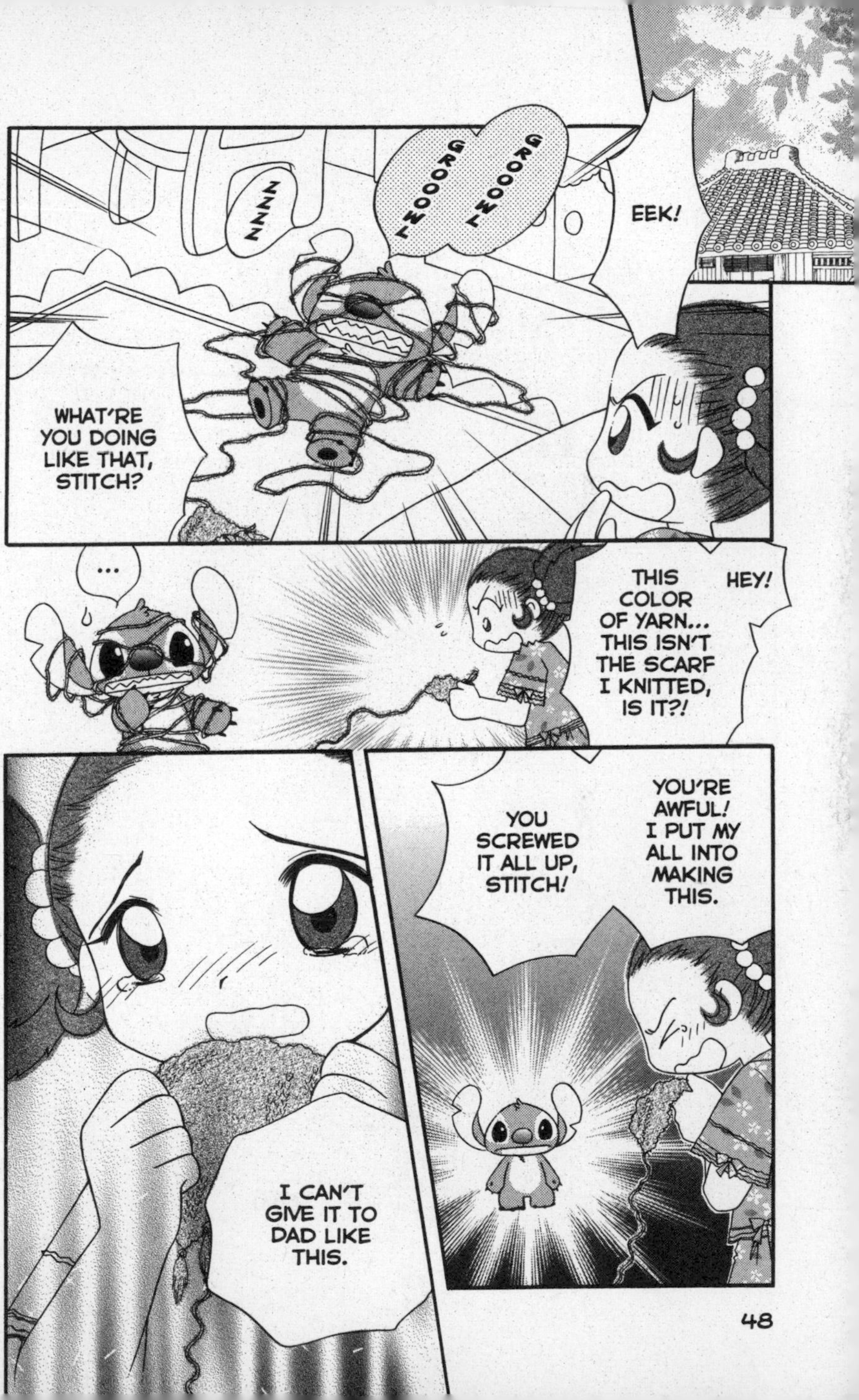
EEK!
GROOOWL GROOOWL
NNNN
WHAT'RE YOU DOING LIKE THAT, STITCH?
HEY!
THIS COLOR OF YARN... THIS ISN'T THE SCARF I KNITTED, IS IT?!
...
YOU'RE AWFUL! I PUT MY ALL INTO MAKING THIS.
YOU SCREWED IT ALL UP, STITCH!
I CAN'T GIVE IT TO DAD LIKE THIS.

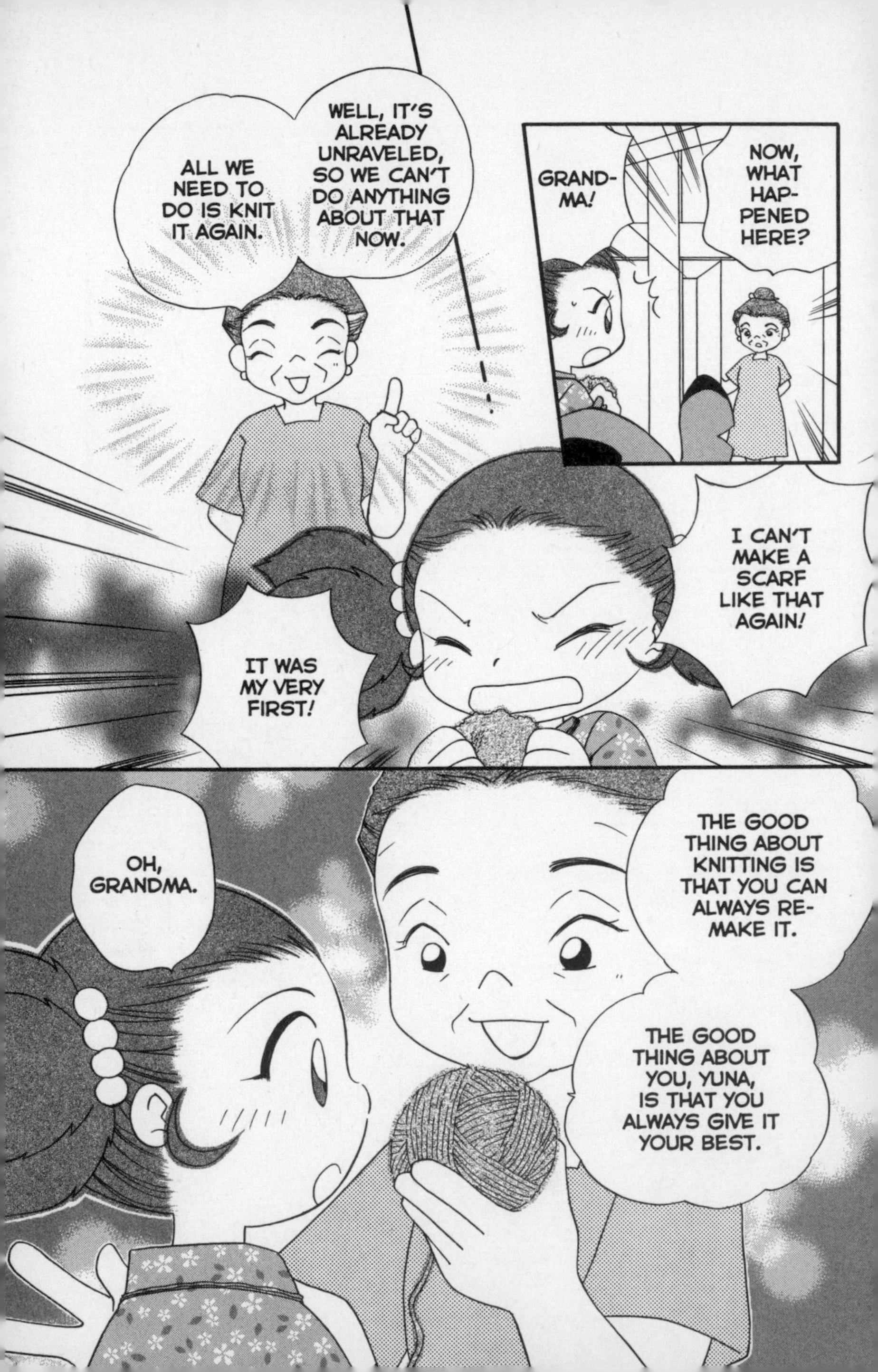
NOW, WHAT HAP-PENED HERE?
GRAND-MA!
WELL, IT'S ALREADY UNRAVELED, SO WE CAN'T DO ANYTHING ABOUT THAT NOW.
ALL WE NEED TO DO IS KNIT IT AGAIN.
I CAN'T MAKE A SCARF LIKE THAT AGAIN!
IT WAS MY VERY FIRST!
THE GOOD THING ABOUT KNITTING IS THAT YOU CAN ALWAYS RE-MAKE IT.
THE GOOD THING ABOUT YOU, YUNA, IS THAT YOU ALWAYS GIVE IT YOUR BEST.
OH, GRANDMA.

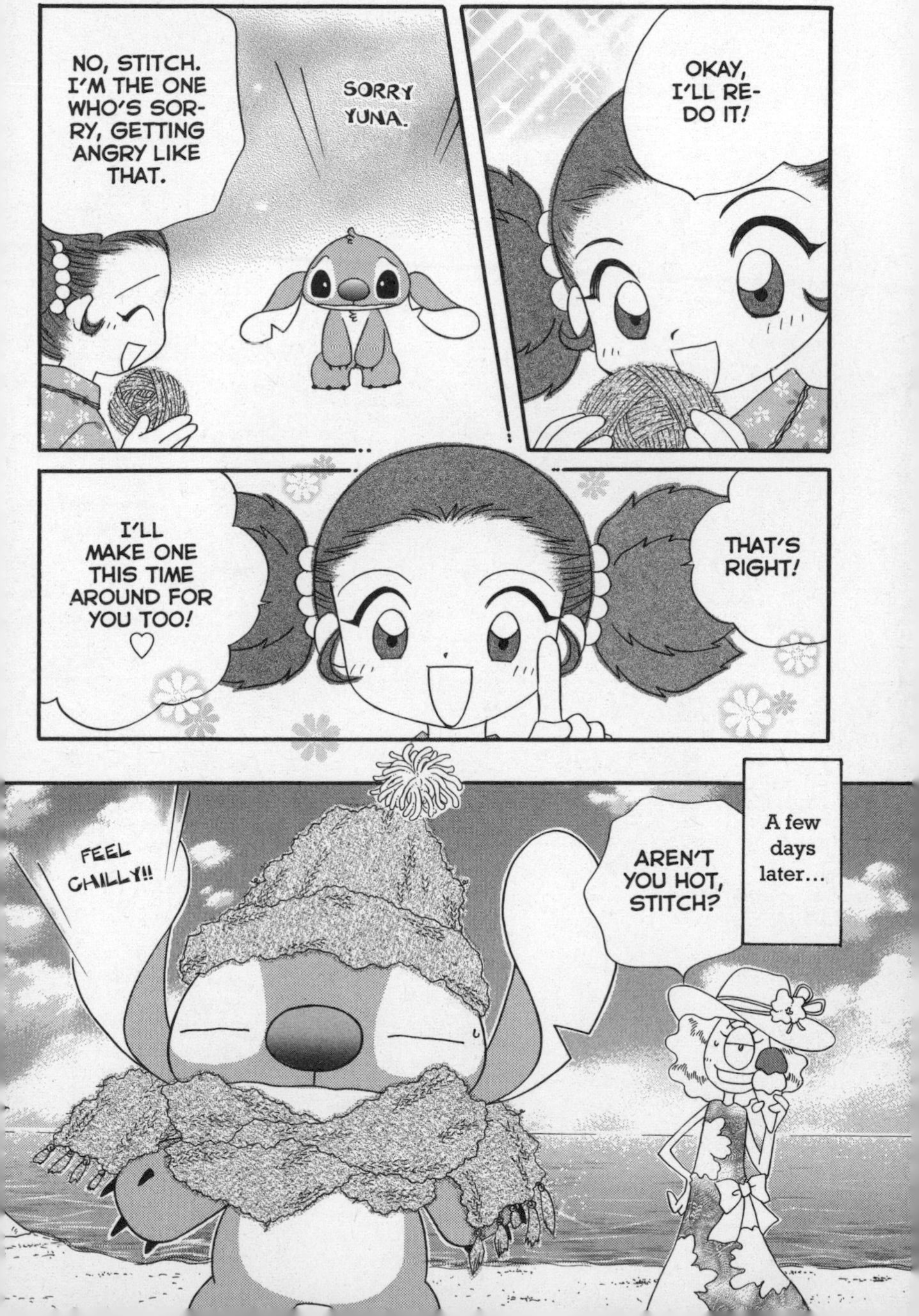
SORRY YUNA.
NO, STITCH. I'M THE ONE WHO'S SOR-RY, GETTING ANGRY LIKE THAT.
OKAY, I'LL RE-DO IT!
THAT'S RIGHT!
I'LL MAKE ONE THIS TIME AROUND FOR YOU TOO! ♡
A few days later…
AREN'T YOU HOT, STITCH?
FEEL CHILLY!!

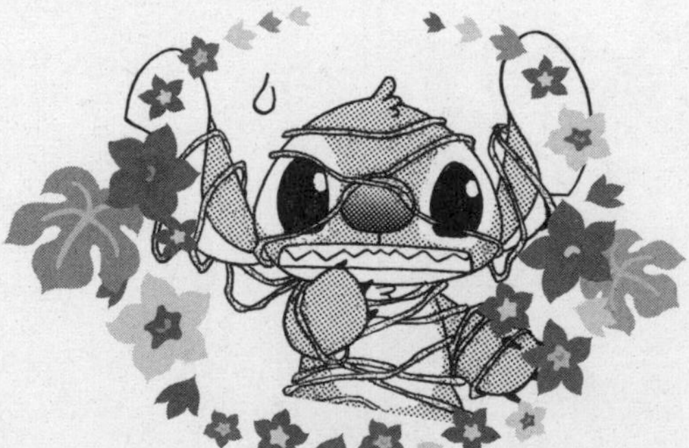

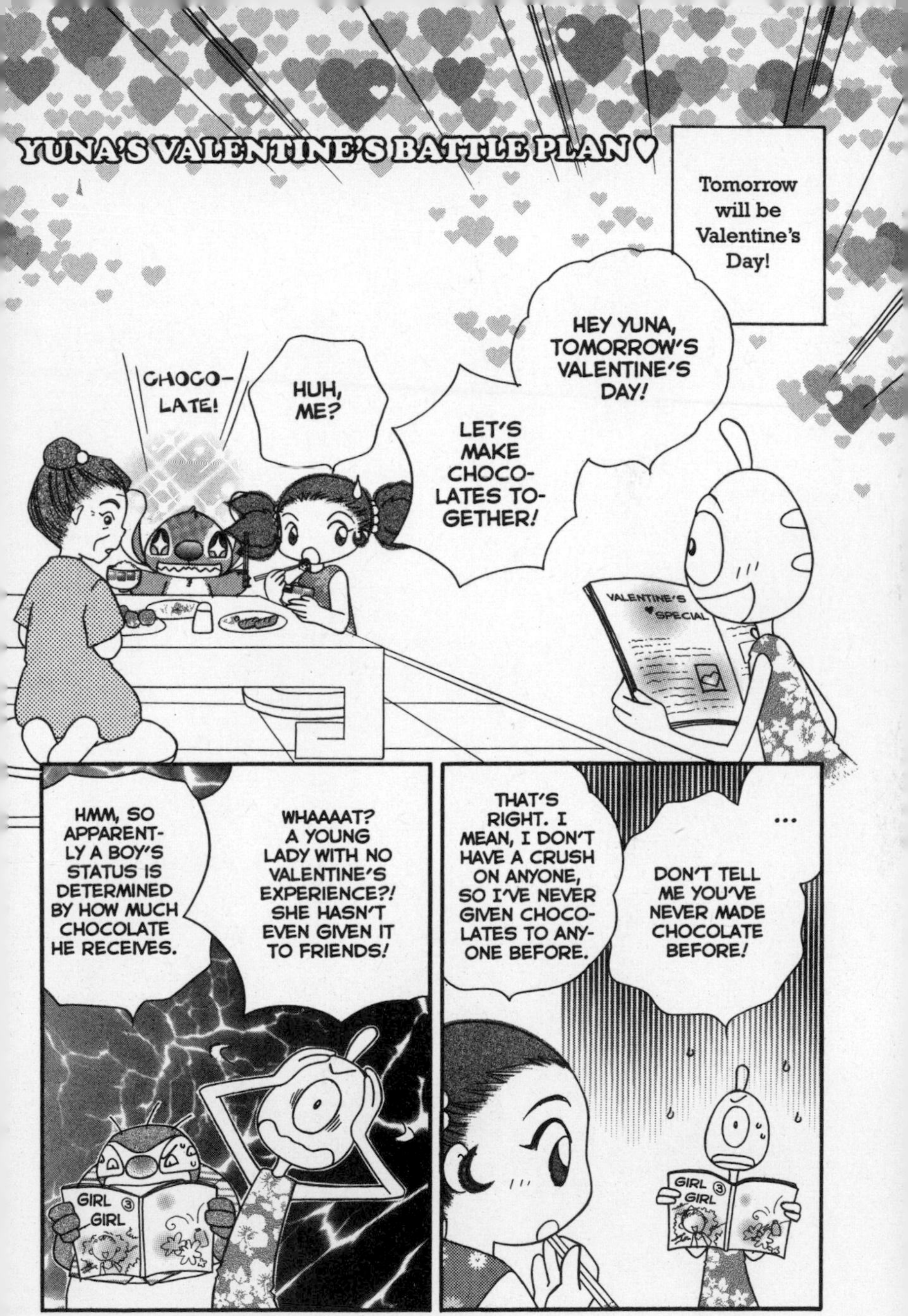
YUNA'S VALENTINE'S BATTLE PLAN ♥
Tomorrow will be Valentine's Day!
HEY YUNA, TOMORROW'S VALENTINE'S DAY!
LET'S MAKE CHOCO-LATES TO-GETHER!
VALENTINE'S ♥ SPECIAL
HUH, ME?
CHOCO-LATE!
...
DON'T TELL ME YOU'VE NEVER MADE CHOCOLATE BEFORE!
THAT'S RIGHT. I MEAN, I DON'T HAVE A CRUSH ON ANYONE, SO I'VE NEVER GIVEN CHOCO-LATES TO ANY-ONE BEFORE.
GIRL ③ GIRL
WHAAAAT? A YOUNG LADY WITH NO VALENTINE'S EXPERIENCE?! SHE HASN'T EVEN GIVEN IT TO FRIENDS!
HMM, SO APPARENT-LY A BOY'S STATUS IS DETERMINED BY HOW MUCH CHOCOLATE HE RECEIVES.
GIRL ③ GIRL

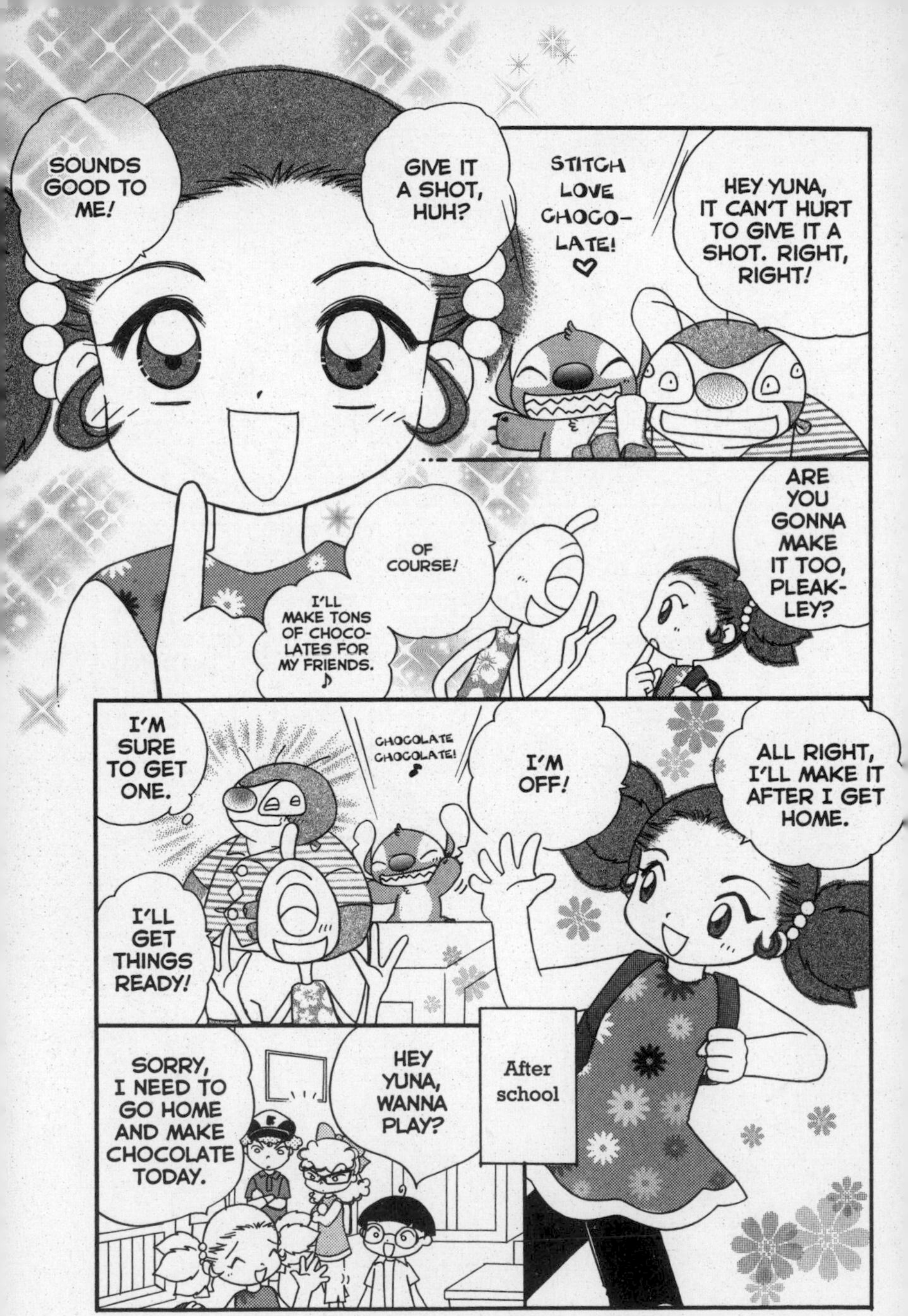
HEY YUNA, IT CAN'T HURT TO GIVE IT A SHOT. RIGHT, RIGHT!
STITCH LOVE CHOCOLATE! ♡
ARE YOU GONNA MAKE IT TOO, PLEAKLEY?
OF COURSE!
I'LL MAKE TONS OF CHOCOLATES FOR MY FRIENDS. ♪
GIVE IT A SHOT, HUH?
SOUNDS GOOD TO ME!
ALL RIGHT, I'LL MAKE IT AFTER I GET HOME.
I'M OFF!
CHOCOLATE CHOCOLATE! ♪
I'M SURE TO GET ONE.
I'LL GET THINGS READY!
After school
HEY YUNA, WANNA PLAY?
SORRY, I NEED TO GO HOME AND MAKE CHOCOLATE TODAY.

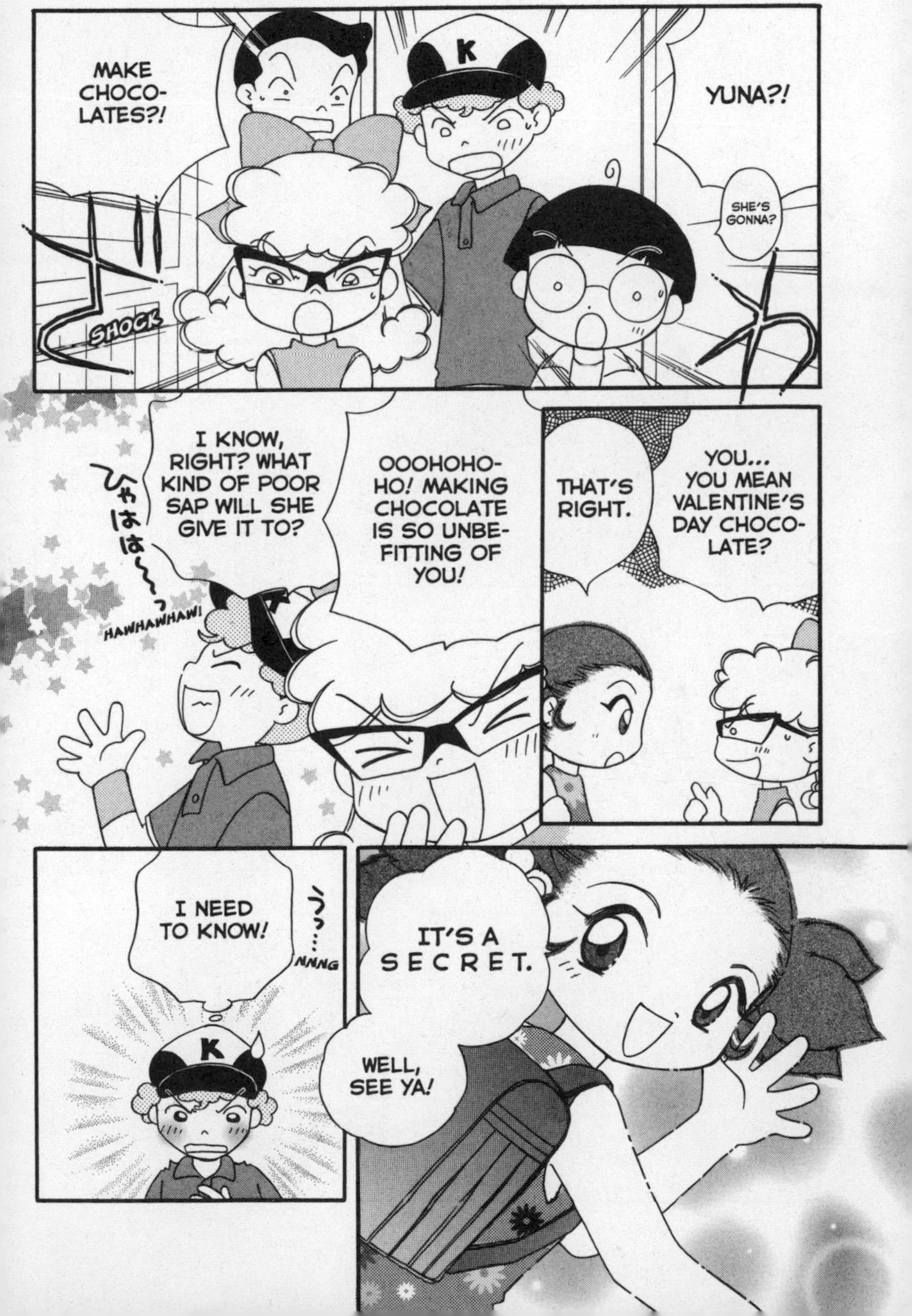
YUNA?!
SHE'S GONNA?
MAKE CHOCO-LATES?!
SHOCK
YOU... YOU MEAN VALENTINE'S DAY CHOCO-LATE?
THAT'S RIGHT.
OOOHOHO-HO! MAKING CHOCOLATE IS SO UNBE-FITTING OF YOU!
I KNOW, RIGHT? WHAT KIND OF POOR SAP WILL SHE GIVE IT TO?
ひゃはは〜〜っ
HAWHAWHAW!
IT'S A SECRET.
WELL, SEE YA!
I NEED TO KNOW!
うっ…
NNNG

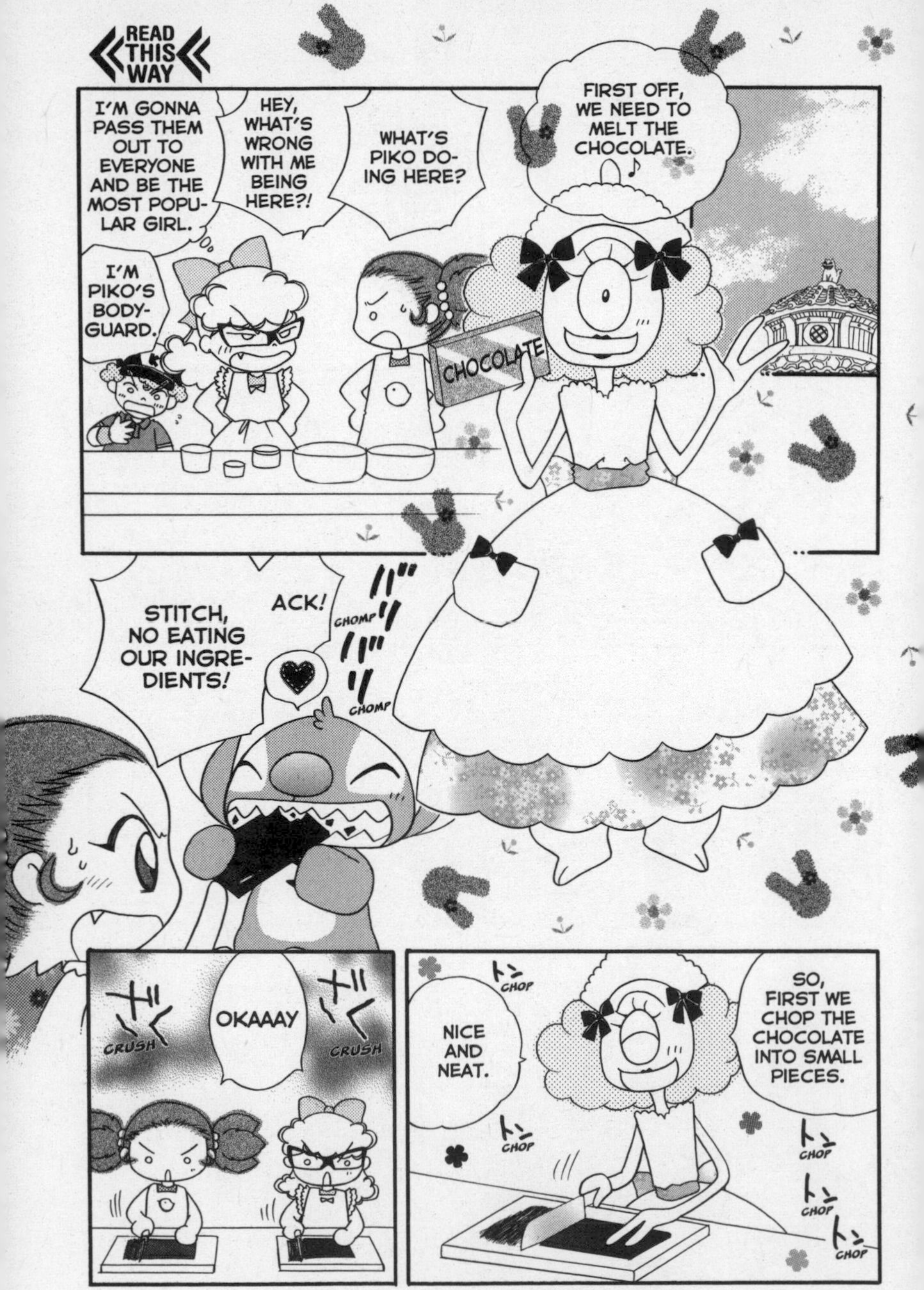
READ THIS WAY
FIRST OFF, WE NEED TO MELT THE CHOCOLATE. ♪
WHAT'S PIKO DOING HERE?
HEY, WHAT'S WRONG WITH ME BEING HERE?!
I'M GONNA PASS THEM OUT TO EVERYONE AND BE THE MOST POPULAR GIRL.
I'M PIKO'S BODYGUARD.
CHOCOLATE
ACK!
バリ GHOMP
バリ GHOMP
STITCH, NO EATING OUR INGREDIENTS!
SO, FIRST WE CHOP THE CHOCOLATE INTO SMALL PIECES.
トン CHOP
NICE AND NEAT.
トン CHOP
トン CHOP
トン CHOP
トン CHOP
ザく CRUSH
OKAAAY
ザく CRUSH

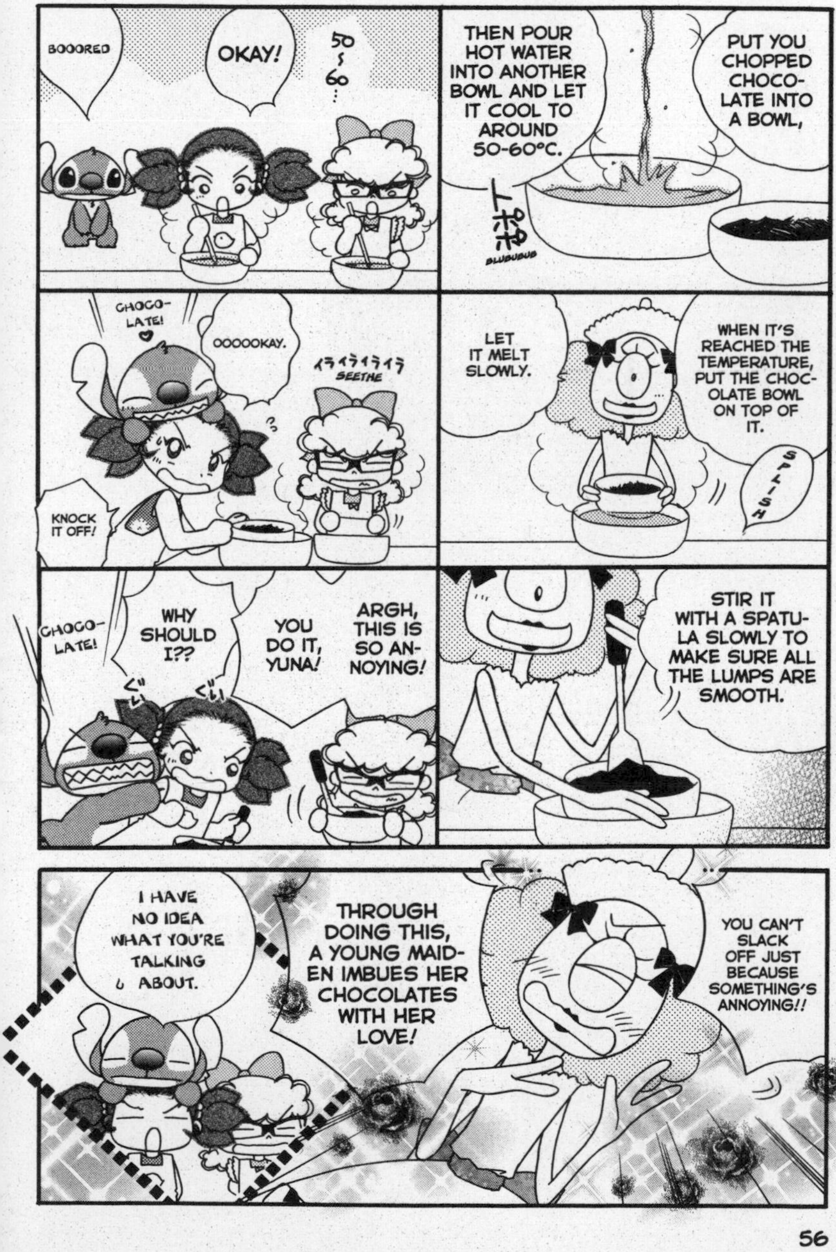
PUT YOU CHOPPED CHOCOLATE INTO A BOWL,
THEN POUR HOT WATER INTO ANOTHER BOWL AND LET IT COOL TO AROUND 50-60°C.
BLUBUBUB
50~60...
OKAY!
BOOORED
WHEN IT'S REACHED THE TEMPERATURE, PUT THE CHOCOLATE BOWL ON TOP OF IT.
SPLISH
LET IT MELT SLOWLY.
イライライライラ
SEETHE
OOOOOKAY.
CHOCOLATE! ♥
KNOCK IT OFF!
STIR IT WITH A SPATULA SLOWLY TO MAKE SURE ALL THE LUMPS ARE SMOOTH.
ARGH, THIS IS SO ANNOYING!
YOU DO IT, YUNA!
WHY SHOULD I??
CHOCOLATE!
YOU CAN'T SLACK OFF JUST BECAUSE SOMETHING'S ANNOYING!!
THROUGH DOING THIS, A YOUNG MAIDEN IMBUES HER CHOCOLATES WITH HER LOVE!
I HAVE NO IDEA WHAT YOU'RE TALKING ABOUT.

READ THIS WAY

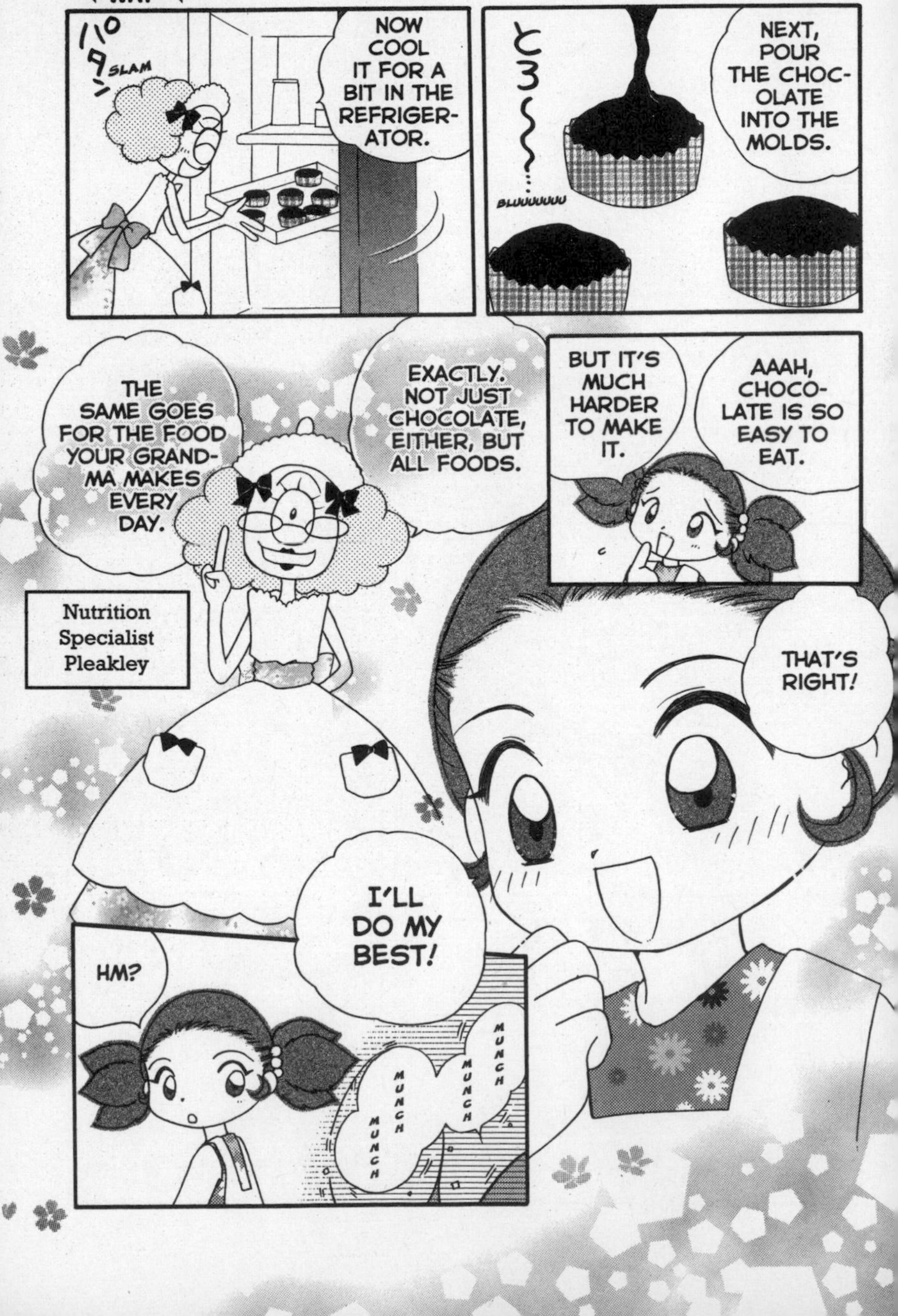
NEXT, POUR THE CHOCOLATE INTO THE MOLDS.
とろ〜…
BLUUUUUUU
NOW COOL IT FOR A BIT IN THE REFRIGERATOR.
パタン
SLAM
AAAH, CHOCOLATE IS SO EASY TO EAT.
BUT IT'S MUCH HARDER TO MAKE IT.
EXACTLY. NOT JUST CHOCOLATE, EITHER, BUT ALL FOODS.
THE SAME GOES FOR THE FOOD YOUR GRANDMA MAKES EVERY DAY.
Nutrition Specialist Pleakley
THAT'S RIGHT!
I'LL DO MY BEST!
MUNCH
MUNCH
MUNCH
MUNCH
HM?

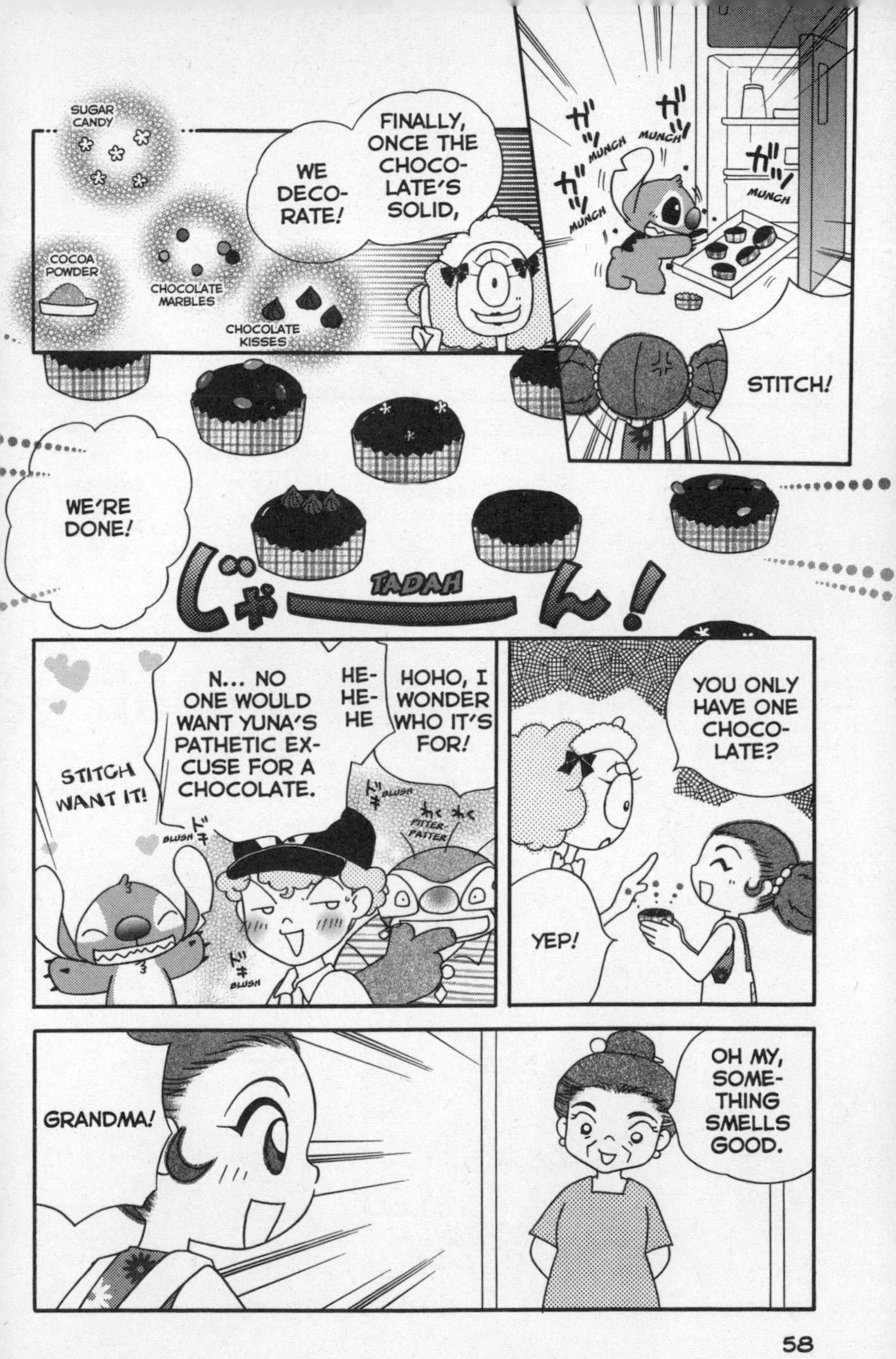
ガツ MUNCH
ガツ MUNCH
ガツ MUNCH
ガツ MUNCH
STITCH!
FINALLY, ONCE THE CHOCOLATE'S SOLID,
WE DECORATE!
SUGAR CANDY
CHOCOLATE MARBLES
COCOA POWDER
CHOCOLATE KISSES
WE'RE DONE!
じゃーーん! TADAH
YOU ONLY HAVE ONE CHOCOLATE?
YEP!
HOHO, I WONDER WHO IT'S FOR!
HE-HE-HE
わく わく PITTER-PATTER
ドキ BLUSH
N... NO ONE WOULD WANT YUNA'S PATHETIC EXCUSE FOR A CHOCOLATE.
ドキ BLUSH
ドキ BLUSH
STITCH WANT IT!
OH MY, SOMETHING SMELLS GOOD.
GRANDMA!

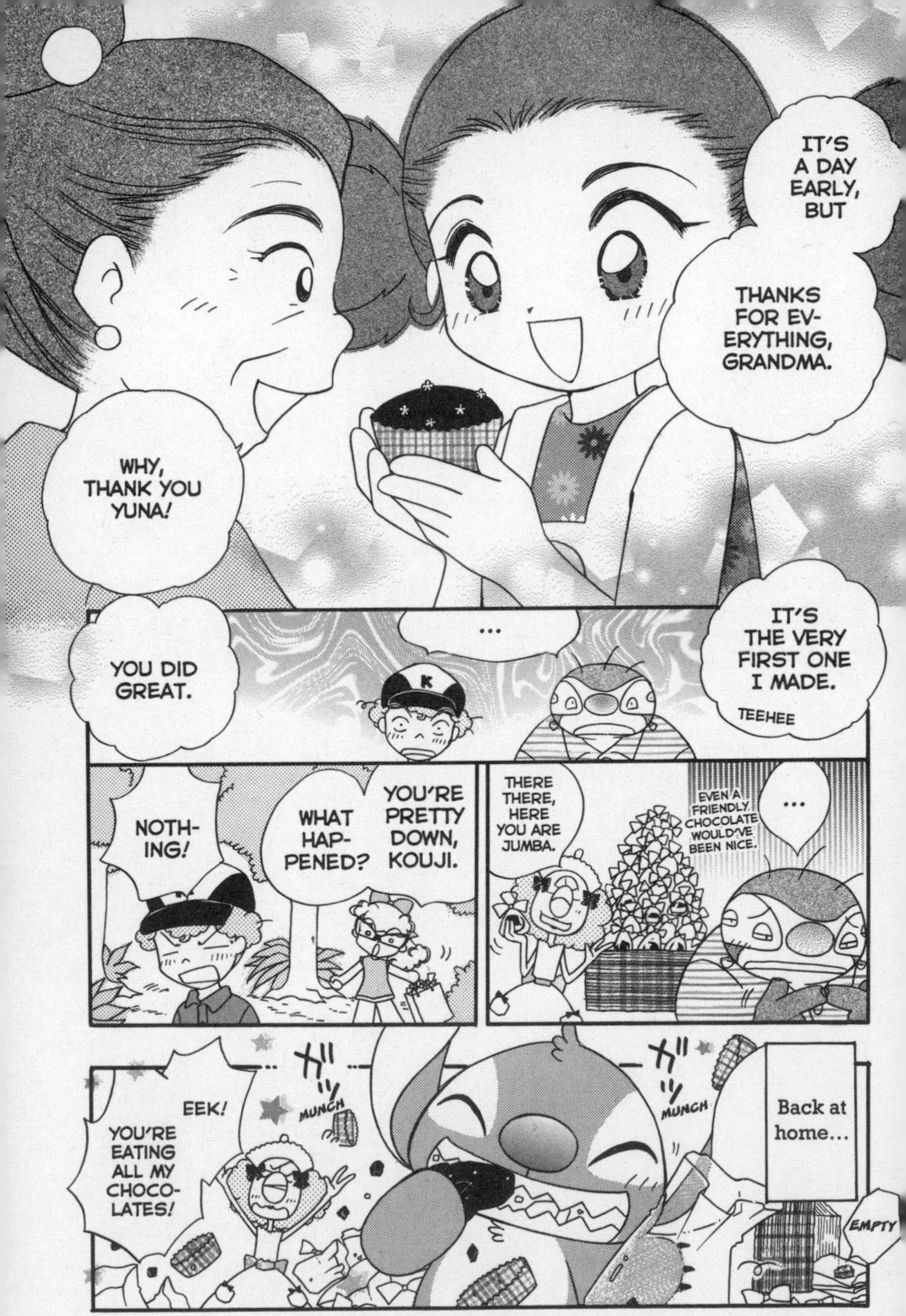

IT'S A DAY EARLY, BUT
THANKS FOR EV-ERYTHING, GRANDMA.
WHY, THANK YOU YUNA!
IT'S THE VERY FIRST ONE I MADE.
TEEHEE
...
YOU DID GREAT.
...
EVEN A FRIENDLY CHOCOLATE WOULD'VE BEEN NICE.
THERE THERE, HERE YOU ARE JUMBA.
YOU'RE PRETTY DOWN, KOUJI.
WHAT HAP-PENED?
NOTH-ING!
Back at home...
EMPTY
ガリ
MUNCH
ガリ
MUNCH
EEK!
YOU'RE EATING ALL MY CHOCO-LATES!

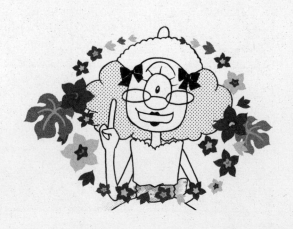

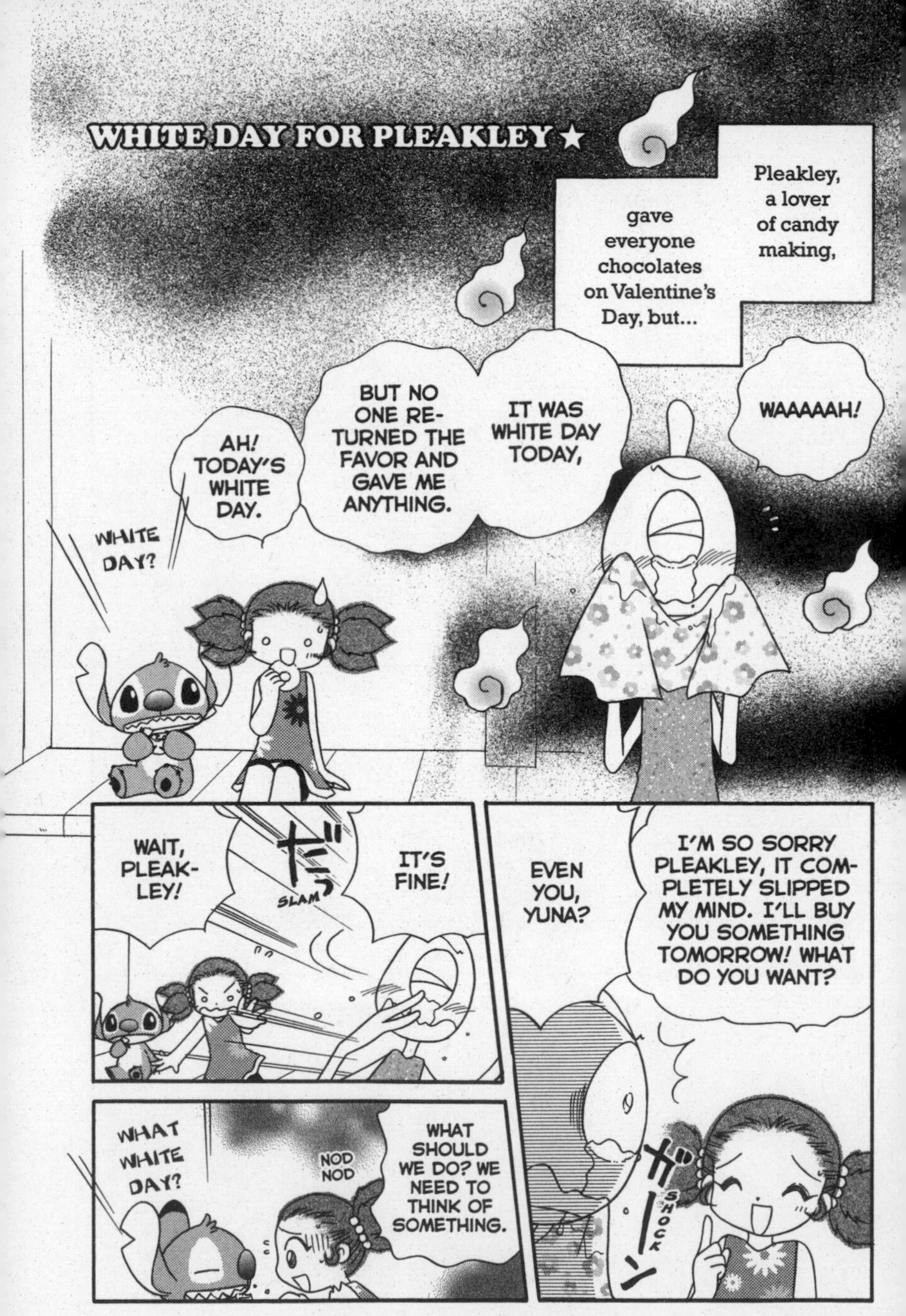
WHITE DAY FOR PLEAKLEY ★
Pleakley, a lover of candy making,
gave everyone chocolates on Valentine's Day, but...
WAAAAAH!
IT WAS WHITE DAY TODAY,
BUT NO ONE RE-TURNED THE FAVOR AND GAVE ME ANYTHING.
AH! TODAY'S WHITE DAY.
WHITE DAY?
I'M SO SORRY PLEAKLEY, IT COM-PLETELY SLIPPED MY MIND. I'LL BUY YOU SOMETHING TOMORROW! WHAT DO YOU WANT?
EVEN YOU, YUNA?
SHOCK
IT'S FINE!
SLAM
WAIT, PLEAK-LEY!
WHAT SHOULD WE DO? WE NEED TO THINK OF SOMETHING.
NOD NOD
WHAT WHITE DAY?

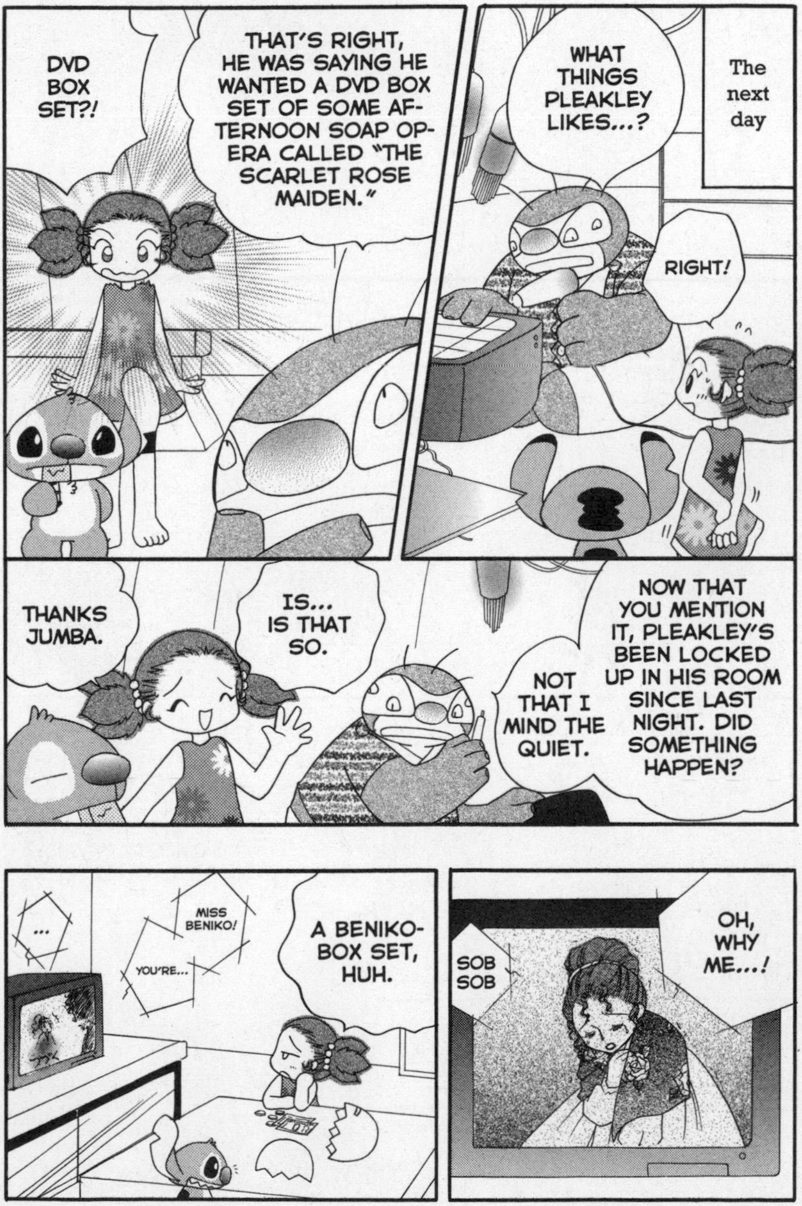
The next day
WHAT THINGS PLEAKLEY LIKES...?
RIGHT!
THAT'S RIGHT, HE WAS SAYING HE WANTED A DVD BOX SET OF SOME AFTERNOON SOAP OPERA CALLED "THE SCARLET ROSE MAIDEN."
DVD BOX SET?!
NOW THAT YOU MENTION IT, PLEAKLEY'S BEEN LOCKED UP IN HIS ROOM SINCE LAST NIGHT. DID SOMETHING HAPPEN?
NOT THAT I MIND THE QUIET.
IS... IS THAT SO.
THANKS JUMBA.
OH, WHY ME...!
SOB SOB
A BENIKO-BOX SET, HUH.
MISS BENIKO!
YOU'RE...
...

READ THIS WAY

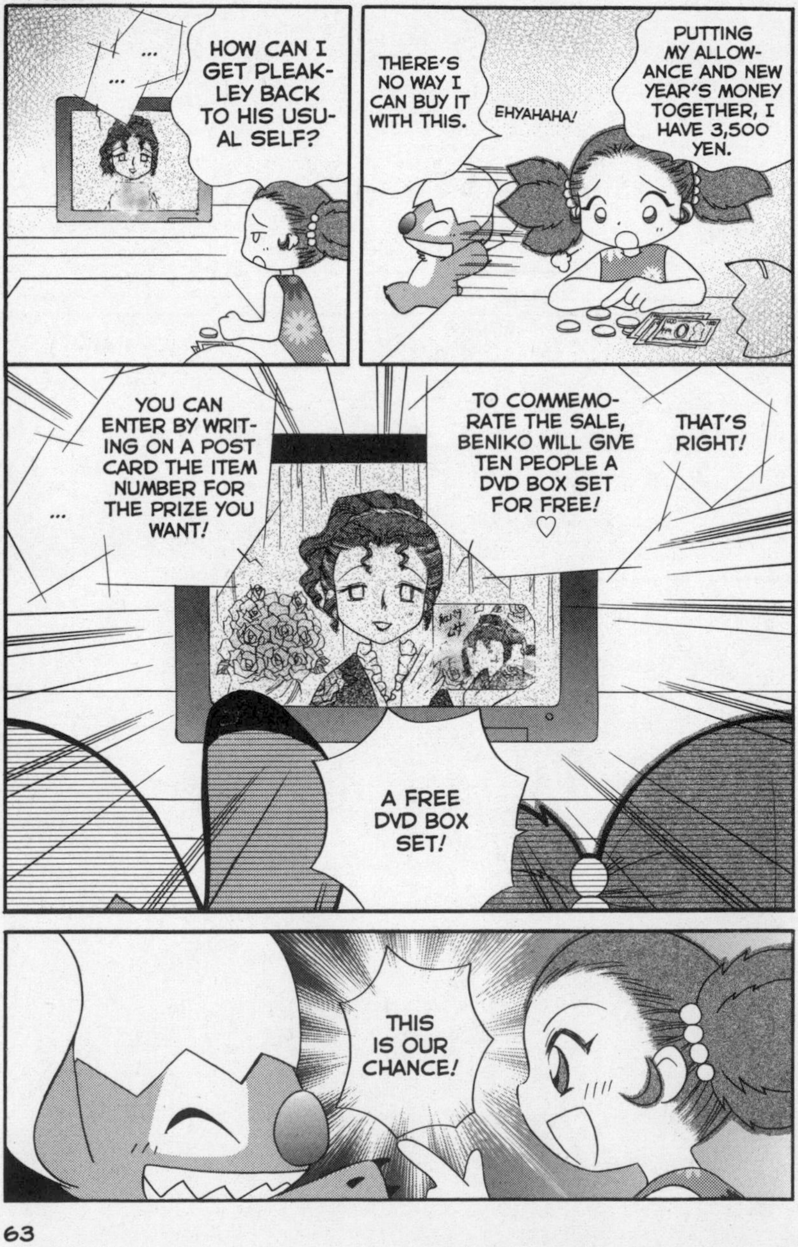
PUTTING MY ALLOW-ANCE AND NEW YEAR'S MONEY TOGETHER, I HAVE 3,500 YEN.
THERE'S NO WAY I CAN BUY IT WITH THIS.
EHYAHAHA!
HOW CAN I GET PLEAK-LEY BACK TO HIS USU-AL SELF?
...
...
THAT'S RIGHT!
TO COMMEMO-RATE THE SALE, BENIKO WILL GIVE TEN PEOPLE A DVD BOX SET FOR FREE! ♡
YOU CAN ENTER BY WRIT-ING ON A POST CARD THE ITEM NUMBER FOR THE PRIZE YOU WANT!
...
A FREE DVD BOX SET!
THIS IS OUR CHANCE!

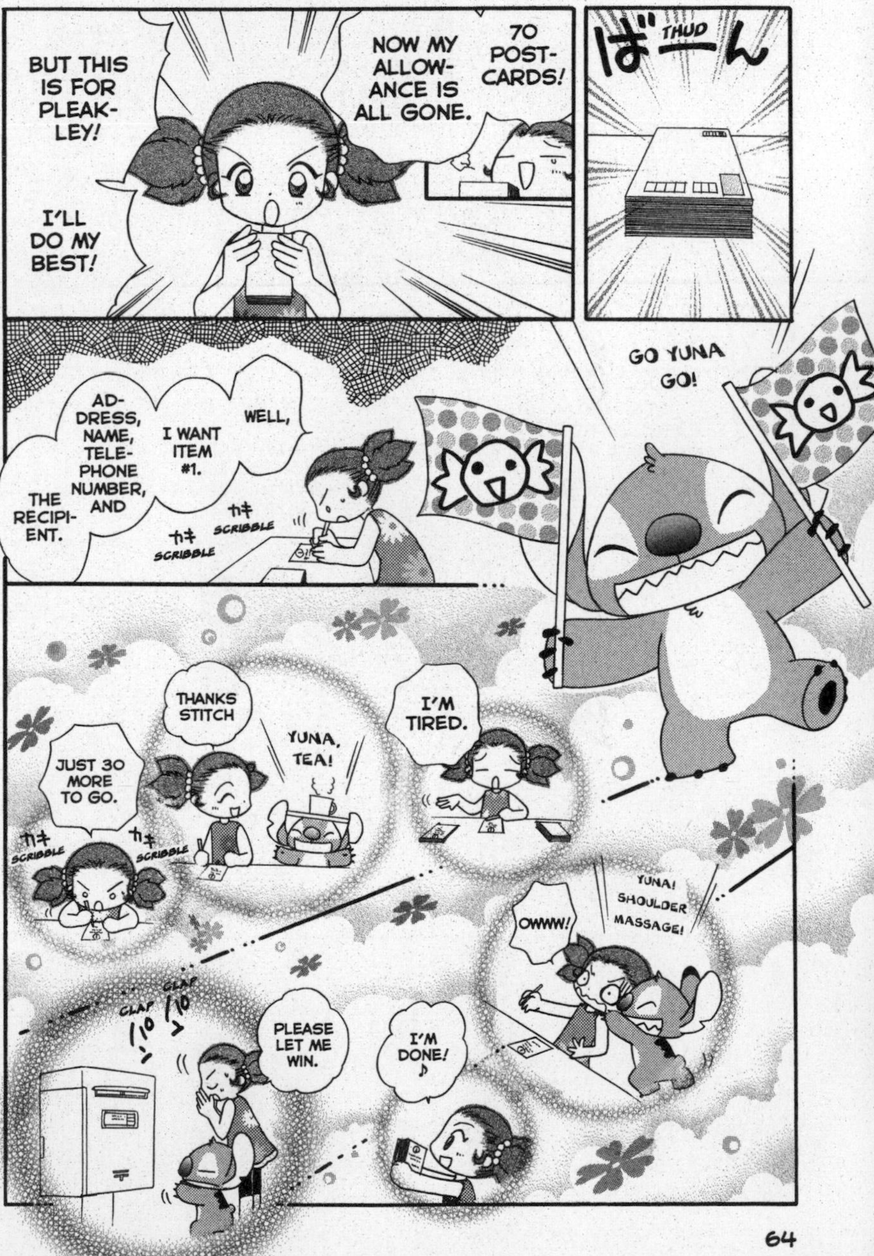
ばーん
THUD
70 POST-CARDS!
NOW MY ALLOW-ANCE IS ALL GONE.
BUT THIS IS FOR PLEAK-LEY!
I'LL DO MY BEST!
GO YUNA GO!
WELL,
I WANT ITEM #1.
AD-DRESS, NAME, TELE-PHONE NUMBER, AND THE RECIPI-ENT.
カキ SCRIBBLE
カキ SCRIBBLE
I'M TIRED.
YUNA, TEA!
THANKS STITCH
JUST 30 MORE TO GO.
カキ SCRIBBLE
カキ SCRIBBLE
YUNA! SHOULDER MASSAGE!
OWWW!
I'M DONE! ♪
PLEASE LET ME WIN.
CLAP
CLAP

READ THIS WAY

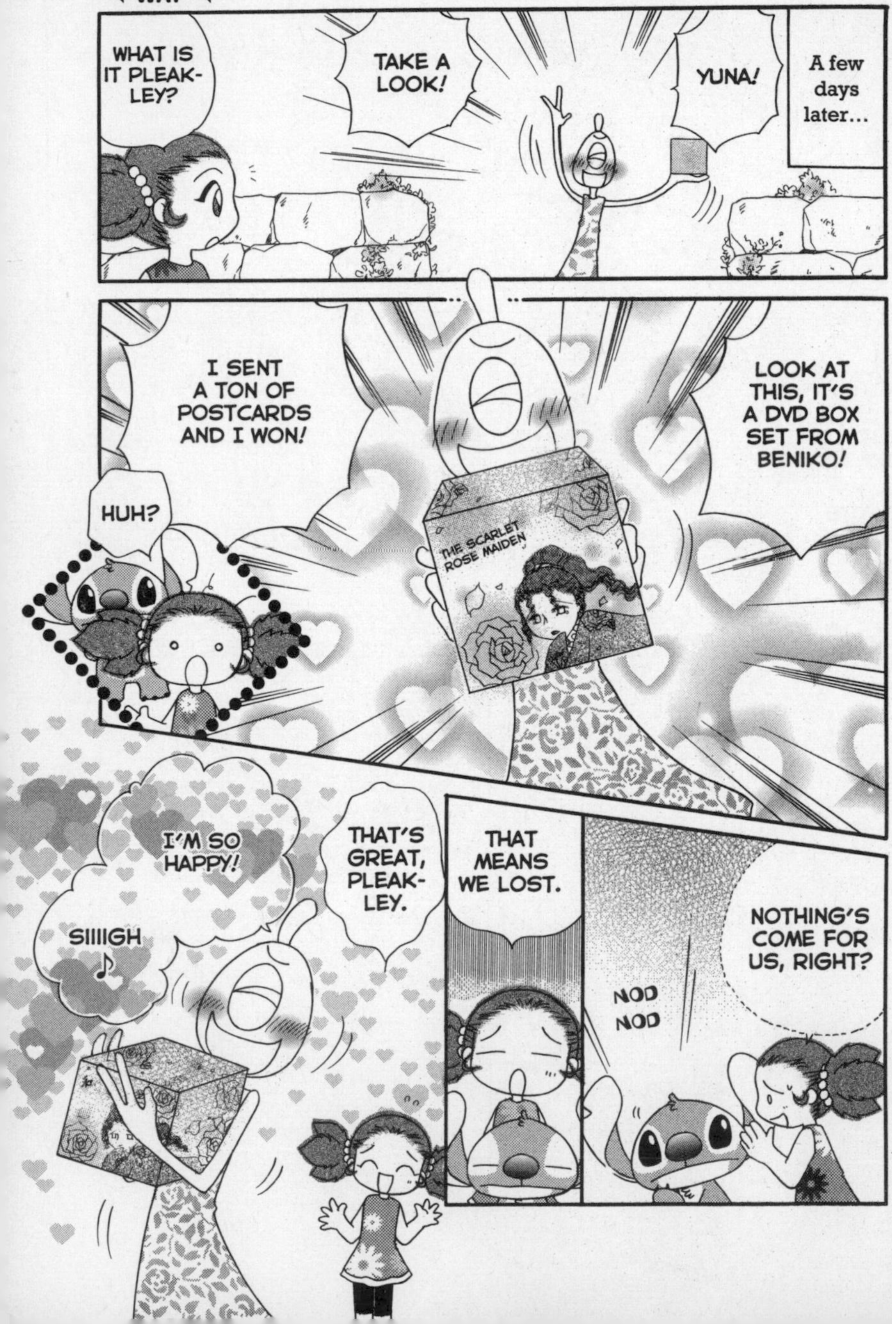
A few days later...
YUNA!
TAKE A LOOK!
WHAT IS IT PLEAK-LEY?
...
LOOK AT THIS, IT'S A DVD BOX SET FROM BENIKO!
I SENT A TON OF POSTCARDS AND I WON!
THE SCARLET ROSE MAIDEN
HUH?
NOTHING'S COME FOR US, RIGHT?
NOD NOD
THAT MEANS WE LOST.
THAT'S GREAT, PLEAK-LEY.
I'M SO HAPPY!
SIIIGH ♪

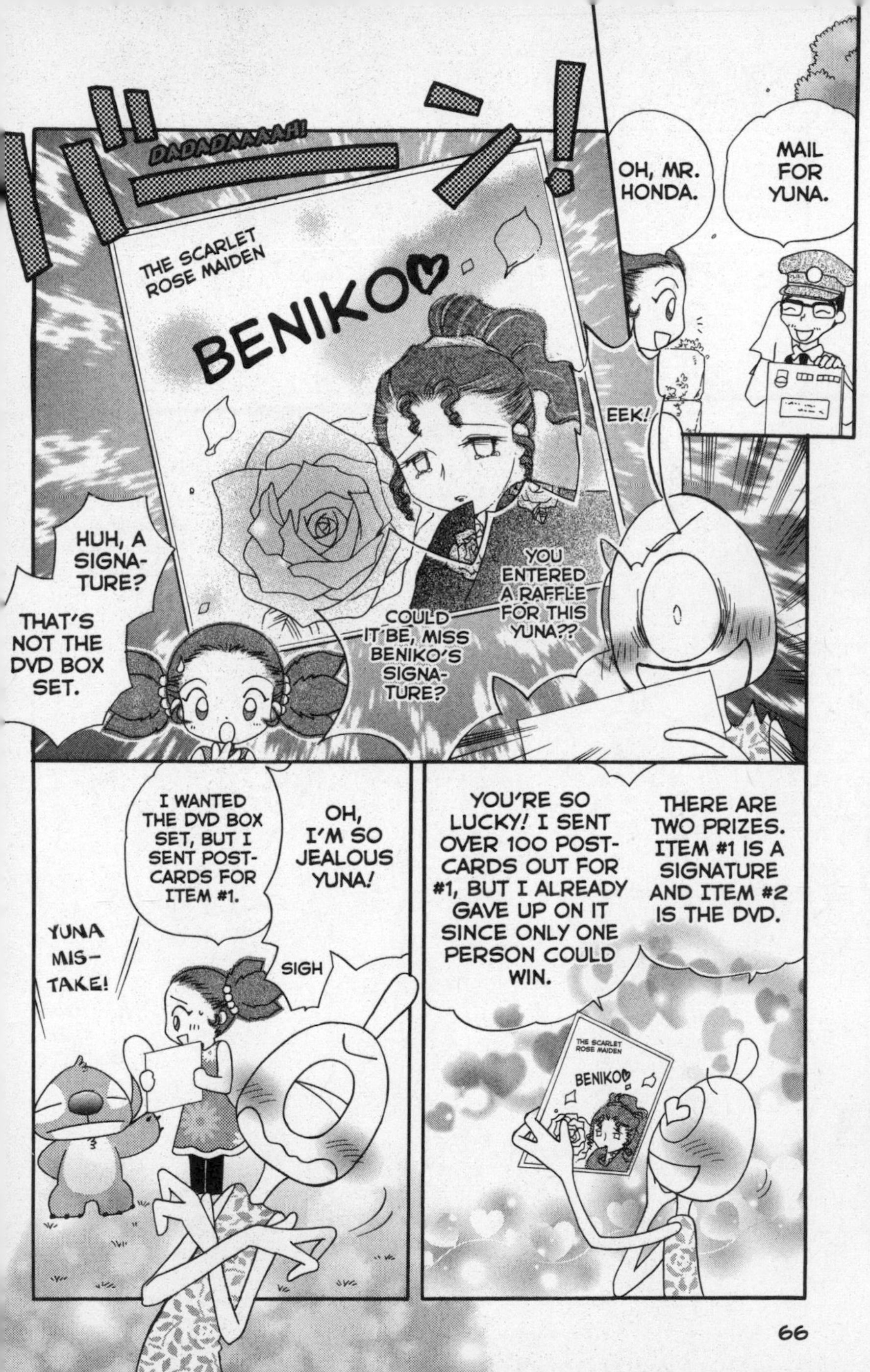
MAIL FOR YUNA.
OH, MR. HONDA.
DADADAAAAAH!
THE SCARLET ROSE MAIDEN
BENIKO
EEK!
YOU ENTERED A RAFFLE FOR THIS YUNA??
COULD IT BE, MISS BENIKO'S SIGNATURE?
HUH, A SIGNATURE?
THAT'S NOT THE DVD BOX SET.
THERE ARE TWO PRIZES. ITEM #1 IS A SIGNATURE AND ITEM #2 IS THE DVD.
YOU'RE SO LUCKY! I SENT OVER 100 POSTCARDS OUT FOR #1, BUT I ALREADY GAVE UP ON IT SINCE ONLY ONE PERSON COULD WIN.
THE SCARLET ROSE MAIDEN
BENIKO
OH, I'M SO JEALOUS YUNA!
I WANTED THE DVD BOX SET, BUT I SENT POSTCARDS FOR ITEM #1.
SIGH
YUNA MISTAKE!

READ THIS WAY

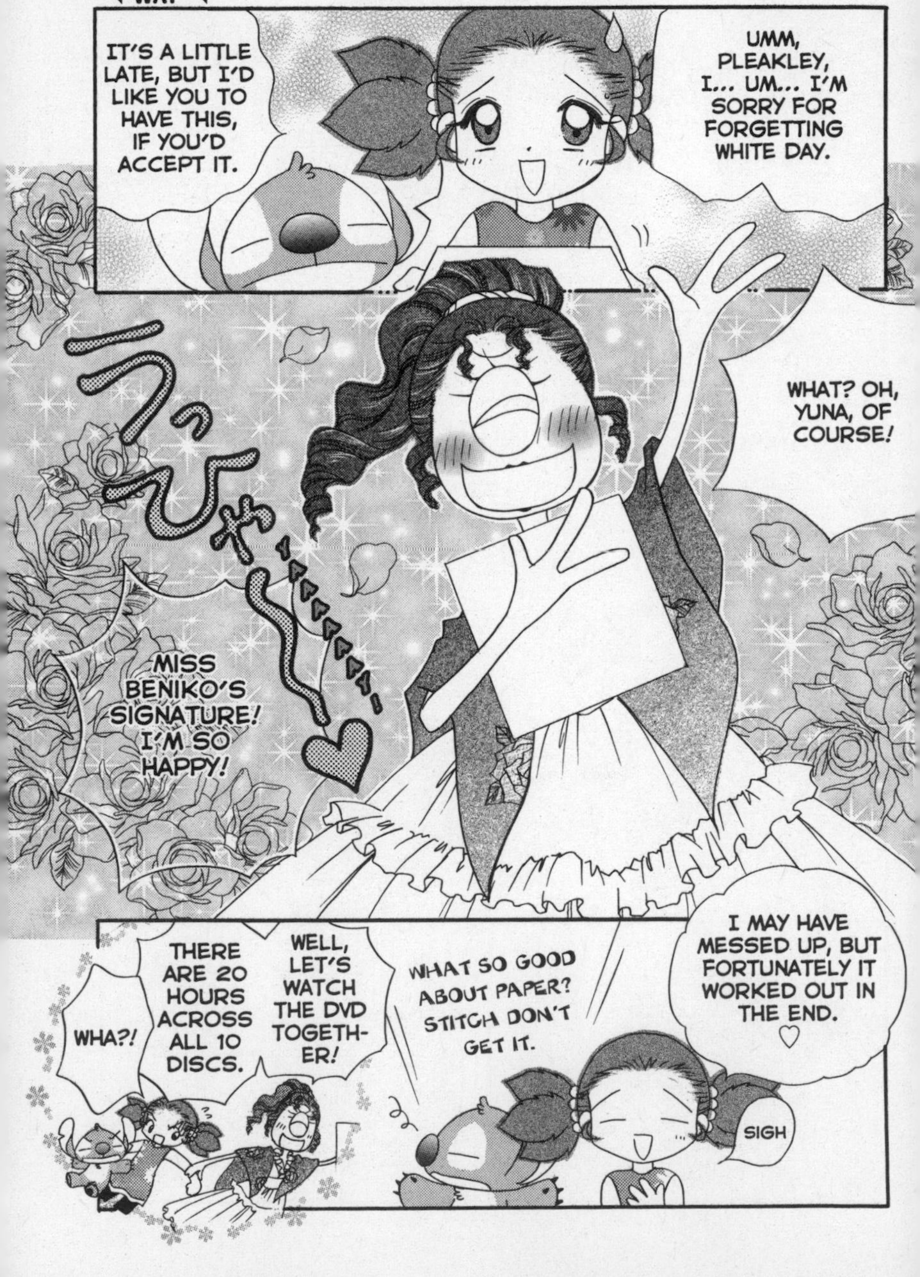

UMM, PLEAKLEY, I... UM... I'M SORRY FOR FORGETTING WHITE DAY.
IT'S A LITTLE LATE, BUT I'D LIKE YOU TO HAVE THIS, IF YOU'D ACCEPT IT.
WHAT? OH, YUNA, OF COURSE!
うっひゃァァァァァ!
MISS BENIKO'S SIGNATURE! I'M SO HAPPY!
I MAY HAVE MESSED UP, BUT FORTUNATELY IT WORKED OUT IN THE END. ♡
SIGH
WHAT SO GOOD ABOUT PAPER? STITCH DON'T GET IT.
WELL, LET'S WATCH THE DVD TOGETH-ER!
THERE ARE 20 HOURS ACROSS ALL 10 DISCS.
WHA?!

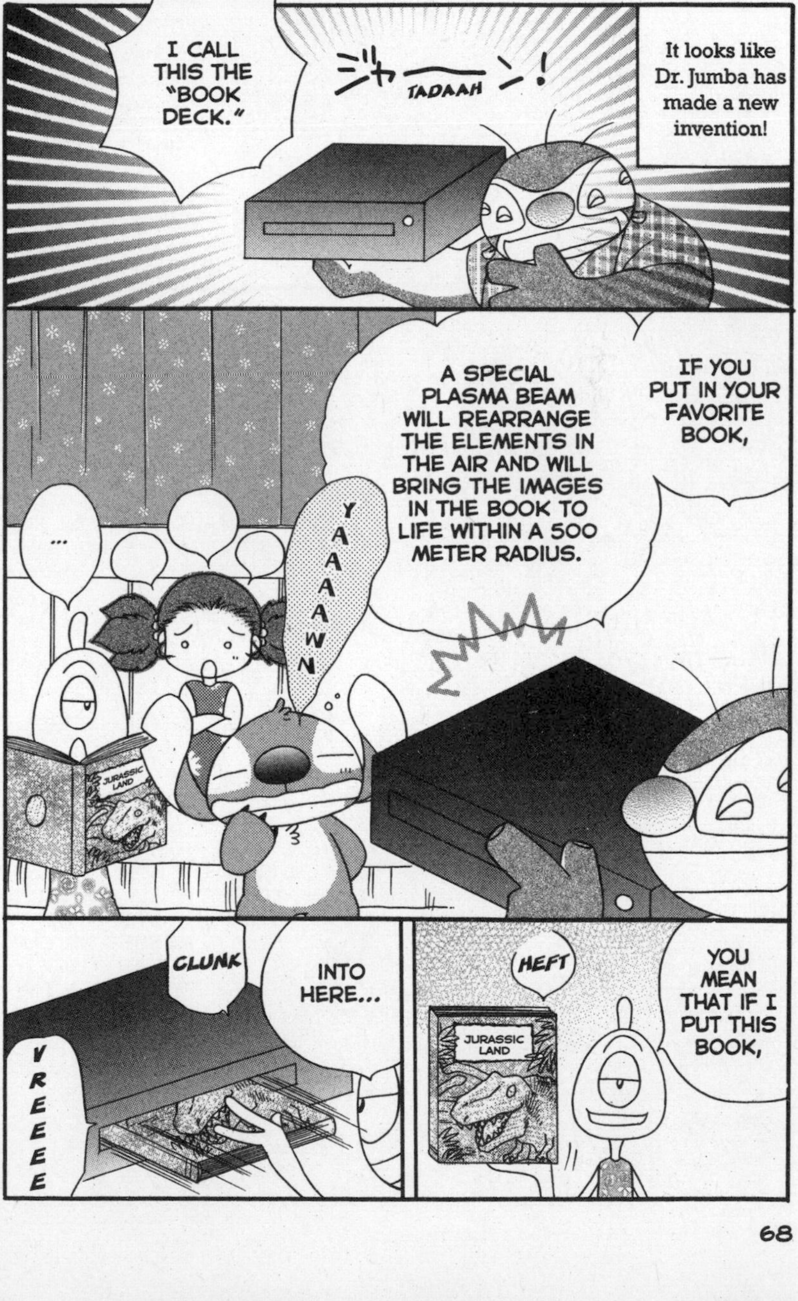
It looks like Dr. Jumba has made a new invention!
ジャーン!
TADAAH
I CALL THIS THE "BOOK DECK."
IF YOU PUT IN YOUR FAVORITE BOOK,
A SPECIAL PLASMA BEAM WILL REARRANGE THE ELEMENTS IN THE AIR AND WILL BRING THE IMAGES IN THE BOOK TO LIFE WITHIN A 500 METER RADIUS.
YAAAAAWN
...
YOU MEAN THAT IF I PUT THIS BOOK,
HEFT
JURASSIC LAND
INTO HERE...
CLUNK
VREEEE

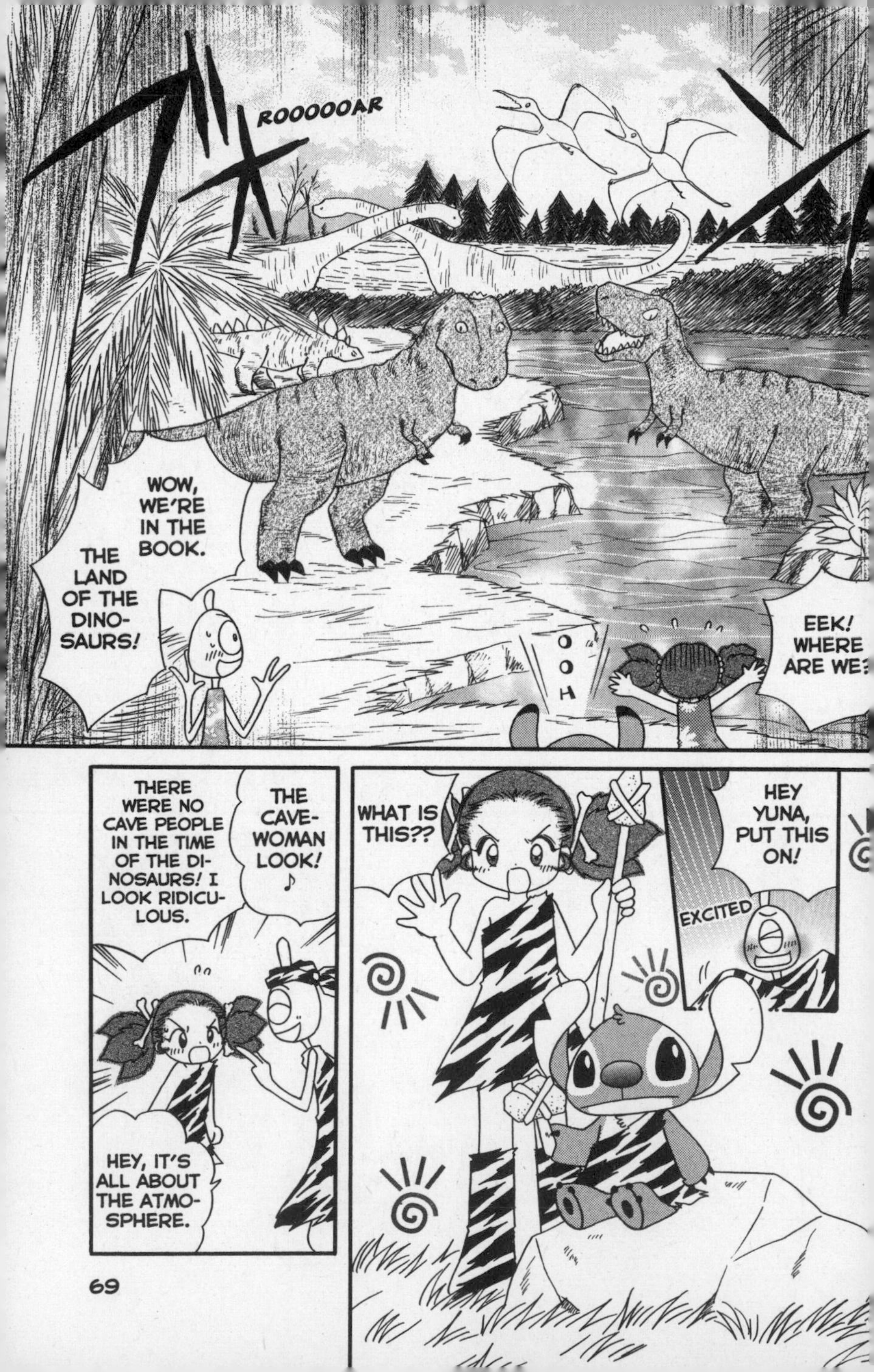
ROOOOOAR
EEK! WHERE ARE WE?
OOH
WOW, WE'RE IN THE BOOK.
THE LAND OF THE DINO-SAURS!
HEY YUNA, PUT THIS ON!
EXCITED
WHAT IS THIS??
THE CAVE-WOMAN LOOK! ♪
THERE WERE NO CAVE PEOPLE IN THE TIME OF THE DI-NOSAURS! I LOOK RIDICU-LOUS.
HEY, IT'S ALL ABOUT THE ATMO-SPHERE.

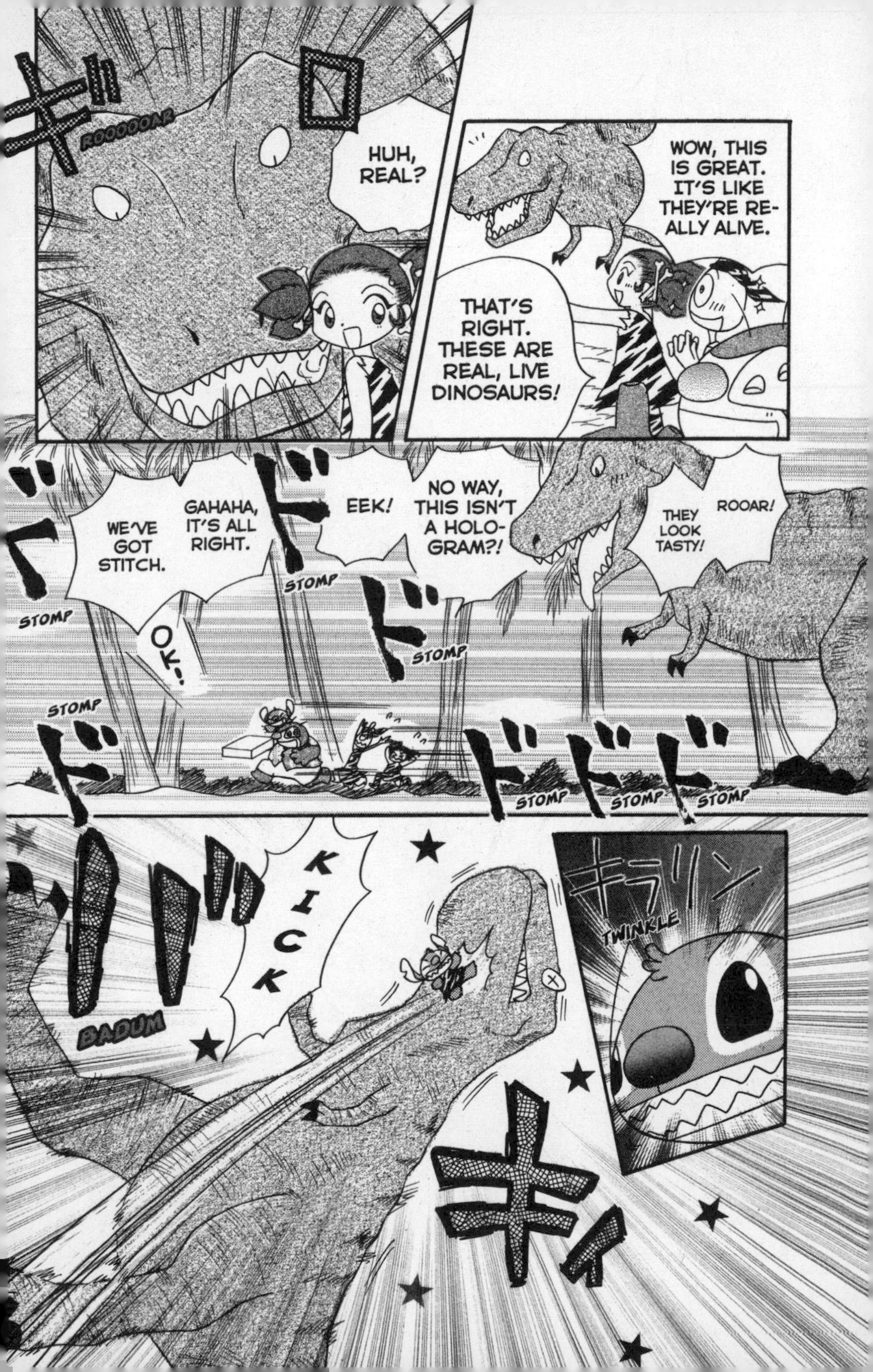
WOW, THIS IS GREAT. IT'S LIKE THEY'RE RE-ALLY ALIVE.
THAT'S RIGHT. THESE ARE REAL, LIVE DINOSAURS!
ROOOOOAR
HUH, REAL?
ROOAR!
THEY LOOK TASTY!
NO WAY, THIS ISN'T A HOLO-GRAM?!
EEK!
STOMP
GAHAHA, IT'S ALL RIGHT.
WE'VE GOT STITCH.
STOMP
OK!
STOMP
STOMP
STOMP
STOMP
STOMP
TWINKLE
KICK
BADUM

READ THIS WAY

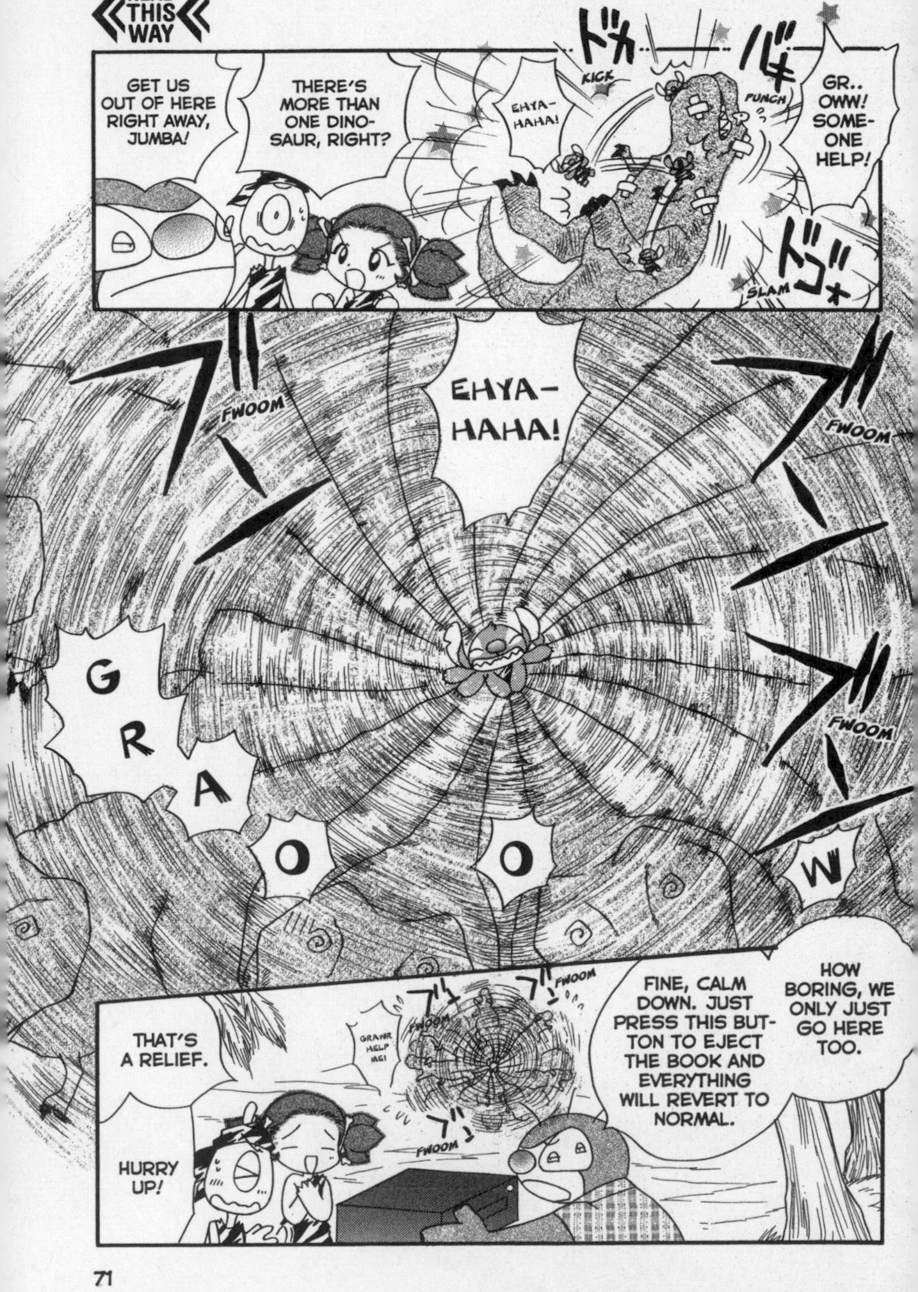
GR.. OWW! SOME-ONE HELP!
PUNCH
EHYA-HAHA!
KICK
THERE'S MORE THAN ONE DINO-SAUR, RIGHT?
GET US OUT OF HERE RIGHT AWAY, JUMBA!
SLAM
EHYA-HAHA!
FWOOM
FWOOM
FWOOM
FWOOM
GRAOOW
HOW BORING, WE ONLY JUST GO HERE TOO.
FINE, CALM DOWN. JUST PRESS THIS BUT-TON TO EJECT THE BOOK AND EVERYTHING WILL REVERT TO NORMAL.
FWOOM
FWOOM
GRAWR HELP ME!
FWOOM
THAT'S A RELIEF.
HURRY UP!

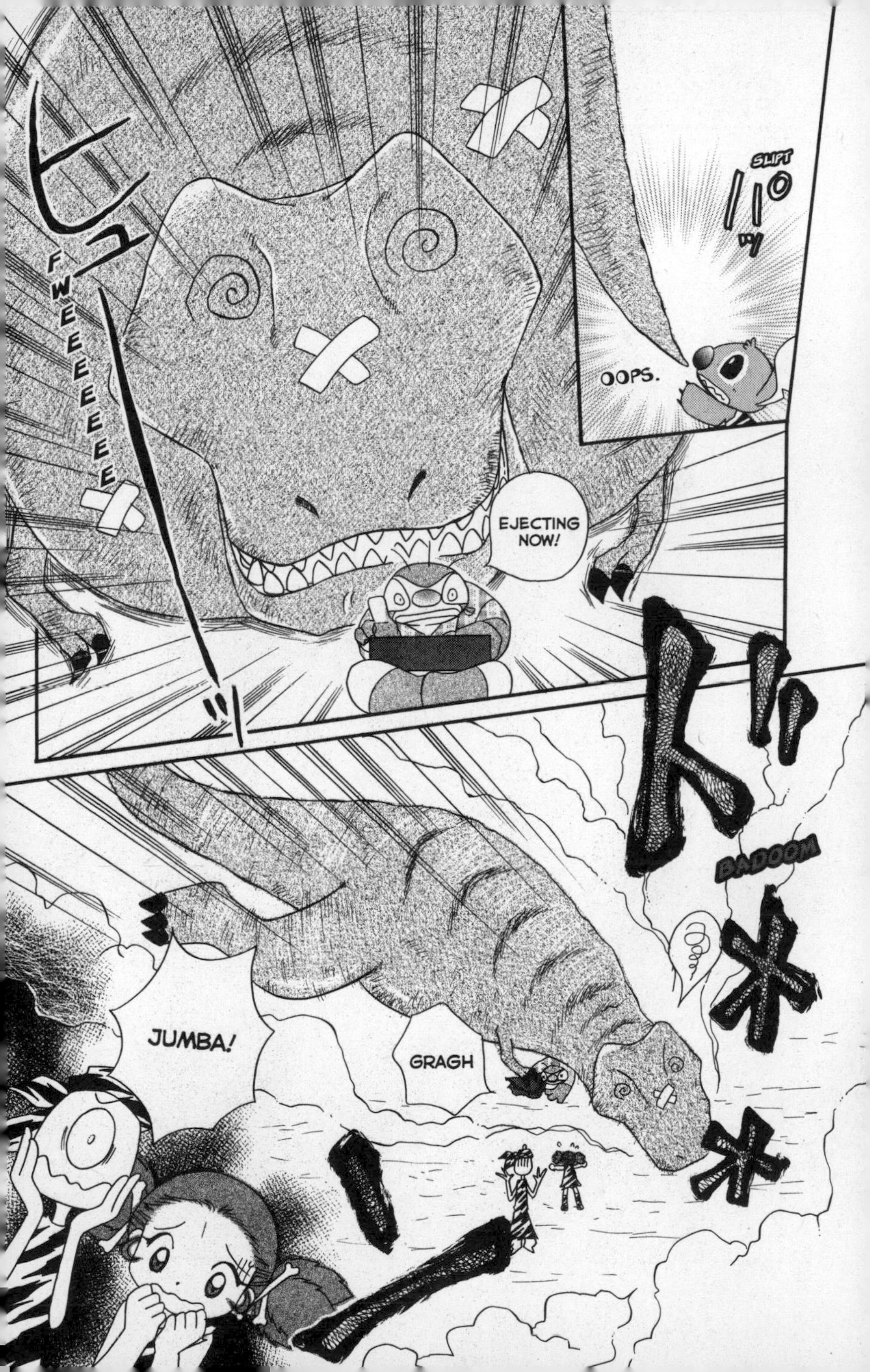
SLIPT
OOPS.
FWEEEEEEEE
EJECTING NOW!
BADOOM
GRAGH
JUMBA!

READ THIS WAY

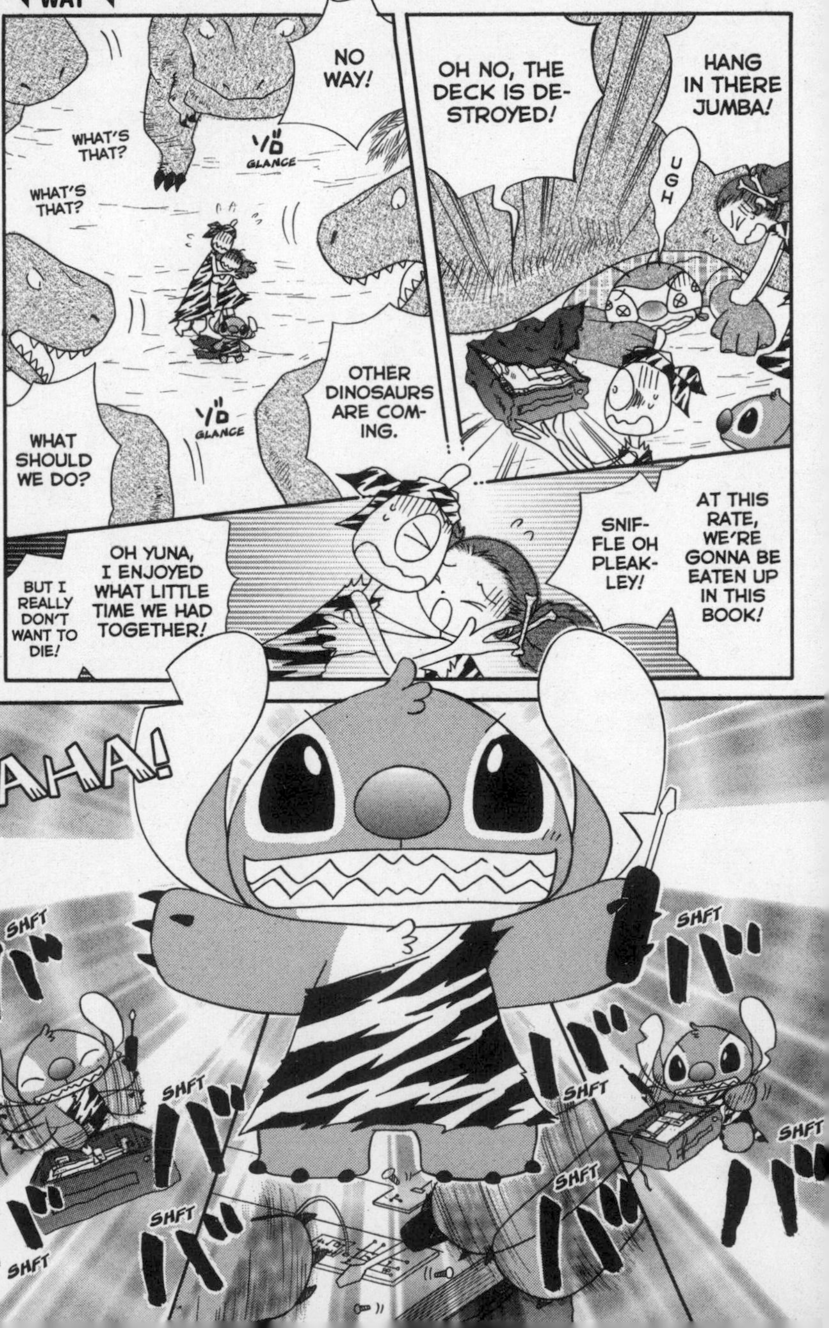
HANG IN THERE JUMBA!
OH NO, THE DECK IS DESTROYED!
UGH
NO WAY!
GLANCE
WHAT'S THAT?
WHAT'S THAT?
OTHER DINOSAURS ARE COMING.
GLANCE
WHAT SHOULD WE DO?
AT THIS RATE, WE'RE GONNA BE EATEN UP IN THIS BOOK!
SNIFFLE OH PLEAKLEY!
OH YUNA, I ENJOYED WHAT LITTLE TIME WE HAD TOGETHER!
BUT I REALLY DON'T WANT TO DIE!
AHA!
SHFT
SHFT
SHFT
SHFT
SHFT
SHFT
SHFT
SHFT

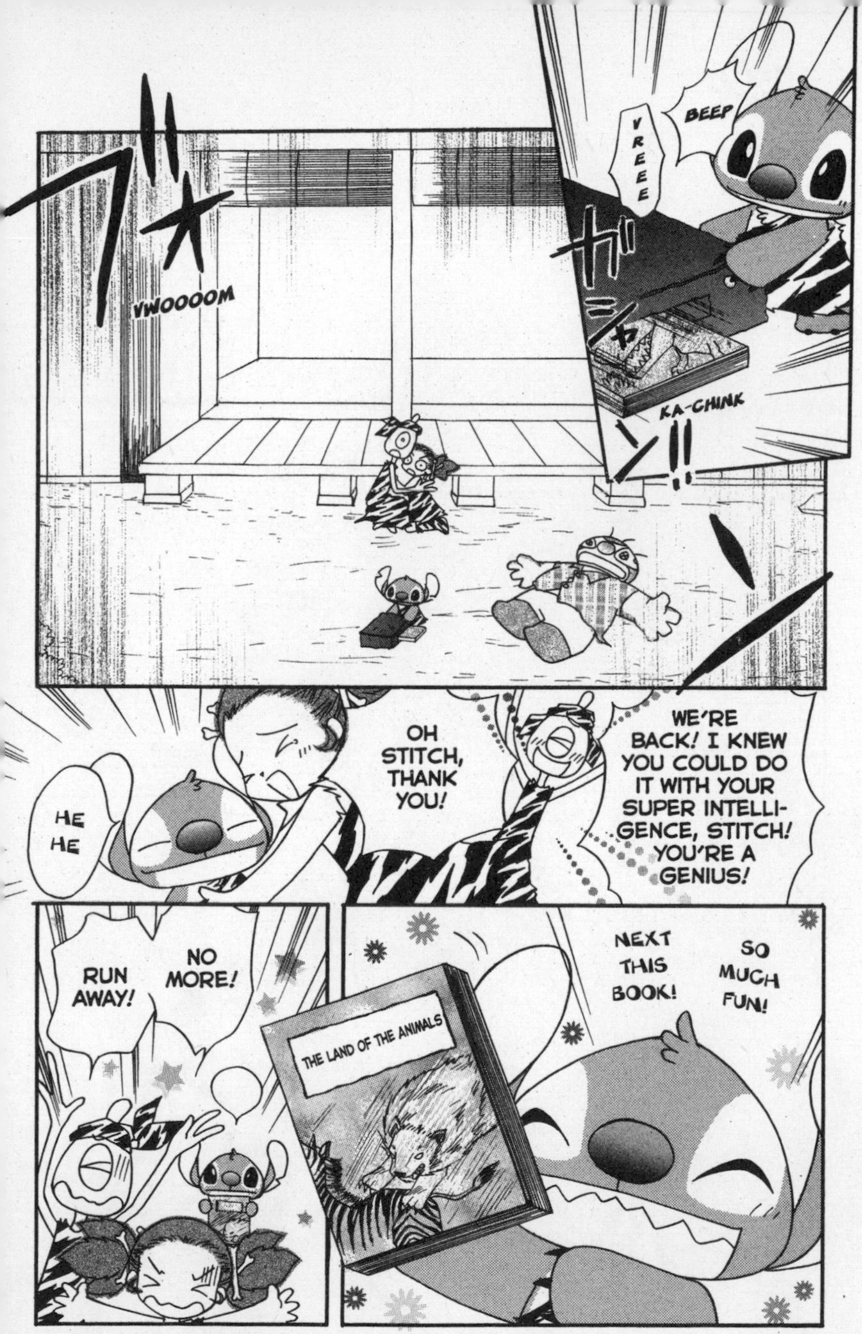
BEEP
VREEE
KA-CHINK
VWOOOOM
WE'RE BACK! I KNEW YOU COULD DO IT WITH YOUR SUPER INTELLIGENCE, STITCH! YOU'RE A GENIUS!
OH STITCH, THANK YOU!
HE HE
SO MUCH FUN!
NEXT THIS BOOK!
THE LAND OF THE ANIMALS
NO MORE!
RUN AWAY!

READ THIS WAY

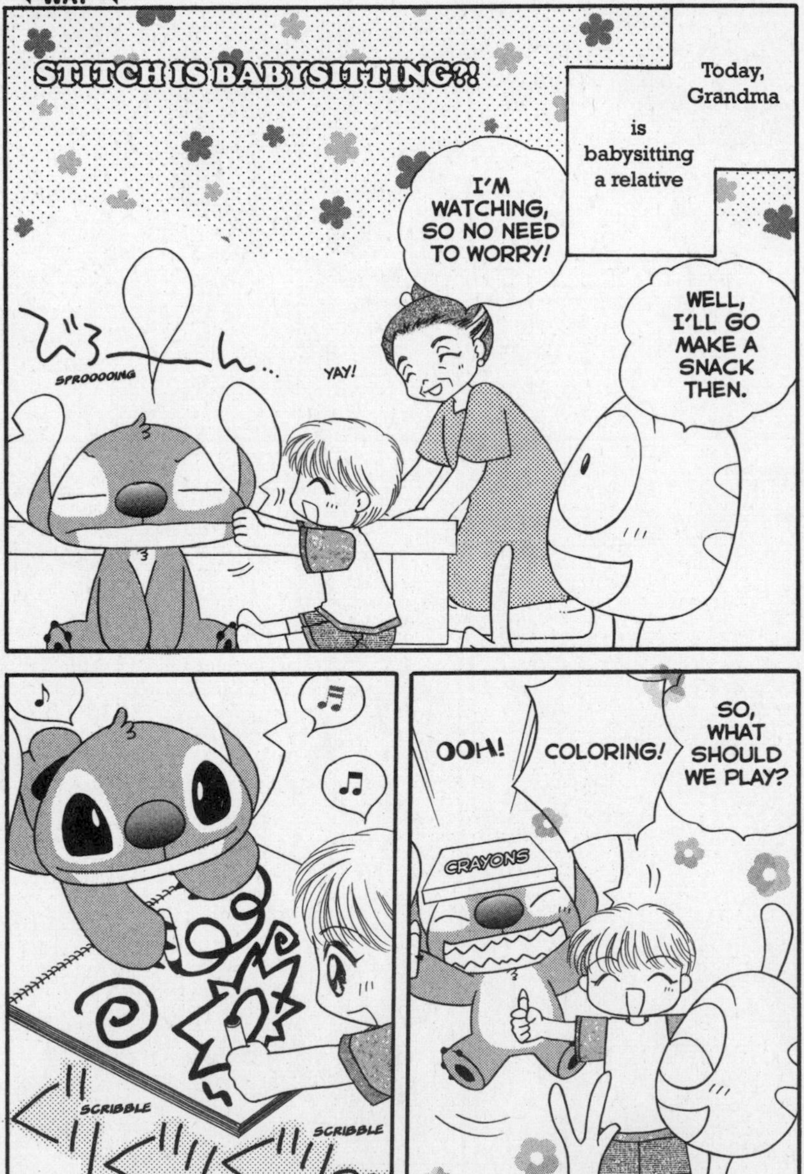
Today, Grandma is babysitting a relative
STITCH IS BABYSITTING?!
I'M WATCHING, SO NO NEED TO WORRY!
WELL, I'LL GO MAKE A SNACK THEN.
YAY!
SPROOOOOING
SO, WHAT SHOULD WE PLAY?
COLORING!
OOH!
CRAYONS
SCRIBBLE
SCRIBBLE

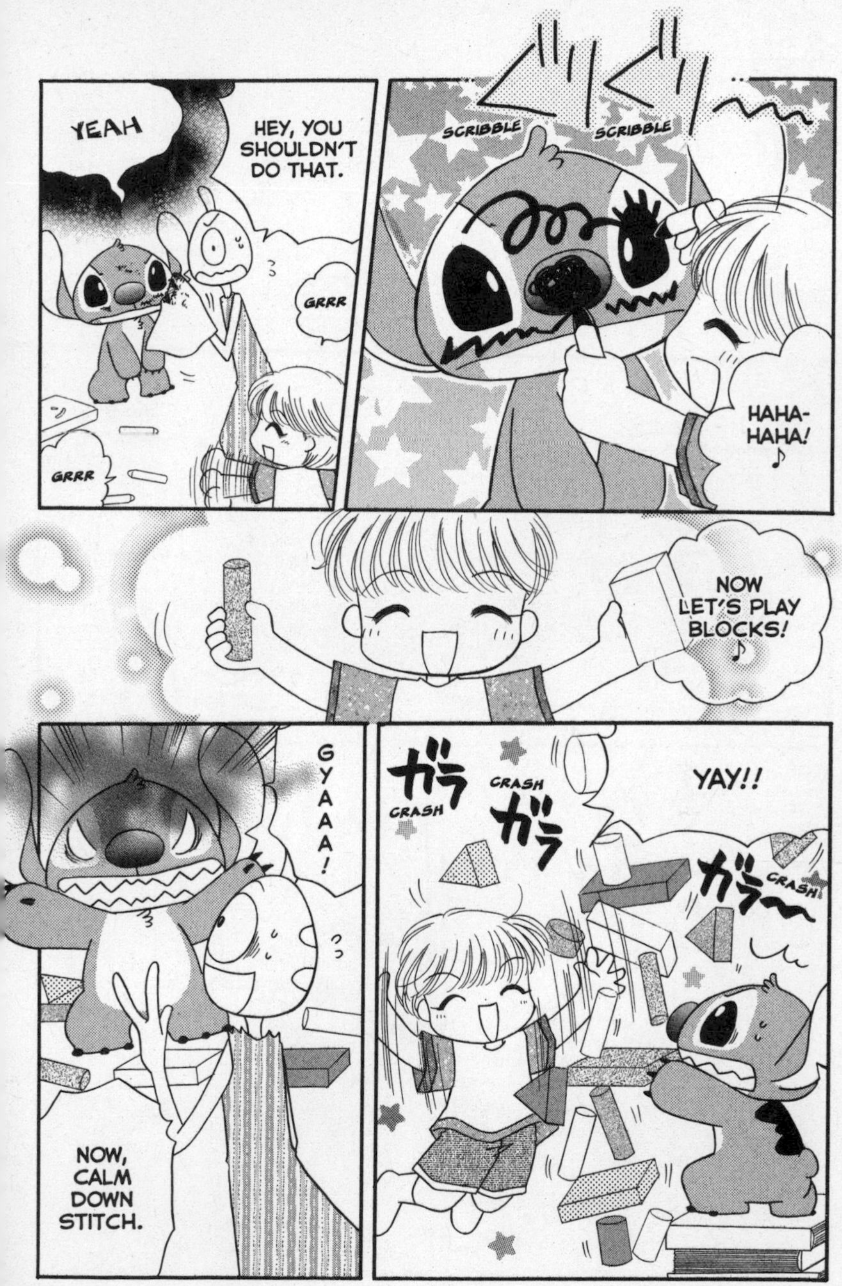
SCRIBBLE
SCRIBBLE
HAHA-HAHA! ♪
HEY, YOU SHOULDN'T DO THAT.
GRRR
YEAH
GRRR
NOW LET'S PLAY BLOCKS! ♪
YAY!!
ガラ
CRASH
ガラ
CRASH
ガラ〜
CRASH
GYAAAA!
NOW, CALM DOWN STITCH.

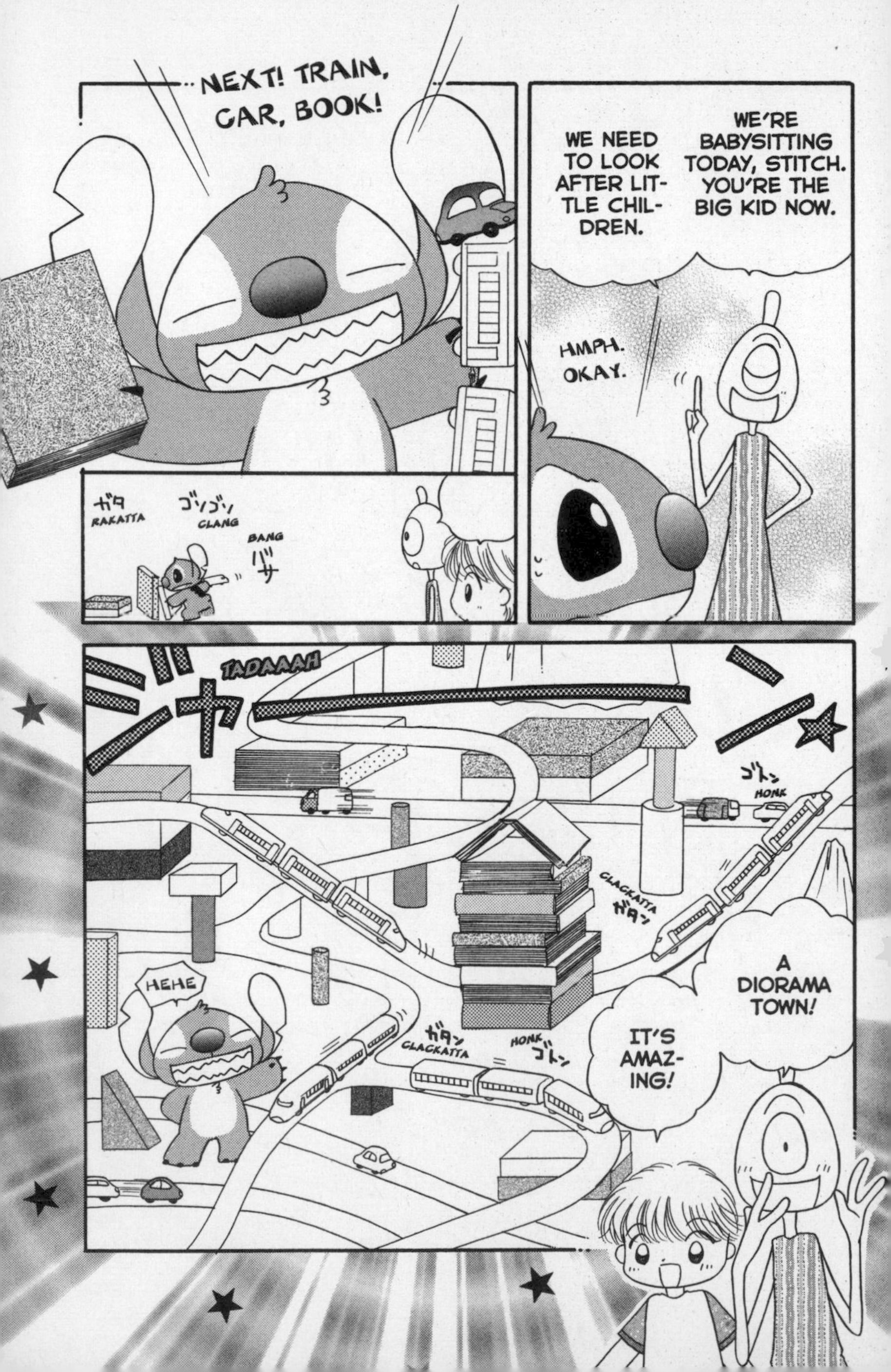
WE'RE BABYSITTING TODAY, STITCH. YOU'RE THE BIG KID NOW.
WE NEED TO LOOK AFTER LITTLE CHILDREN.
HMPH. OKAY.
...NEXT! TRAIN, CAR, BOOK!
ガタ RAKATTA
ゴソゴソ CLANG
バサ BANG
シャーン TADAAAH
ゴトン HONK
ガタン CLACKATTA
A DIORAMA TOWN!
IT'S AMAZING!
HEHE
ガタン CLACKATTA
HONK ゴトン

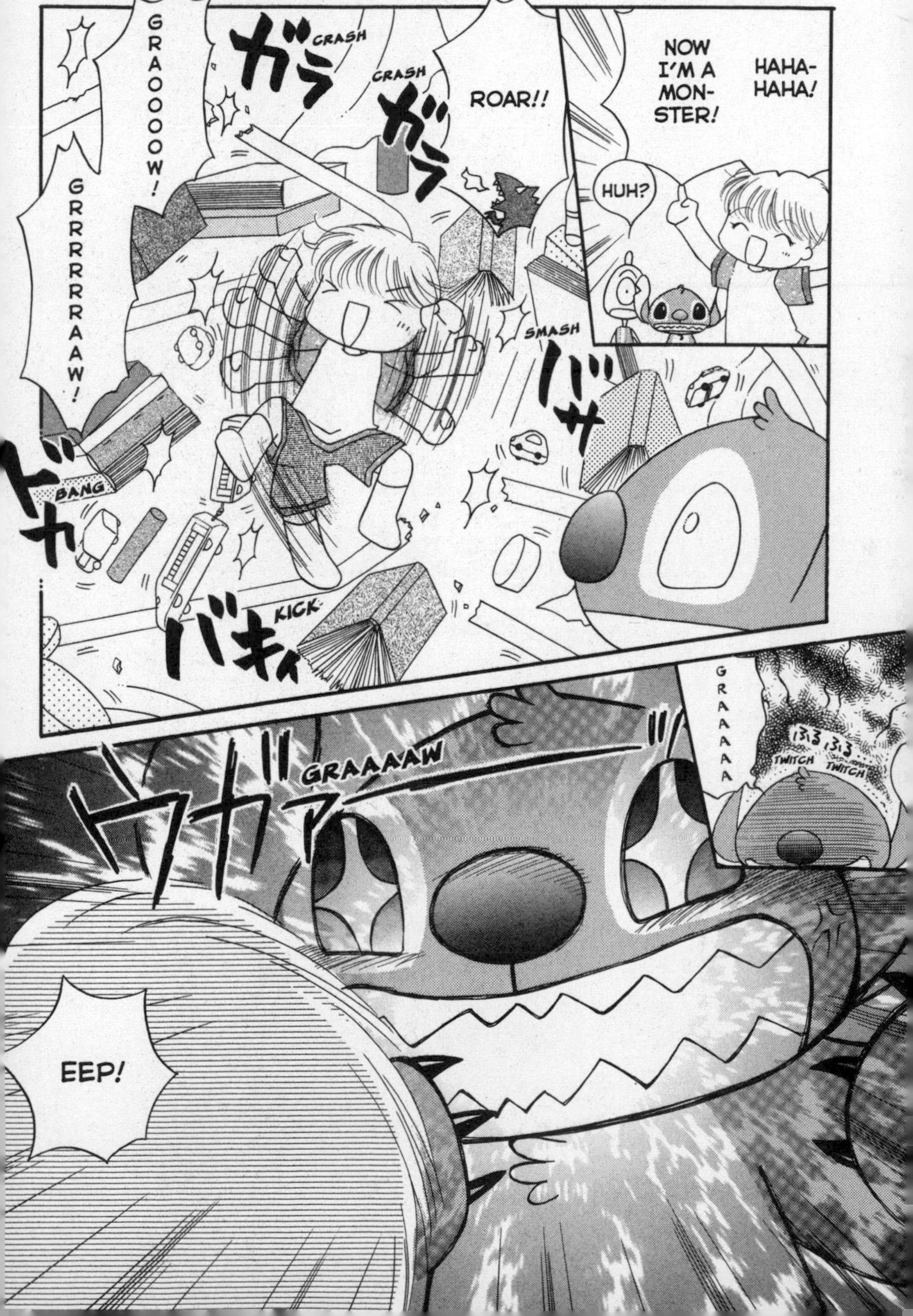
HAHA-HAHA!
NOW I'M A MON-STER!
HUH?
ROAR!!
ガラ CRASH
ガラ CRASH
GRAOOOOOW!
GRRRRRRRAAW!
バサ SMASH
ドカ BANG
バキィ KICK
GRAAAAAA
TWITCH TWITCH
ウガァ GRAAAAW
EEP!

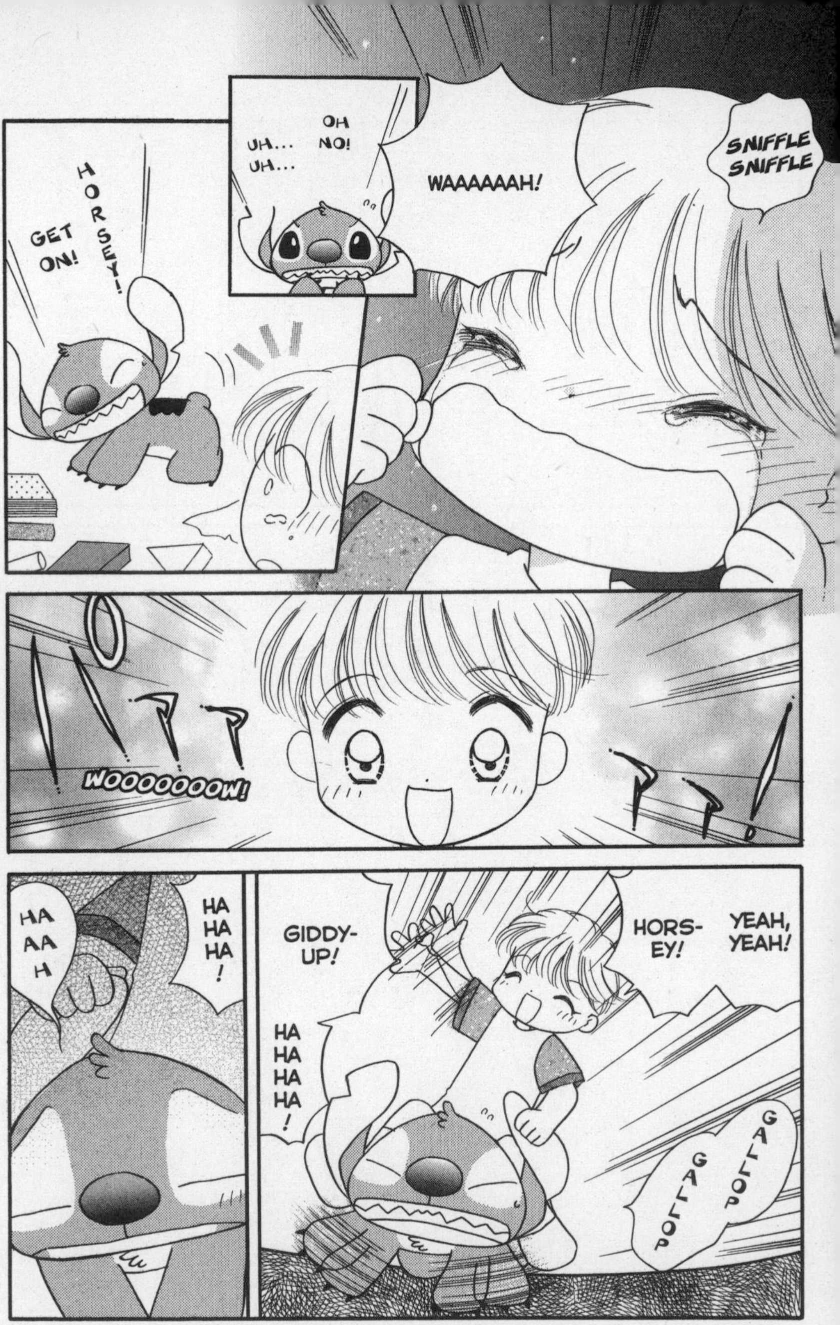
SNIFFLE SNIFFLE
WAAAAAAH!
OH NO!
UH... UH...
HORSEY!
GET ON!
WOOOOOOOW!
YEAH, YEAH!
HORS-EY!
GIDDY-UP!
HA HA HA HA HA HA HA!
GALLOP GALLOP
HA HA HA HA!
HA AA H

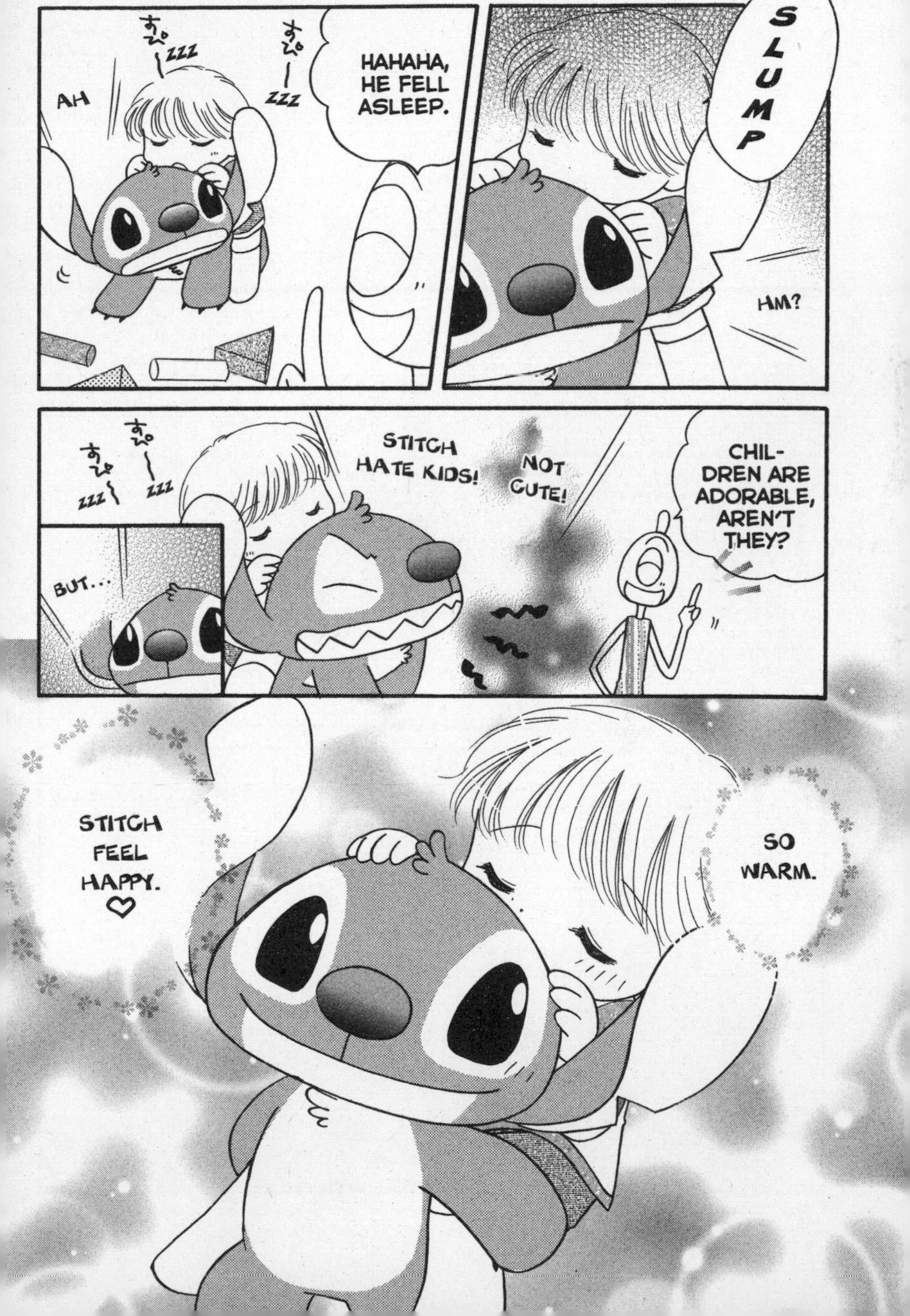
HM?
SLUMP
AH
すぴ〜 ZZZ
すぴ〜 ZZZ
HAHAHA, HE FELL ASLEEP.
CHIL-DREN ARE ADORABLE, AREN'T THEY?
NOT CUTE!
STITCH HATE KIDS!
すぴ〜 ZZZ
すぴ〜 ZZZ
BUT...
SO WARM.
STITCH FEEL HAPPY. ♡

PIKO'S CLASS NEWSPAPER♪

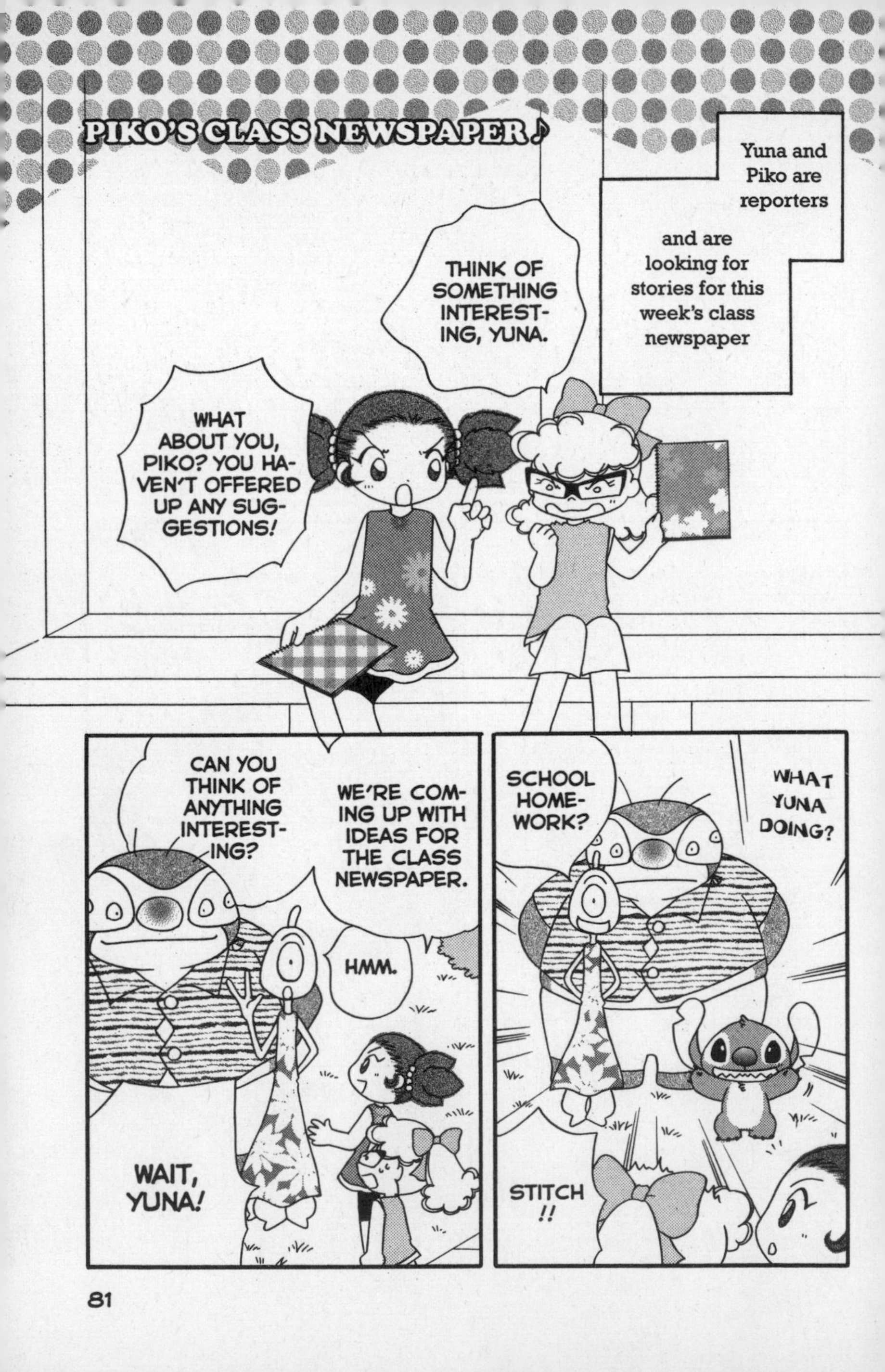

Yuna and Piko are reporters
and are looking for stories for this week's class newspaper
THINK OF SOMETHING INTEREST-ING, YUNA.
WHAT ABOUT YOU, PIKO? YOU HA-VEN'T OFFERED UP ANY SUG-GESTIONS!
WHAT YUNA DOING?
SCHOOL HOME-WORK?
STITCH !!
WE'RE COM-ING UP WITH IDEAS FOR THE CLASS NEWSPAPER.
CAN YOU THINK OF ANYTHING INTEREST-ING?
HMM.
WAIT, YUNA!

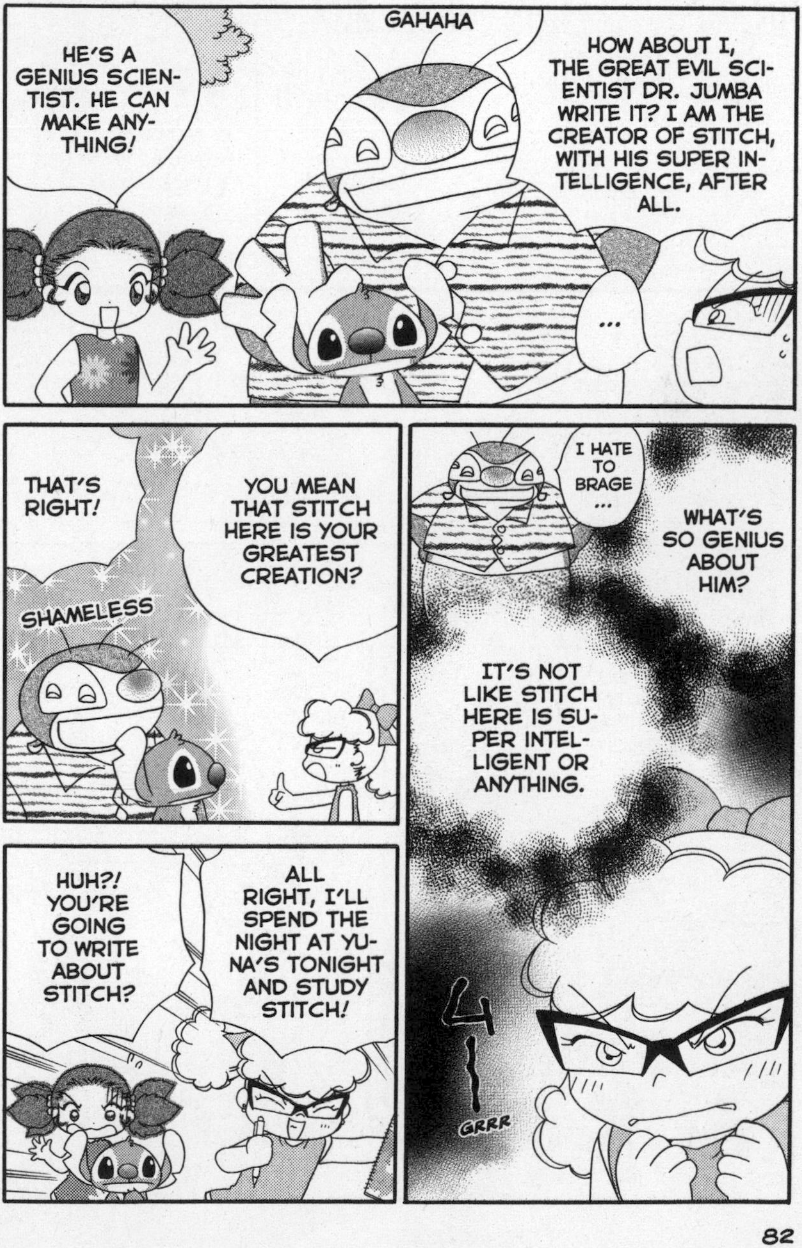
HOW ABOUT I, THE GREAT EVIL SCIENTIST DR. JUMBA WRITE IT? I AM THE CREATOR OF STITCH, WITH HIS SUPER INTELLIGENCE, AFTER ALL.
GAHAHA
HE'S A GENIUS SCIENTIST. HE CAN MAKE ANYTHING!
...
WHAT'S SO GENIUS ABOUT HIM?
I HATE TO BRAGE ...
IT'S NOT LIKE STITCH HERE IS SUPER INTELLIGENT OR ANYTHING.
GRRR
YOU MEAN THAT STITCH HERE IS YOUR GREATEST CREATION?
THAT'S RIGHT!
SHAMELESS
ALL RIGHT, I'LL SPEND THE NIGHT AT YUNA'S TONIGHT AND STUDY STITCH!
HUH?! YOU'RE GOING TO WRITE ABOUT STITCH?

READ THIS WAY

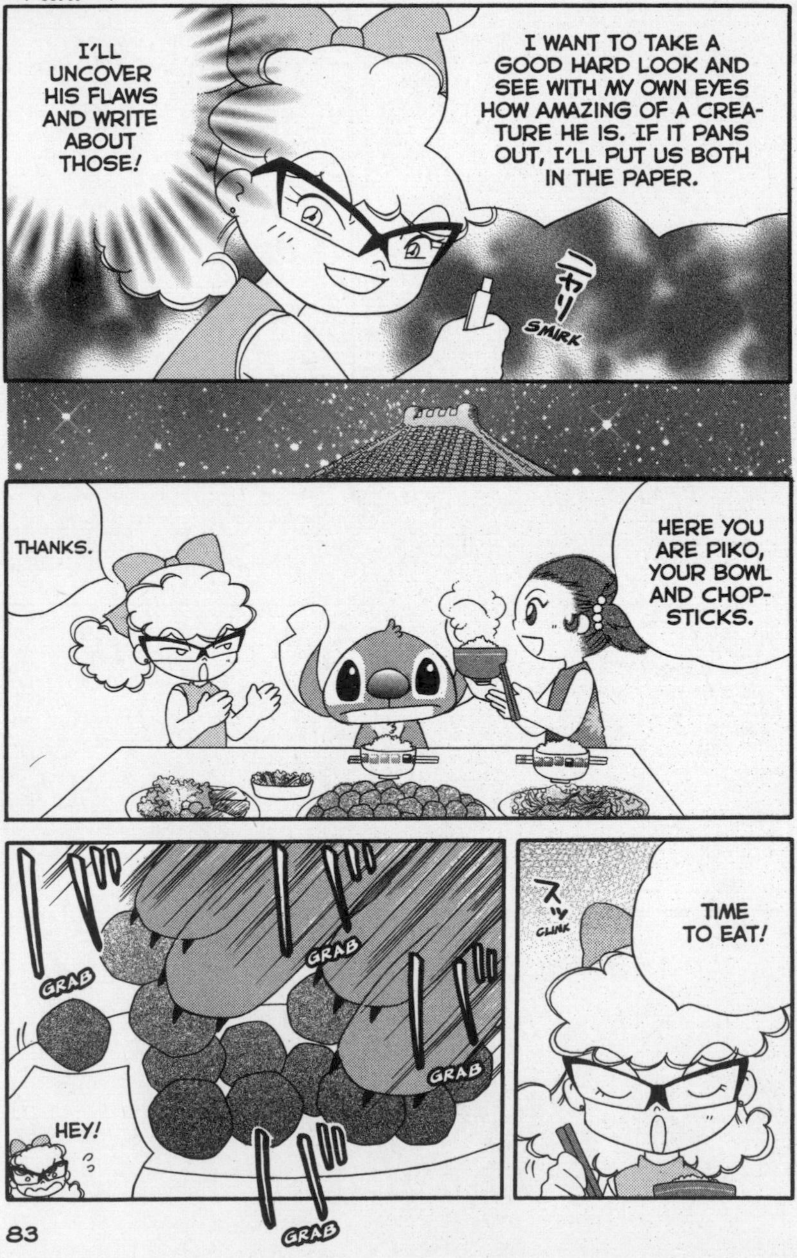
I WANT TO TAKE A GOOD HARD LOOK AND SEE WITH MY OWN EYES HOW AMAZING OF A CREATURE HE IS. IF IT PANS OUT, I'LL PUT US BOTH IN THE PAPER.
I'LL UNCOVER HIS FLAWS AND WRITE ABOUT THOSE!
ニヤリ
SMIRK
HERE YOU ARE PIKO, YOUR BOWL AND CHOPSTICKS.
THANKS.
TIME TO EAT!
スッ
CLINK
GRAB
GRAB
GRAB
HEY!
GRAB

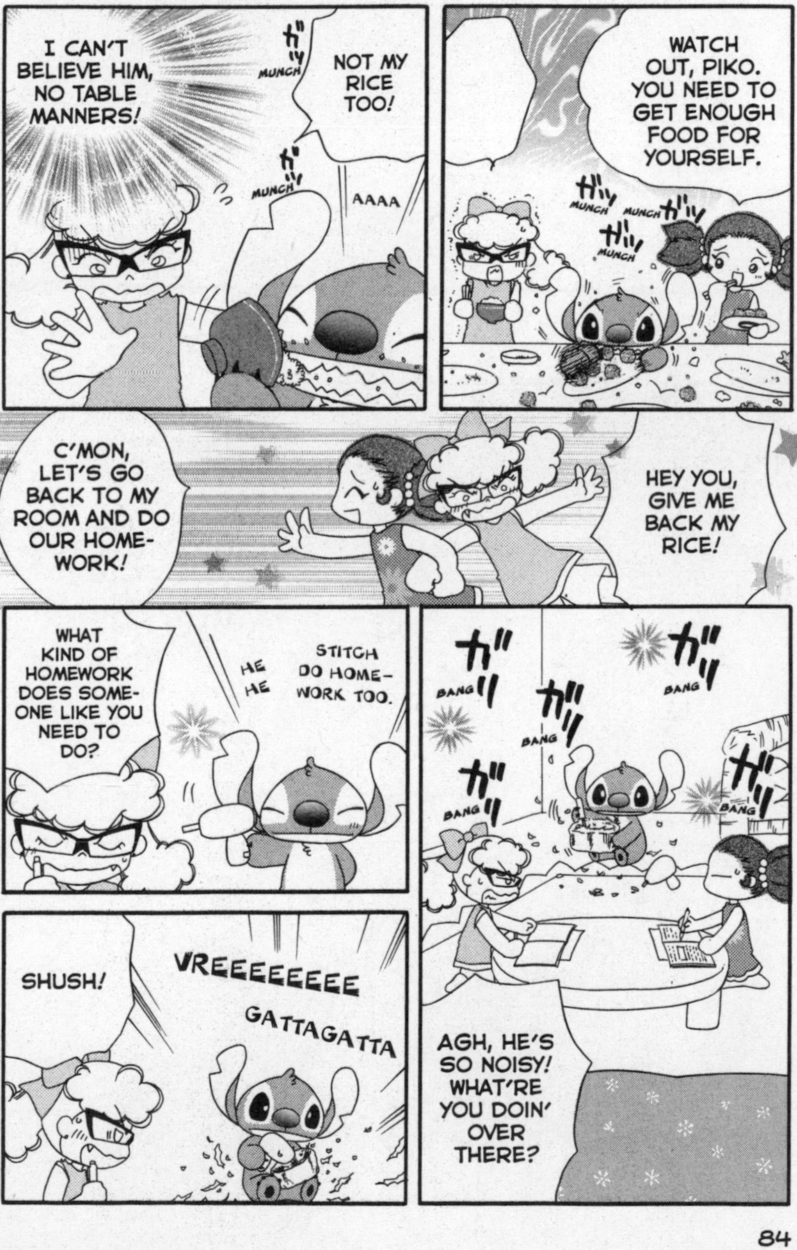
WATCH OUT, PIKO. YOU NEED TO GET ENOUGH FOOD FOR YOURSELF.
MUNCH
MUNCH
MUNCH
NOT MY RICE TOO!
MUNCH
I CAN'T BELIEVE HIM, NO TABLE MANNERS!
MUNCH
AAAA
HEY YOU, GIVE ME BACK MY RICE!
C'MON, LET'S GO BACK TO MY ROOM AND DO OUR HOME-WORK!
BANG
BANG
BANG
BANG
BANG
AGH, HE'S SO NOISY! WHAT'RE YOU DOIN' OVER THERE?
STITCH DO HOME-WORK TOO.
HE HE
WHAT KIND OF HOMEWORK DOES SOME-ONE LIKE YOU NEED TO DO?
VREEEEEEEEE
GATTAGATTA
SHUSH!

READ THIS WAY

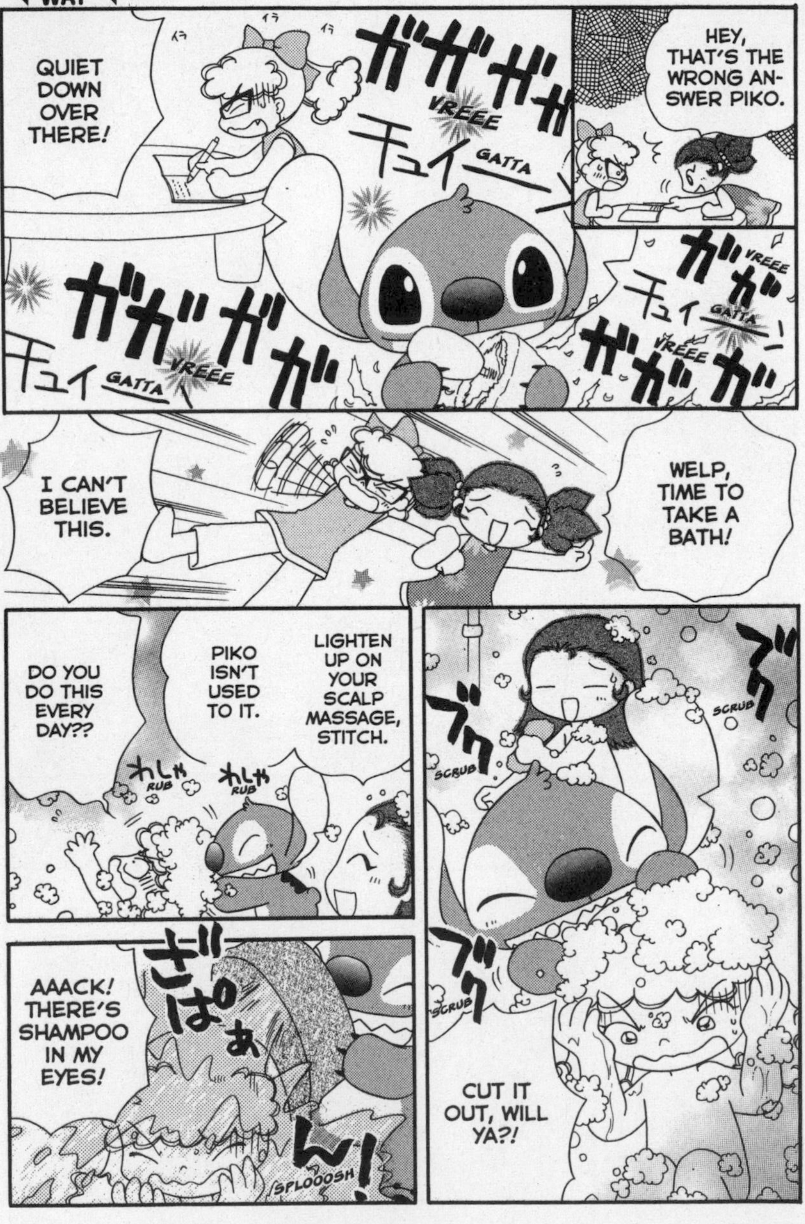
HEY, THAT'S THE WRONG AN-SWER PIKO.
QUIET DOWN OVER THERE!
イラ イラ イラ
ガガガガ
VREEE
チュイー
GATTA
ガガ
VREEE
チュイ
GATTA
ガガガ
VREEE
ガガガガ
チュイ
GATTA
VREEE
WELP, TIME TO TAKE A BATH!
I CAN'T BELIEVE THIS.
ゴシ
SCRUB
ゴシ
SCRUB
ゴシ
SCRUB
CUT IT OUT, WILL YA?!
LIGHTEN UP ON YOUR SCALP MASSAGE, STITCH.
PIKO ISN'T USED TO IT.
DO YOU DO THIS EVERY DAY??
わしゃ
RUB
わしゃ
RUB
AAACK! THERE'S SHAMPOO IN MY EYES!
ざぱぁん!
SPLOOOSH

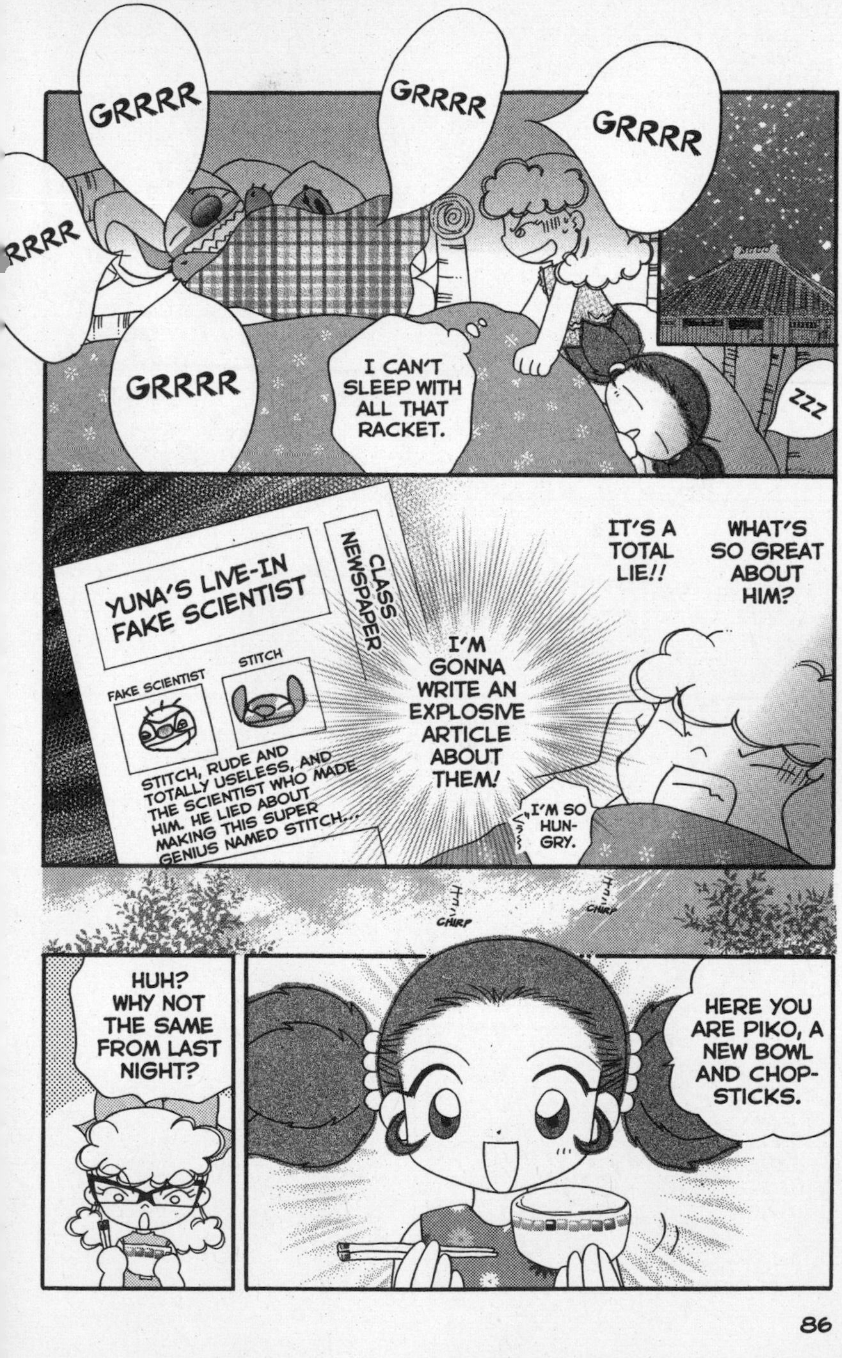
GRRRR
GRRRR
GRRRR
RRRR
ZZZ
I CAN'T SLEEP WITH ALL THAT RACKET.
GRRRR
WHAT'S SO GREAT ABOUT HIM?
IT'S A TOTAL LIE!!
CLASS NEWSPAPER
YUNA'S LIVE-IN FAKE SCIENTIST
STITCH
FAKE SCIENTIST
STITCH, RUDE AND TOTALLY USELESS, AND THE SCIENTIST WHO MADE HIM. HE LIED ABOUT MAKING THIS SUPER GENIUS NAMED STITCH...
I'M GONNA WRITE AN EXPLOSIVE ARTICLE ABOUT THEM!
I'M SO HUN-GRY.
CHIRP
CHIRP
HERE YOU ARE PIKO, A NEW BOWL AND CHOP-STICKS.
HUH? WHY NOT THE SAME FROM LAST NIGHT?

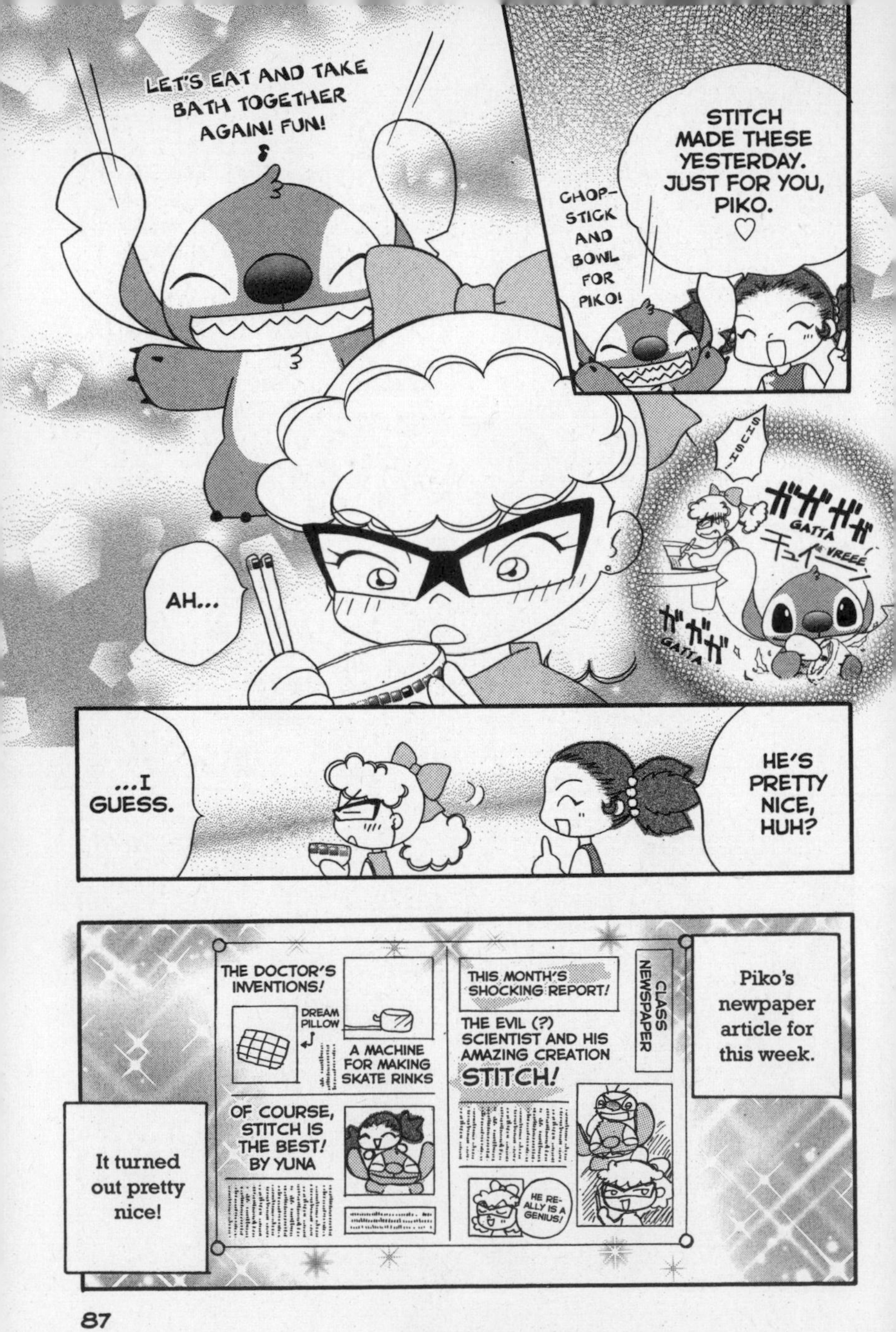

STITCH MADE THESE YESTERDAY. JUST FOR YOU, PIKO. ♡
CHOP-STICK AND BOWL FOR PIKO!
LET'S EAT AND TAKE BATH TOGETHER AGAIN! FUN!
AH...
SHUSH-
GATTA
VREEE
GATTA
HE'S PRETTY NICE, HUH?
...I GUESS.
Piko's newpaper article for this week.
CLASS NEWSPAPER
THIS MONTH'S SHOCKING REPORT!
THE EVIL (?) SCIENTIST AND HIS AMAZING CREATION
STITCH!
HE REALLY IS A GENIUS!
THE DOCTOR'S INVENTIONS!
DREAM PILLOW
A MACHINE FOR MAKING SKATE RINKS
OF COURSE, STITCH IS THE BEST! BY YUNA
It turned out pretty nice!

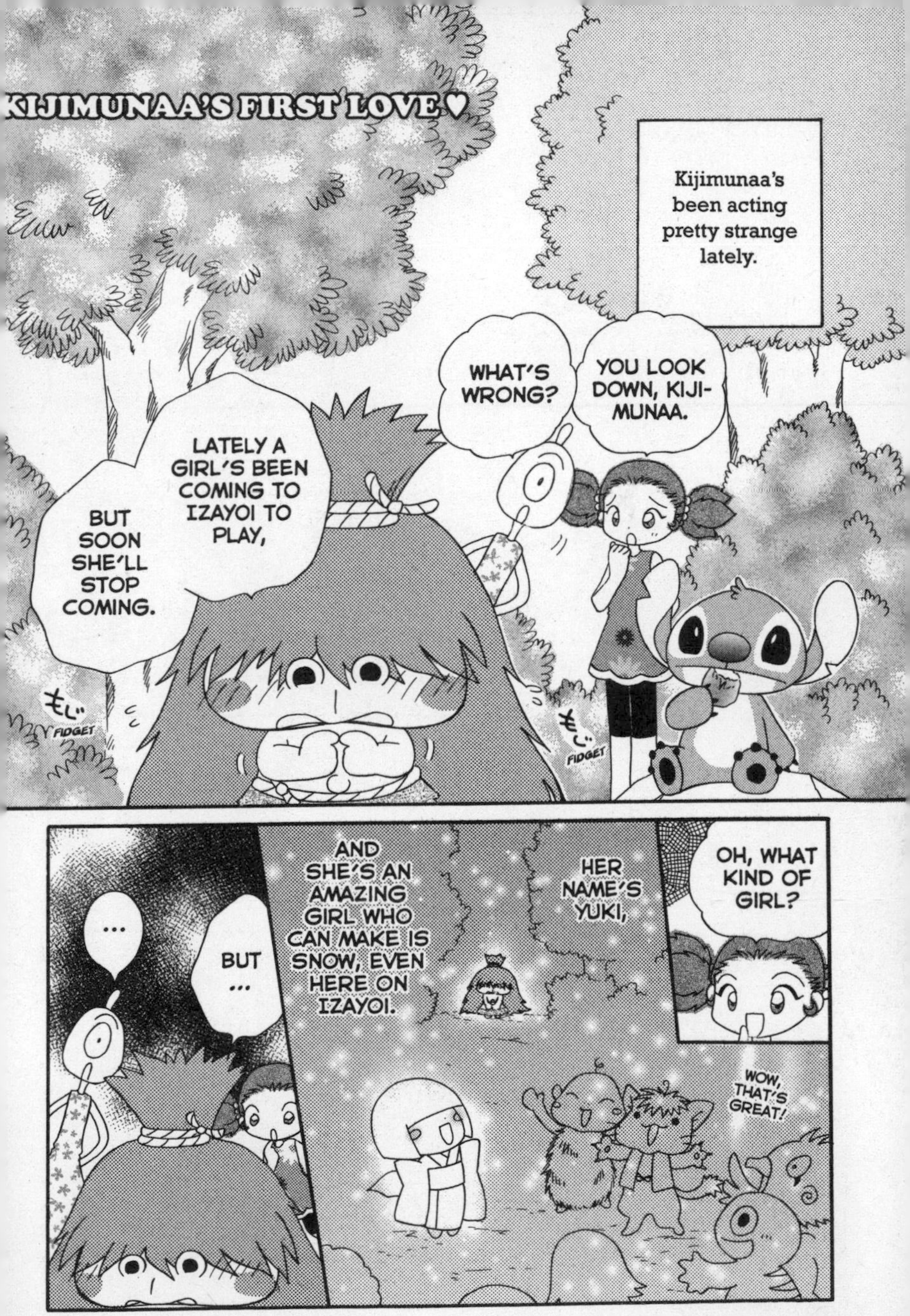
KIJIMUNAA'S FIRST LOVE♥
Kijimunaa's been acting pretty strange lately.
YOU LOOK DOWN, KIJI-MUNAA.
WHAT'S WRONG?
LATELY A GIRL'S BEEN COMING TO IZAYOI TO PLAY,
BUT SOON SHE'LL STOP COMING.
もじ FIDGET
もじ FIDGET
OH, WHAT KIND OF GIRL?
HER NAME'S YUKI,
AND SHE'S AN AMAZING GIRL WHO CAN MAKE IS SNOW, EVEN HERE ON IZAYOI.
WOW, THAT'S GREAT!
BUT ...
...

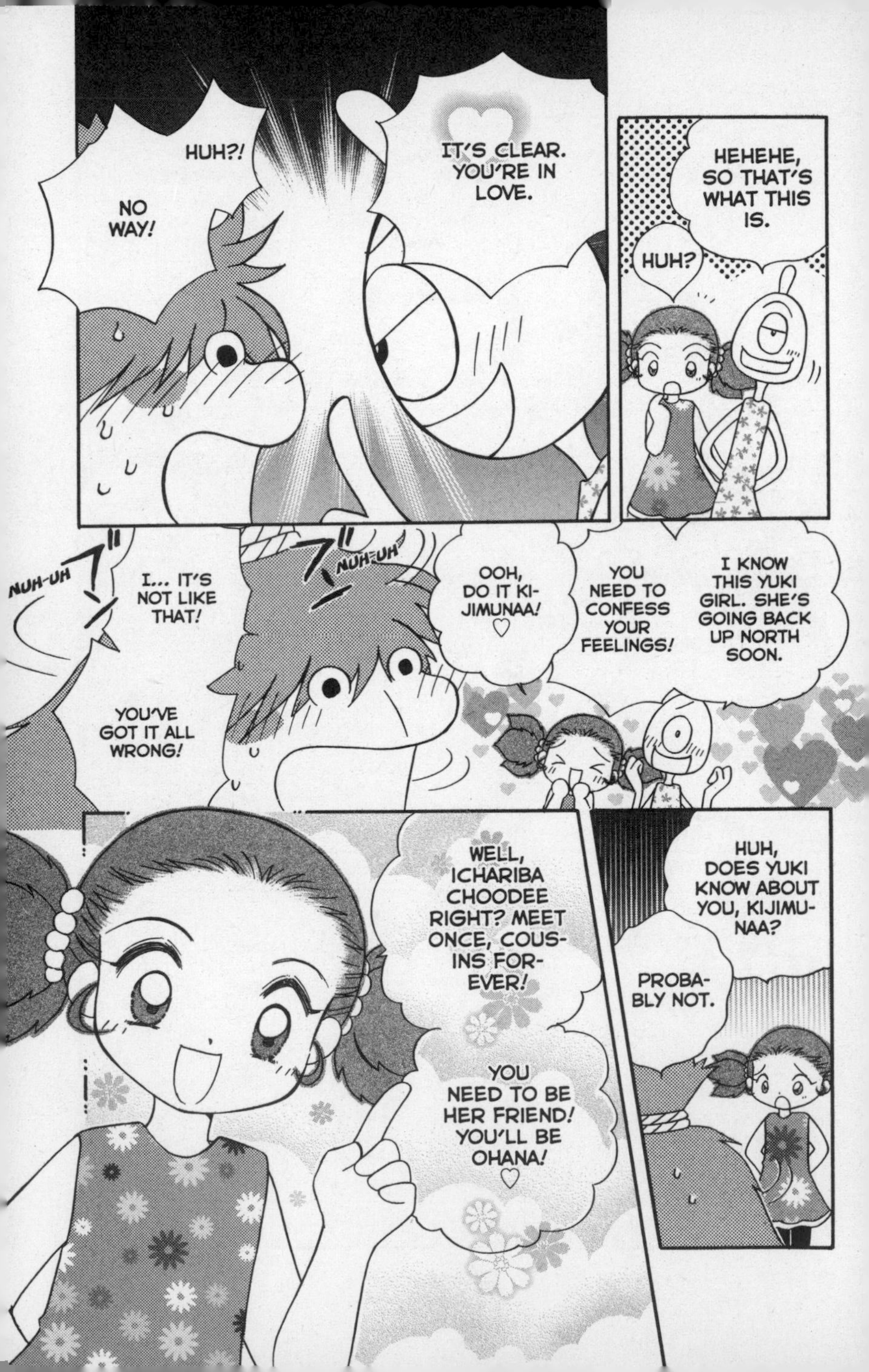
HEHEHE, SO THAT'S WHAT THIS IS.
HUH?
IT'S CLEAR. YOU'RE IN LOVE.
HUH?!
NO WAY!
I KNOW THIS YUKI GIRL. SHE'S GOING BACK UP NORTH SOON.
YOU NEED TO CONFESS YOUR FEELINGS!
OOH, DO IT KI-JIMUNAA! ♡
NUH-UH
I... IT'S NOT LIKE THAT!
NUH-UH
YOU'VE GOT IT ALL WRONG!
HUH, DOES YUKI KNOW ABOUT YOU, KIJIMU-NAA?
PROBA-BLY NOT.
WELL, ICHARIBA CHOODEE RIGHT? MEET ONCE, COUS-INS FOR-EVER!
YOU NEED TO BE HER FRIEND! YOU'LL BE OHANA! ♡

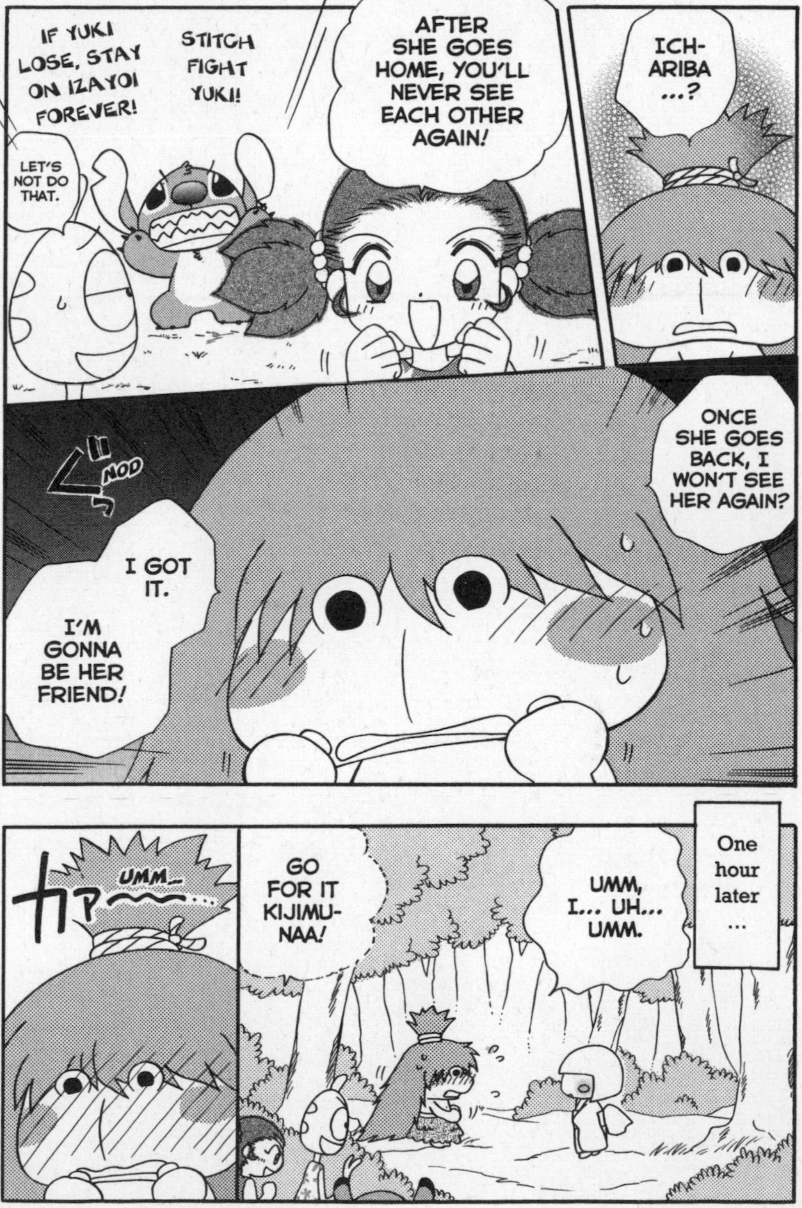
ICH-ARIBA ...?
AFTER SHE GOES HOME, YOU'LL NEVER SEE EACH OTHER AGAIN!
STITCH FIGHT YUKI!
IF YUKI LOSE, STAY ON IZAYOI FOREVER!
LET'S NOT DO THAT.
ONCE SHE GOES BACK, I WON'T SEE HER AGAIN?
NOD
I GOT IT.
I'M GONNA BE HER FRIEND!
One hour later ...
UMM, I... UH... UMM.
GO FOR IT KIJIMUNAA!
UMM...
カア〜〜

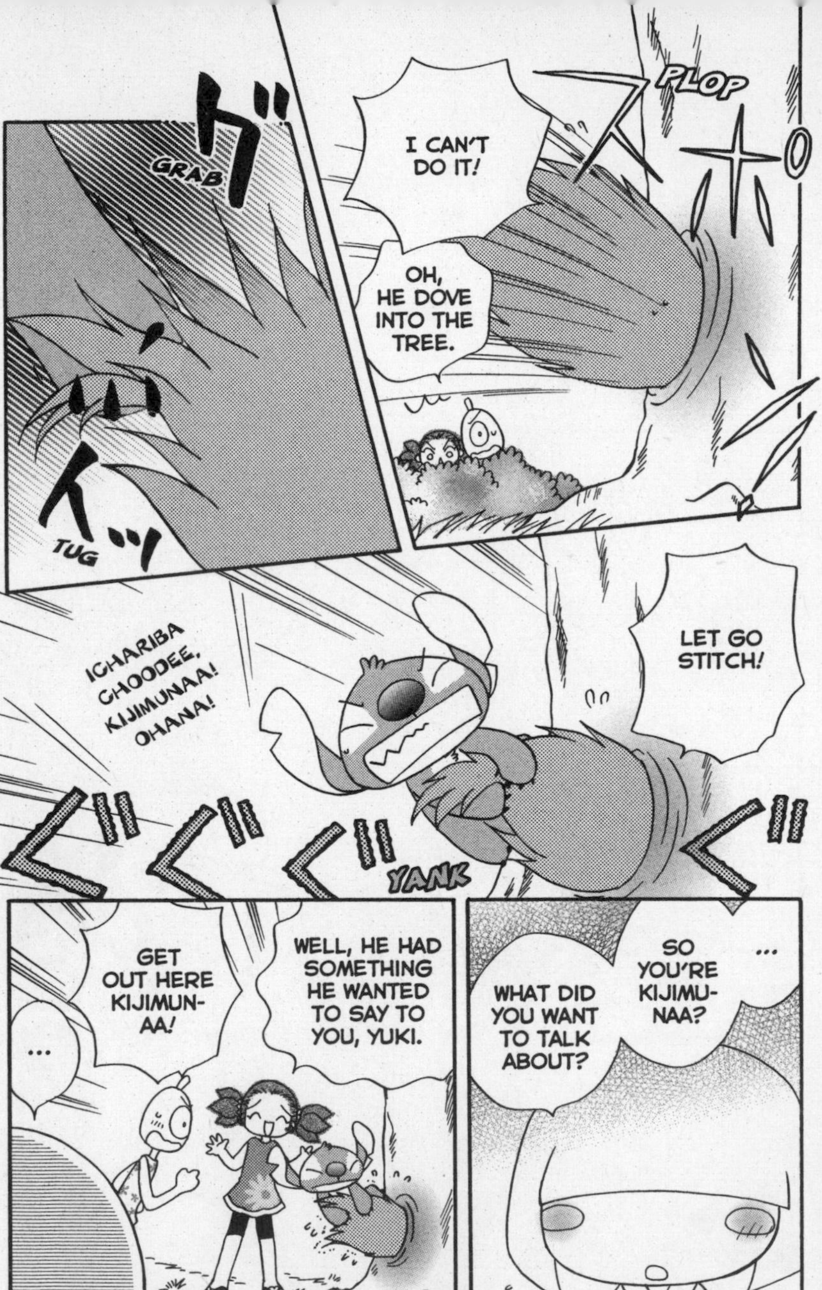
PLOP
I CAN'T DO IT!
OH, HE DOVE INTO THE TREE.
GRAB
TUG
LET GO STITCH!
ICHARIBA CHOODEE, KIJIMUNAA! OHANA!
YANK
...
SO YOU'RE KIJIMUNAA?
WHAT DID YOU WANT TO TALK ABOUT?
WELL, HE HAD SOMETHING HE WANTED TO SAY TO YOU, YUKI.
GET OUT HERE KIJIMUNAA!
...

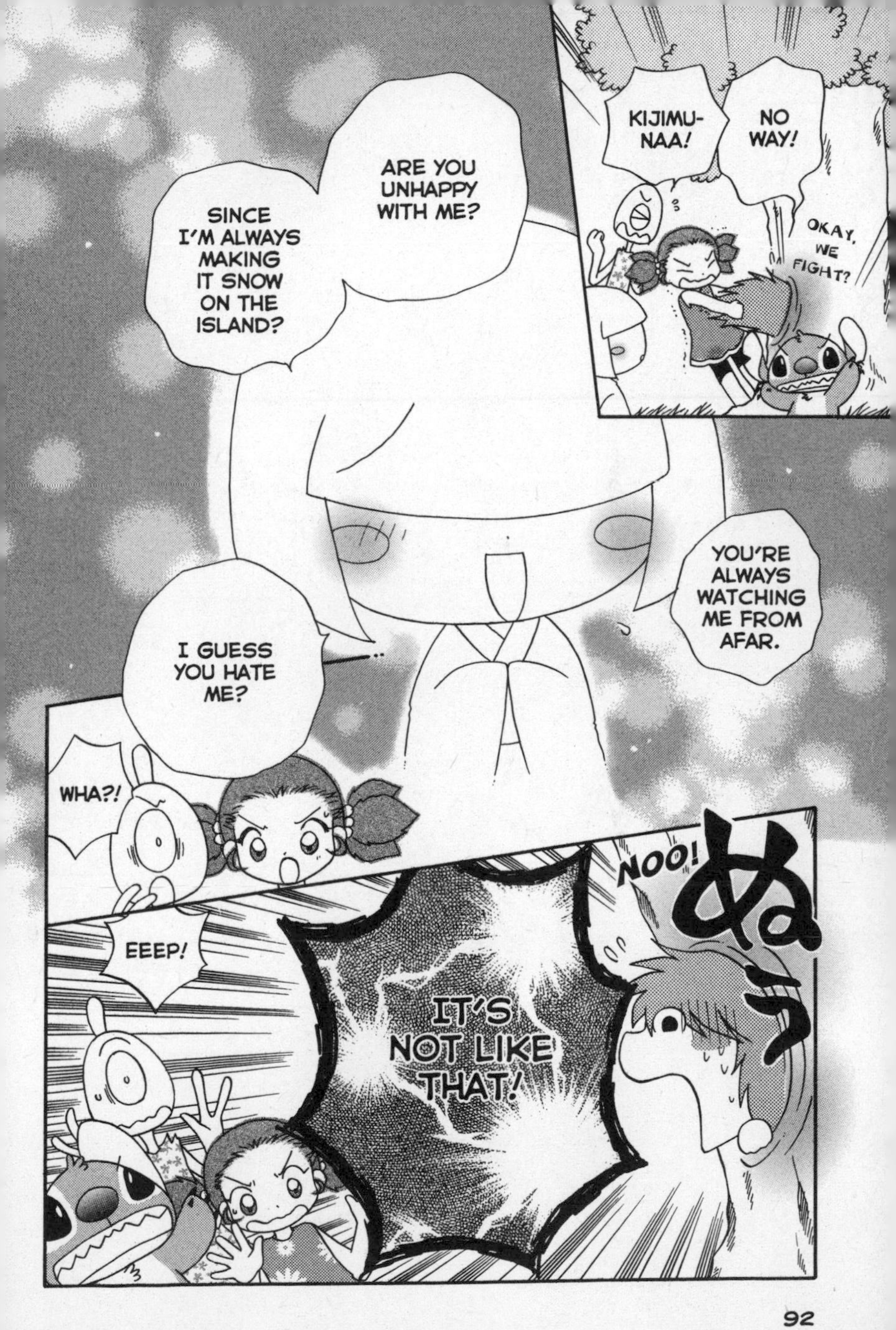
NO WAY!
KIJIMUNAA!
OKAY, WE FIGHT?
ARE YOU UNHAPPY WITH ME?
SINCE I'M ALWAYS MAKING IT SNOW ON THE ISLAND?
YOU'RE ALWAYS WATCHING ME FROM AFAR.
I GUESS YOU HATE ME?
WHA?!
NOO!
ぬっ
IT'S NOT LIKE THAT!
EEEP!

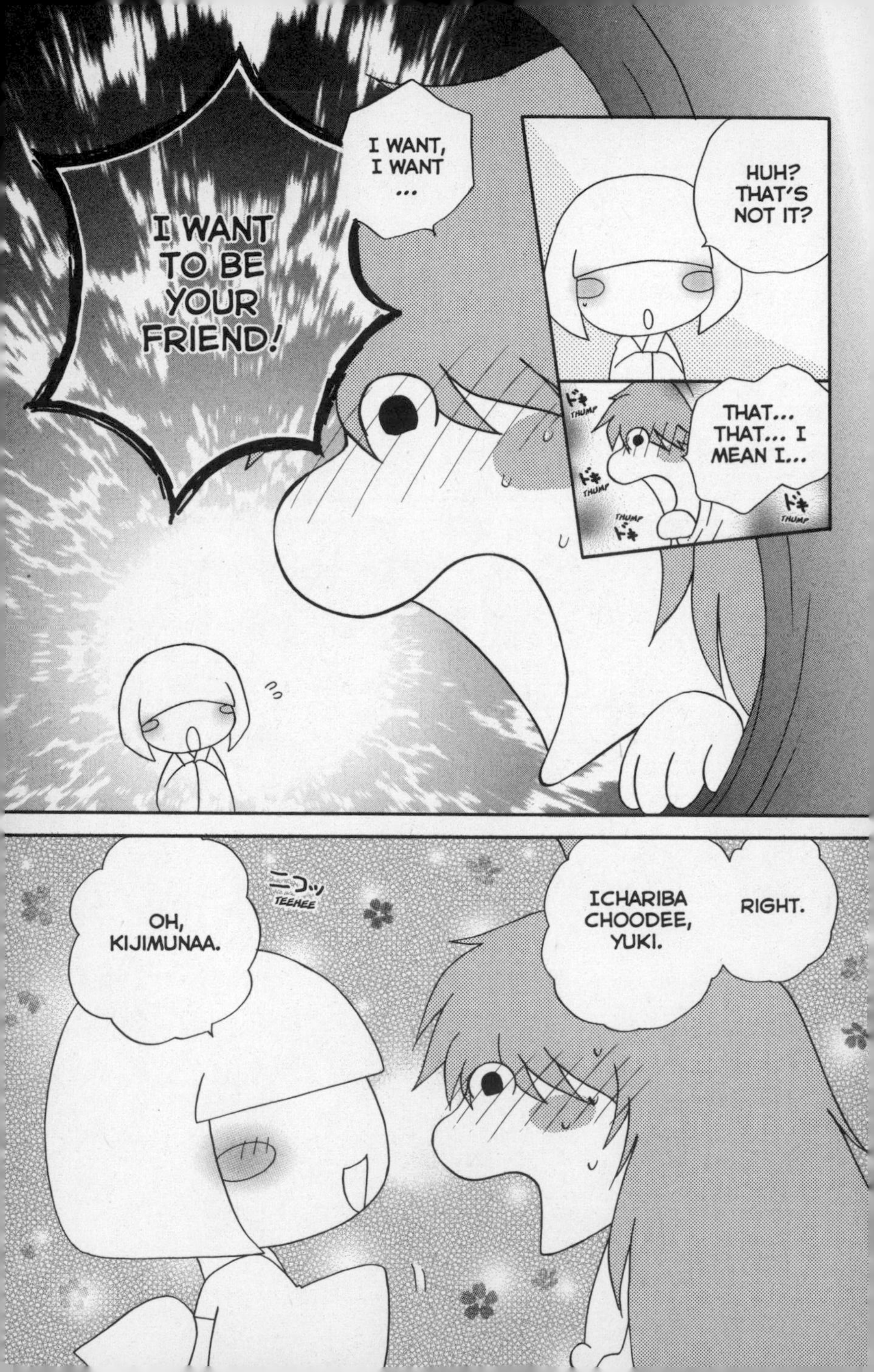
HUH? THAT'S NOT IT?
ドキ THUMP
THAT... THAT... I MEAN I...
ドキ THUMP
ドキ THUMP
ドキ THUMP
I WANT, I WANT ...
I WANT TO BE YOUR FRIEND!
RIGHT.
ICHARIBA CHOODEE, YUKI.
ニコッ TEEHEE
OH, KIJIMUNAA.

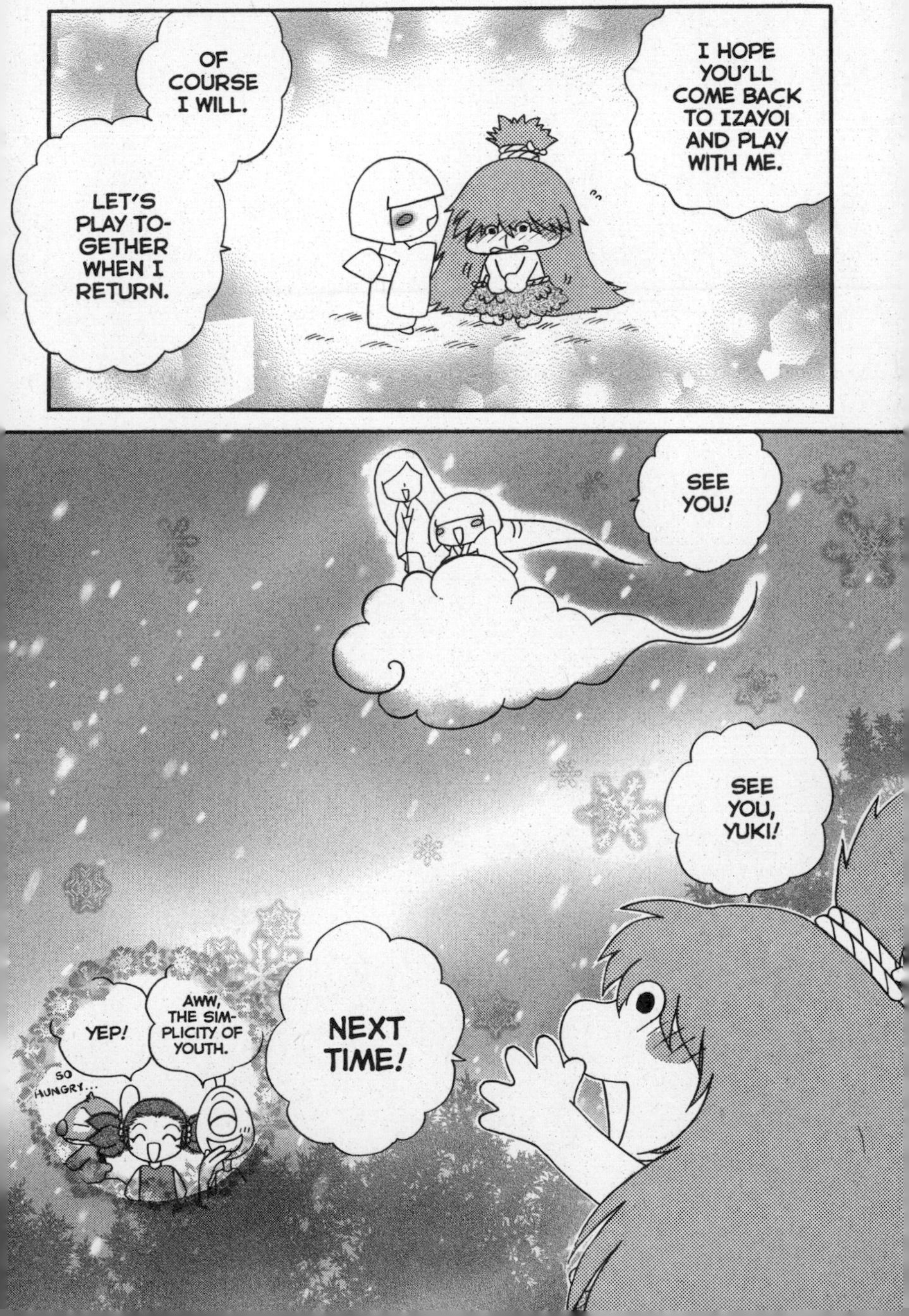
I HOPE YOU'LL COME BACK TO IZAYOI AND PLAY WITH ME.
OF COURSE I WILL.
LET'S PLAY TO-GETHER WHEN I RETURN.
SEE YOU!
SEE YOU, YUKI!
NEXT TIME!
AWW, THE SIM-PLICITY OF YOUTH.
YEP!
SO HUNGRY...

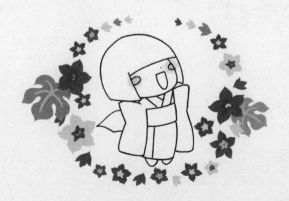

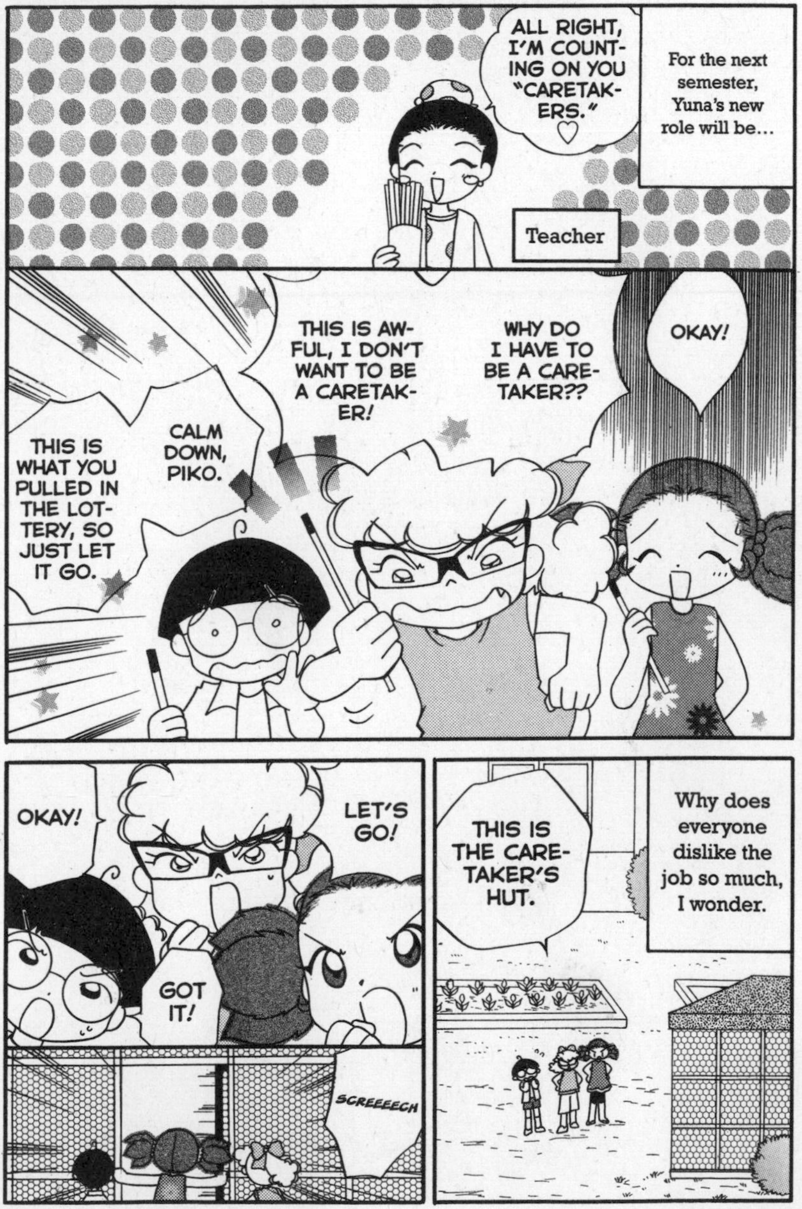
For the next semester, Yuna's new role will be…
ALL RIGHT, I'M COUNTING ON YOU "CARETAKERS." ♡
Teacher
OKAY!
WHY DO I HAVE TO BE A CARETAKER??
THIS IS AWFUL, I DON'T WANT TO BE A CARETAKER!
CALM DOWN, PIKO.
THIS IS WHAT YOU PULLED IN THE LOTTERY, SO JUST LET IT GO.
Why does everyone dislike the job so much, I wonder.
THIS IS THE CARETAKER'S HUT.
LET'S GO!
OKAY!
GOT IT!
SCREEEEECH

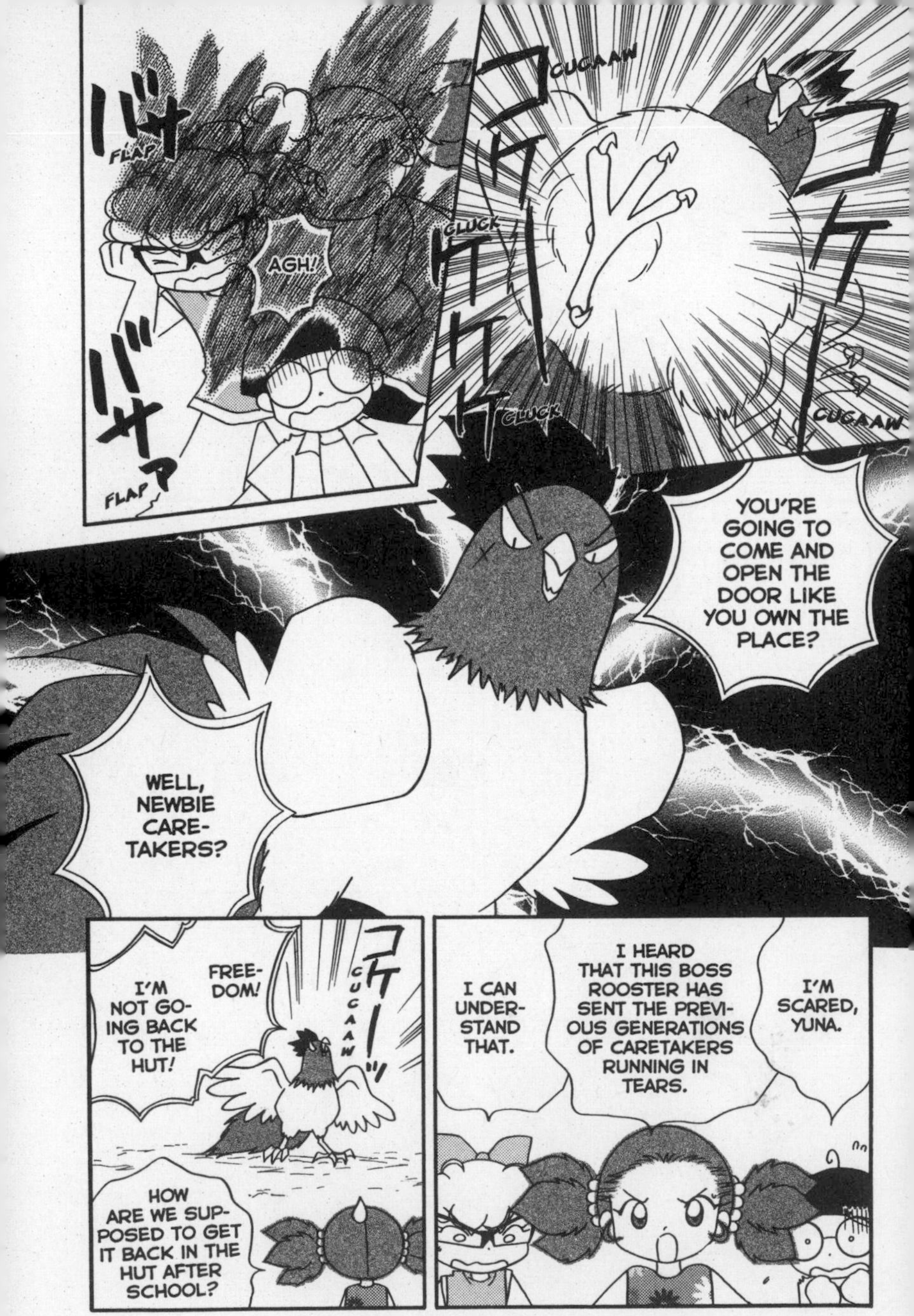
CUGAAW
GLUCK
GLUCK
CUGAAW
FLAP
AGH!
FLAP
YOU'RE GOING TO COME AND OPEN THE DOOR LIKE YOU OWN THE PLACE?
WELL, NEWBIE CARETAKERS?
I'M SCARED, YUNA.
I HEARD THAT THIS BOSS ROOSTER HAS SENT THE PREVIOUS GENERATIONS OF CARETAKERS RUNNING IN TEARS.
I CAN UNDERSTAND THAT.
CUGAAW
FREEDOM!
I'M NOT GOING BACK TO THE HUT!
HOW ARE WE SUPPOSED TO GET IT BACK IN THE HUT AFTER SCHOOL?

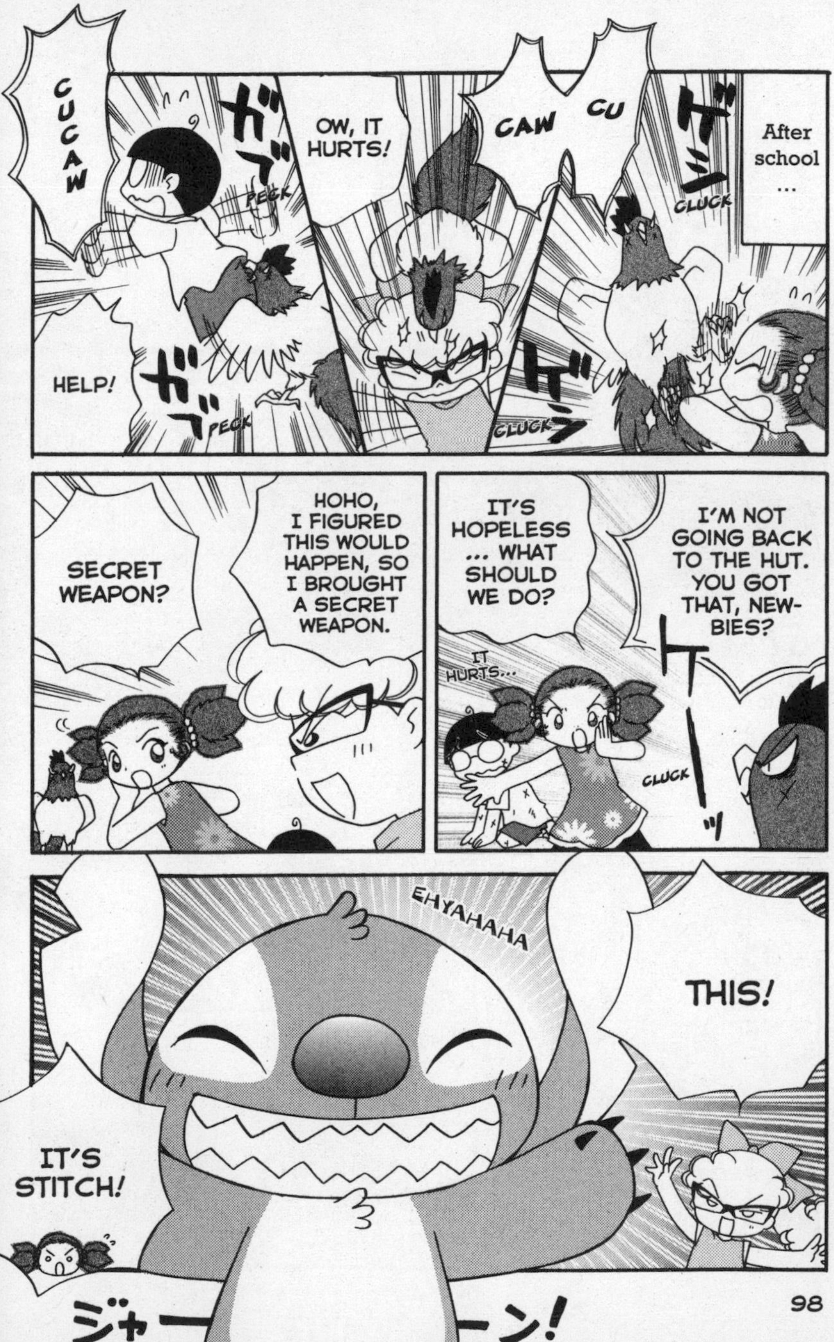
After school ...
CU
CAW
ゲッ
CLUCK
ゲッ
CLUCK
OW, IT HURTS!
CUCAW
ガブ
PECK
HELP!
ガブ
PECK
I'M NOT GOING BACK TO THE HUT. YOU GOT THAT, NEW-BIES?
ケーッ
CLUCK
IT'S HOPELESS ... WHAT SHOULD WE DO?
IT HURTS...
HOHO, I FIGURED THIS WOULD HAPPEN, SO I BROUGHT A SECRET WEAPON.
SECRET WEAPON?
THIS!
EHYAHAHA
IT'S STITCH!
ジャーーン!
TADAAAH

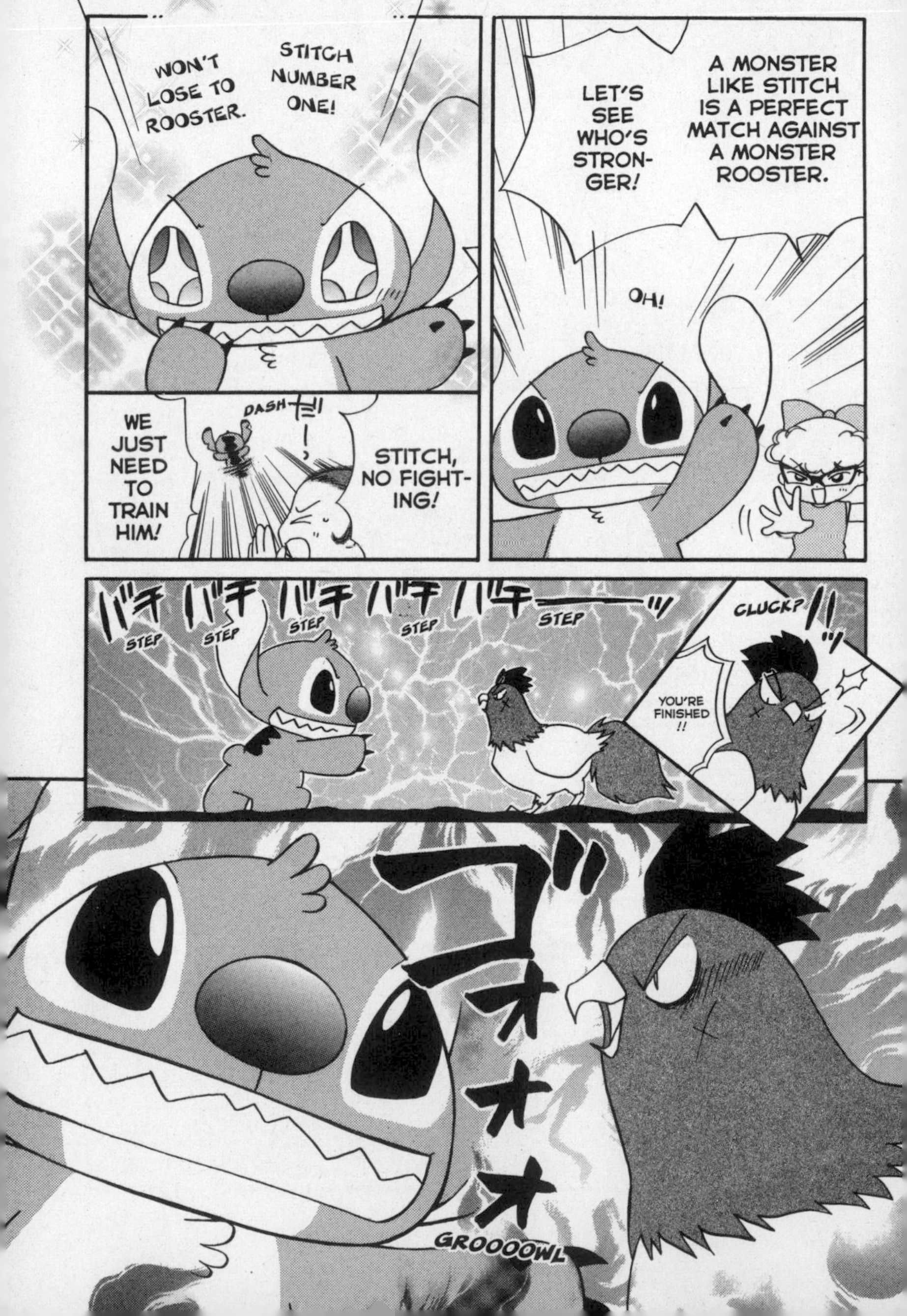
A MONSTER LIKE STITCH IS A PERFECT MATCH AGAINST A MONSTER ROOSTER.
LET'S SEE WHO'S STRONGER!
OH!
STITCH NUMBER ONE!
WON'T LOSE TO ROOSTER.
STITCH, NO FIGHTING!
DASH
WE JUST NEED TO TRAIN HIM!
GLUCK?
YOU'RE FINISHED !!
バチ バチ バチ バチ バチー
STEP STEP STEP STEP STEP
ゴオオオ
GROOOOWL

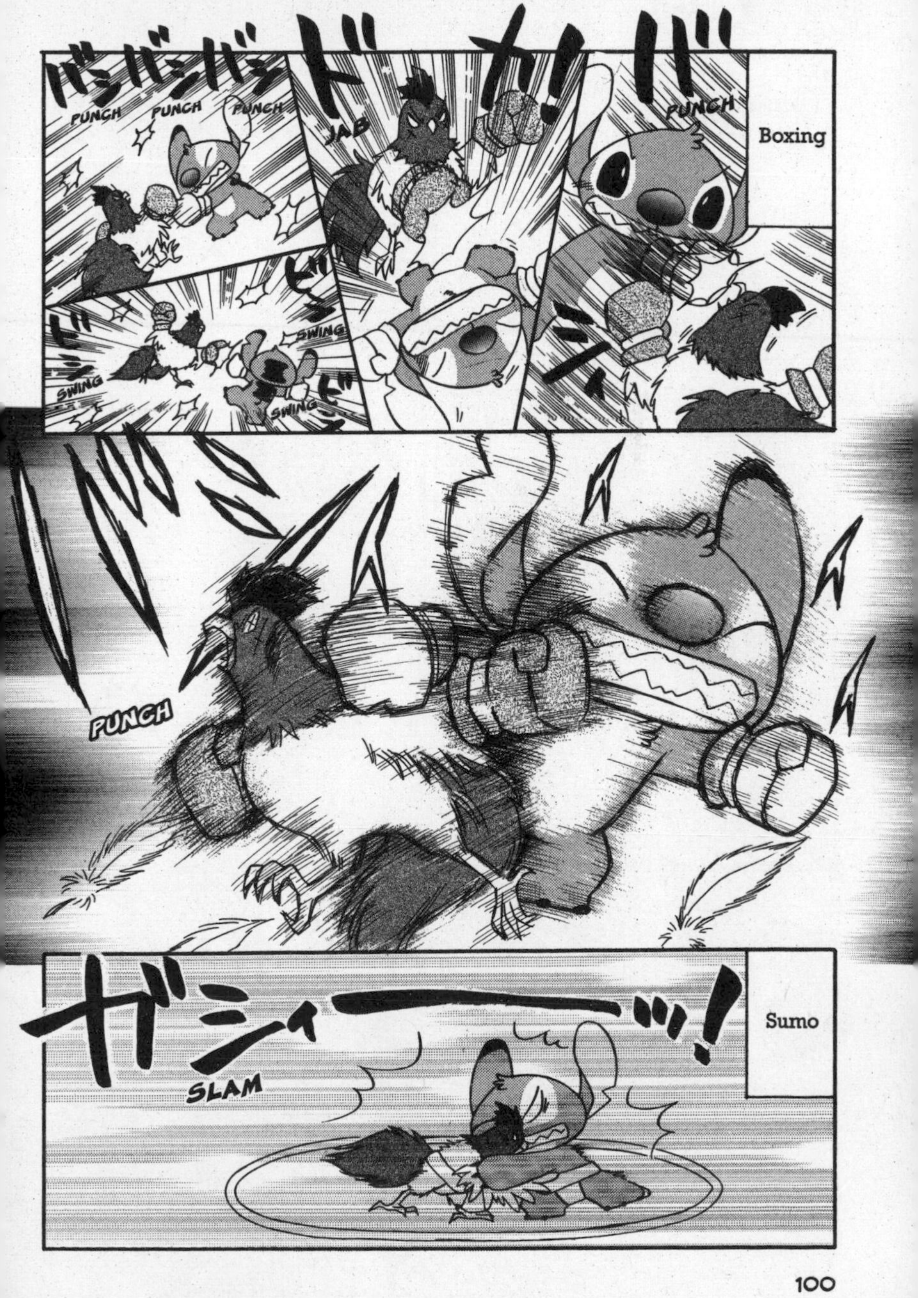

Boxing
PUNCH
JAB
PUNCH
PUNCH
PUNCH
SWING
SWING
SWING
PUNCH
Sumo
SLAM

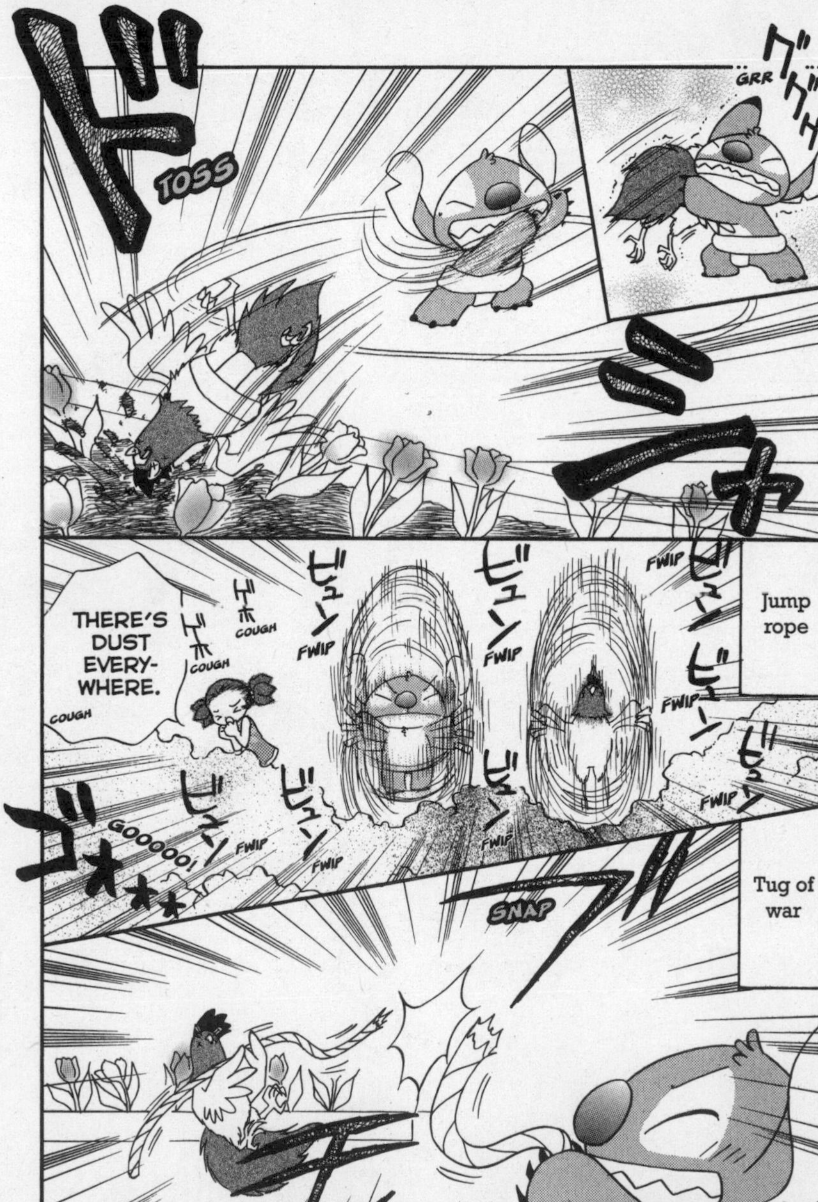
GRR
TOSS
Jump rope
FWIP
FWIP
FWIP
FWIP
THERE'S DUST EVERY-WHERE.
COUGH
COUGH
COUGH
FWIP
FWIP
FWIP
FWIP
GOOOOO!
Tug of war
SNAP

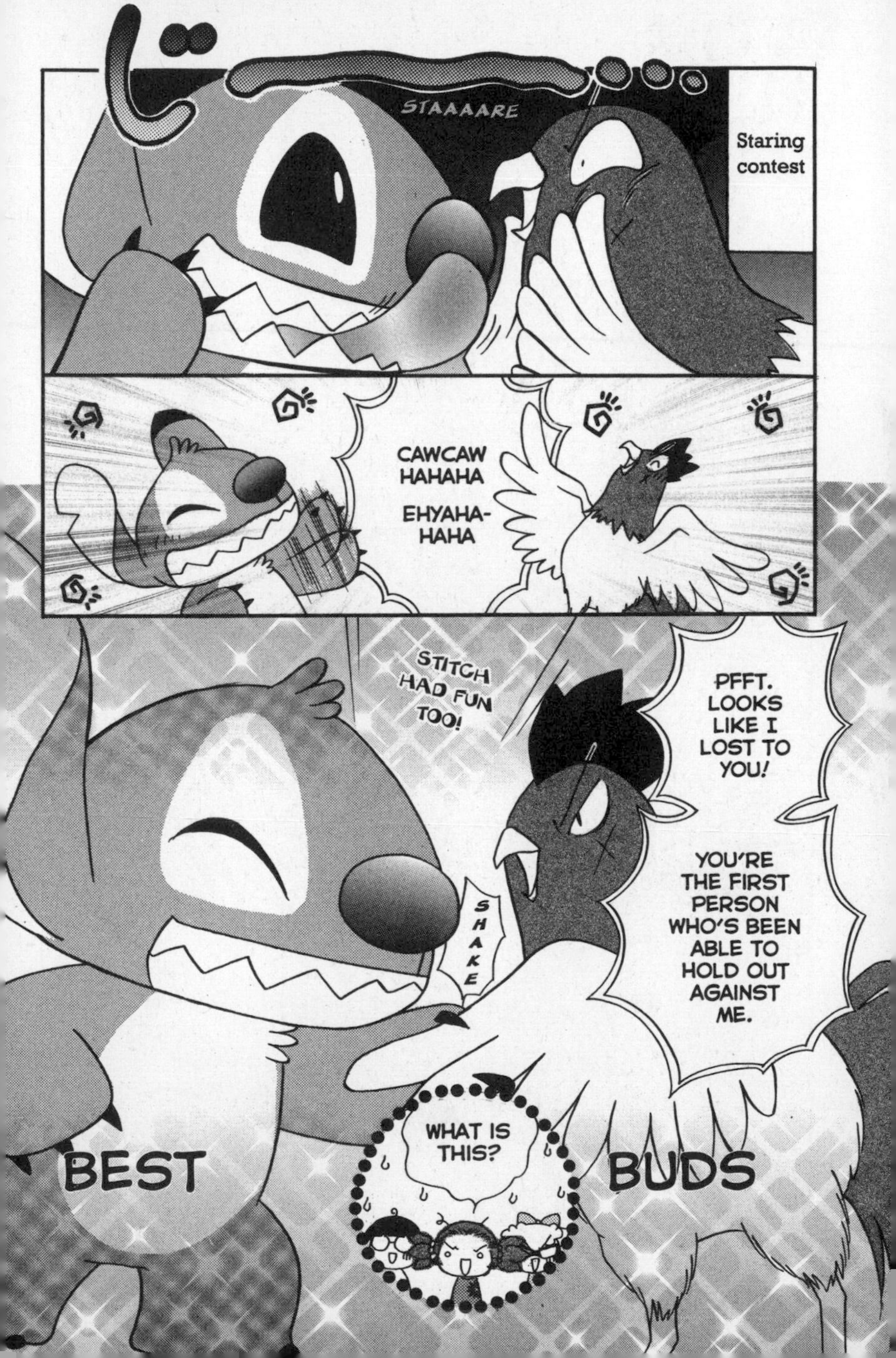
Staring contest
STAAAARE
CAWCAW HAHAHA
EHYAHA-HAHA
PFFT. LOOKS LIKE I LOST TO YOU!
YOU'RE THE FIRST PERSON WHO'S BEEN ABLE TO HOLD OUT AGAINST ME.
STITCH HAD FUN TOO!
SHAKE
WHAT IS THIS?
BEST
BUDS

READ THIS WAY

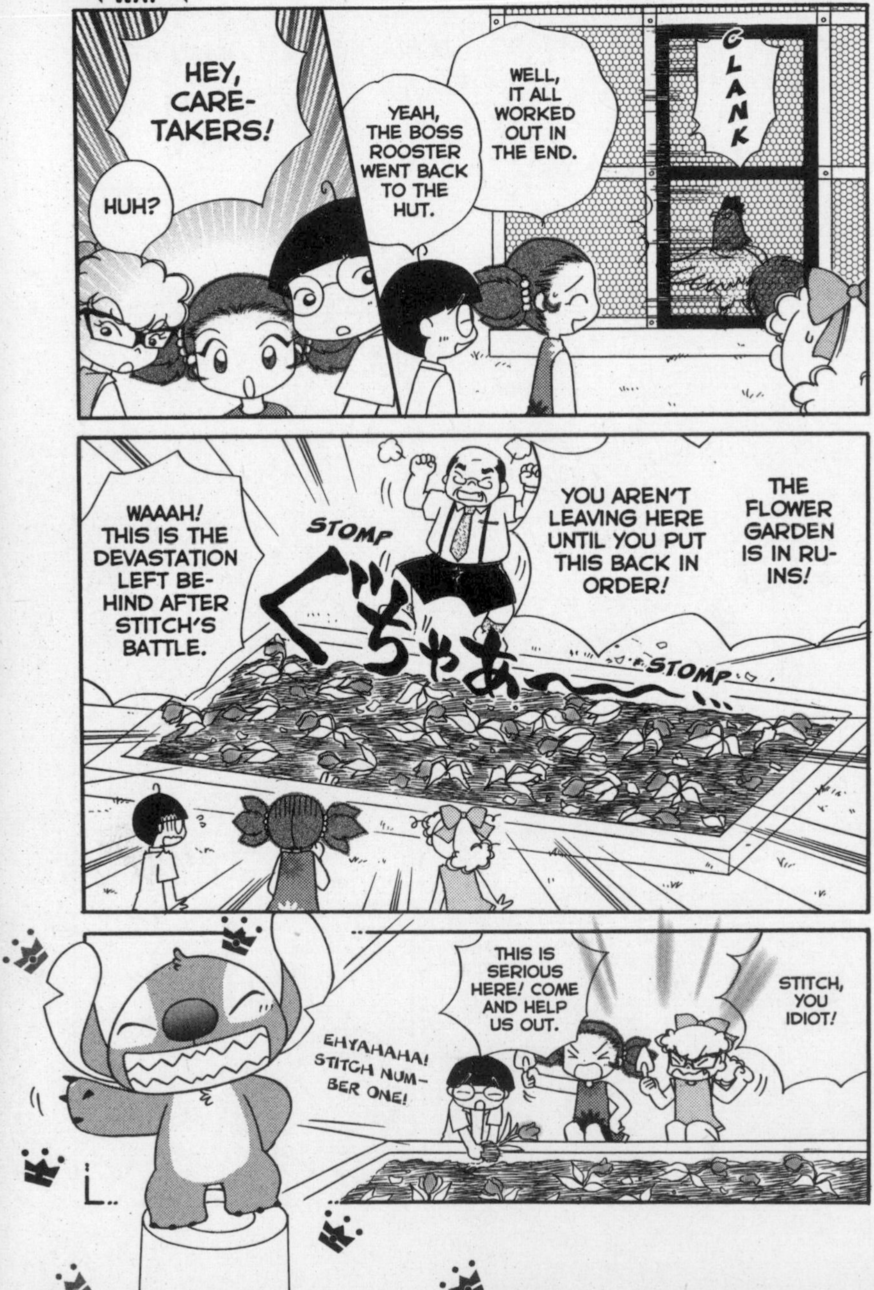
CLANK
WELL, IT ALL WORKED OUT IN THE END.
YEAH, THE BOSS ROOSTER WENT BACK TO THE HUT.
HEY, CARE-TAKERS!
HUH?
THE FLOWER GARDEN IS IN RU-INS!
YOU AREN'T LEAVING HERE UNTIL YOU PUT THIS BACK IN ORDER!
STOMP
STOMP
ぐちゃあ〜
WAAAH! THIS IS THE DEVASTATION LEFT BE-HIND AFTER STITCH'S BATTLE.
STITCH, YOU IDIOT!
THIS IS SERIOUS HERE! COME AND HELP US OUT.
EHYAHAHA! STITCH NUM-BER ONE!

CLOSE CALL ON THE FIELDTRIP!

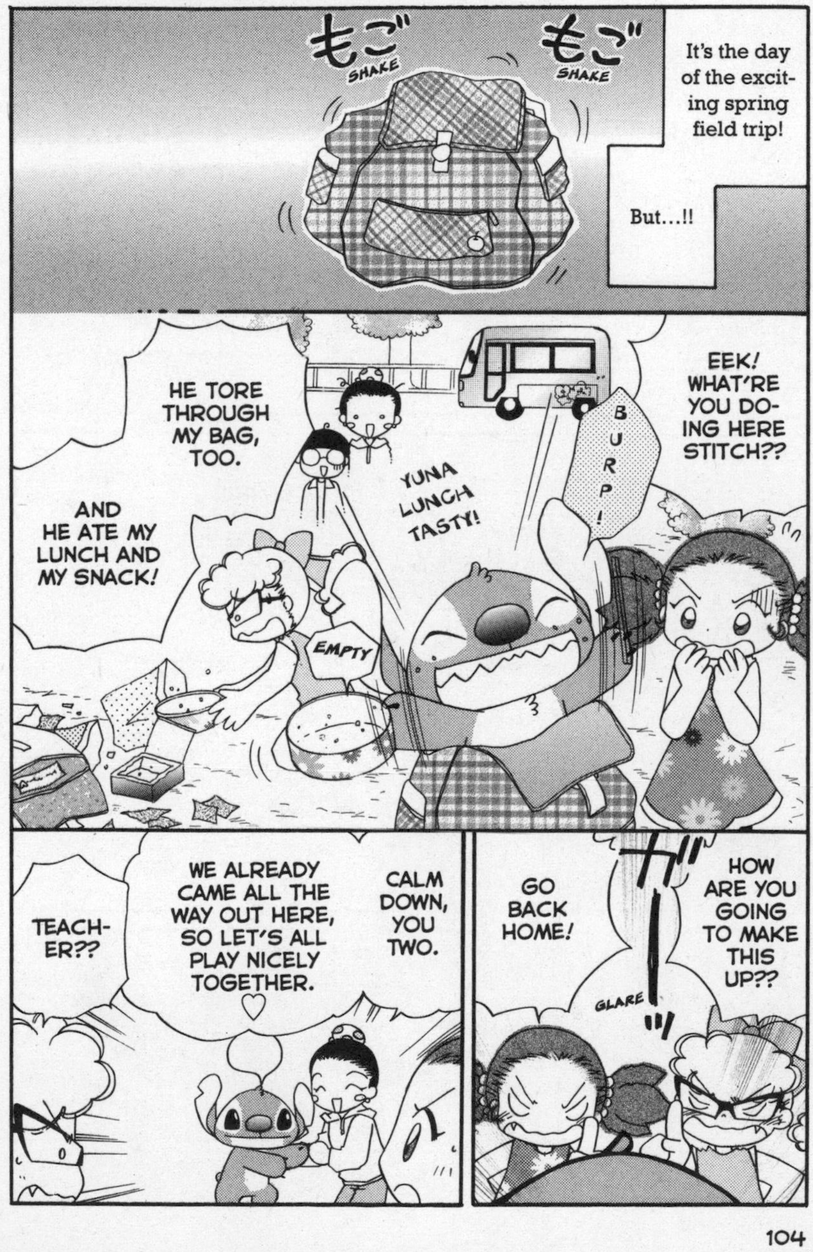
It's the day of the exciting spring field trip!
But...!!
もご
SHAKE
もご
SHAKE
EEK! WHAT'RE YOU DOING HERE STITCH??
BURP!
YUNA LUNCH TASTY!
HE TORE THROUGH MY BAG, TOO.
AND HE ATE MY LUNCH AND MY SNACK!
EMPTY
HOW ARE YOU GOING TO MAKE THIS UP??
GO BACK HOME!
GLARE
CALM DOWN, YOU TWO.
WE ALREADY CAME ALL THE WAY OUT HERE, SO LET'S ALL PLAY NICELY TOGETHER. ♡
TEACHER??

READ THIS WAY

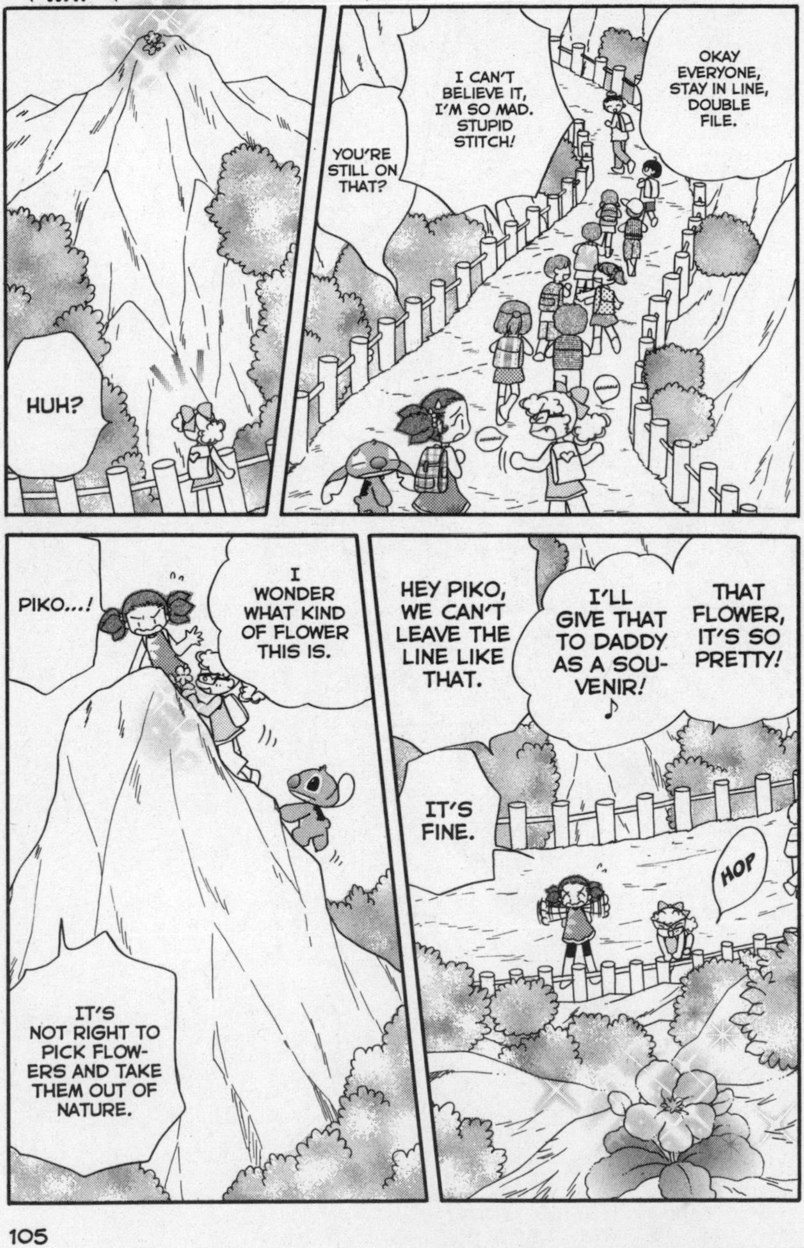
OKAY EVERYONE, STAY IN LINE, DOUBLE FILE.
I CAN'T BELIEVE IT, I'M SO MAD. STUPID STITCH!
YOU'RE STILL ON THAT?
HUH?
THAT FLOWER, IT'S SO PRETTY!
I'LL GIVE THAT TO DADDY AS A SOU-VENIR! ♪
HEY PIKO, WE CAN'T LEAVE THE LINE LIKE THAT.
IT'S FINE.
HOP
I WONDER WHAT KIND OF FLOWER THIS IS.
PIKO...!
IT'S NOT RIGHT TO PICK FLOW-ERS AND TAKE THEM OUT OF NATURE.

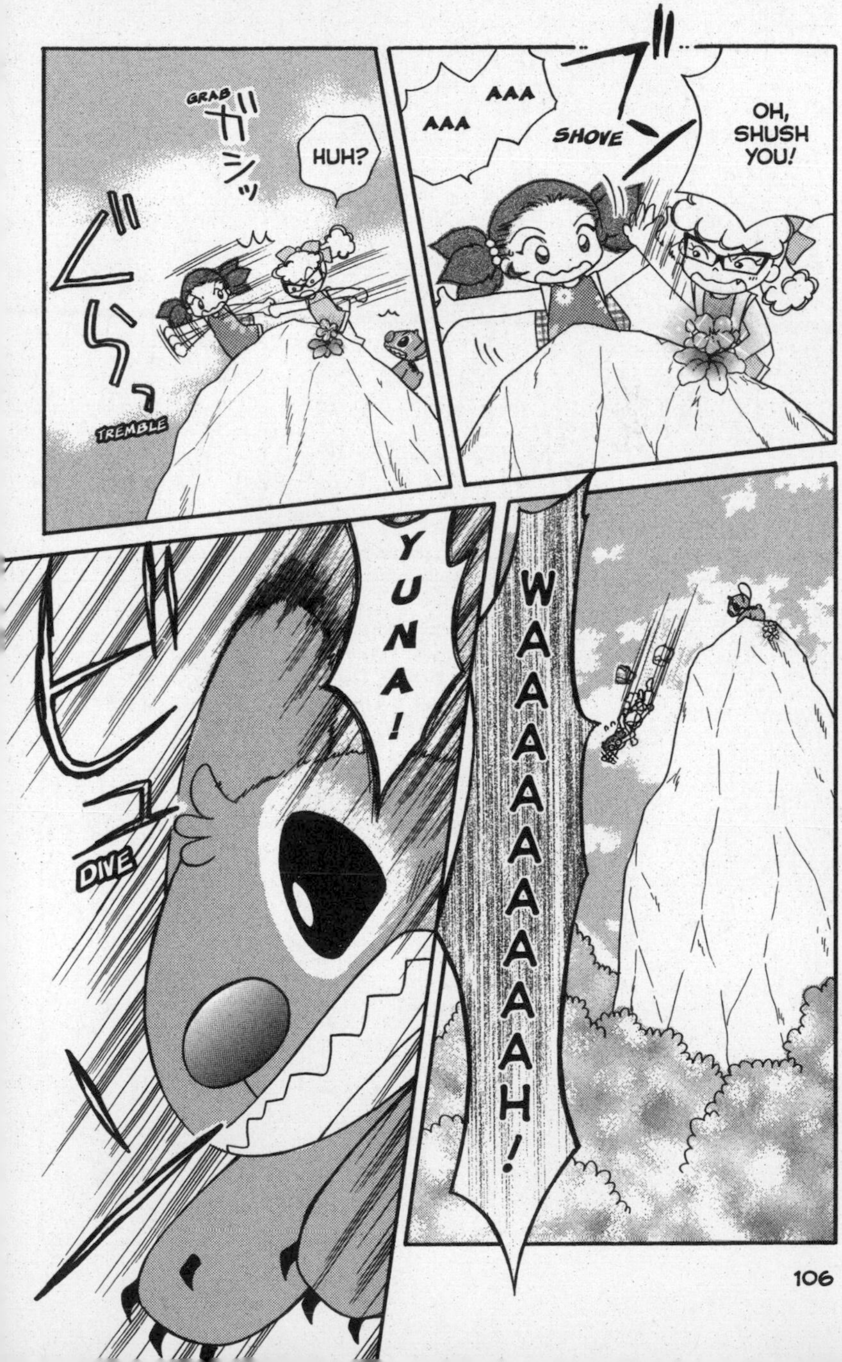
OH, SHUSH YOU!
SHOVE
AAA
AAA
HUH?
GRAB
TREMBLE
WAAAAAAAAAAH!
YUNA!
DIVE

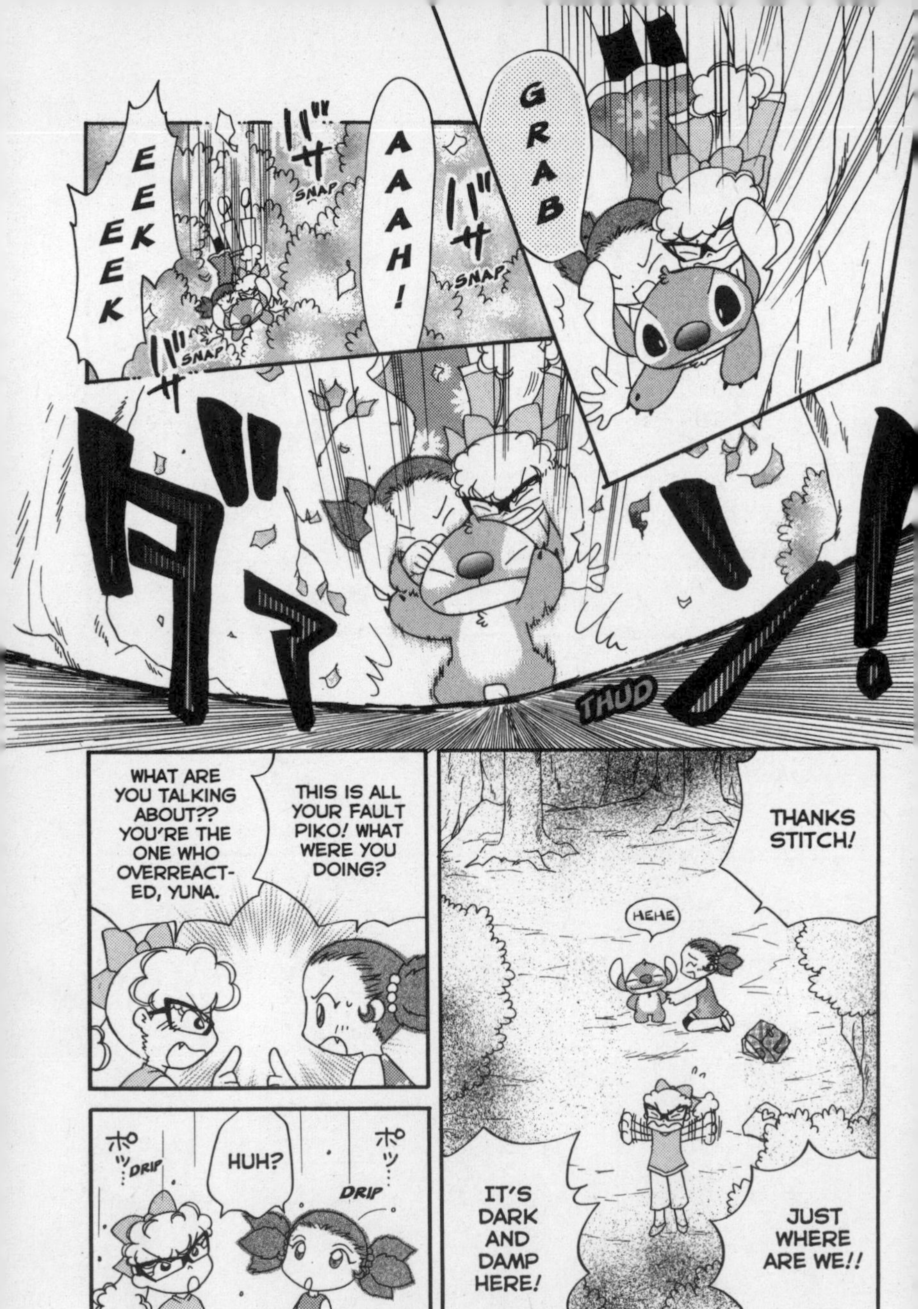
GRAB
AAAH!
バサ
SNAP
バサ
SNAP
EEEK EEK
バサ
SNAP
ダアン!
THUD
THANKS STITCH!
HEHE
JUST WHERE ARE WE!!
IT'S DARK AND DAMP HERE!
THIS IS ALL YOUR FAULT PIKO! WHAT WERE YOU DOING?
WHAT ARE YOU TALKING ABOUT?? YOU'RE THE ONE WHO OVERREACT-ED, YUNA.
ポツ…
DRIP
HUH?
ポツ…
DRIP

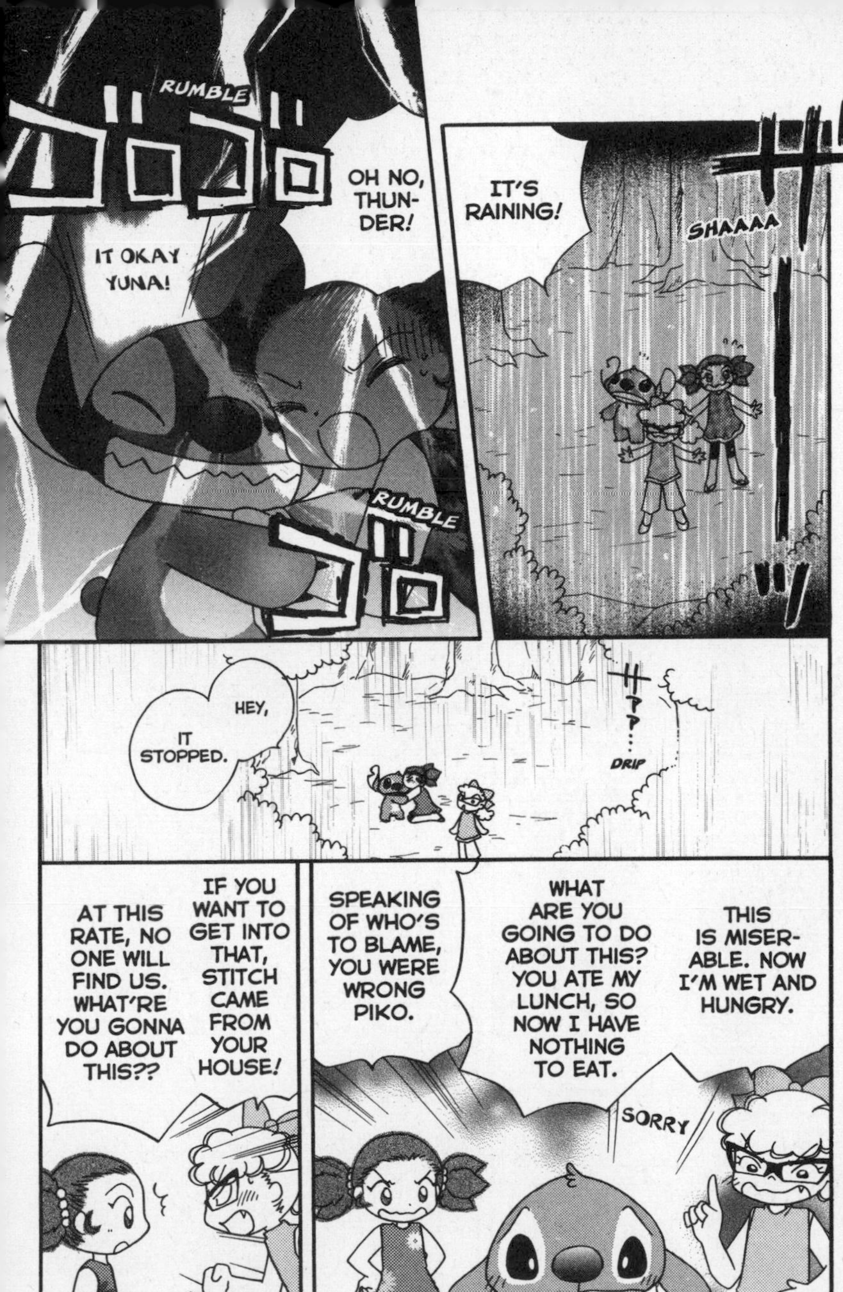
IT'S RAINING!
SHAAAA
RUMBLE
OH NO, THUN-DER!
IT OKAY YUNA!
RUMBLE
HEY, IT STOPPED.
DRIP
THIS IS MISER-ABLE. NOW I'M WET AND HUNGRY.
WHAT ARE YOU GOING TO DO ABOUT THIS? YOU ATE MY LUNCH, SO NOW I HAVE NOTHING TO EAT.
SORRY
SPEAKING OF WHO'S TO BLAME, YOU WERE WRONG PIKO.
IF YOU WANT TO GET INTO THAT, STITCH CAME FROM YOUR HOUSE!
AT THIS RATE, NO ONE WILL FIND US. WHAT'RE YOU GONNA DO ABOUT THIS??

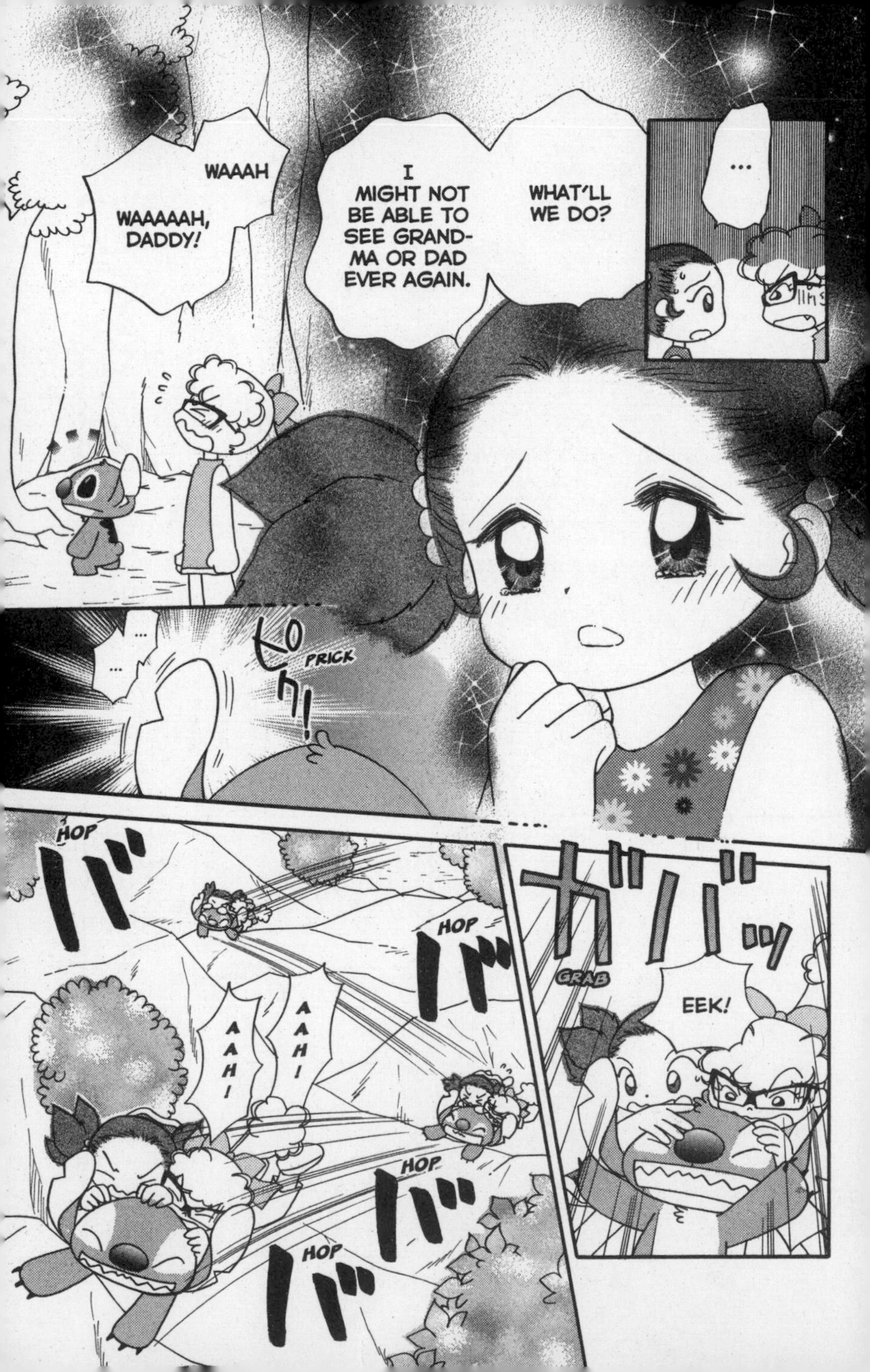
...
WHAT'LL WE DO?
I MIGHT NOT BE ABLE TO SEE GRAND-MA OR DAD EVER AGAIN.
WAAAH
WAAAAAH, DADDY!
...
...
PRICK
GRAB
EEK!
HOP
HOP
AAH!
AAH!
HOP
HOP

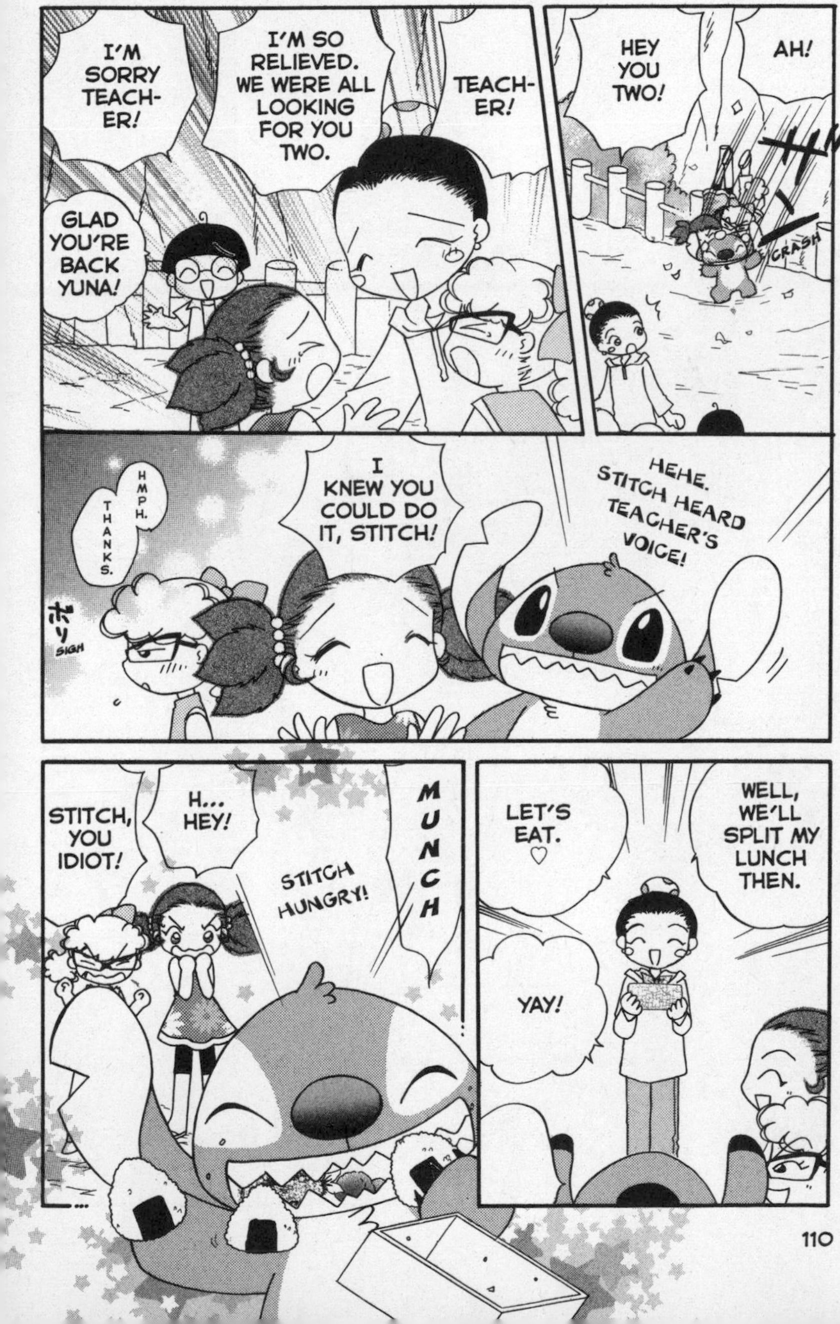
AH!
HEY YOU TWO!
CRASH
TEACHER!
I'M SO RELIEVED. WE WERE ALL LOOKING FOR YOU TWO.
I'M SORRY TEACHER!
GLAD YOU'RE BACK YUNA!
HEHE. STITCH HEARD TEACHER'S VOICE!
I KNEW YOU COULD DO IT, STITCH!
HMPH. THANKS.
ポリ SIGH
WELL, WE'LL SPLIT MY LUNCH THEN.
LET'S EAT. ♡
YAY!
MUNCH
STITCH HUNGRY!
H... HEY!
STITCH, YOU IDIOT!

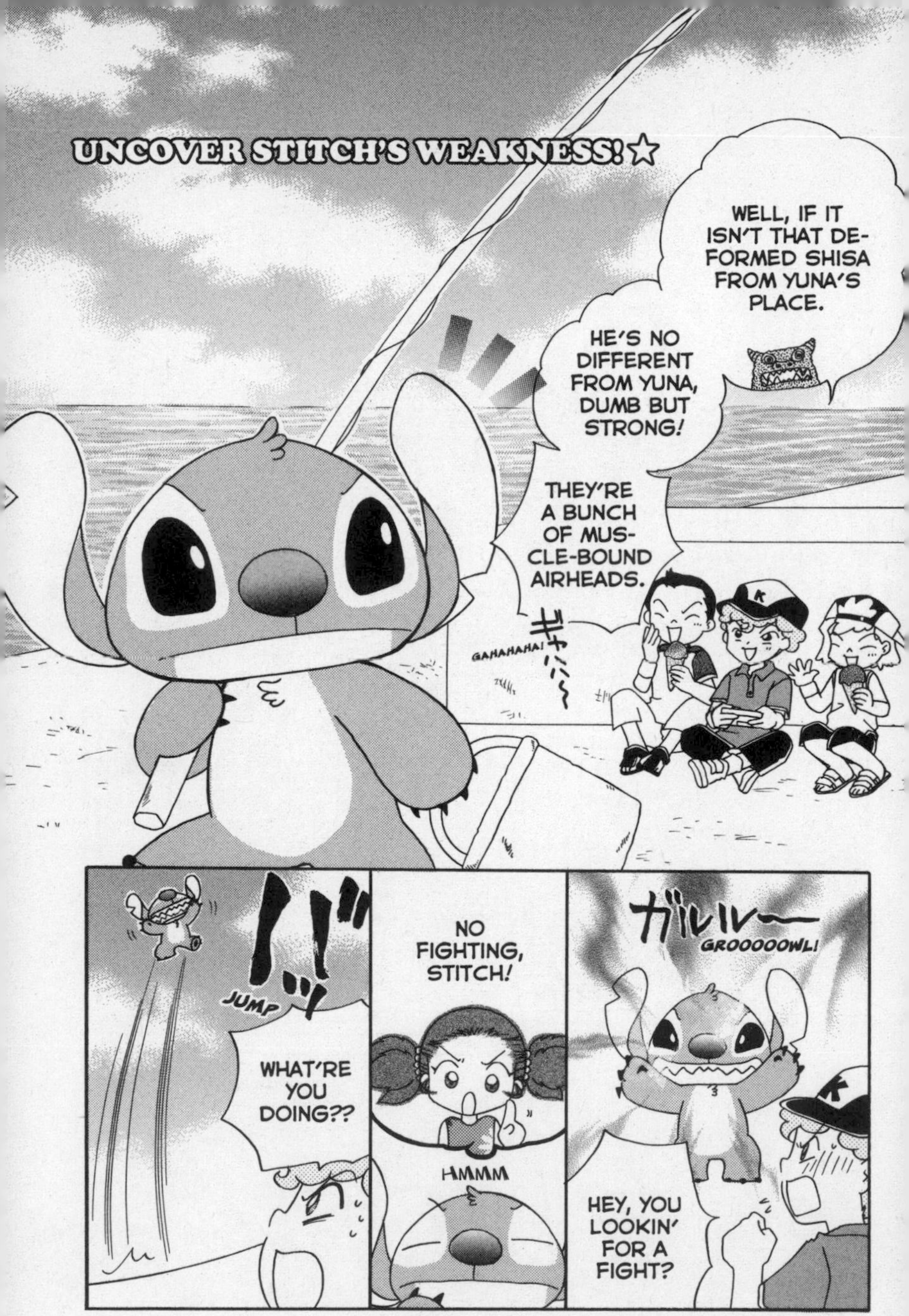
UNCOVER STITCH'S WEAKNESS!☆
WELL, IF IT ISN'T THAT DEFORMED SHISA FROM YUNA'S PLACE.
HE'S NO DIFFERENT FROM YUNA, DUMB BUT STRONG!
THEY'RE A BUNCH OF MUSCLE-BOUND AIRHEADS.
ギャハハ~
GAHAHAHA!
ガルルー
GROOOOOWL!
HEY, YOU LOOKIN' FOR A FIGHT?
NO FIGHTING, STITCH!
HMMM
JUMP
WHAT'RE YOU DOING??

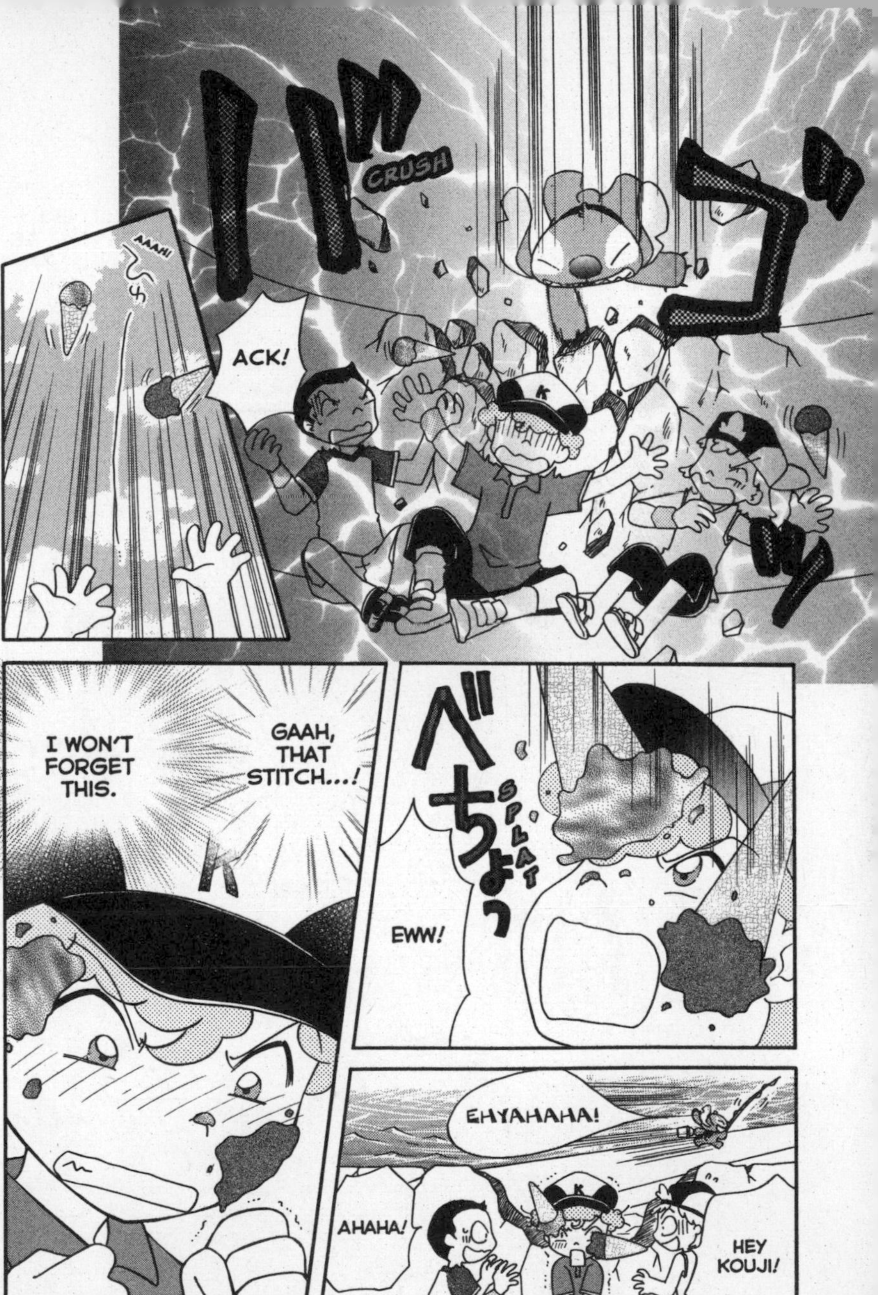
CRUSH
ACK!
AAAH!
べちょっ
SPLAT
EWW!
EHYAHAHA!
HEY KOUJI!
AHAHA!
GAAH, THAT STITCH...!
I WON'T FORGET THIS.

READ THIS WAY

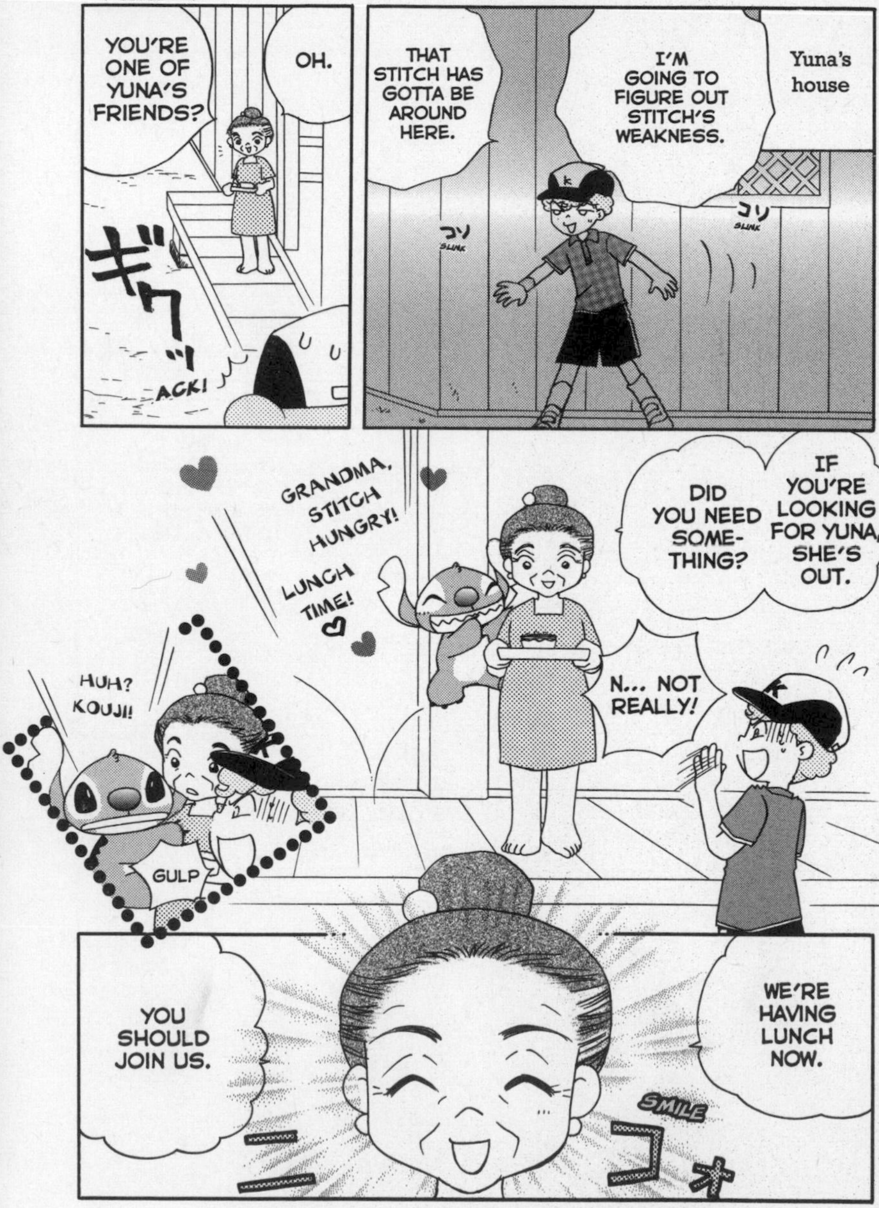

Yuna's house
I'M GOING TO FIGURE OUT STITCH'S WEAKNESS.
THAT STITCH HAS GOTTA BE AROUND HERE.
コソ
SLINK
コソ
SLINK
OH.
YOU'RE ONE OF YUNA'S FRIENDS?
ギクッ
ACK!
IF YOU'RE LOOKING FOR YUNA, SHE'S OUT.
DID YOU NEED SOME-THING?
N... NOT REALLY!
GRANDMA, STITCH HUNGRY!
LUNCH TIME!
HUH? KOUJI!
GULP
WE'RE HAVING LUNCH NOW.
SMILE
YOU SHOULD JOIN US.

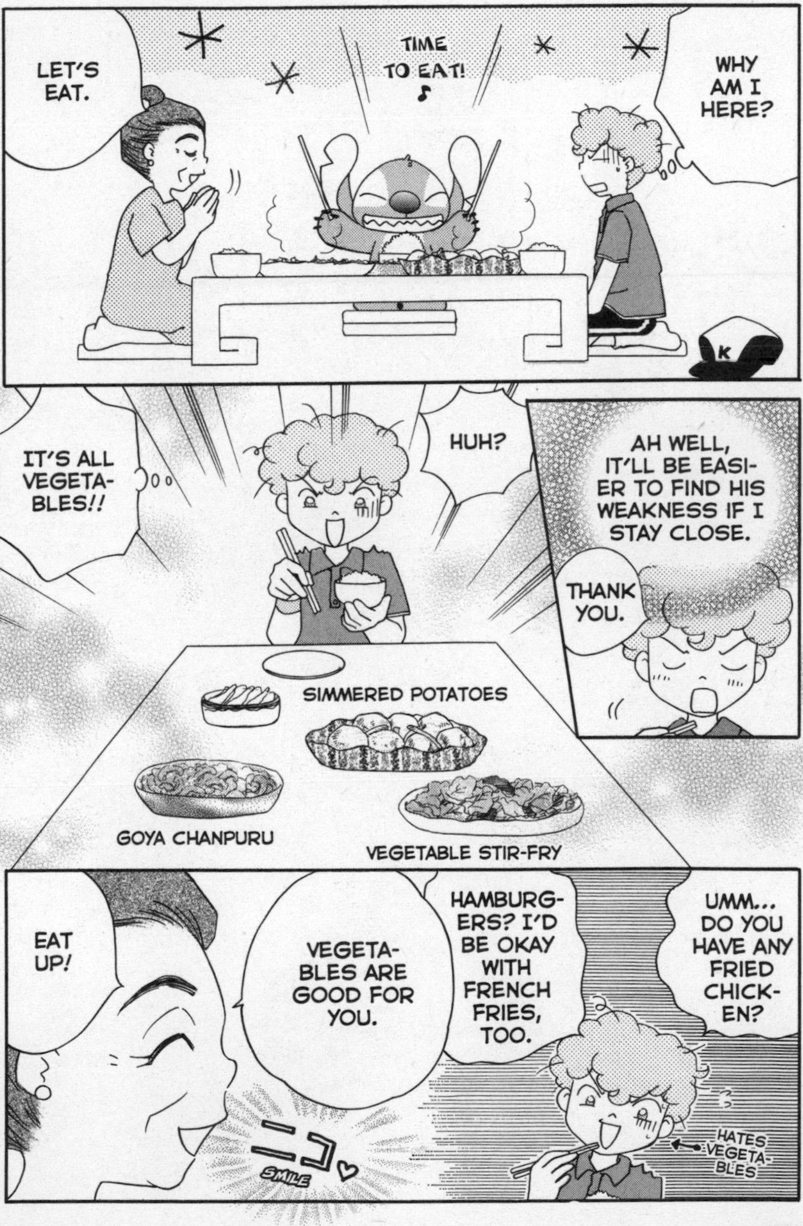
WHY AM I HERE?
TIME TO EAT! ♪
LET'S EAT.
AH WELL, IT'LL BE EASIER TO FIND HIS WEAKNESS IF I STAY CLOSE.
THANK YOU.
HUH?
IT'S ALL VEGETABLES!!
SIMMERED POTATOES
VEGETABLE STIR-FRY
GOYA CHANPURU
UMM... DO YOU HAVE ANY FRIED CHICKEN?
HAMBURGERS? I'D BE OKAY WITH FRENCH FRIES, TOO.
HATES VEGETABLES
VEGETABLES ARE GOOD FOR YOU.
EAT UP!
SMILE

READ THIS WAY

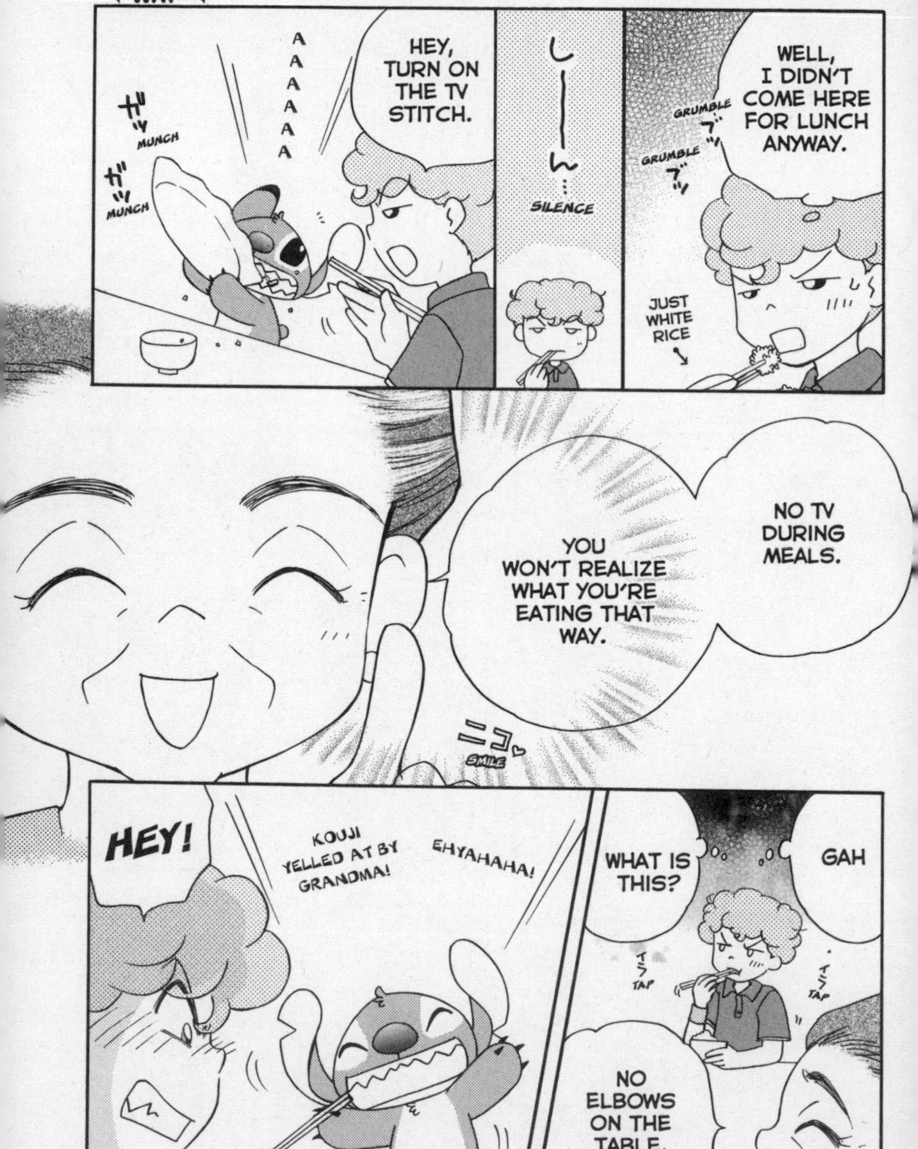
WELL, I DIDN'T COME HERE FOR LUNCH ANYWAY.
ブツ GRUMBLE
ブツ GRUMBLE
JUST WHITE RICE
しーん…
SILENCE
HEY, TURN ON THE TV STITCH.
AAAAAAA
ガツ MUNCH
ガツ MUNCH
NO TV DURING MEALS.
YOU WON'T REALIZE WHAT YOU'RE EATING THAT WAY.
ニコ
SMILE
GAH
WHAT IS THIS?
イラ TAP
イラ TAP
NO ELBOWS ON THE TABLE, KOUJI!
EHYAHAHA!
KOUJI YELLED AT BY GRANDMA!
HEY!

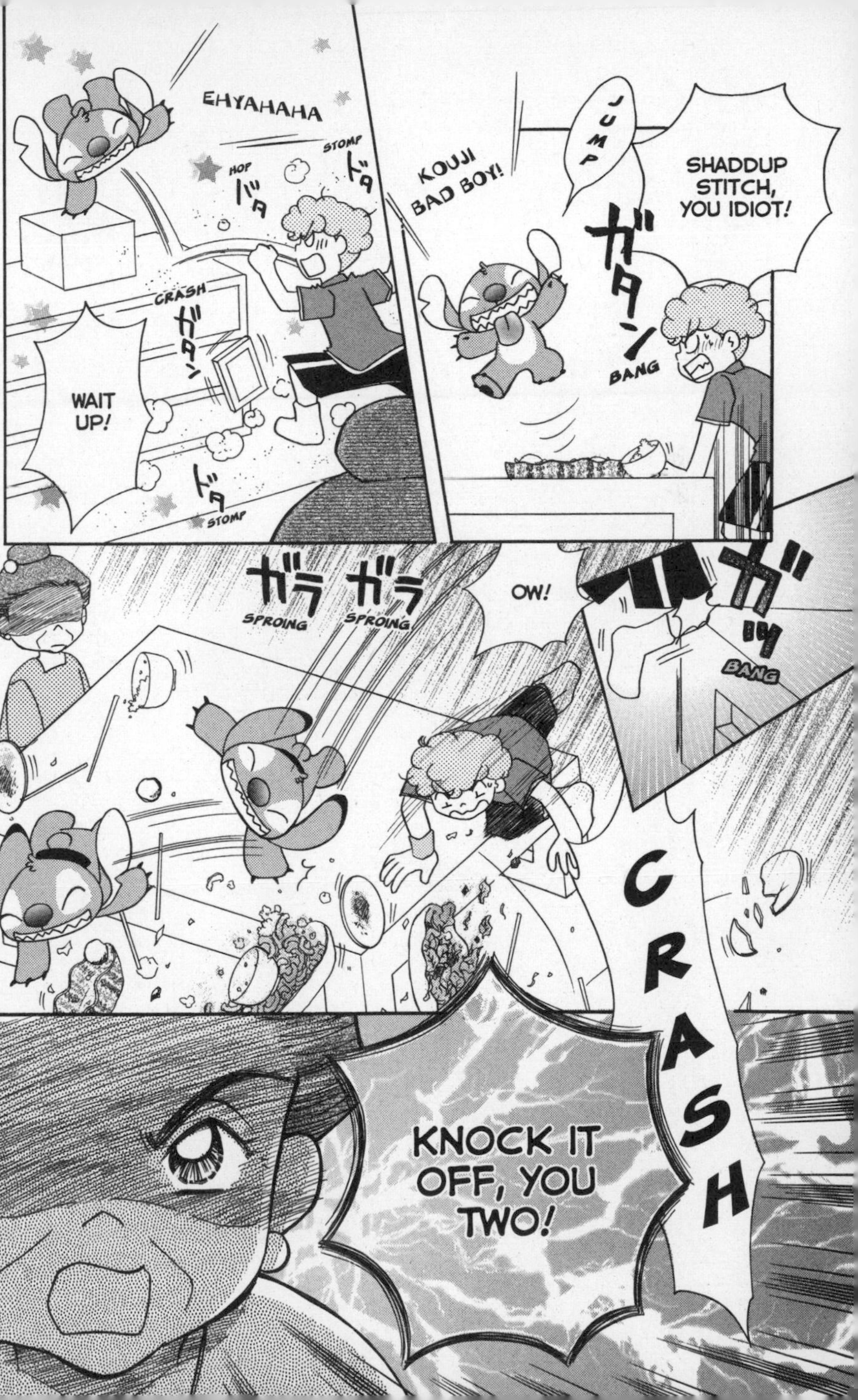
SHADDUP STITCH, YOU IDIOT!
JUMP
KOUJI BAD BOY!
ガタン
BANG
EHYAHAHA
STOMP
ドタ
HOP
ドタ
CRASH
ガタン
WAIT UP!
ドタ
STOMP
ガッ
BANG
OW!
ガラ
SPROING
ガラ
SPROING
CRASH
KNOCK IT OFF, YOU TWO!

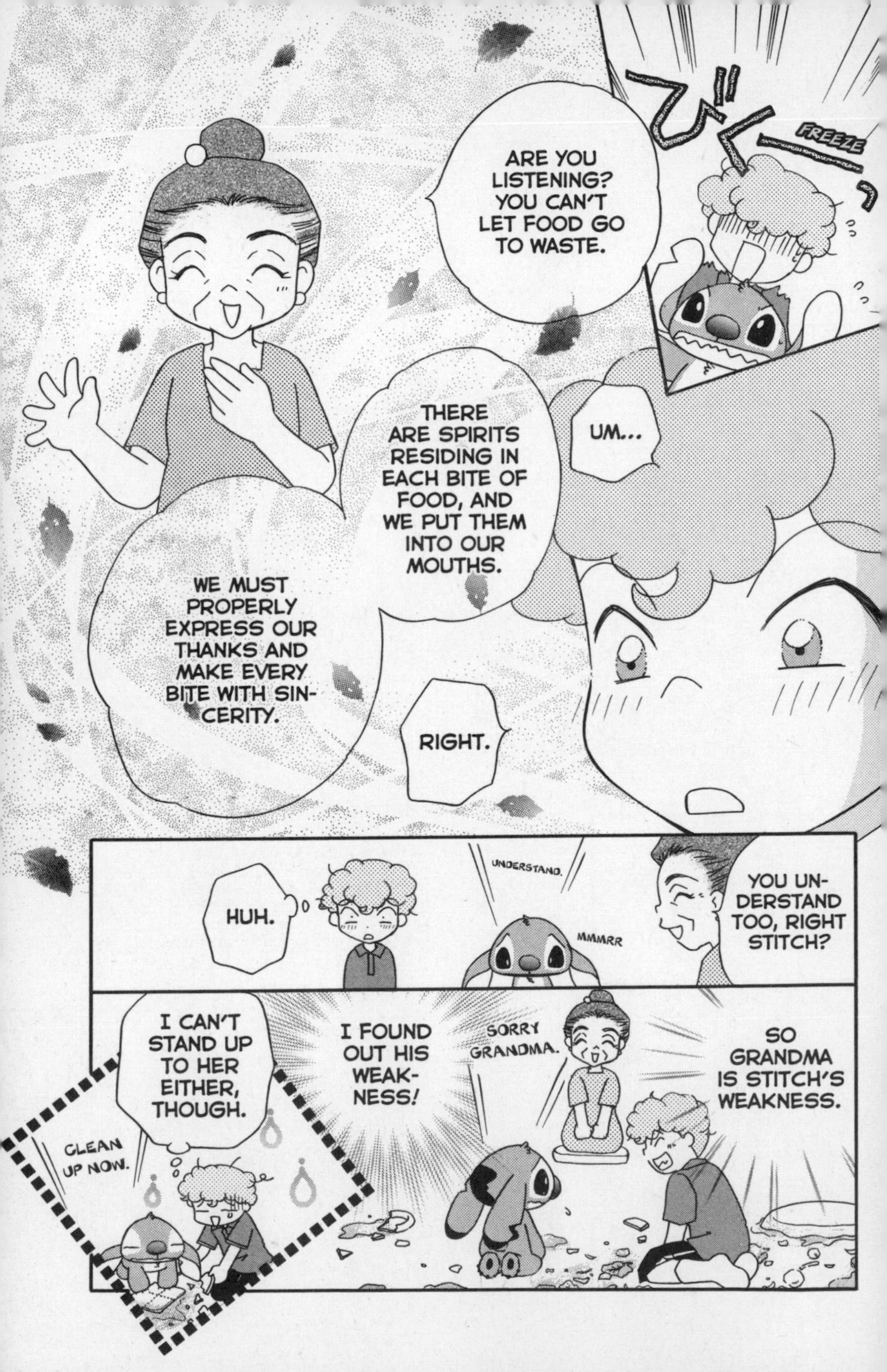

ARE YOU LISTENING? YOU CAN'T LET FOOD GO TO WASTE.
FREEZE
UM...
THERE ARE SPIRITS RESIDING IN EACH BITE OF FOOD, AND WE PUT THEM INTO OUR MOUTHS.
WE MUST PROPERLY EXPRESS OUR THANKS AND MAKE EVERY BITE WITH SIN-CERITY.
RIGHT.
YOU UN-DERSTAND TOO, RIGHT STITCH?
UNDERSTAND.
MMMRR
HUH.
SO GRANDMA IS STITCH'S WEAKNESS.
SORRY GRANDMA.
I FOUND OUT HIS WEAK-NESS!
I CAN'T STAND UP TO HER EITHER, THOUGH.
CLEAN UP NOW.

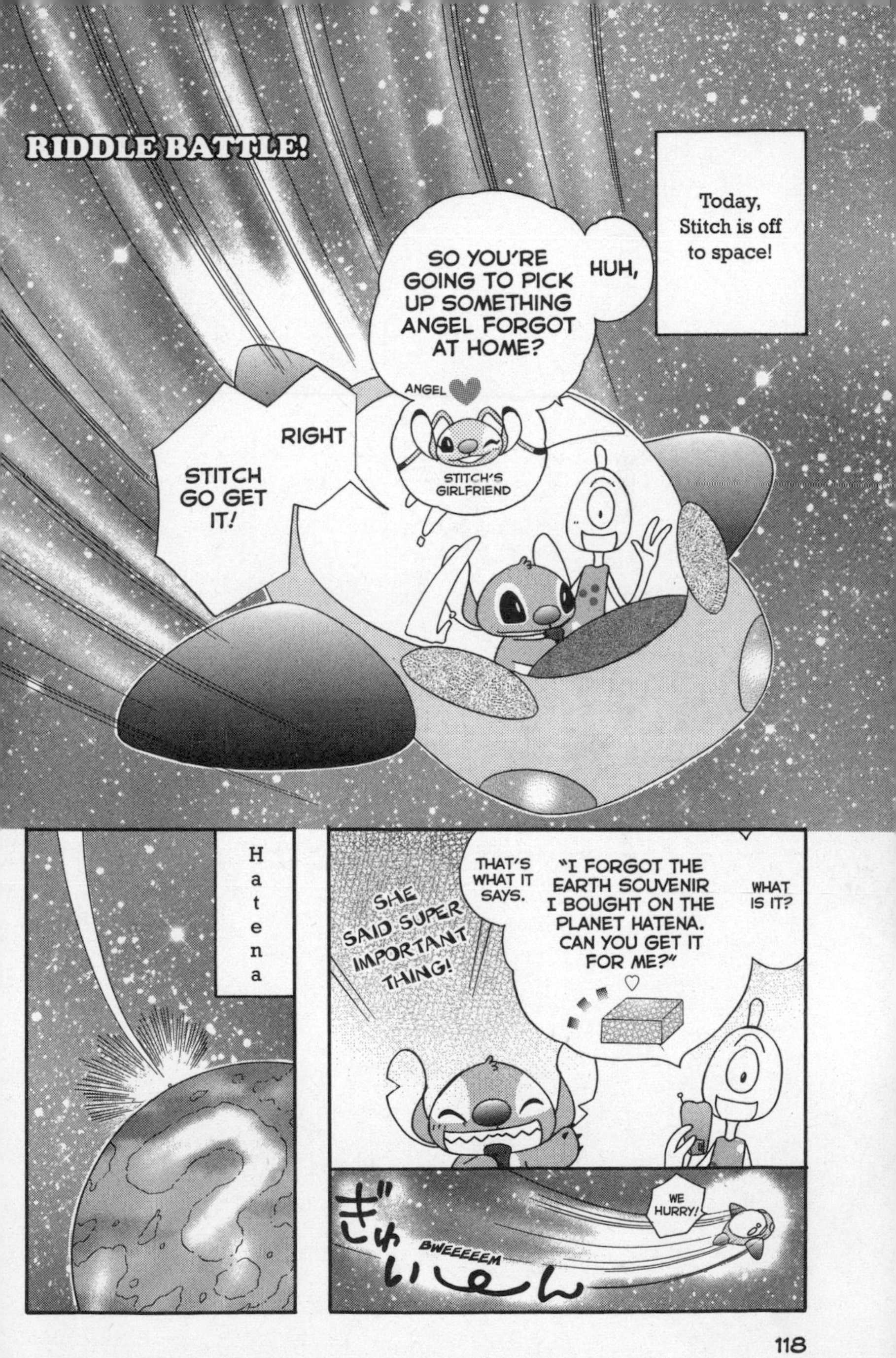
RIDDLE BATTLE!
Today, Stitch is off to space!
HUH,
SO YOU'RE GOING TO PICK UP SOMETHING ANGEL FORGOT AT HOME?
ANGEL
STITCH'S GIRLFRIEND
RIGHT
STITCH GO GET IT!
WHAT IS IT?
"I FORGOT THE EARTH SOUVENIR I BOUGHT ON THE PLANET HATENA. CAN YOU GET IT FOR ME?"
THAT'S WHAT IT SAYS.
SHE SAID SUPER IMPORTANT THING!
WE HURRY!
BWEEEEEM
ぎゅいーん
Hatena

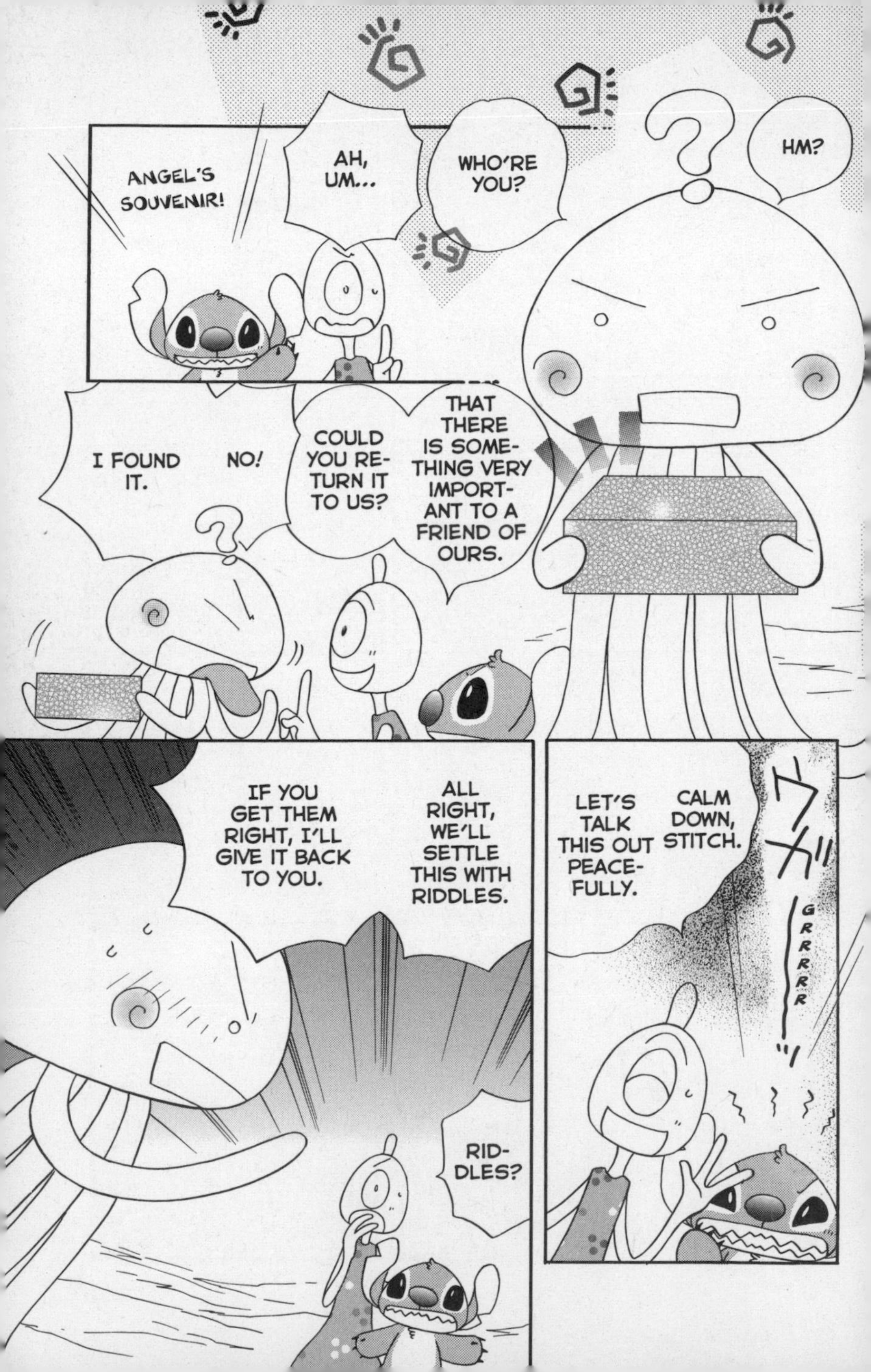
HM?
WHO'RE YOU?
AH, UM...
ANGEL'S SOUVENIR!
THAT THERE IS SOMETHING VERY IMPORTANT TO A FRIEND OF OURS.
COULD YOU RETURN IT TO US?
NO!
I FOUND IT.
CALM DOWN, STITCH.
LET'S TALK THIS OUT PEACEFULLY.
GRRRRR
ALL RIGHT, WE'LL SETTLE THIS WITH RIDDLES.
IF YOU GET THEM RIGHT, I'LL GIVE IT BACK TO YOU.
RIDDLES?

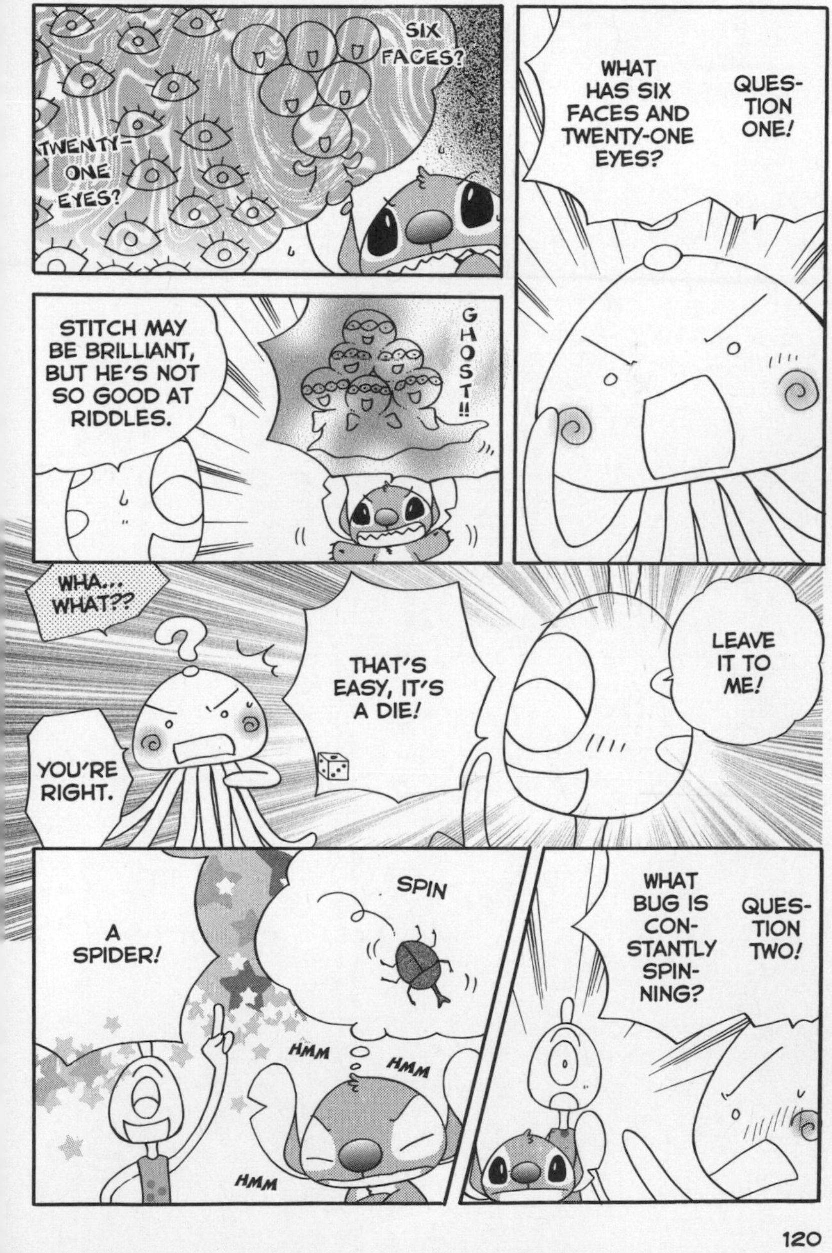
QUES-TION ONE!
WHAT HAS SIX FACES AND TWENTY-ONE EYES?
SIX FACES?
TWENTY-ONE EYES?
GHOST!!
STITCH MAY BE BRILLIANT, BUT HE'S NOT SO GOOD AT RIDDLES.
LEAVE IT TO ME!
THAT'S EASY, IT'S A DIE!
WHA... WHAT??
YOU'RE RIGHT.
QUES-TION TWO!
WHAT BUG IS CON-STANTLY SPIN-NING?
SPIN
HMM
HMM
HMM
A SPIDER!

READ THIS WAY

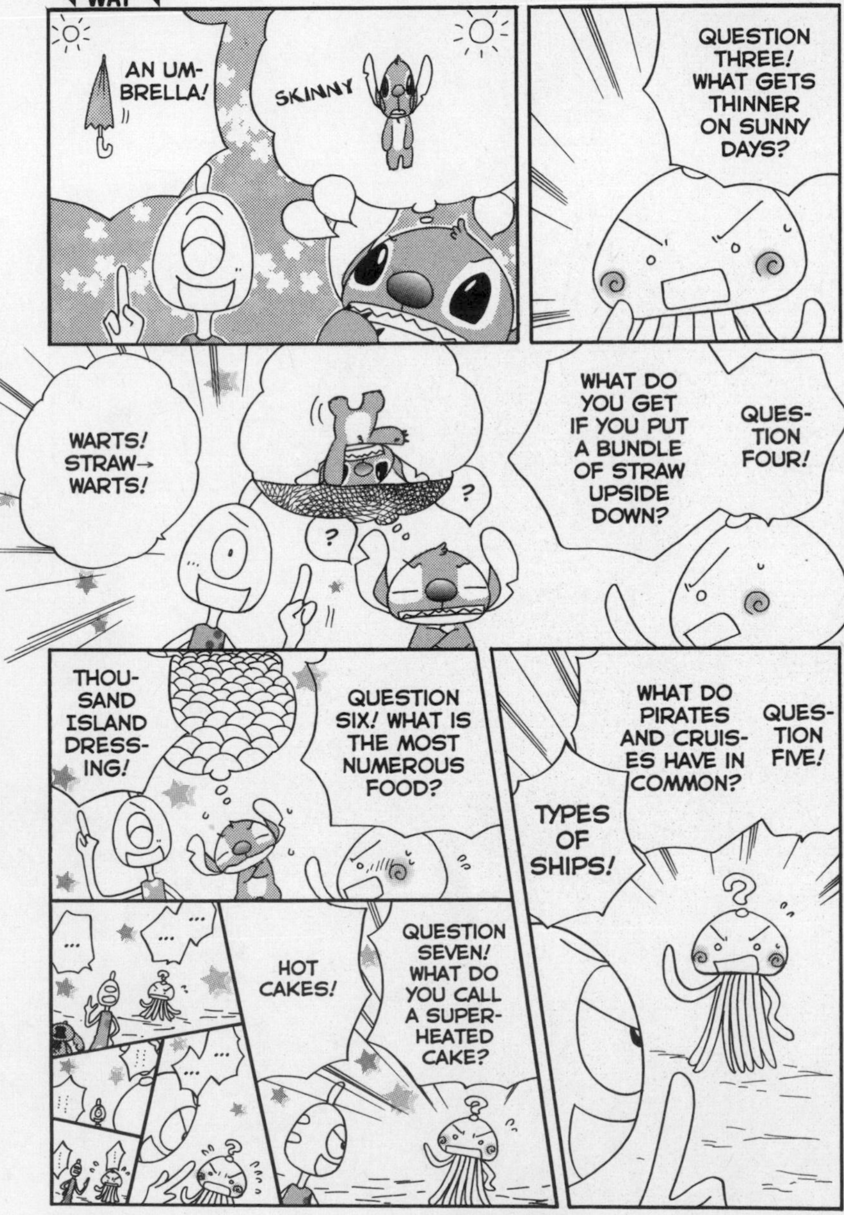
QUESTION THREE! WHAT GETS THINNER ON SUNNY DAYS?
SKINNY
AN UM-BRELLA!
QUES-TION FOUR!
WHAT DO YOU GET IF YOU PUT A BUNDLE OF STRAW UPSIDE DOWN?
WARTS! STRAW→WARTS!
QUES-TION FIVE!
WHAT DO PIRATES AND CRUIS-ES HAVE IN COMMON?
TYPES OF SHIPS!
QUESTION SIX! WHAT IS THE MOST NUMEROUS FOOD?
THOU-SAND ISLAND DRESS-ING!
QUESTION SEVEN! WHAT DO YOU CALL A SUPER-HEATED CAKE?
HOT CAKES!

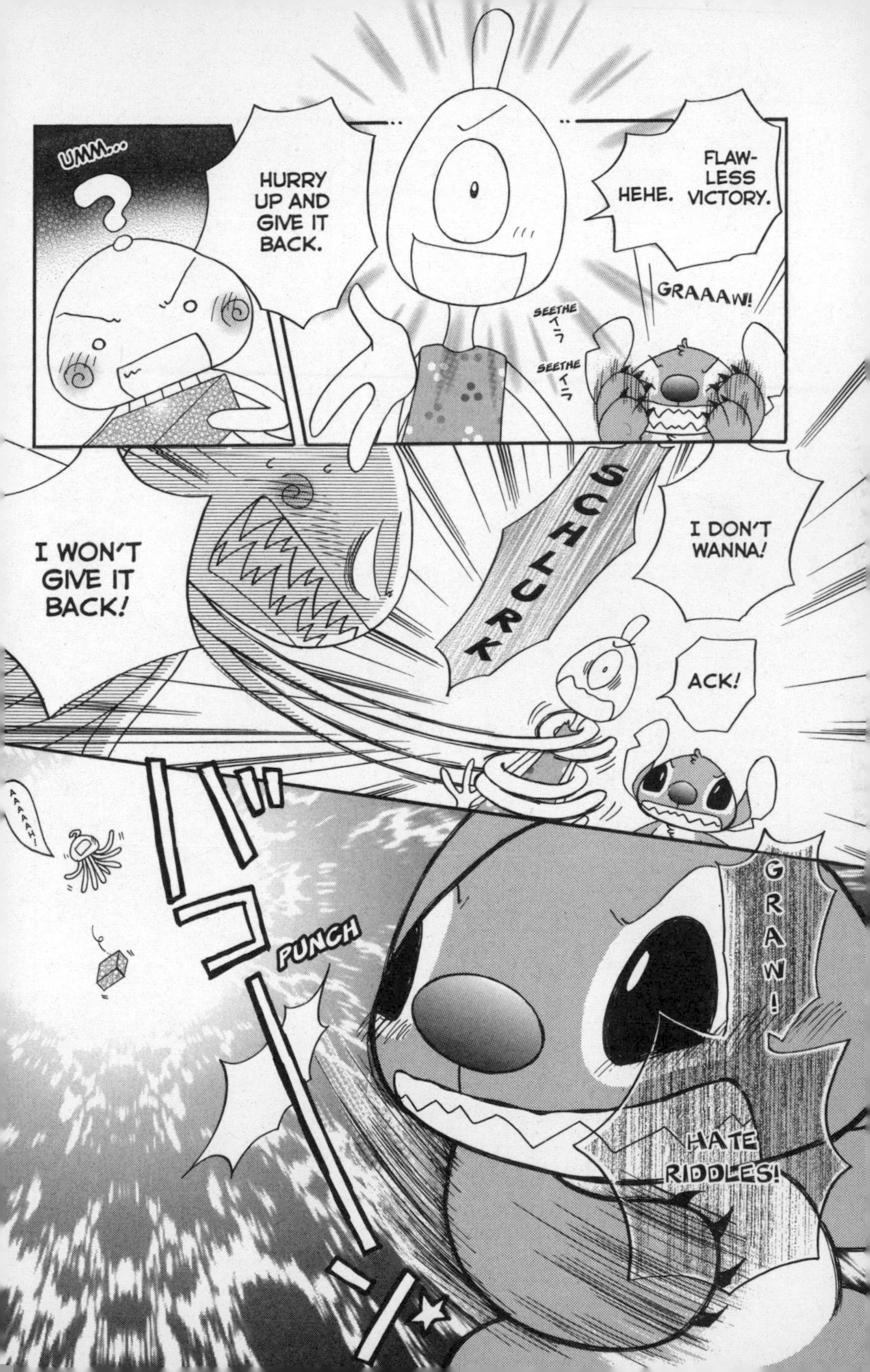
HEHE. FLAW-LESS VICTORY.
GRAAAW!
SEETHE イラ
SEETHE イラ
HURRY UP AND GIVE IT BACK.
UMM...
I DON'T WANNA!
SCHLURK
I WON'T GIVE IT BACK!
ACK!
GRAW!
HATE RIDDLES!
PUNCH
AAAAH!

READ THIS WAY

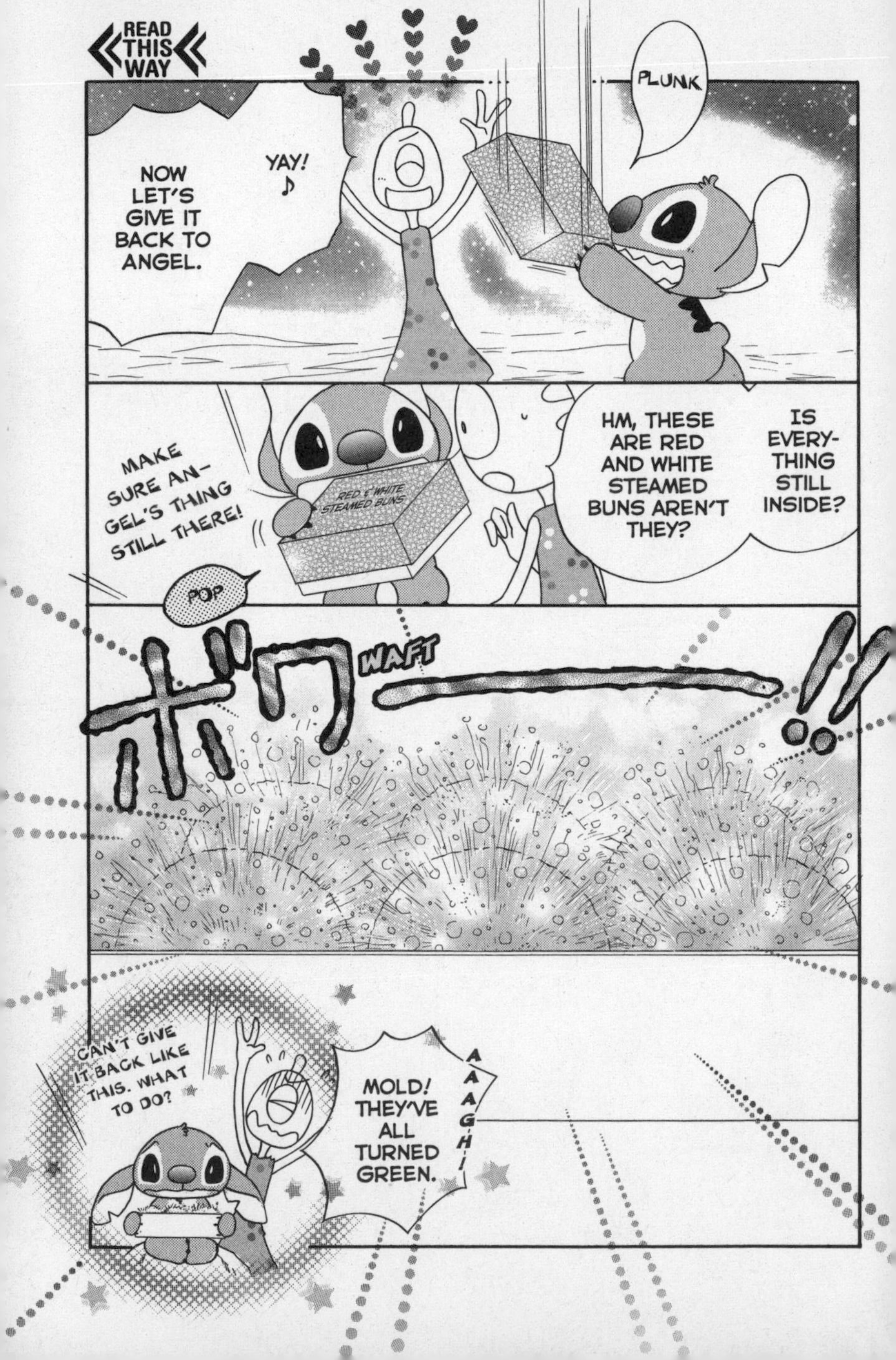
PLUNK
YAY! ♪
NOW LET'S GIVE IT BACK TO ANGEL.
IS EVERY-THING STILL INSIDE?
HM, THESE ARE RED AND WHITE STEAMED BUNS AREN'T THEY?
MAKE SURE AN-GEL'S THING STILL THERE!
RED & WHITE STEAMED BUNS
POP
ボワーー!!
WAFT
AAAGH!
MOLD! THEY'VE ALL TURNED GREEN.
CAN'T GIVE IT BACK LIKE THIS. WHAT TO DO?

EMERGENCY DOG HUNT!

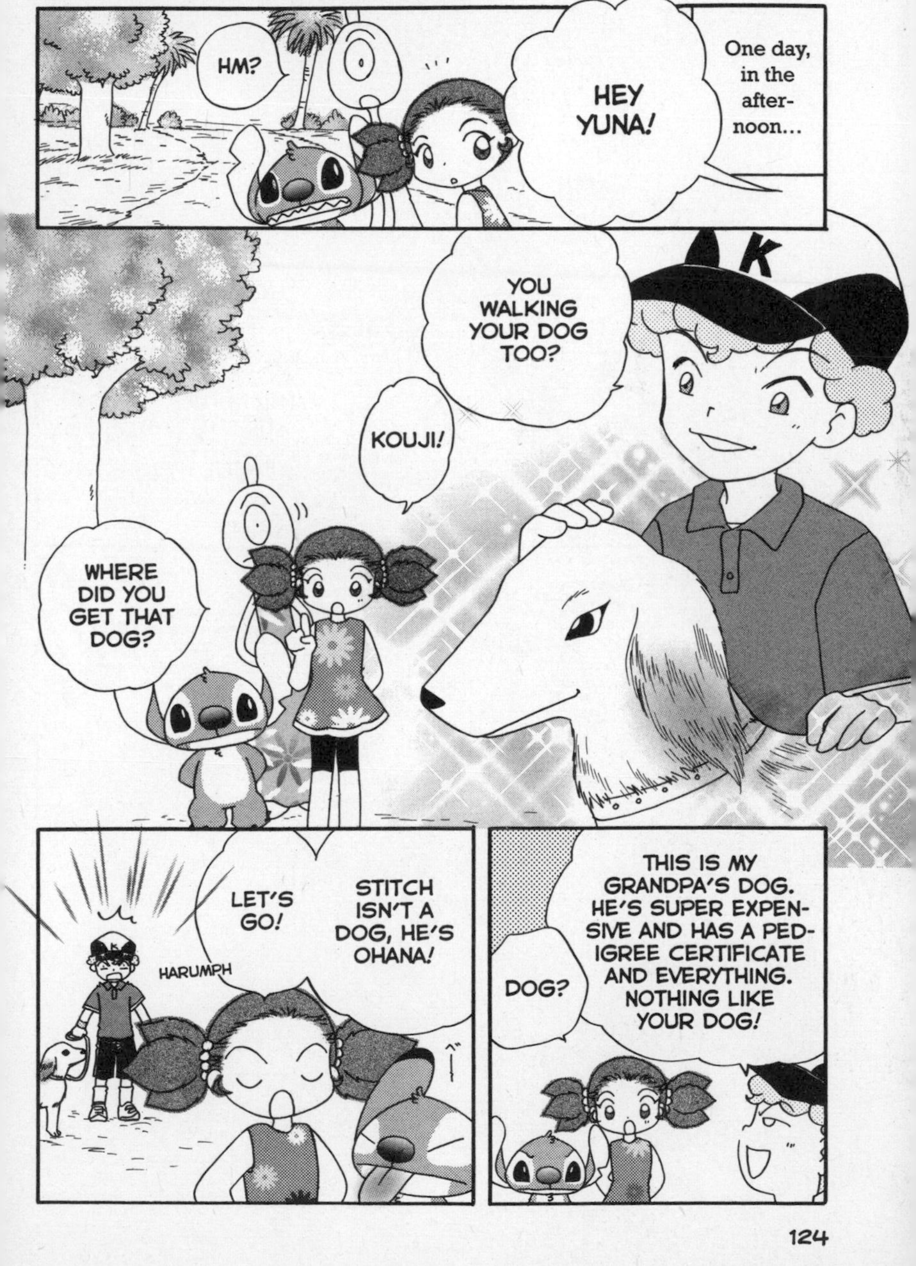
One day, in the after-noon...
HEY YUNA!
HM?
YOU WALKING YOUR DOG TOO?
KOUJI!
WHERE DID YOU GET THAT DOG?
THIS IS MY GRANDPA'S DOG. HE'S SUPER EXPEN-SIVE AND HAS A PED-IGREE CERTIFICATE AND EVERYTHING. NOTHING LIKE YOUR DOG!
DOG?
STITCH ISN'T A DOG, HE'S OHANA!
LET'S GO!
HARUMPH

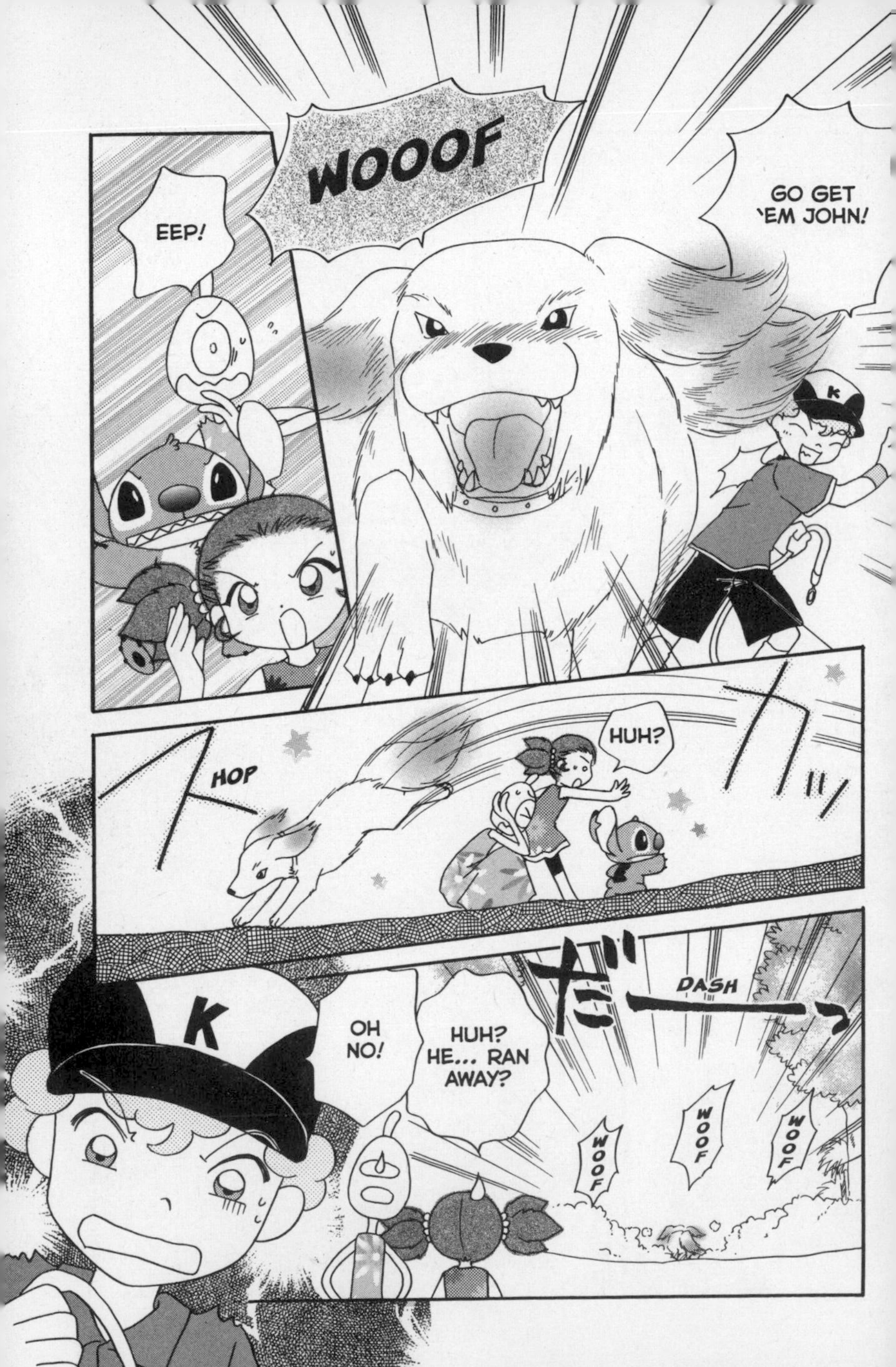
GO GET 'EM JOHN!
WOOOF
EEP!
HUH?
HOP
DASH
WOOF
WOOF
WOOF
HUH? HE... RAN AWAY?
OH NO!

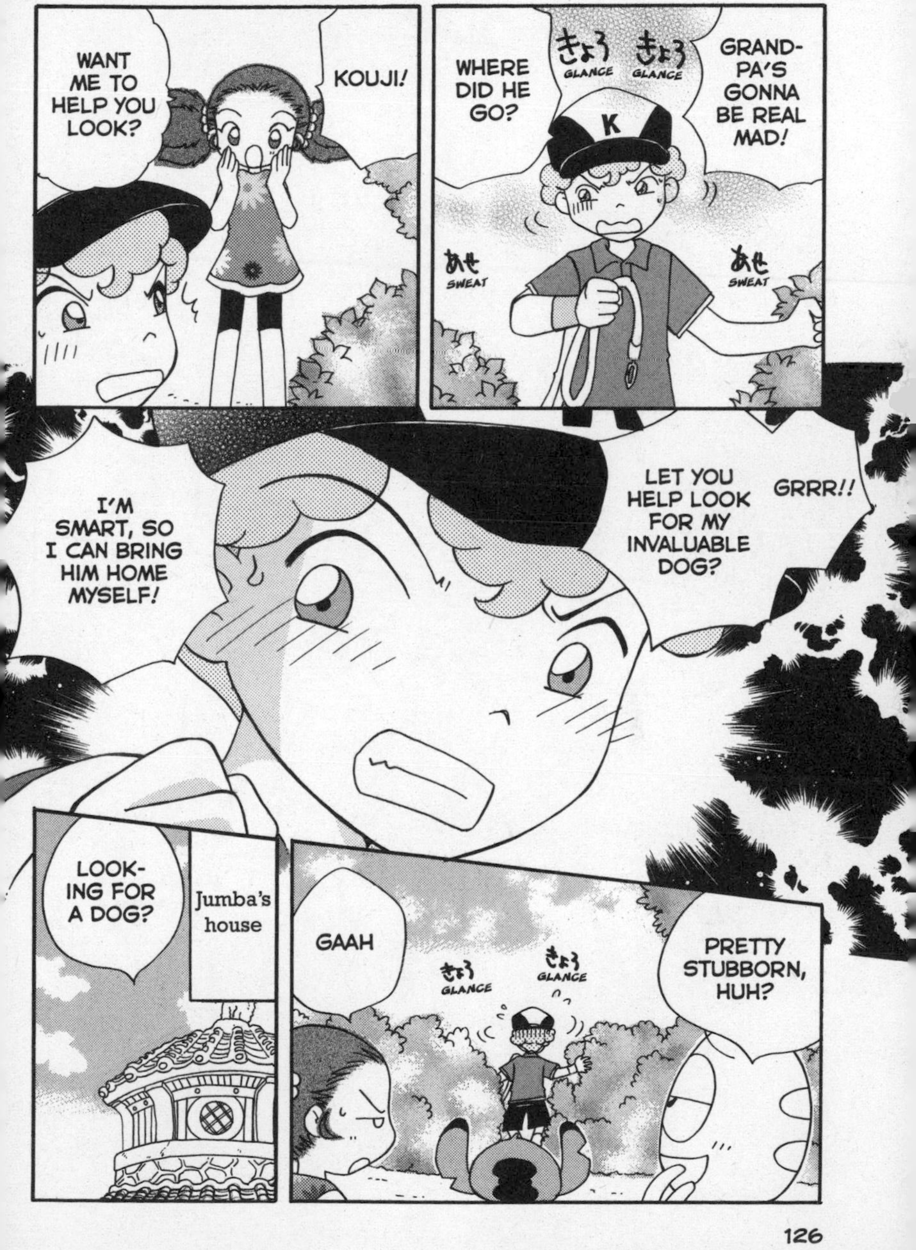
GRAND-PA'S GONNA BE REAL MAD!
きょろ GLANCE
きょろ GLANCE
WHERE DID HE GO?
あせ SWEAT
あせ SWEAT
KOUJI!
WANT ME TO HELP YOU LOOK?
GRRR!!
LET YOU HELP LOOK FOR MY INVALUABLE DOG?
I'M SMART, SO I CAN BRING HIM HOME MYSELF!
PRETTY STUBBORN, HUH?
きょろ GLANCE
きょろ GLANCE
GAAH
Jumba's house
LOOKING FOR A DOG?

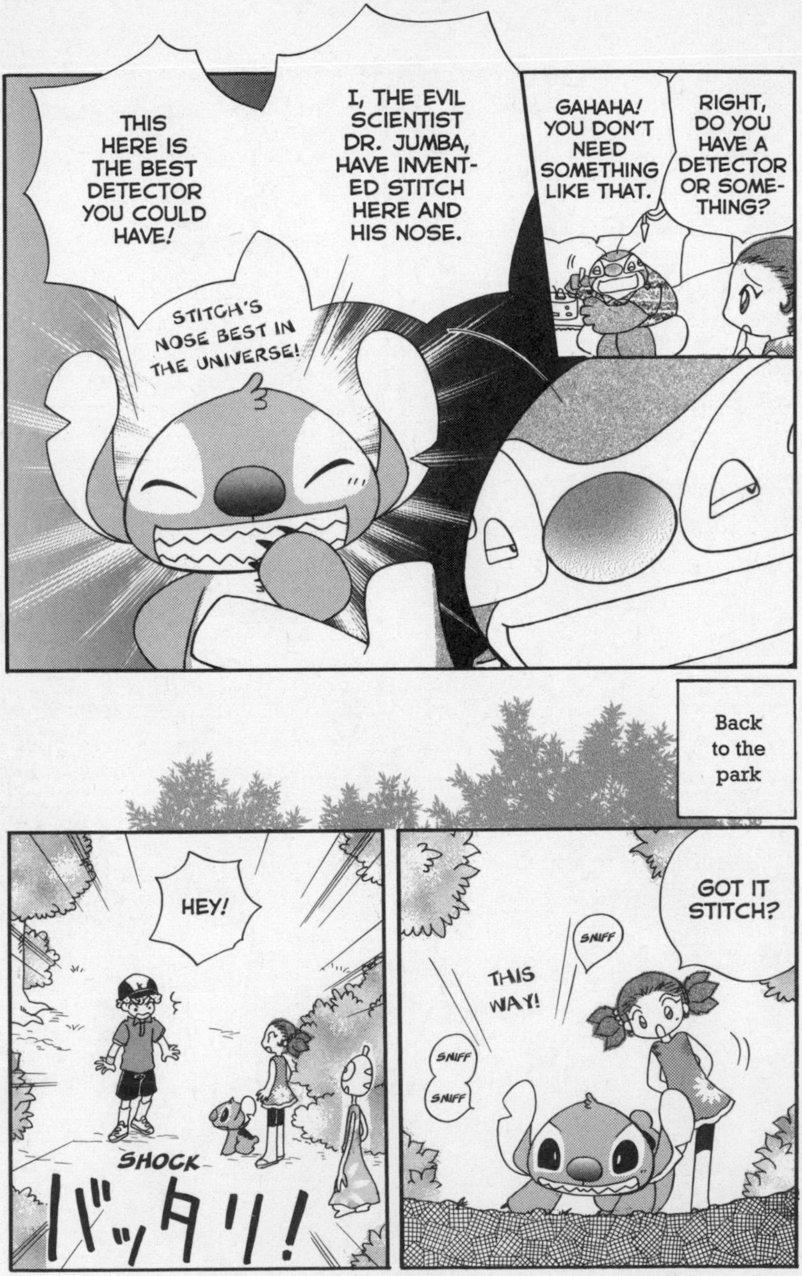
RIGHT, DO YOU HAVE A DETECTOR OR SOMETHING?
GAHAHA! YOU DON'T NEED SOMETHING LIKE THAT.
I, THE EVIL SCIENTIST DR. JUMBA, HAVE INVENTED STITCH HERE AND HIS NOSE.
THIS HERE IS THE BEST DETECTOR YOU COULD HAVE!
STITCH'S NOSE BEST IN THE UNIVERSE!
Back to the park
GOT IT STITCH?
SNIFF
THIS WAY!
SNIFF
SNIFF
HEY!
SHOCK
バッタリ!

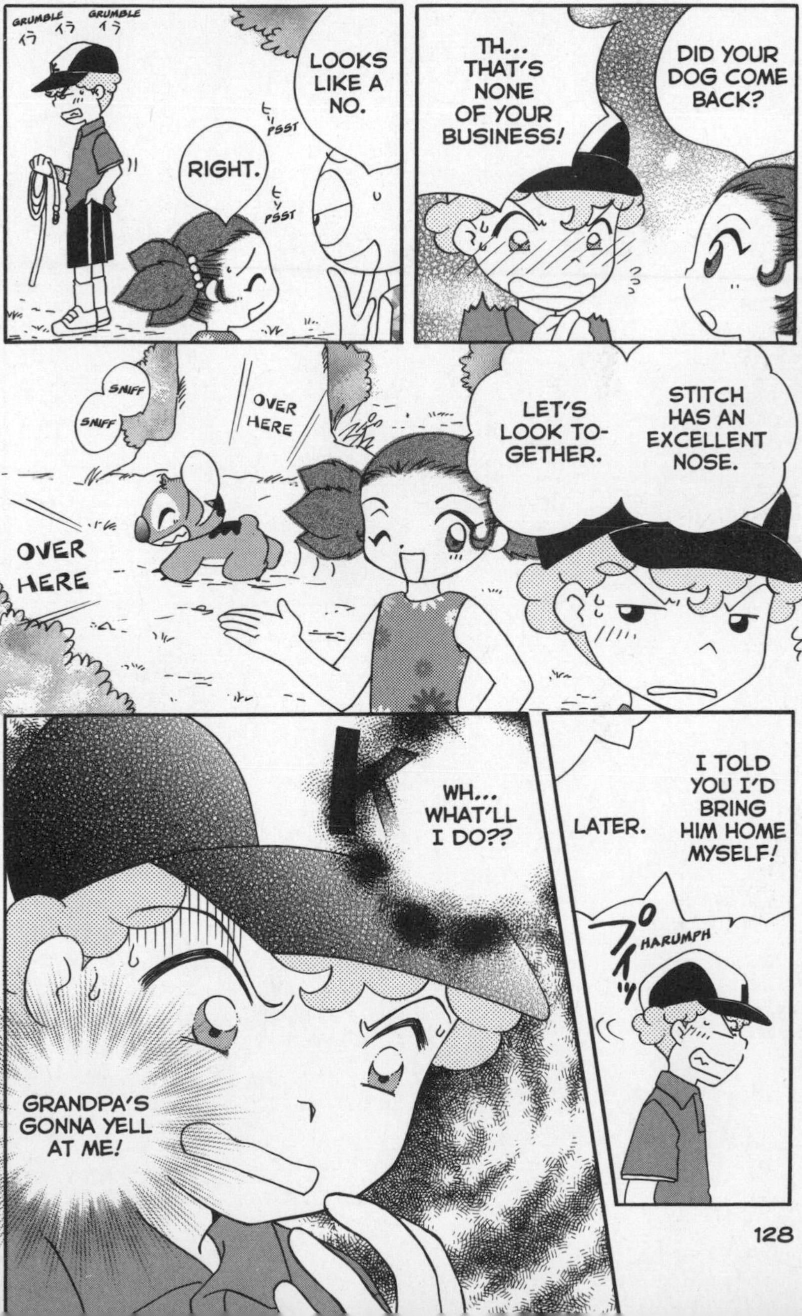
DID YOUR DOG COME BACK?
TH... THAT'S NONE OF YOUR BUSINESS!
LOOKS LIKE A NO.
ヒソ
PSST
RIGHT.
ヒソ
PSST
GRUMBLE
GRUMBLE
イラ イラ イラ
STITCH HAS AN EXCELLENT NOSE.
LET'S LOOK TO-GETHER.
OVER HERE
SNIFF
SNIFF
OVER HERE
I TOLD YOU I'D BRING HIM HOME MYSELF!
LATER.
プイッ
HARUMPH
WH... WHAT'LL I DO??
GRANDPA'S GONNA YELL AT ME!

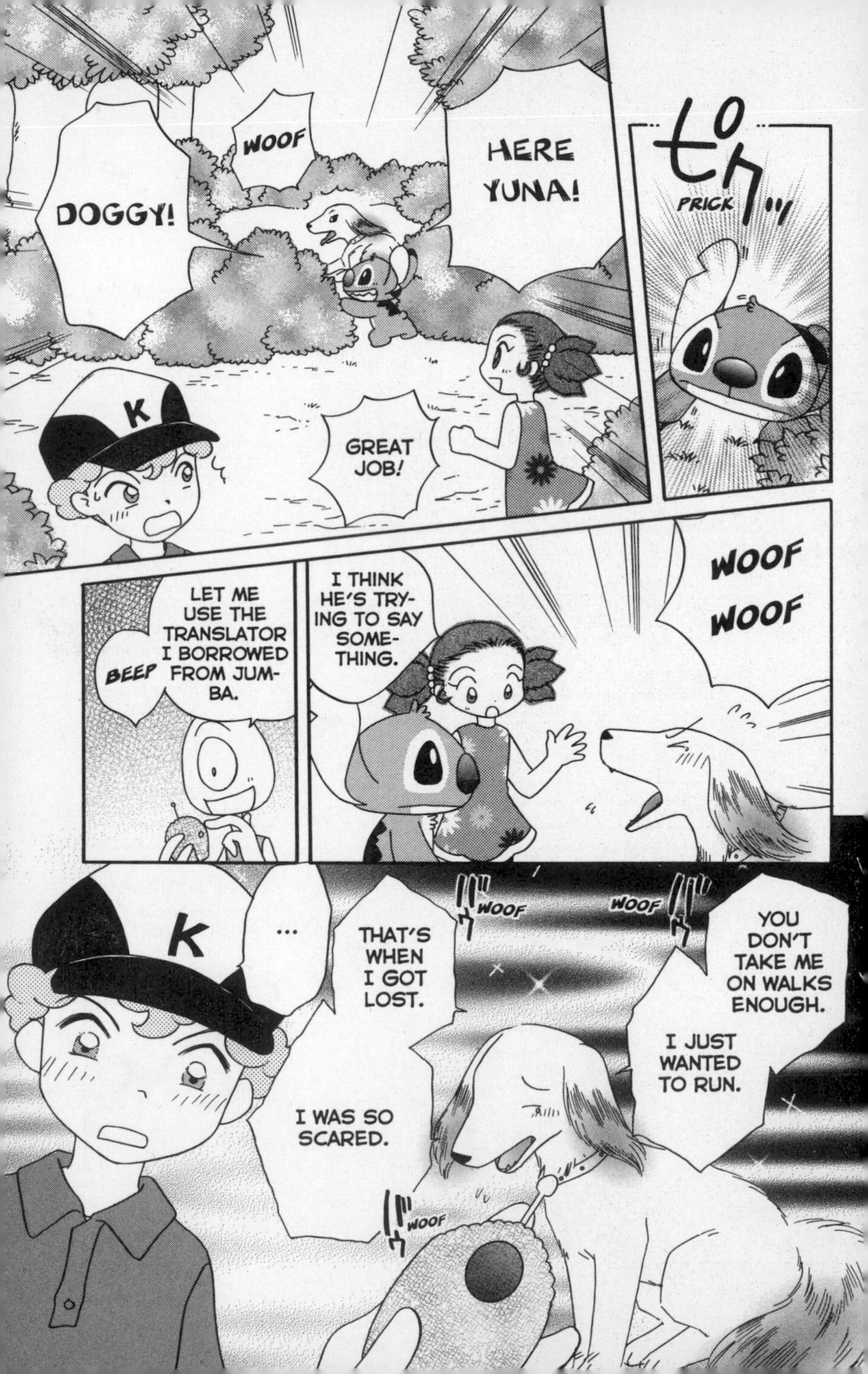

ピクッ
PRICK
HERE YUNA!
WOOF
DOGGY!
GREAT JOB!
WOOF WOOF
I THINK HE'S TRY-ING TO SAY SOME-THING.
LET ME USE THE TRANSLATOR I BORROWED FROM JUM-BA.
BEEP
WOOF
YOU DON'T TAKE ME ON WALKS ENOUGH.
I JUST WANTED TO RUN.
WOOF
THAT'S WHEN I GOT LOST.
...
I WAS SO SCARED.
WOOF

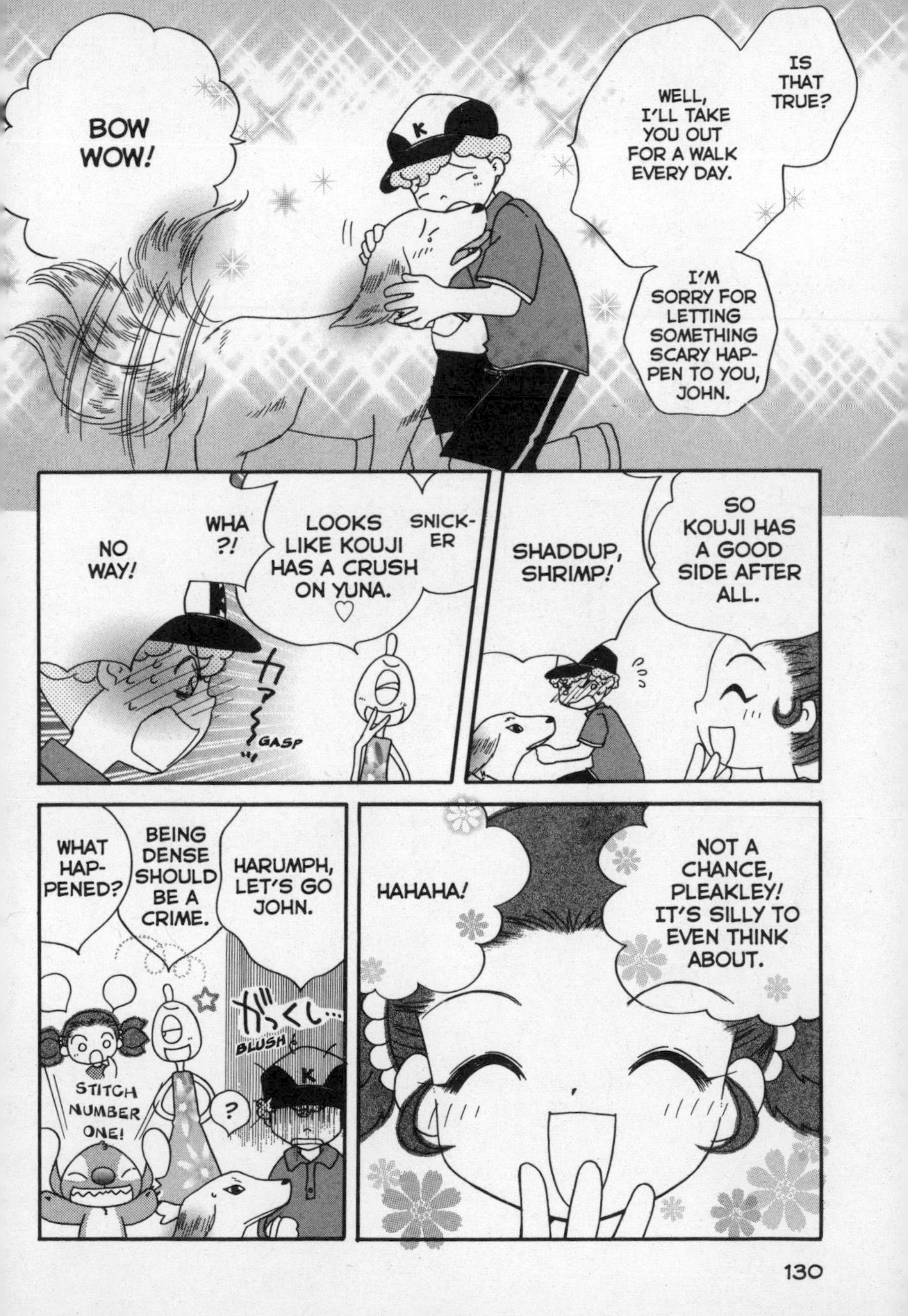
IS THAT TRUE?
WELL, I'LL TAKE YOU OUT FOR A WALK EVERY DAY.
I'M SORRY FOR LETTING SOMETHING SCARY HAP-PEN TO YOU, JOHN.
BOW WOW!
SO KOUJI HAS A GOOD SIDE AFTER ALL.
SHADDUP, SHRIMP!
SNICK-ER
LOOKS LIKE KOUJI HAS A CRUSH ON YUNA. ♡
WHA ?!
NO WAY!
カァ～
GASP
NOT A CHANCE, PLEAKLEY! IT'S SILLY TO EVEN THINK ABOUT.
HAHAHA!
HARUMPH, LET'S GO JOHN.
BEING DENSE SHOULD BE A CRIME.
WHAT HAP-PENED?
がっくし…
BLUSH
?
STITCH NUMBER ONE!

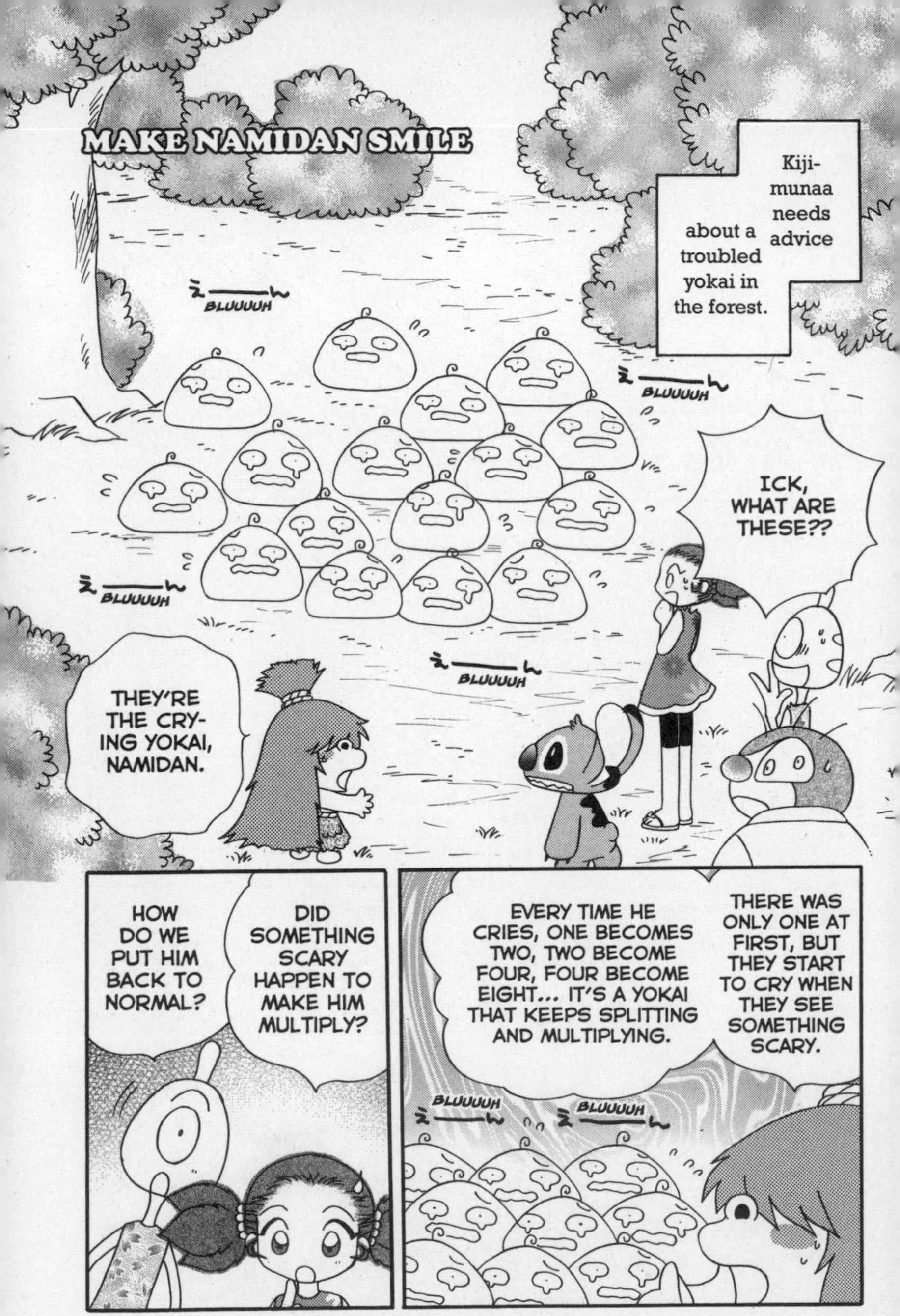
MAKE NAMIDAN SMILE
Kiji-munaa needs advice about a troubled yokai in the forest.
え——ん BLUUUUH
え——ん BLUUUUH
ICK, WHAT ARE THESE??
え——ん BLUUUUH
え——ん BLUUUUH
THEY'RE THE CRY-ING YOKAI, NAMIDAN.
THERE WAS ONLY ONE AT FIRST, BUT THEY START TO CRY WHEN THEY SEE SOMETHING SCARY.
EVERY TIME HE CRIES, ONE BECOMES TWO, TWO BECOME FOUR, FOUR BECOME EIGHT... IT'S A YOKAI THAT KEEPS SPLITTING AND MULTIPLYING.
え——ん BLUUUUH
え——ん BLUUUUH
DID SOMETHING SCARY HAPPEN TO MAKE HIM MULTIPLY?
HOW DO WE PUT HIM BACK TO NORMAL?

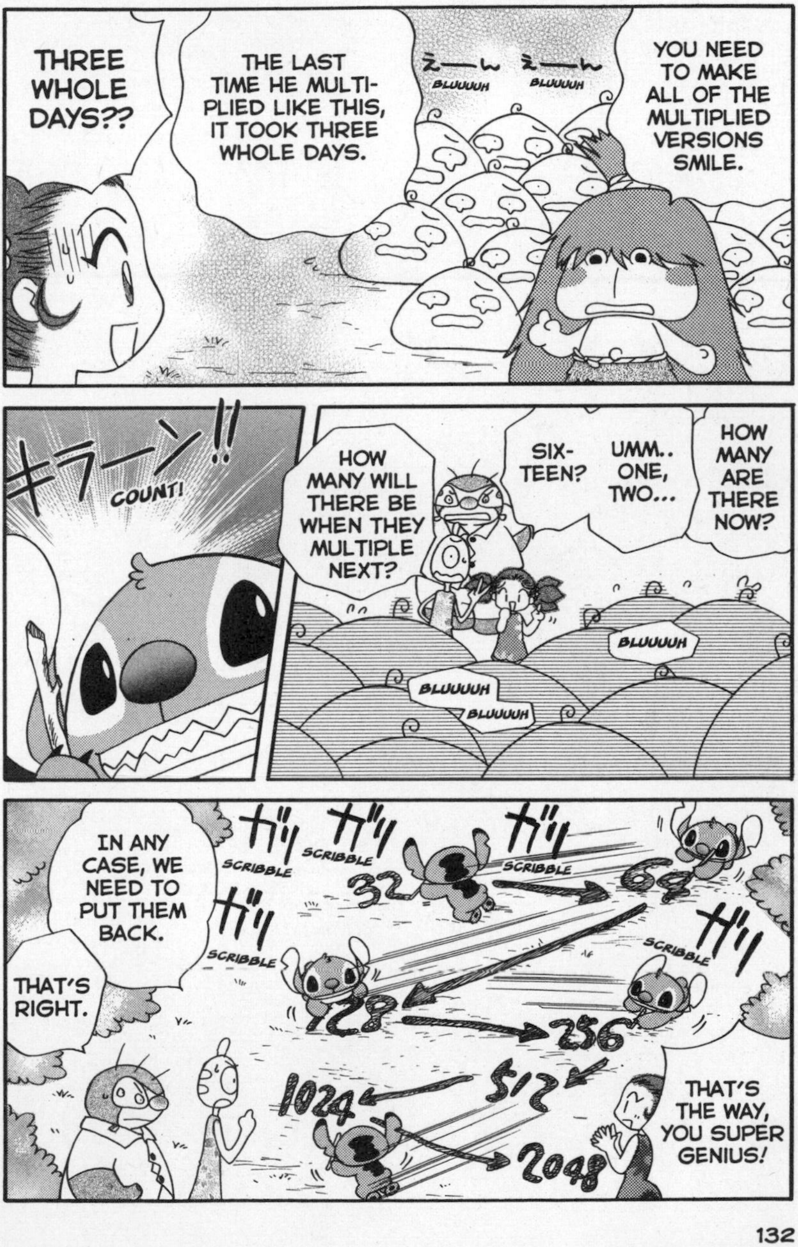
YOU NEED TO MAKE ALL OF THE MULTIPLIED VERSIONS SMILE.
えーん えーん
BLUUUUH BLUUUUH
THE LAST TIME HE MULTI-PLIED LIKE THIS, IT TOOK THREE WHOLE DAYS.
THREE WHOLE DAYS??
HOW MANY ARE THERE NOW?
UMM.. ONE, TWO...
SIX-TEEN?
HOW MANY WILL THERE BE WHEN THEY MULTIPLE NEXT?
BLUUUUH
BLUUUUH
BLUUUUH
キラーン!!
COUNT!
ガリ
SCRIBBLE
ガリ
SCRIBBLE
ガリ
SCRIBBLE
ガリ
SCRIBBLE
ガリ
SCRIBBLE
32
64
128
256
512
1024
2048
THAT'S THE WAY, YOU SUPER GENIUS!
IN ANY CASE, WE NEED TO PUT THEM BACK.
THAT'S RIGHT.

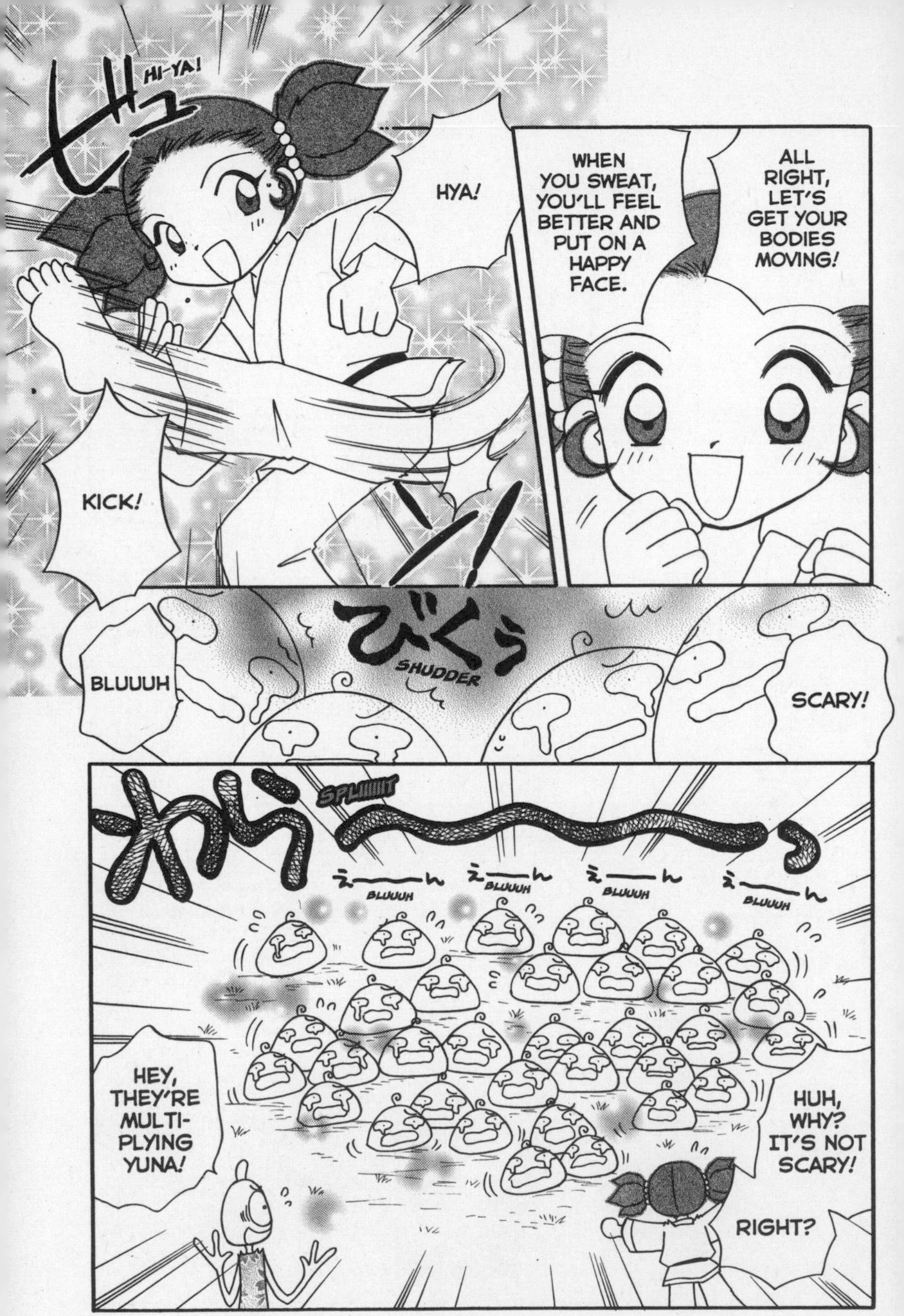

ALL RIGHT, LET'S GET YOUR BODIES MOVING!
WHEN YOU SWEAT, YOU'LL FEEL BETTER AND PUT ON A HAPPY FACE.
HI-YA!
HYA!
KICK!
SCARY!
SHUDDER
BLUUUH
SPLIIIIT
BLUUUH
BLUUUH
BLUUUH
BLUUUH
HUH, WHY? IT'S NOT SCARY!
RIGHT?
HEY, THEY'RE MULTI-PLYING YUNA!

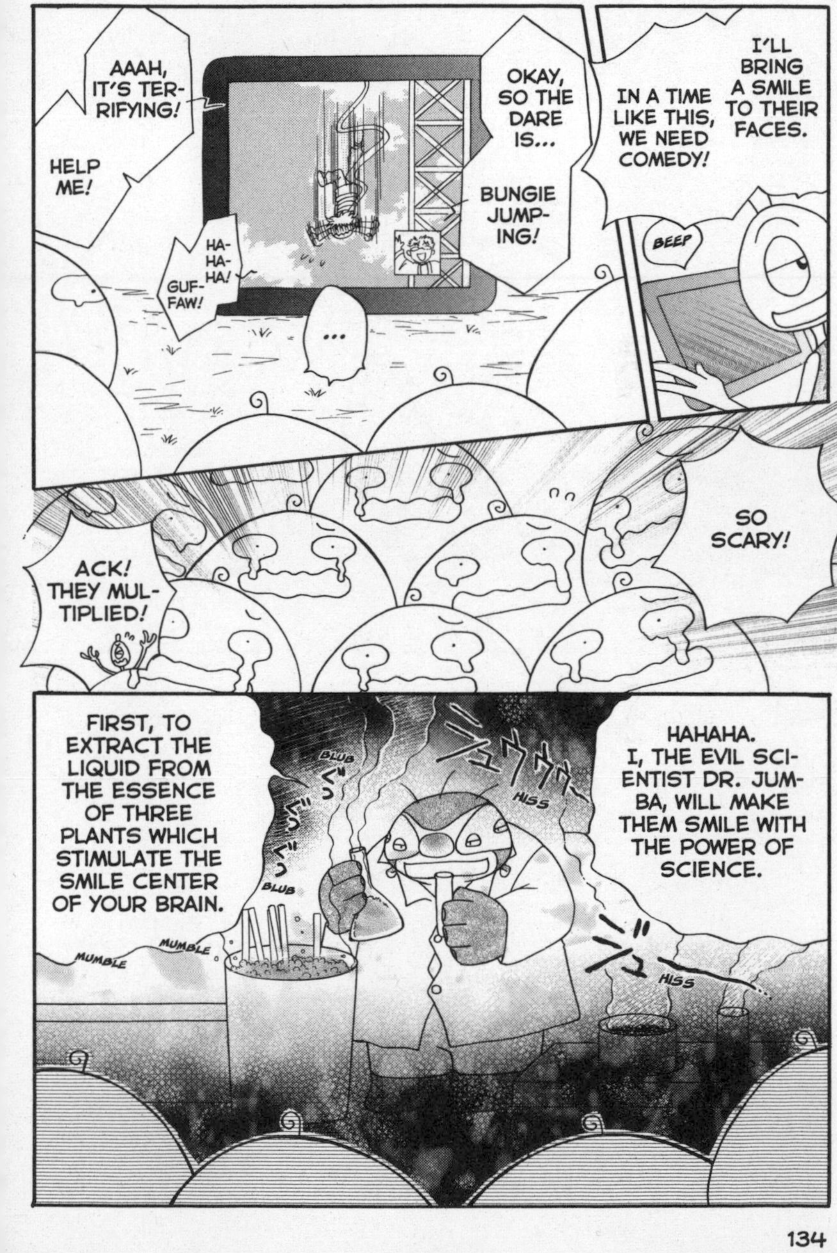

IN A TIME LIKE THIS, WE NEED COMEDY!
I'LL BRING A SMILE TO THEIR FACES.
BEEP
OKAY, SO THE DARE IS...
BUNGIE JUMPING!
AAAH, IT'S TERRIFYING!
HELP ME!
HA-HA-HA!
GUF-FAW!
...
SO SCARY!
ACK! THEY MULTIPLIED!
HAHAHA. I, THE EVIL SCIENTIST DR. JUMBA, WILL MAKE THEM SMILE WITH THE POWER OF SCIENCE.
HISS
HISS
BLUB
BLUB
FIRST, TO EXTRACT THE LIQUID FROM THE ESSENCE OF THREE PLANTS WHICH STIMULATE THE SMILE CENTER OF YOUR BRAIN.
MUMBLE
MUMBLE

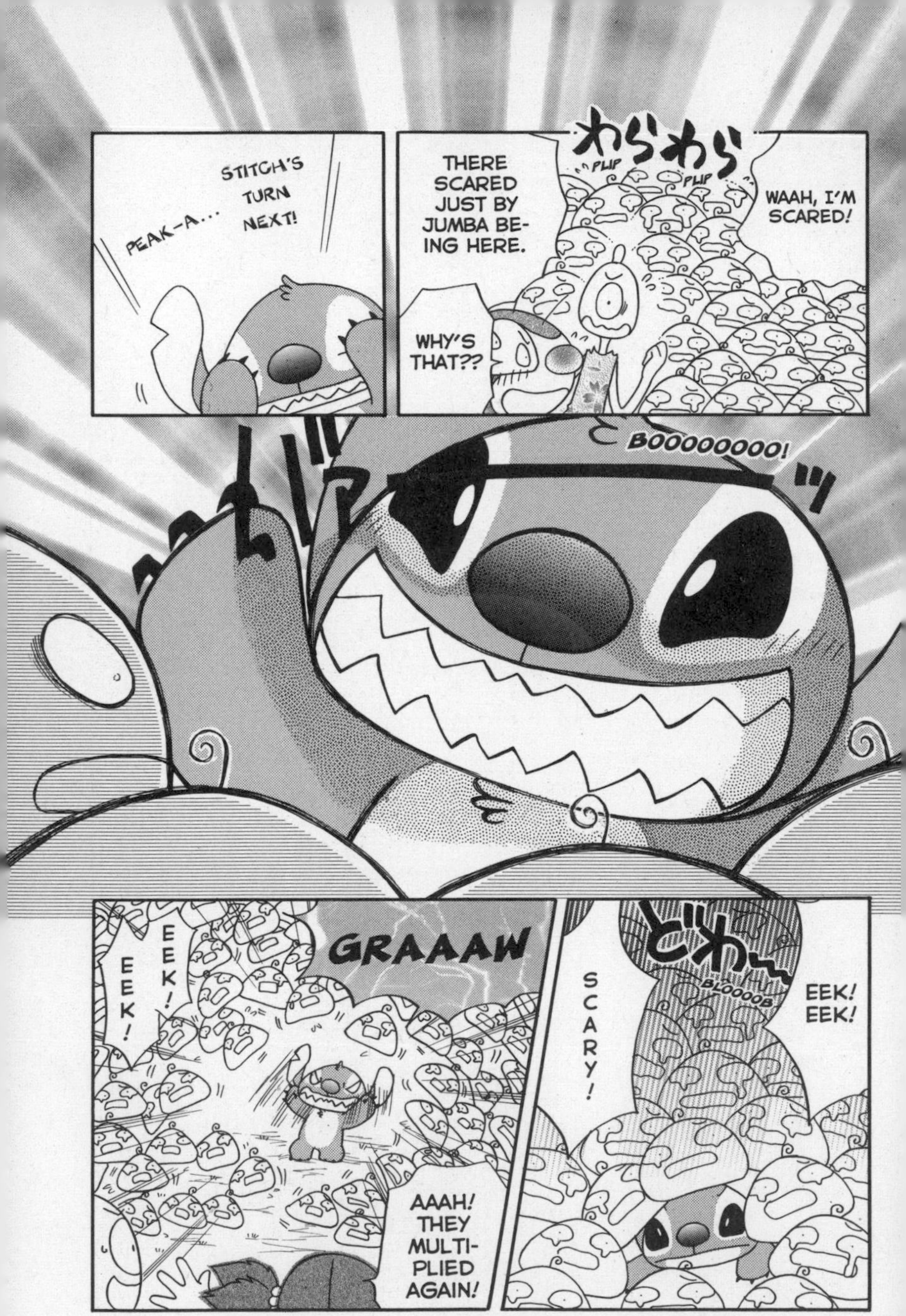
わらわら
PLIP
PLIP
WAAH, I'M SCARED!
THERE SCARED JUST BY JUMBA BE-ING HERE.
WHY'S THAT??
STITCH'S TURN NEXT!
PEAK-A...
BOOOOOOOO!
どわ~
BLOOOOB
EEK! EEK!
SCARY!
GRAAAW
EEK!
EEK!
AAAH! THEY MULTI-PLIED AGAIN!

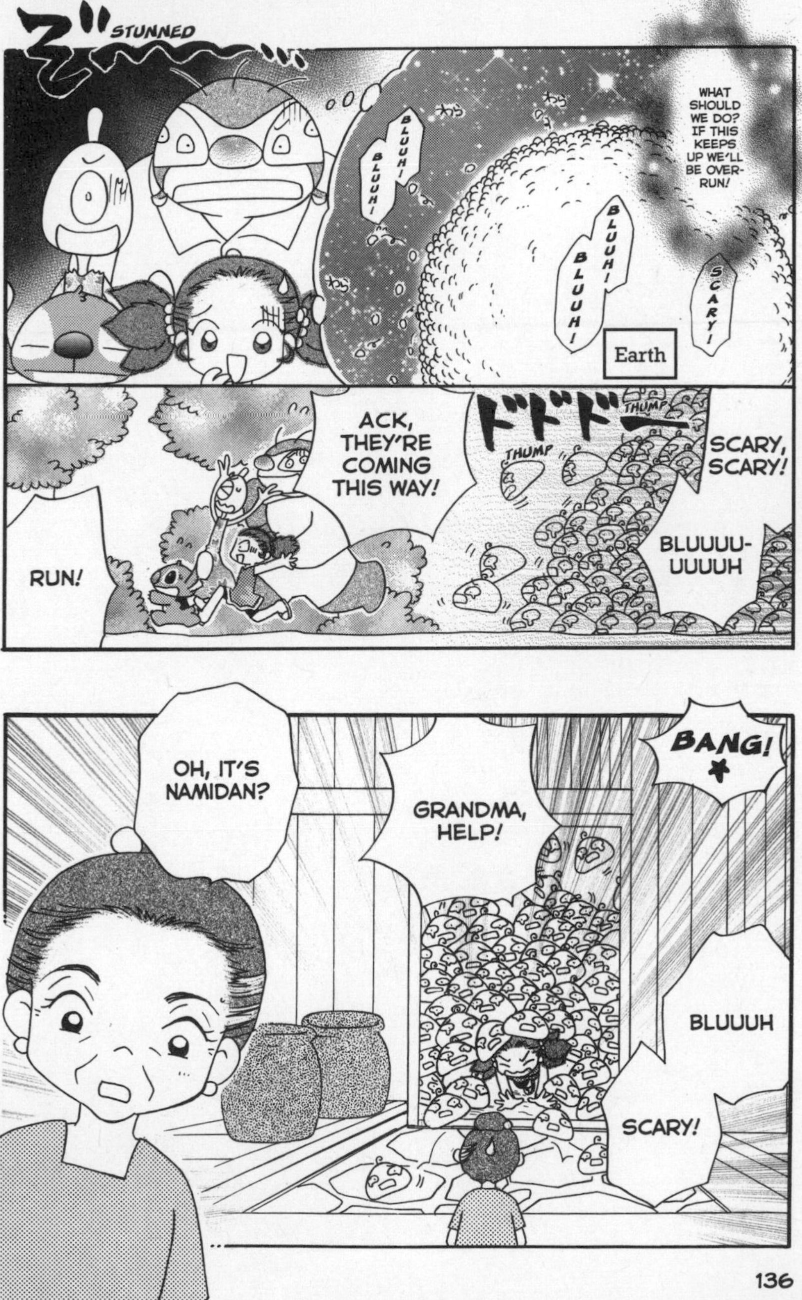
STUNNED
WHAT SHOULD WE DO? IF THIS KEEPS UP WE'LL BE OVER-RUN!
SCARY!
BLUUHI! BLUUHI!
BLUUHI! BLUUHI!
Earth
SCARY, SCARY!
BLUUUU-UUUUH
ドドドー
THUMP
THUMP
ACK, THEY'RE COMING THIS WAY!
RUN!
BANG!
GRANDMA, HELP!
OH, IT'S NAMIDAN?
BLUUUH
SCARY!

READ THIS WAY

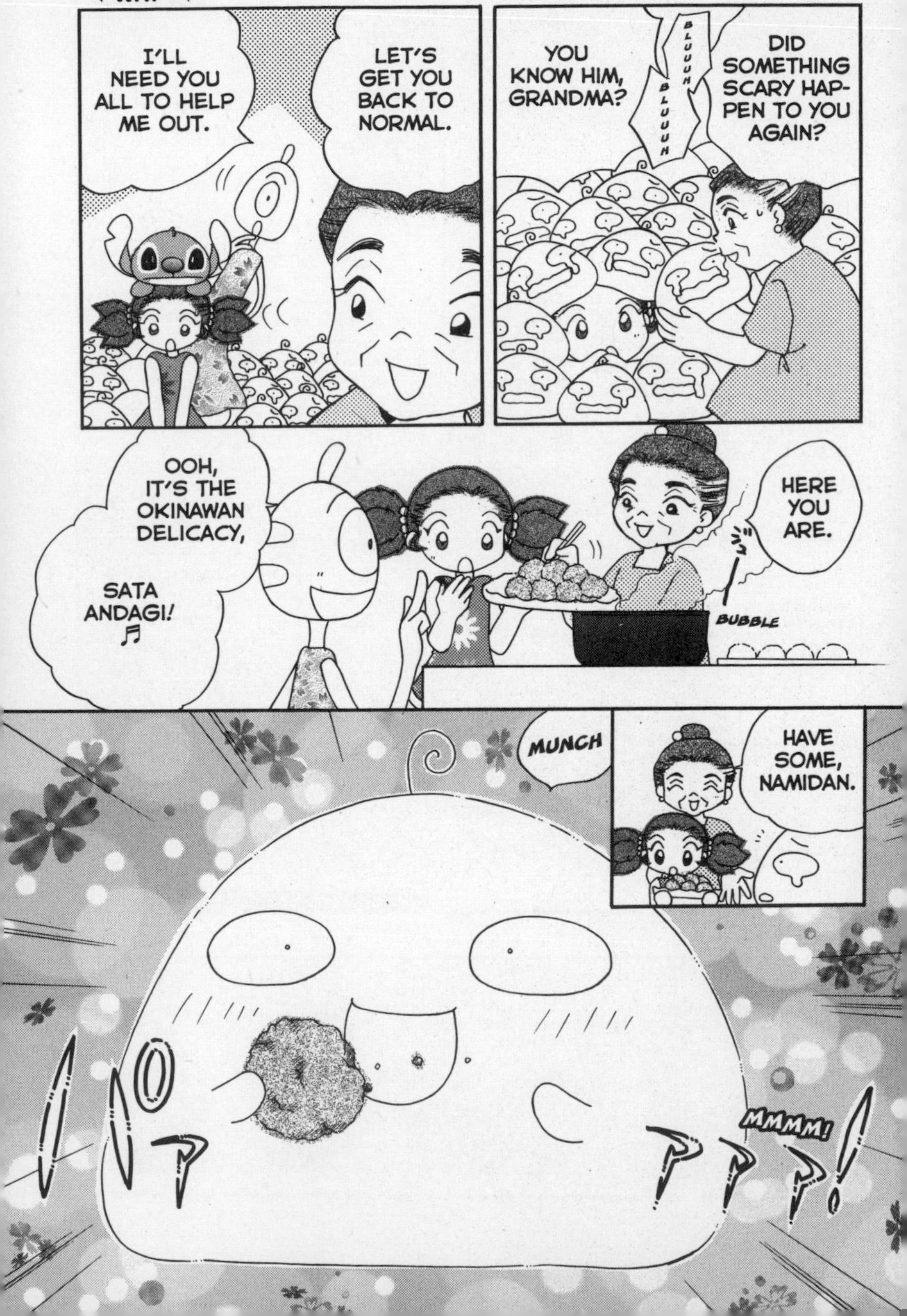

DID SOMETHING SCARY HAP-PEN TO YOU AGAIN?
BLUUUH
BLUUUH
YOU KNOW HIM, GRANDMA?
LET'S GET YOU BACK TO NORMAL.
I'LL NEED YOU ALL TO HELP ME OUT.
HERE YOU ARE.
BUBBLE
OOH, IT'S THE OKINAWAN DELICACY,
SATA ANDAGI! ♬
HAVE SOME, NAMIDAN.
MUNCH
MMMM!

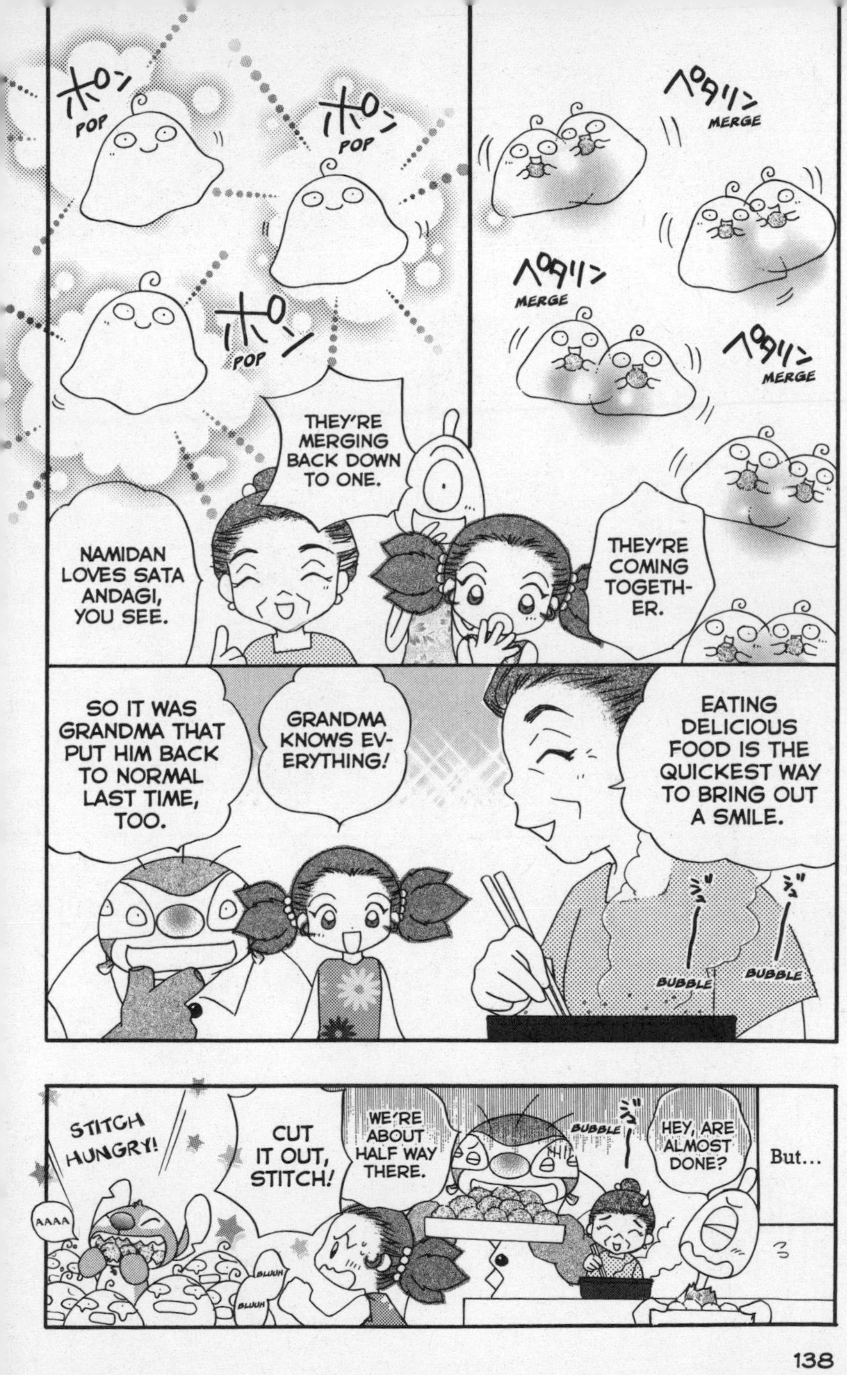
ペタリン
MERGE
ペタリン
MERGE
ペタリン
MERGE
THEY'RE COMING TOGETH-ER.
ポン
POP
ポン
POP
ポン
POP
THEY'RE MERGING BACK DOWN TO ONE.
NAMIDAN LOVES SATA ANDAGI, YOU SEE.
EATING DELICIOUS FOOD IS THE QUICKEST WAY TO BRING OUT A SMILE.
BUBBLE
BUBBLE
GRANDMA KNOWS EV-ERYTHING!
SO IT WAS GRANDMA THAT PUT HIM BACK TO NORMAL LAST TIME, TOO.
But…
HEY, ARE ALMOST DONE?
BUBBLE
WE'RE ABOUT HALF WAY THERE.
CUT IT OUT, STITCH!
STITCH HUNGRY!
AAAA
BLUUH
BLUUH

TOPPLE THE CAVITY BACTERIA ARMY!

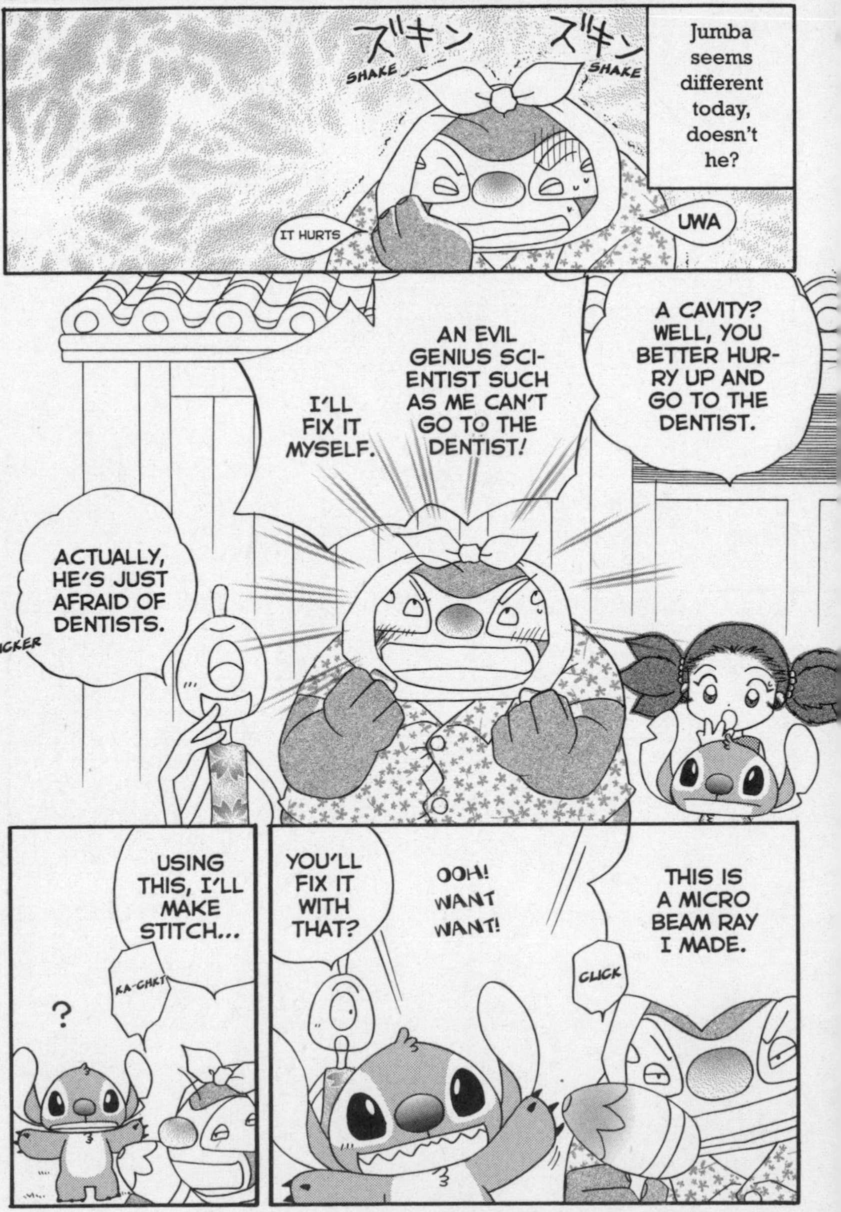
Jumba seems different today, doesn't he?
ズキン
SHAKE
ズキン
SHAKE
UWA
IT HURTS
A CAVITY? WELL, YOU BETTER HURRY UP AND GO TO THE DENTIST.
AN EVIL GENIUS SCIENTIST SUCH AS ME CAN'T GO TO THE DENTIST!
I'LL FIX IT MYSELF.
ACTUALLY, HE'S JUST AFRAID OF DENTISTS.
SNICKER
THIS IS A MICRO BEAM RAY I MADE.
CLICK
OOH! WANT WANT!
YOU'LL FIX IT WITH THAT?
USING THIS, I'LL MAKE STITCH...
KA-CHK!
?

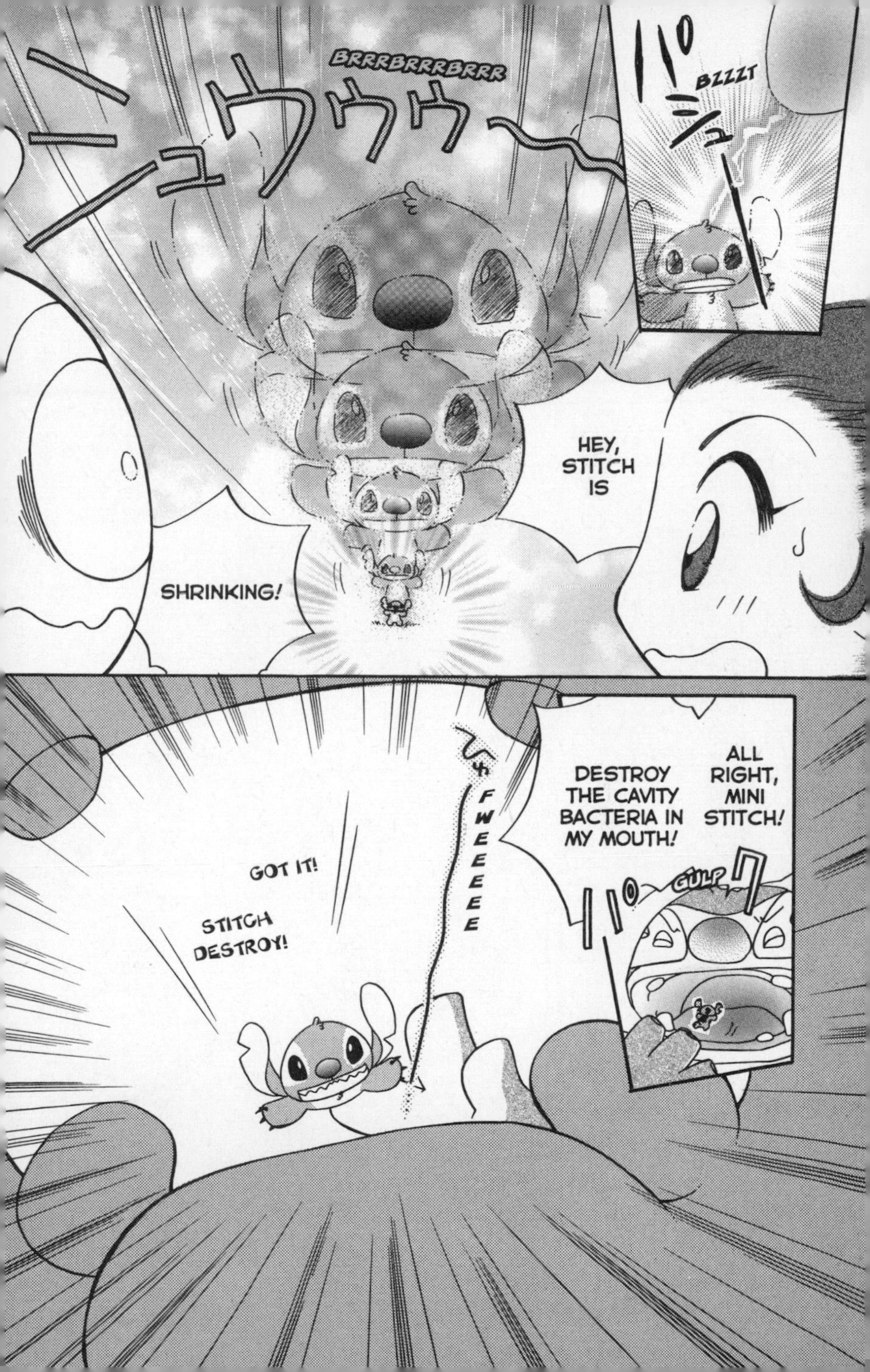
パシュ
BZZZT
シュウウウ～
BRRRBRRRBRRR
HEY, STITCH IS
SHRINKING!
ALL RIGHT, MINI STITCH!
DESTROY THE CAVITY BACTERIA IN MY MOUTH!
パ
GULP
ぴゅ
FWEEEEEE
GOT IT!
STITCH DESTROY!

READ THIS WAY

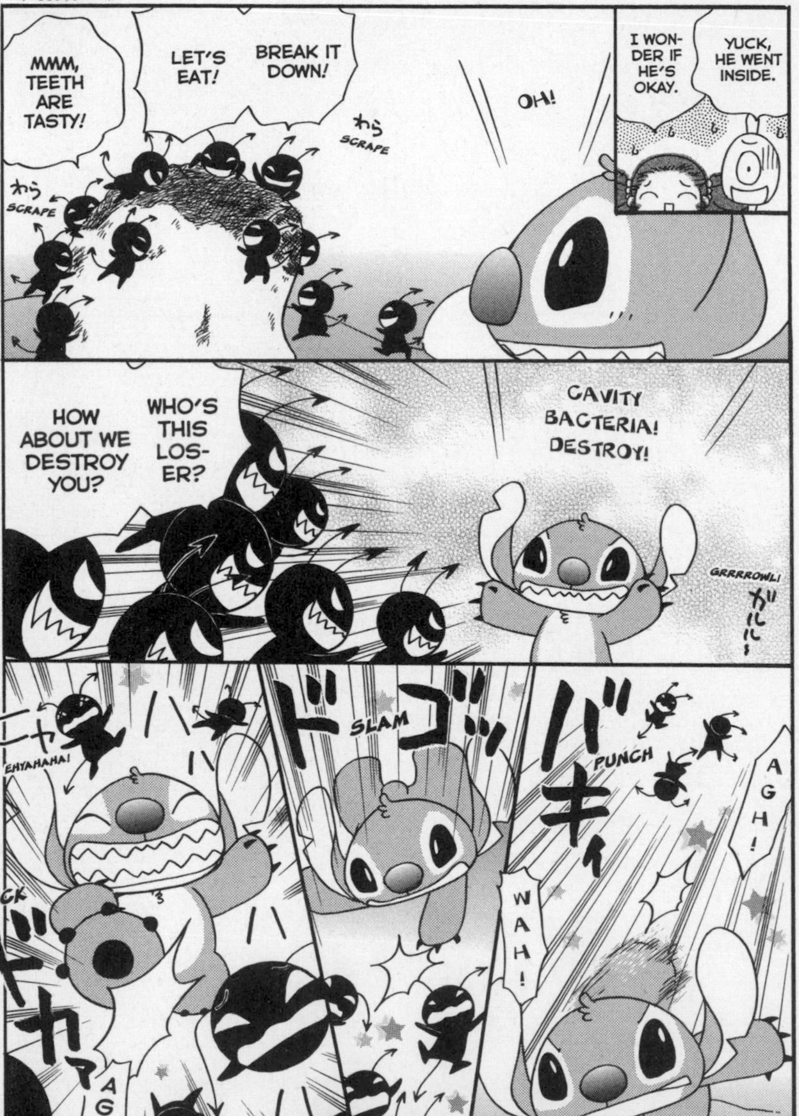

YUCK, HE WENT INSIDE.
I WONDER IF HE'S OKAY.
OH!
わら SCRAPE
BREAK IT DOWN!
LET'S EAT!
MMM, TEETH ARE TASTY!
わら SCRAPE
CAVITY BACTERIA! DESTROY!
ガルル~ GRRRROWL!
WHO'S THIS LOSER?
HOW ABOUT WE DESTROY YOU?
バキィ PUNCH
AGH!
WAH!
ドゴッ SLAM
ヒャハハ EHYAHAHA!
ドカァ KICK
AGH!

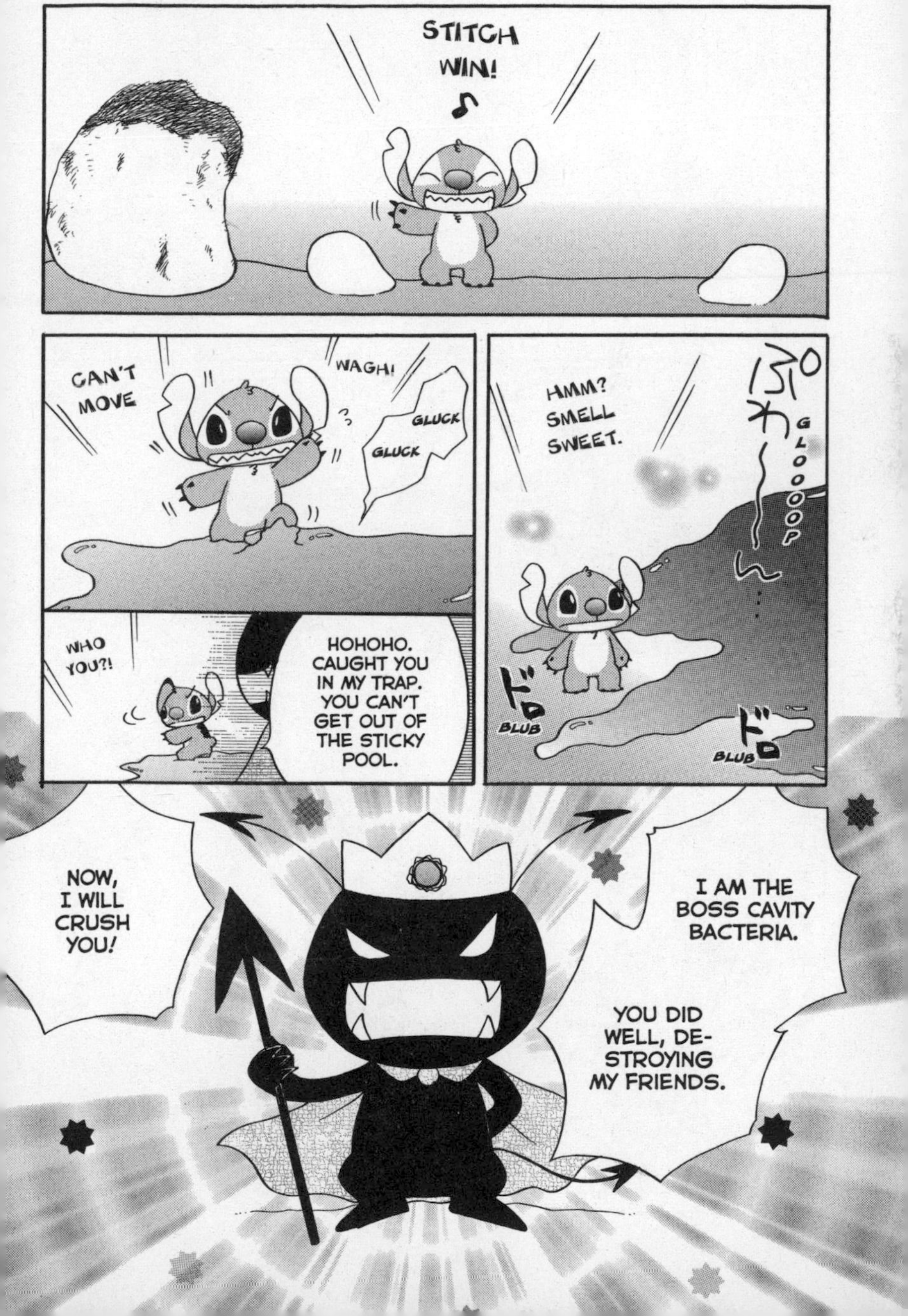
STITCH WIN! ♪
ぷわ〜ん…
GLOOOOOP
HMM? SMELL SWEET.
ドロ BLUB
ドロ BLUB
WAGH!
GLUCK GLUCK
CAN'T MOVE
HOHOHO. CAUGHT YOU IN MY TRAP. YOU CAN'T GET OUT OF THE STICKY POOL.
WHO YOU?!
I AM THE BOSS CAVITY BACTERIA.
YOU DID WELL, DE-STROYING MY FRIENDS.
NOW, I WILL CRUSH YOU!

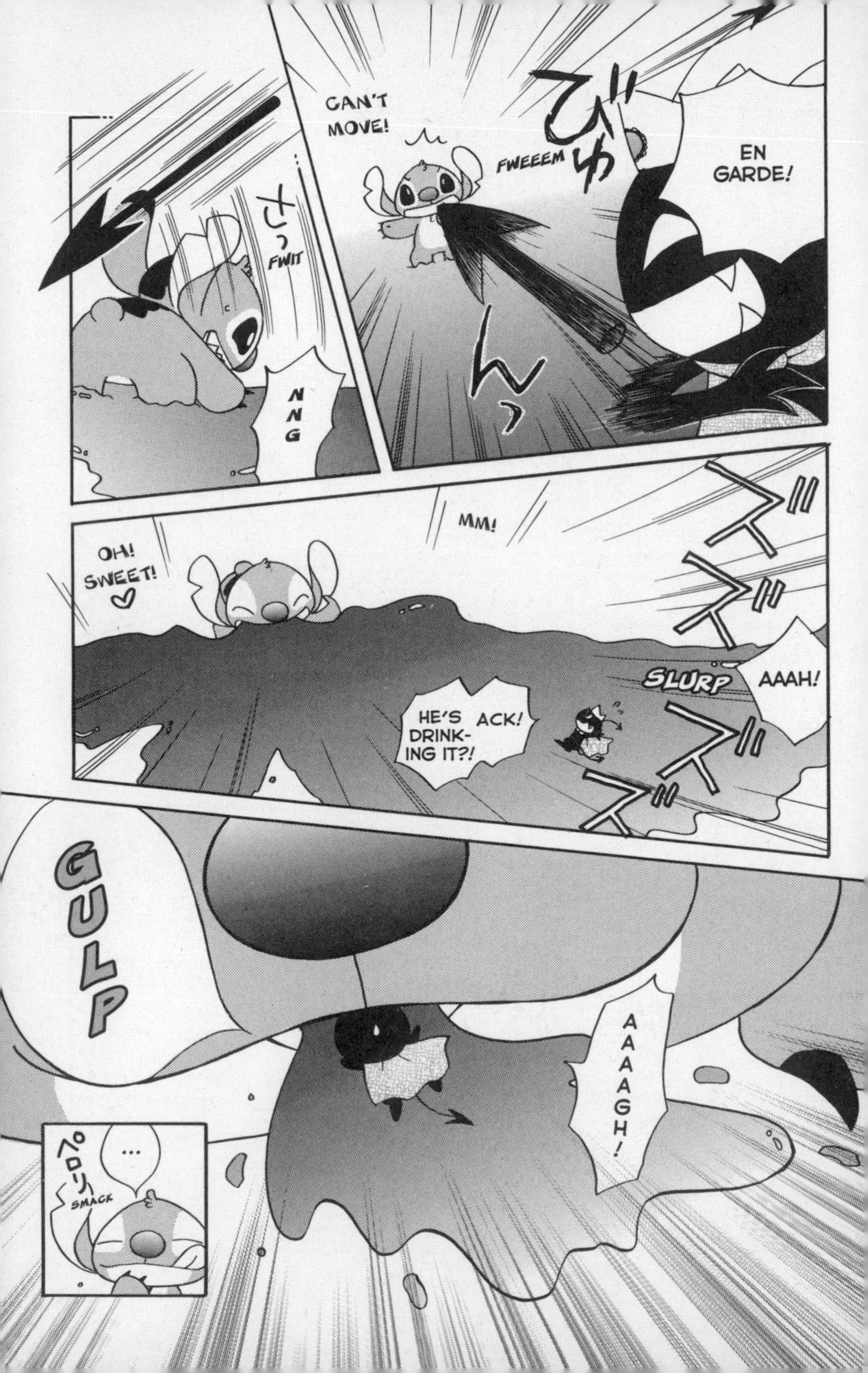

EN GARDE!
びゅ
FWEEEM
CAN'T MOVE!
んっ
…
さっ
FWIT
NNG
ズズズズ
SLURP
MM!
AAAH!
ACK!
HE'S DRINKING IT?!
OH! SWEET! ♥
AAAAAGH!
GULP
…
ペロリ
SMACK

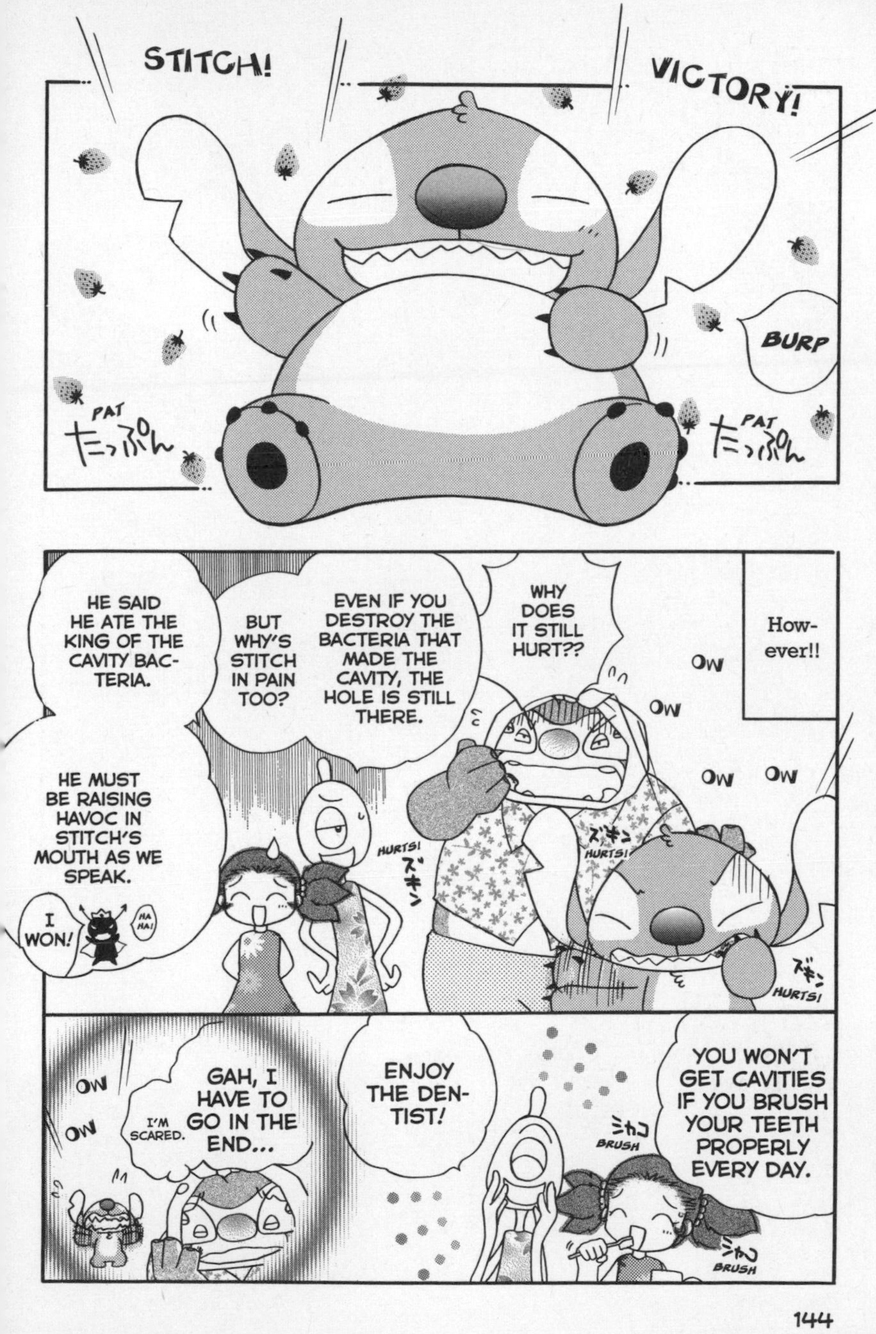
STITCH!
VICTORY!
BURP
PAT たっぷん
PAT たっぷん
How-ever!!
WHY DOES IT STILL HURT??
OW
OW
OW
OW
EVEN IF YOU DESTROY THE BACTERIA THAT MADE THE CAVITY, THE HOLE IS STILL THERE.
BUT WHY'S STITCH IN PAIN TOO?
HE SAID HE ATE THE KING OF THE CAVITY BAC-TERIA.
ズキン HURTS!
ズキン HURTS!
HURTS! ズキン
HE MUST BE RAISING HAVOC IN STITCH'S MOUTH AS WE SPEAK.
HA HA!
I WON!
YOU WON'T GET CAVITIES IF YOU BRUSH YOUR TEETH PROPERLY EVERY DAY.
シャコ BRUSH
シャコ BRUSH
ENJOY THE DEN-TIST!
GAH, I HAVE TO GO IN THE END...
I'M SCARED.
OW
OW

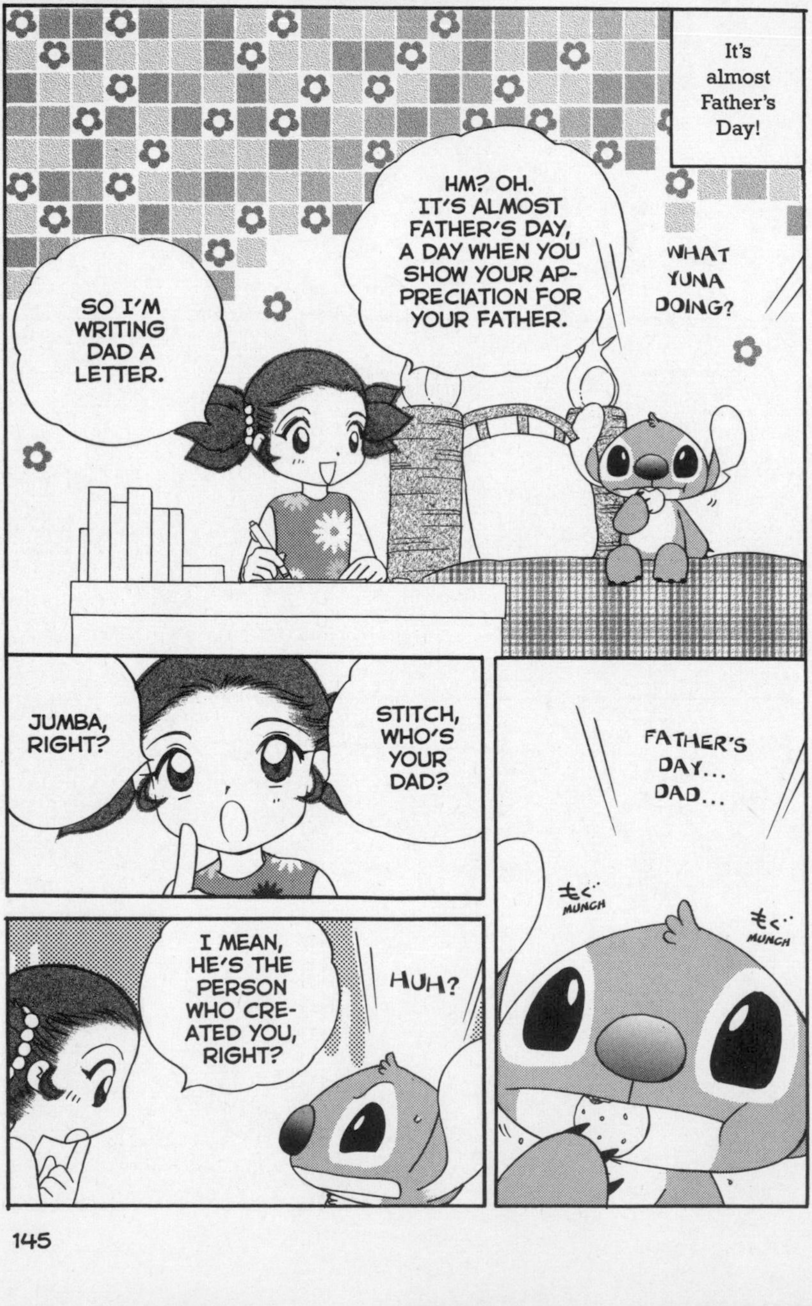
It's almost Father's Day!
WHAT YUNA DOING?
HM? OH. IT'S ALMOST FATHER'S DAY, A DAY WHEN YOU SHOW YOUR AP-PRECIATION FOR YOUR FATHER.
SO I'M WRITING DAD A LETTER.
FATHER'S DAY... DAD...
もぐ‥ MUNCH
もぐ‥ MUNCH
STITCH, WHO'S YOUR DAD?
JUMBA, RIGHT?
HUH?
I MEAN, HE'S THE PERSON WHO CRE-ATED YOU, RIGHT?

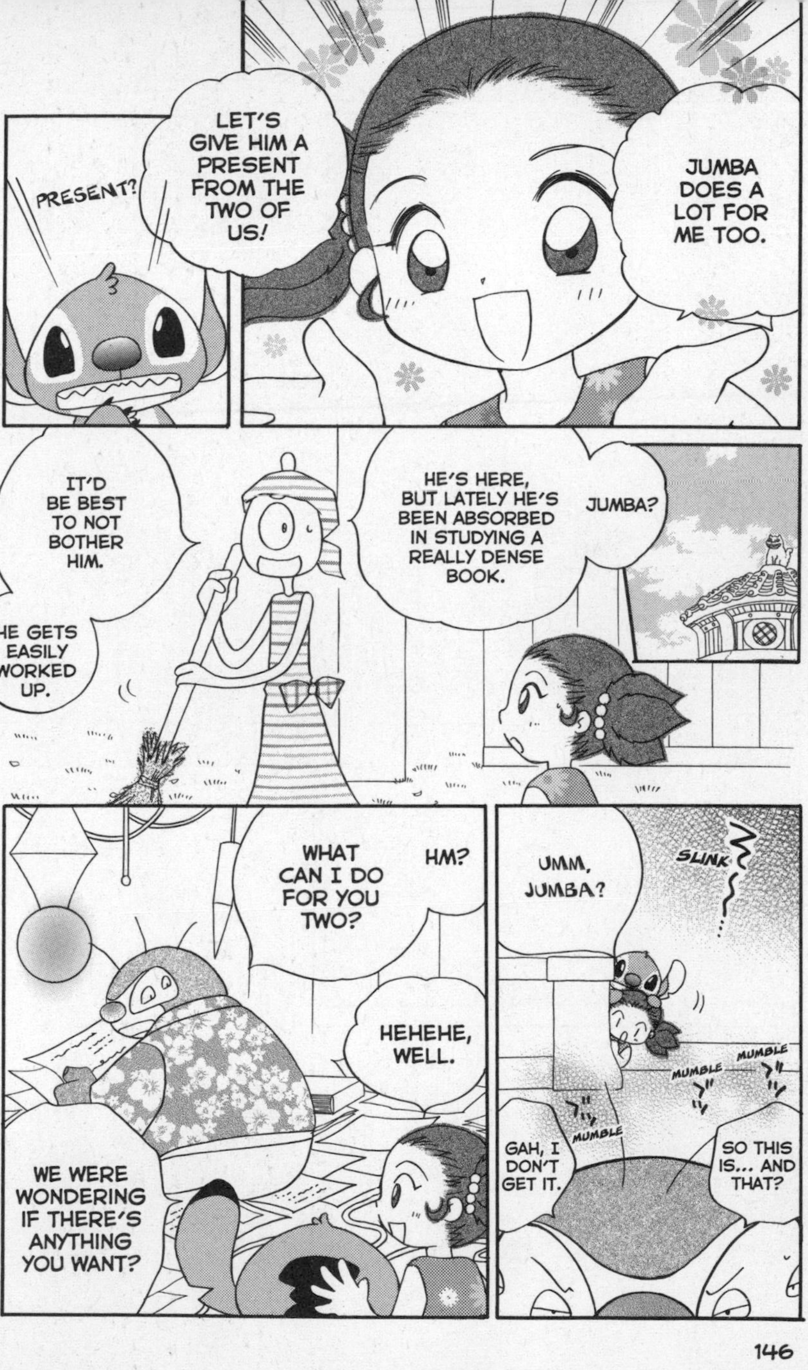
JUMBA DOES A LOT FOR ME TOO.
LET'S GIVE HIM A PRESENT FROM THE TWO OF US!
PRESENT?
JUMBA?
HE'S HERE, BUT LATELY HE'S BEEN ABSORBED IN STUDYING A REALLY DENSE BOOK.
IT'D BE BEST TO NOT BOTHER HIM.
HE GETS EASILY WORKED UP.
SLINK
UMM, JUMBA?
MUMBLE
MUMBLE
SO THIS IS... AND THAT?
MUMBLE
GAH, I DON'T GET IT.
HM?
WHAT CAN I DO FOR YOU TWO?
HEHEHE, WELL.
WE WERE WONDERING IF THERE'S ANYTHING YOU WANT?

READ THIS WAY

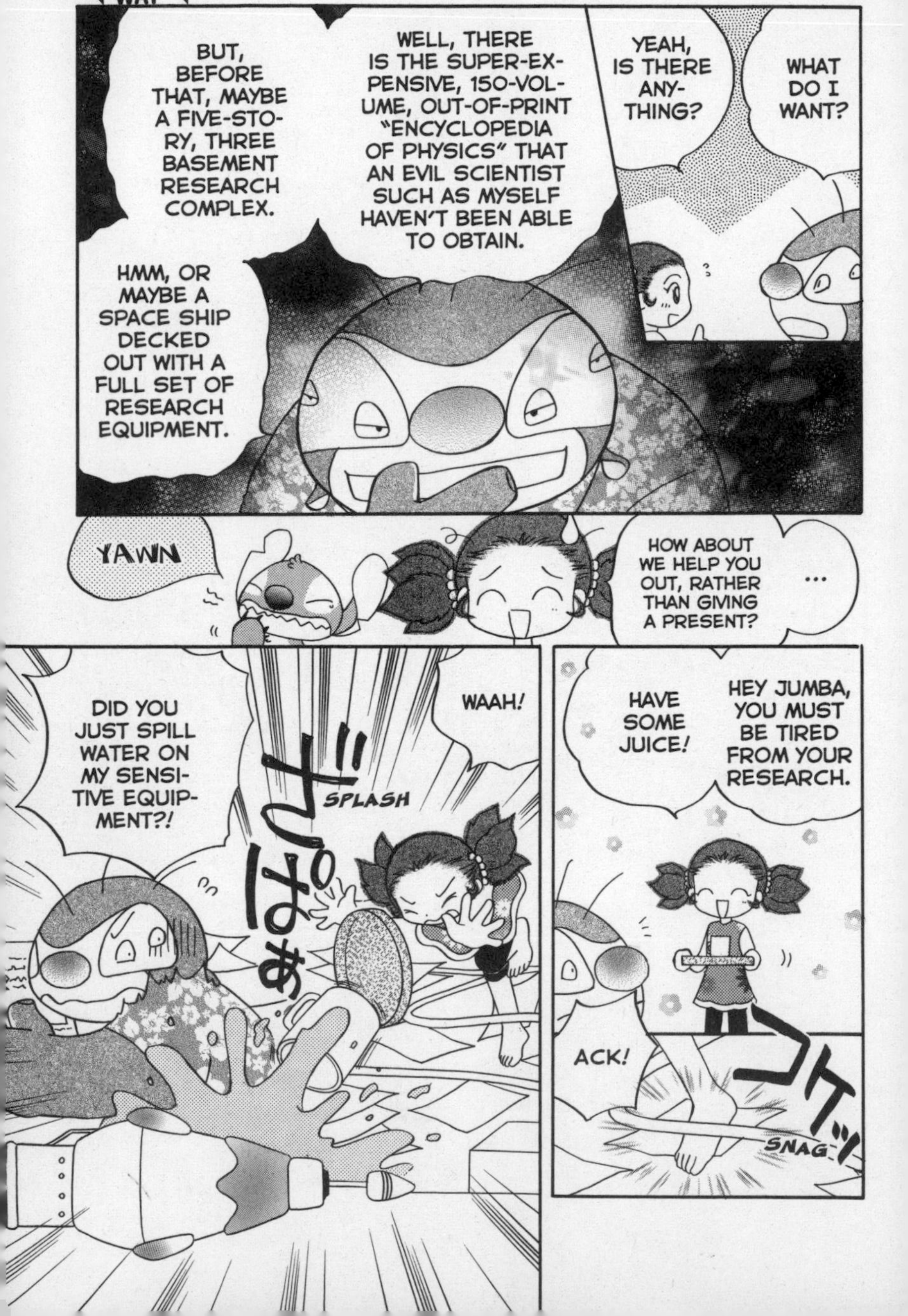
WHAT DO I WANT?
YEAH, IS THERE ANYTHING?
WELL, THERE IS THE SUPER-EXPENSIVE, 150-VOLUME, OUT-OF-PRINT "ENCYCLOPEDIA OF PHYSICS" THAT AN EVIL SCIENTIST SUCH AS MYSELF HAVEN'T BEEN ABLE TO OBTAIN.
BUT, BEFORE THAT, MAYBE A FIVE-STORY, THREE BASEMENT RESEARCH COMPLEX.
HMM, OR MAYBE A SPACE SHIP DECKED OUT WITH A FULL SET OF RESEARCH EQUIPMENT.
...
HOW ABOUT WE HELP YOU OUT, RATHER THAN GIVING A PRESENT?
YAWN
HEY JUMBA, YOU MUST BE TIRED FROM YOUR RESEARCH.
HAVE SOME JUICE!
ACK!
コケッ
SNAG
WAAH!
ざぱあ
SPLASH
DID YOU JUST SPILL WATER ON MY SENSITIVE EQUIPMENT?!

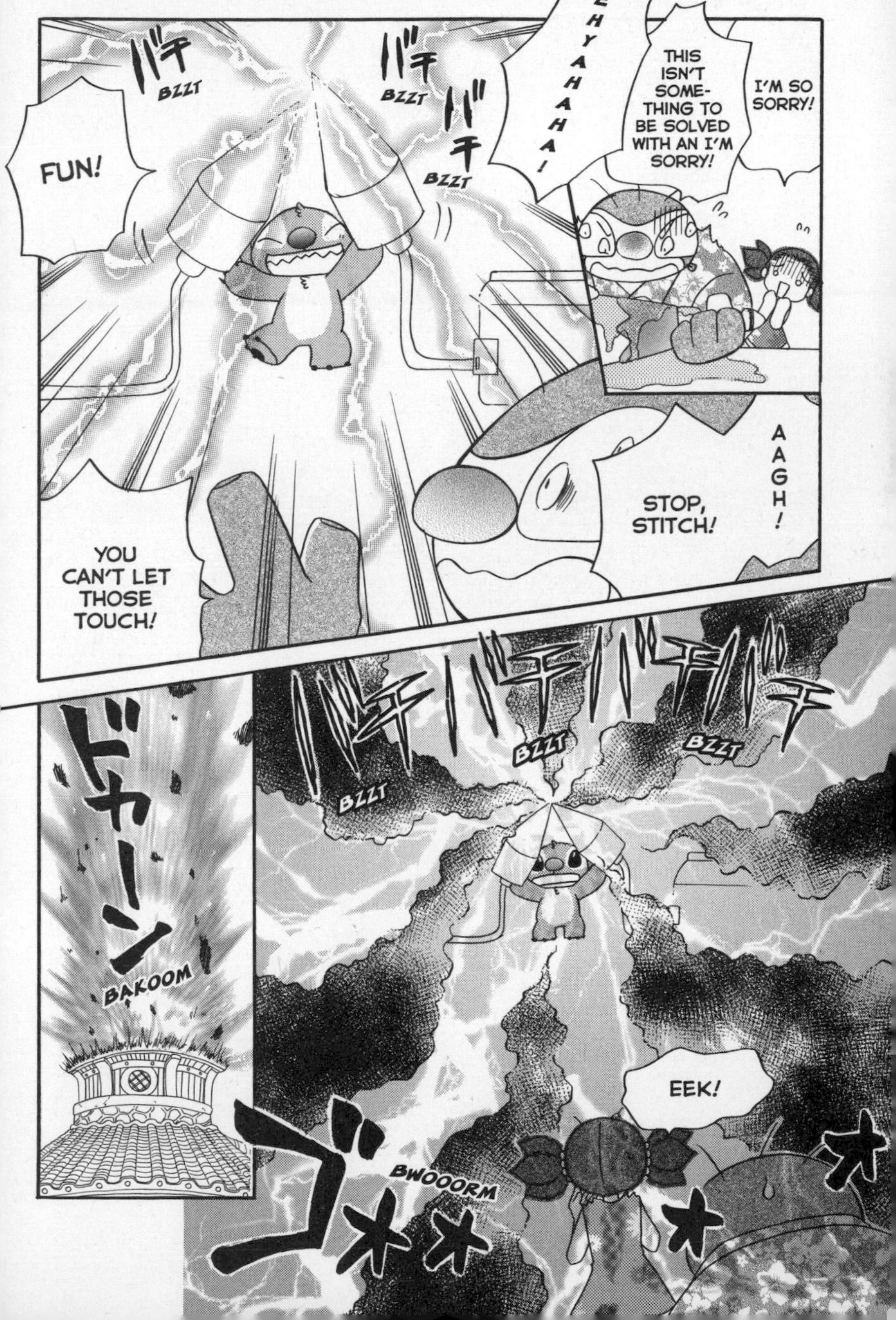
I'M SO SORRY!
THIS ISN'T SOME-THING TO BE SOLVED WITH AN I'M SORRY!
EHYAHAHA!
BZZT
BZZT
BZZT
FUN!
AAGH!
STOP, STITCH!
YOU CAN'T LET THOSE TOUCH!
BZZT
BZZT
BZZT
EEK!
BWOOORM
BAKOOM

READ THIS WAY

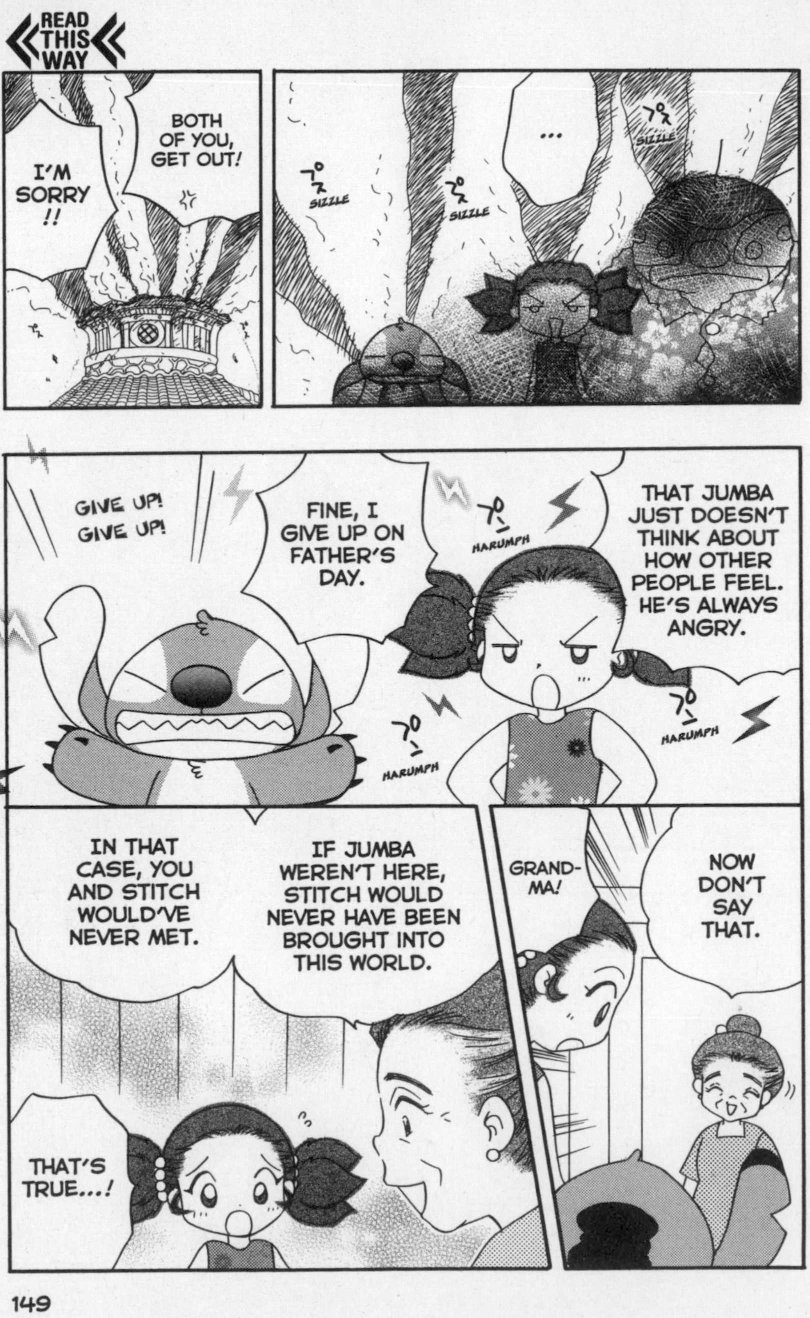
...
SIZZLE
SIZZLE
SIZZLE
BOTH OF YOU, GET OUT!
I'M SORRY!!
THAT JUMBA JUST DOESN'T THINK ABOUT HOW OTHER PEOPLE FEEL. HE'S ALWAYS ANGRY.
HARUMPH
HARUMPH
HARUMPH
FINE, I GIVE UP ON FATHER'S DAY.
GIVE UP! GIVE UP!
NOW DON'T SAY THAT.
GRAND-MA!
IF JUMBA WEREN'T HERE, STITCH WOULD NEVER HAVE BEEN BROUGHT INTO THIS WORLD.
IN THAT CASE, YOU AND STITCH WOULD'VE NEVER MET.
THAT'S TRUE...!

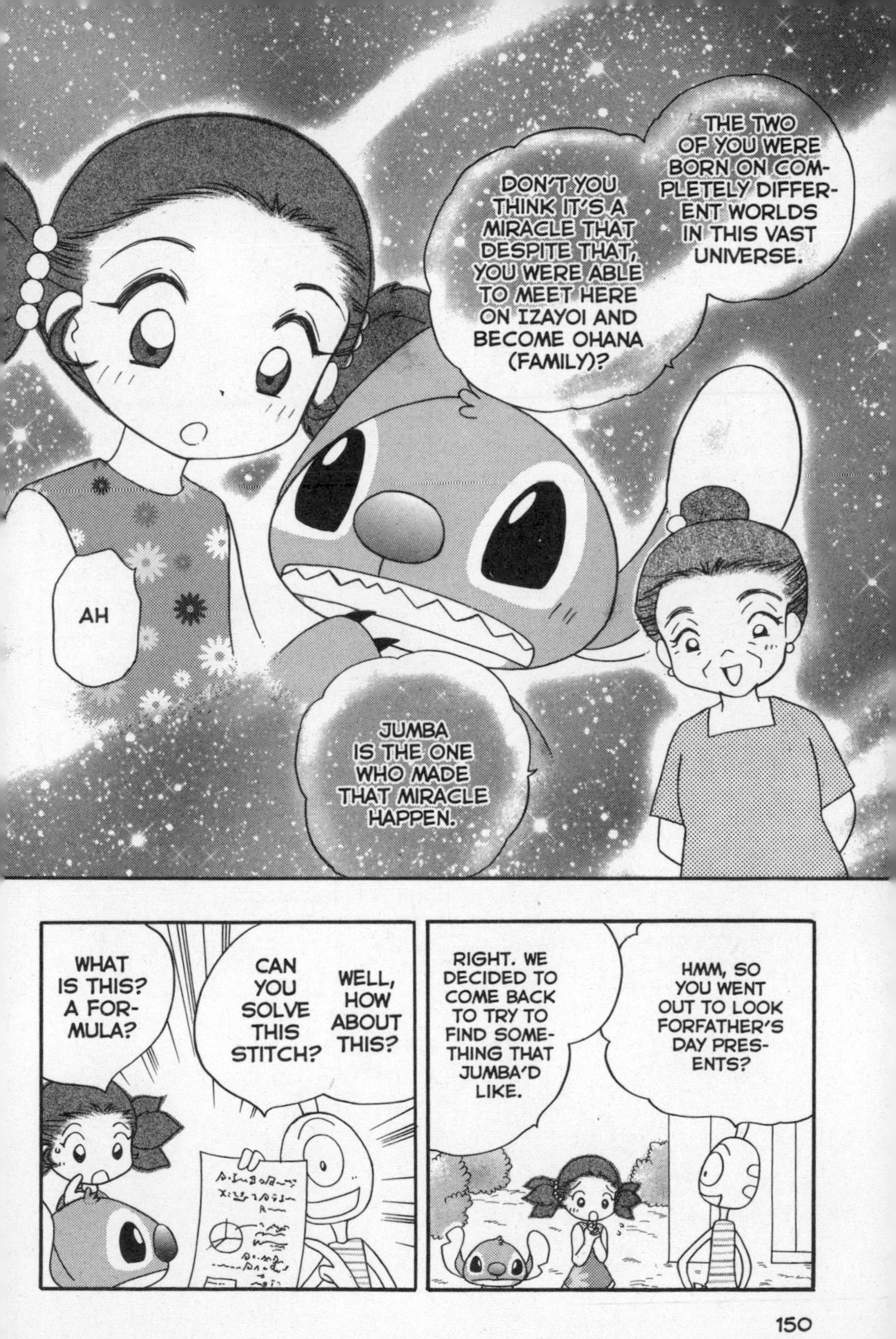
THE TWO OF YOU WERE BORN ON COMPLETELY DIFFERENT WORLDS IN THIS VAST UNIVERSE.
DON'T YOU THINK IT'S A MIRACLE THAT DESPITE THAT, YOU WERE ABLE TO MEET HERE ON IZAYOI AND BECOME OHANA (FAMILY)?
AH
JUMBA IS THE ONE WHO MADE THAT MIRACLE HAPPEN.
HMM, SO YOU WENT OUT TO LOOK FORFATHER'S DAY PRESENTS?
RIGHT. WE DECIDED TO COME BACK TO TRY TO FIND SOMETHING THAT JUMBA'D LIKE.
WELL, HOW ABOUT THIS?
CAN YOU SOLVE THIS STITCH?
WHAT IS THIS? A FORMULA?

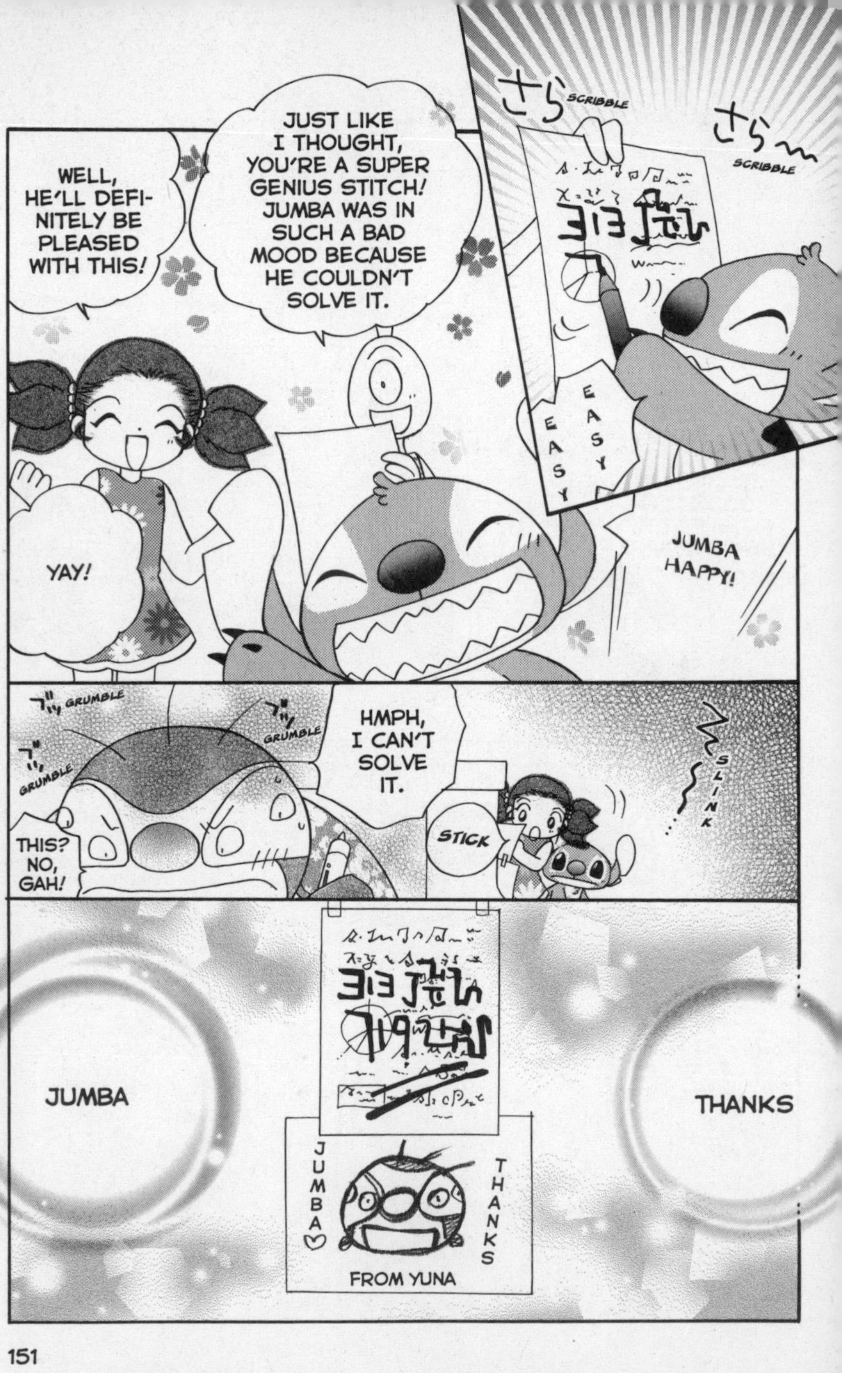
さら SCRIBBLE
さら~ SCRIBBLE
EASY EASY
JUST LIKE I THOUGHT, YOU'RE A SUPER GENIUS STITCH! JUMBA WAS IN SUCH A BAD MOOD BECAUSE HE COULDN'T SOLVE IT.
WELL, HE'LL DEFINITELY BE PLEASED WITH THIS!
JUMBA HAPPY!
YAY!
SLINK
STICK
HMPH, I CAN'T SOLVE IT.
GRUMBLE
GRUMBLE
GRUMBLE
THIS? NO, GAH!
THANKS
JUMBA THANKS FROM YUNA
JUMBA

PLEAKLEY'S SUPER FANTASY☆

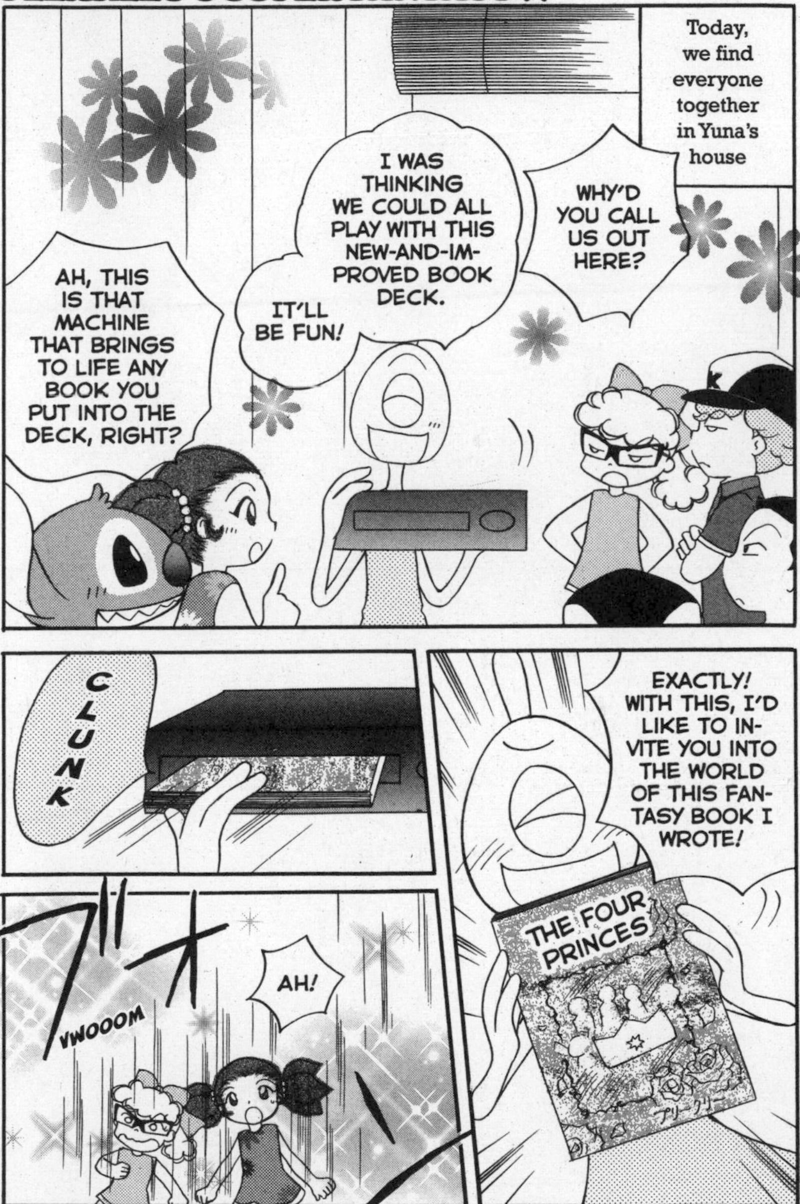
Today, we find everyone together in Yuna's house
WHY'D YOU CALL US OUT HERE?
I WAS THINKING WE COULD ALL PLAY WITH THIS NEW-AND-IM-PROVED BOOK DECK.
IT'LL BE FUN!
AH, THIS IS THAT MACHINE THAT BRINGS TO LIFE ANY BOOK YOU PUT INTO THE DECK, RIGHT?
EXACTLY! WITH THIS, I'D LIKE TO IN-VITE YOU INTO THE WORLD OF THIS FAN-TASY BOOK I WROTE!
THE FOUR PRINCES
CLUNK
VWOOOM
AH!

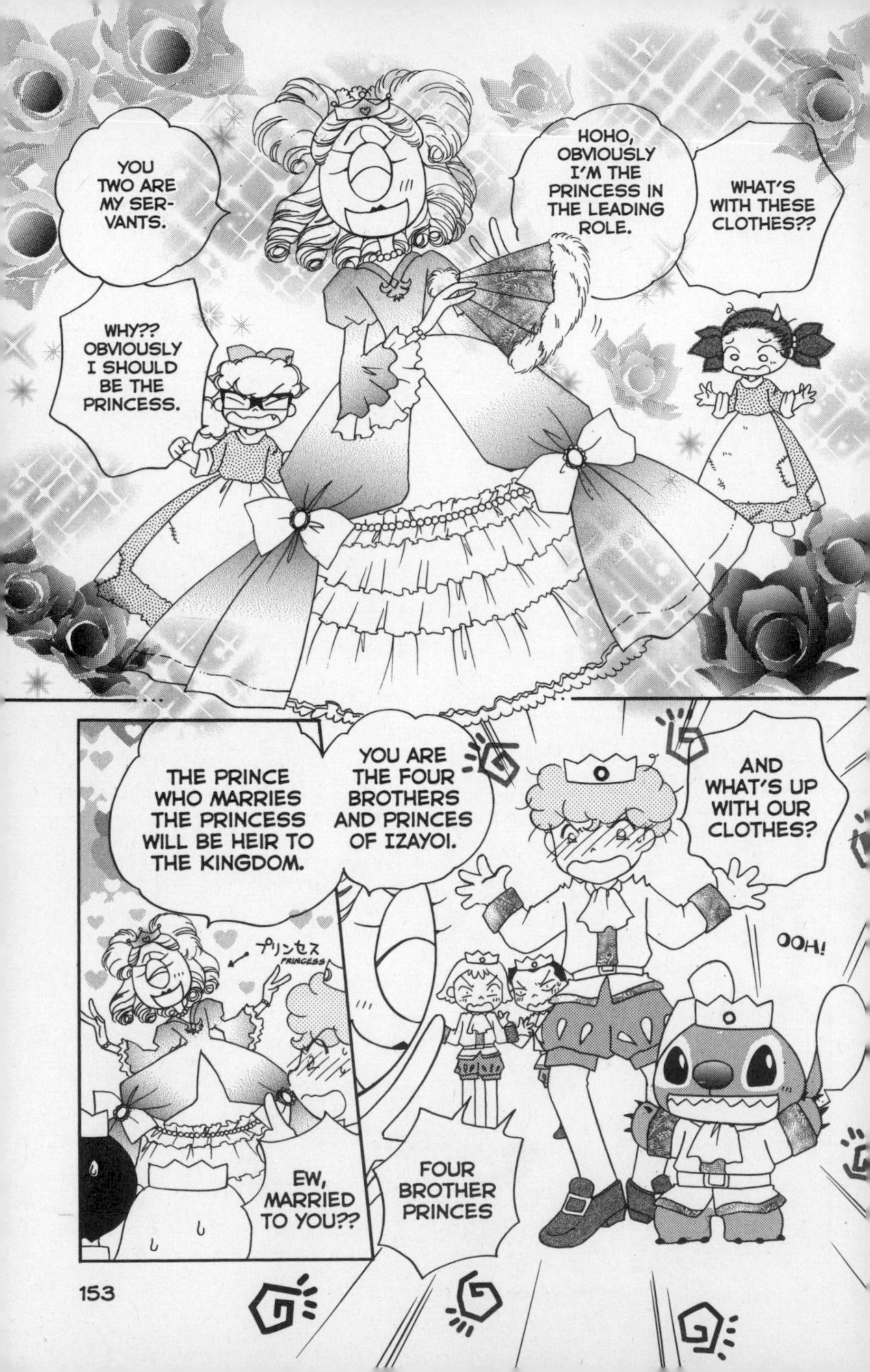
WHAT'S WITH THESE CLOTHES??
HOHO, OBVIOUSLY I'M THE PRINCESS IN THE LEADING ROLE.
YOU TWO ARE MY SERVANTS.
WHY?? OBVIOUSLY I SHOULD BE THE PRINCESS.
...
AND WHAT'S UP WITH OUR CLOTHES?
YOU ARE THE FOUR BROTHERS AND PRINCES OF IZAYOI.
THE PRINCE WHO MARRIES THE PRINCESS WILL BE HEIR TO THE KINGDOM.
OOH!
FOUR BROTHER PRINCES
プリンセス PRINCESS
EW, MARRIED TO YOU??

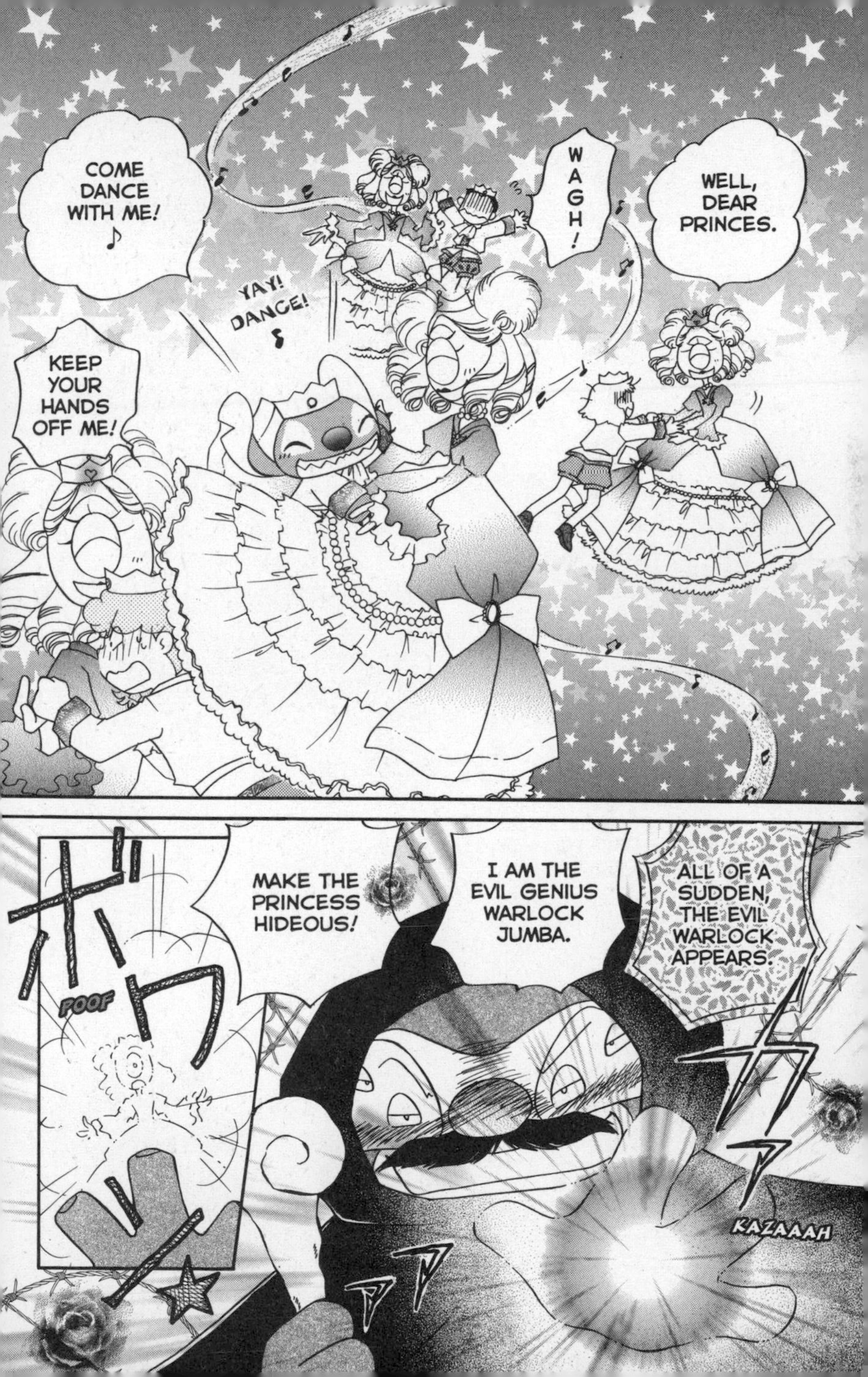
WELL, DEAR PRINCES.
WAGH!
COME DANCE WITH ME! ♪
YAY! DANCE!
KEEP YOUR HANDS OFF ME!
ALL OF A SUDDEN, THE EVIL WARLOCK APPEARS.
I AM THE EVIL GENIUS WARLOCK JUMBA.
MAKE THE PRINCESS HIDEOUS!
KAZAAAH
POOF

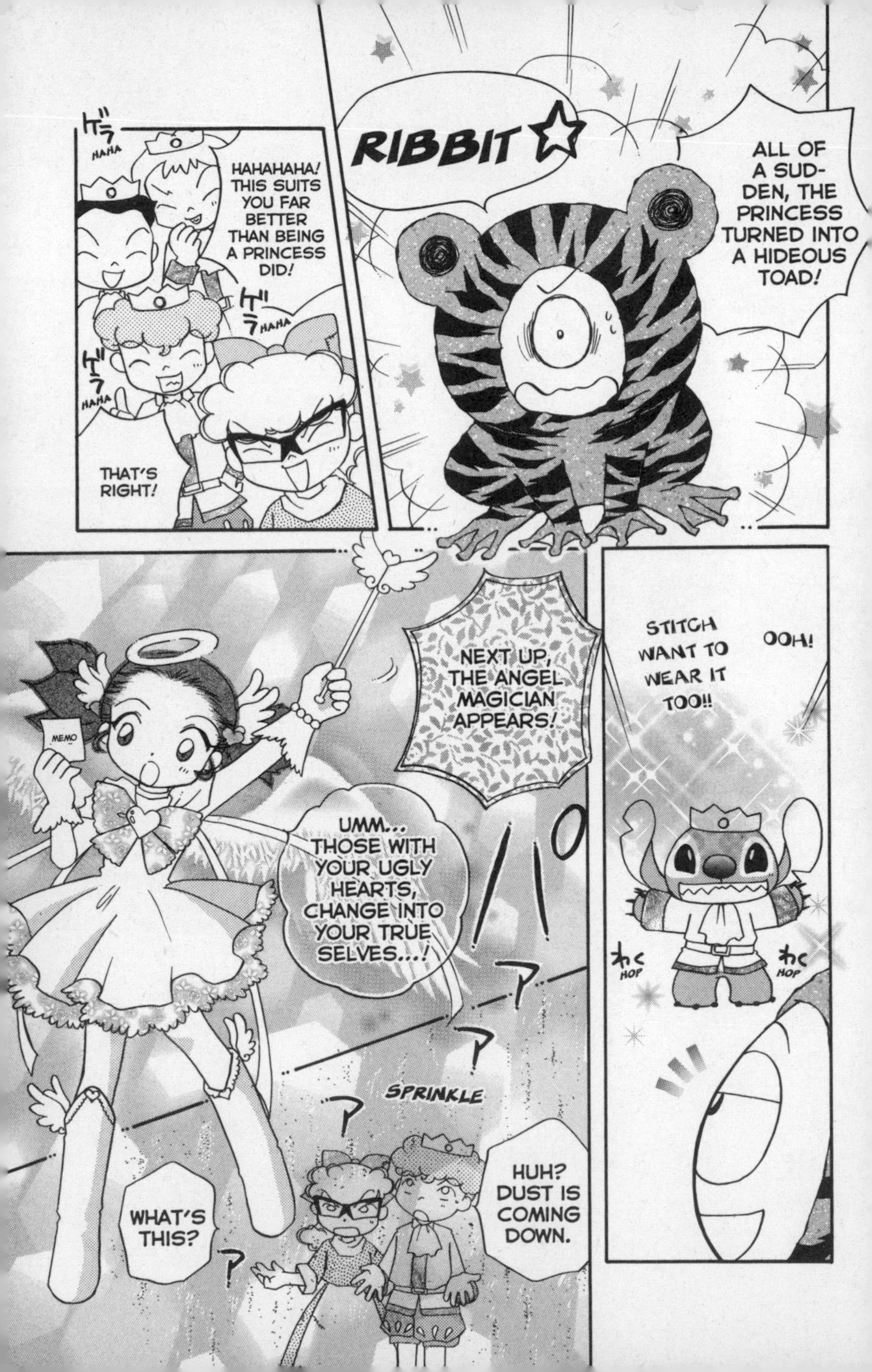
ALL OF A SUD-DEN, THE PRINCESS TURNED INTO A HIDEOUS TOAD!
RIBBIT☆
ゲラ HAHA
HAHAHAHA! THIS SUITS YOU FAR BETTER THAN BEING A PRINCESS DID!
ゲラ HAHA
ゲラ HAHA
THAT'S RIGHT!
OOH!
STITCH WANT TO WEAR IT TOO!!
わく HOP
わく HOP
NEXT UP, THE ANGEL MAGICIAN APPEARS!
MEMO
UMM... THOSE WITH YOUR UGLY HEARTS, CHANGE INTO YOUR TRUE SELVES...!
SPRINKLE
HUH? DUST IS COMING DOWN.
WHAT'S THIS?

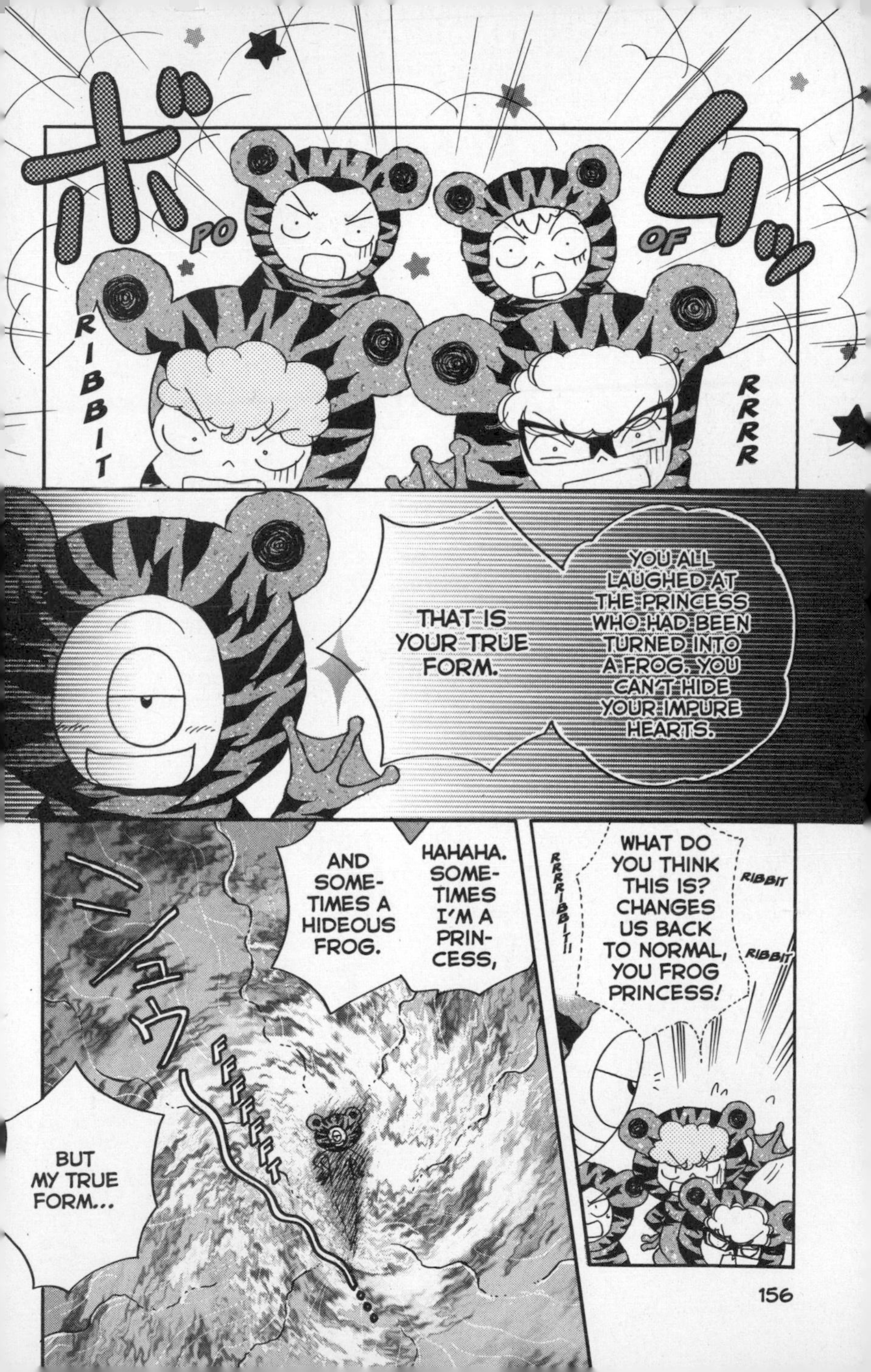
PO OF
RRRR
RIBBIT
YOU ALL LAUGHED AT THE PRINCESS WHO HAD BEEN TURNED INTO A FROG. YOU CAN'T HIDE YOUR IMPURE HEARTS.
THAT IS YOUR TRUE FORM.
WHAT DO YOU THINK THIS IS? CHANGES US BACK TO NORMAL, YOU FROG PRINCESS!
RIBBIT
RIBBIT
RRRRIBBIT!!
HAHAHA. SOMETIMES I'M A PRINCESS,
AND SOMETIMES A HIDEOUS FROG.
FFFFFFT
BUT MY TRUE FORM...

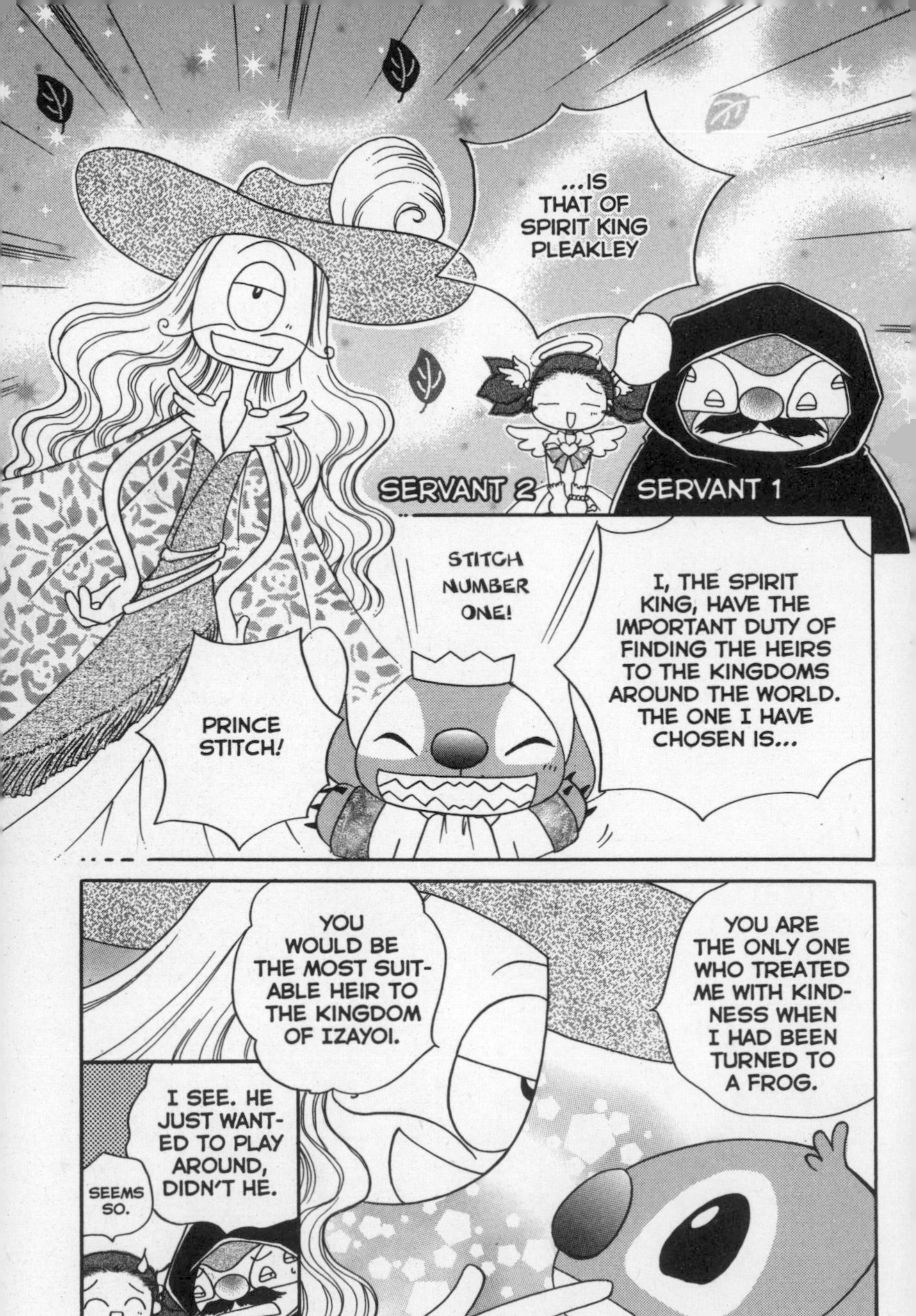
...IS THAT OF SPIRIT KING PLEAKLEY
SERVANT 1
SERVANT 2
I, THE SPIRIT KING, HAVE THE IMPORTANT DUTY OF FINDING THE HEIRS TO THE KINGDOMS AROUND THE WORLD. THE ONE I HAVE CHOSEN IS...
STITCH NUMBER ONE!
PRINCE STITCH!
YOU ARE THE ONLY ONE WHO TREATED ME WITH KINDNESS WHEN I HAD BEEN TURNED TO A FROG.
YOU WOULD BE THE MOST SUITABLE HEIR TO THE KINGDOM OF IZAYOI.
I SEE. HE JUST WANTED TO PLAY AROUND, DIDN'T HE.
SEEMS SO.

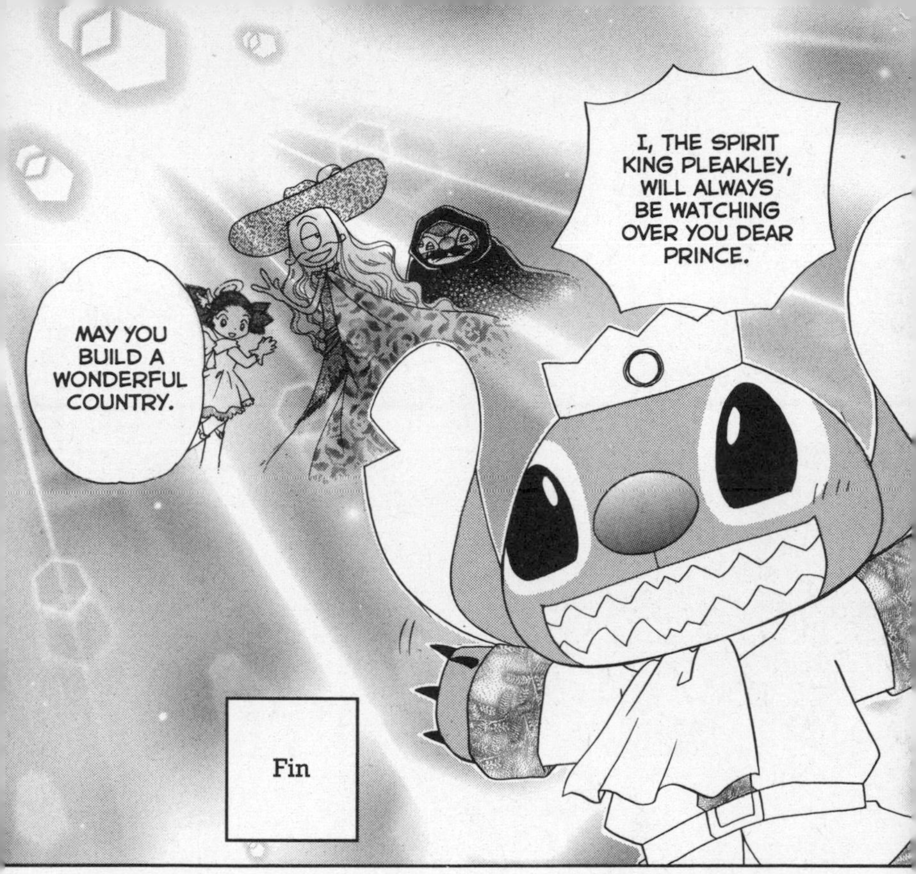
I, THE SPIRIT KING PLEAKLEY, WILL ALWAYS BE WATCHING OVER YOU DEAR PRINCE.
MAY YOU BUILD A WONDERFUL COUNTRY.
Fin

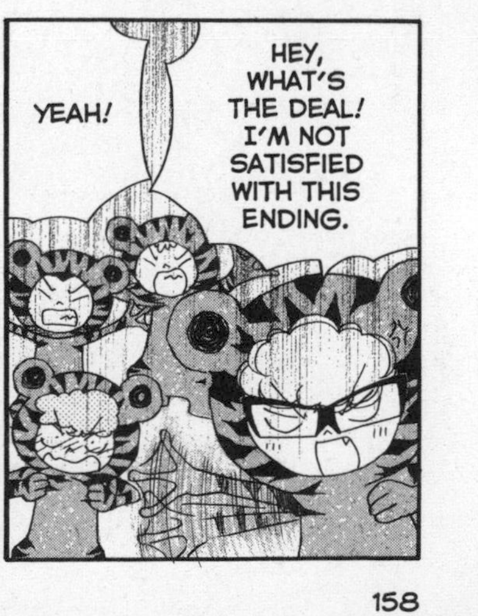
HEY, WHAT'S THE DEAL! I'M NOT SATISFIED WITH THIS ENDING.
YEAH!

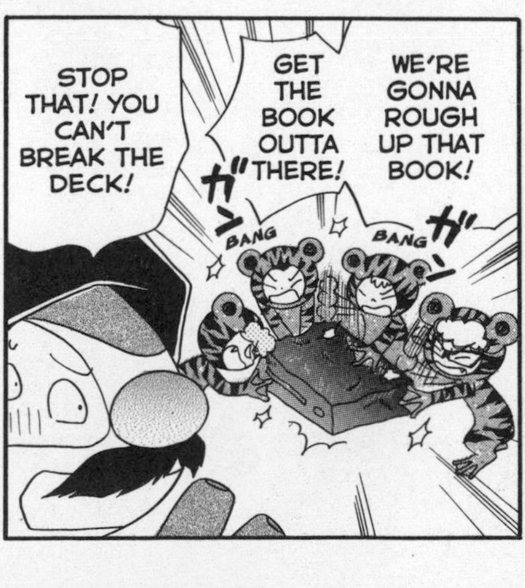
WE'RE GONNA ROUGH UP THAT BOOK!
GET THE BOOK OUTTA THERE!
ガン
BANG
ガン
BANG
STOP THAT! YOU CAN'T BREAK THE DECK!

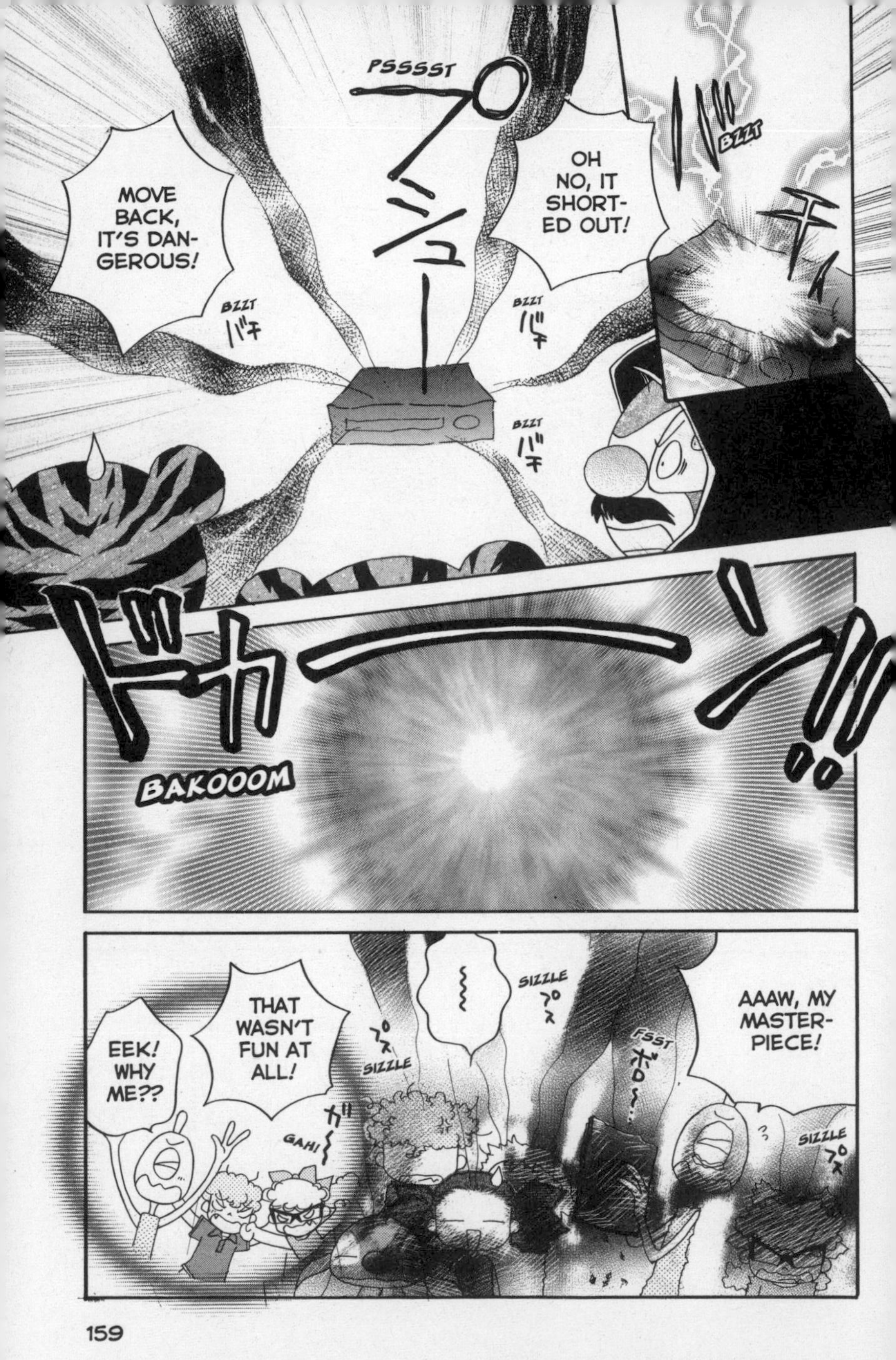
BZZT
PSSSST
プシュー
OH NO, IT SHORTED OUT!
MOVE BACK, IT'S DANGEROUS!
BZZT
バチ
BZZT
バチ
BZZT
バチ
ドカーーン!!
BAKOOOM
AAAW, MY MASTERPIECE!
SIZZLE
SIZZLE
FSST
...
SIZZLE
THAT WASN'T FUN AT ALL!
EEK! WHY ME??
GAH!

MAKING A WISH WITH THE HAREHARE YOKAI!

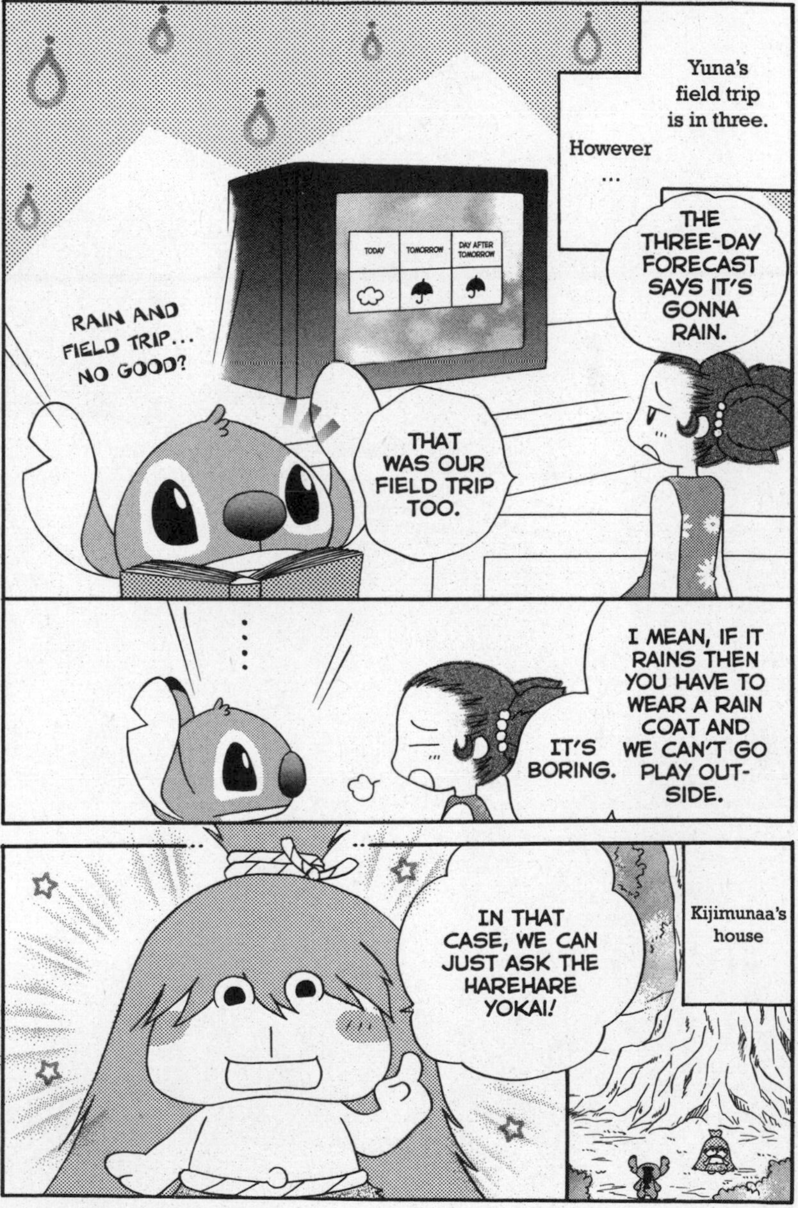
Yuna's field trip is in three.
However ...
THE THREE-DAY FORECAST SAYS IT'S GONNA RAIN.
TODAY
TOMORROW
DAY AFTER TOMORROW
THAT WAS OUR FIELD TRIP TOO.
RAIN AND FIELD TRIP... NO GOOD?
I MEAN, IF IT RAINS THEN YOU HAVE TO WEAR A RAIN COAT AND WE CAN'T GO PLAY OUT-SIDE.
IT'S BORING.
....
Kijimunaa's house
IN THAT CASE, WE CAN JUST ASK THE HAREHARE YOKAI!
...
...

READ THIS WAY

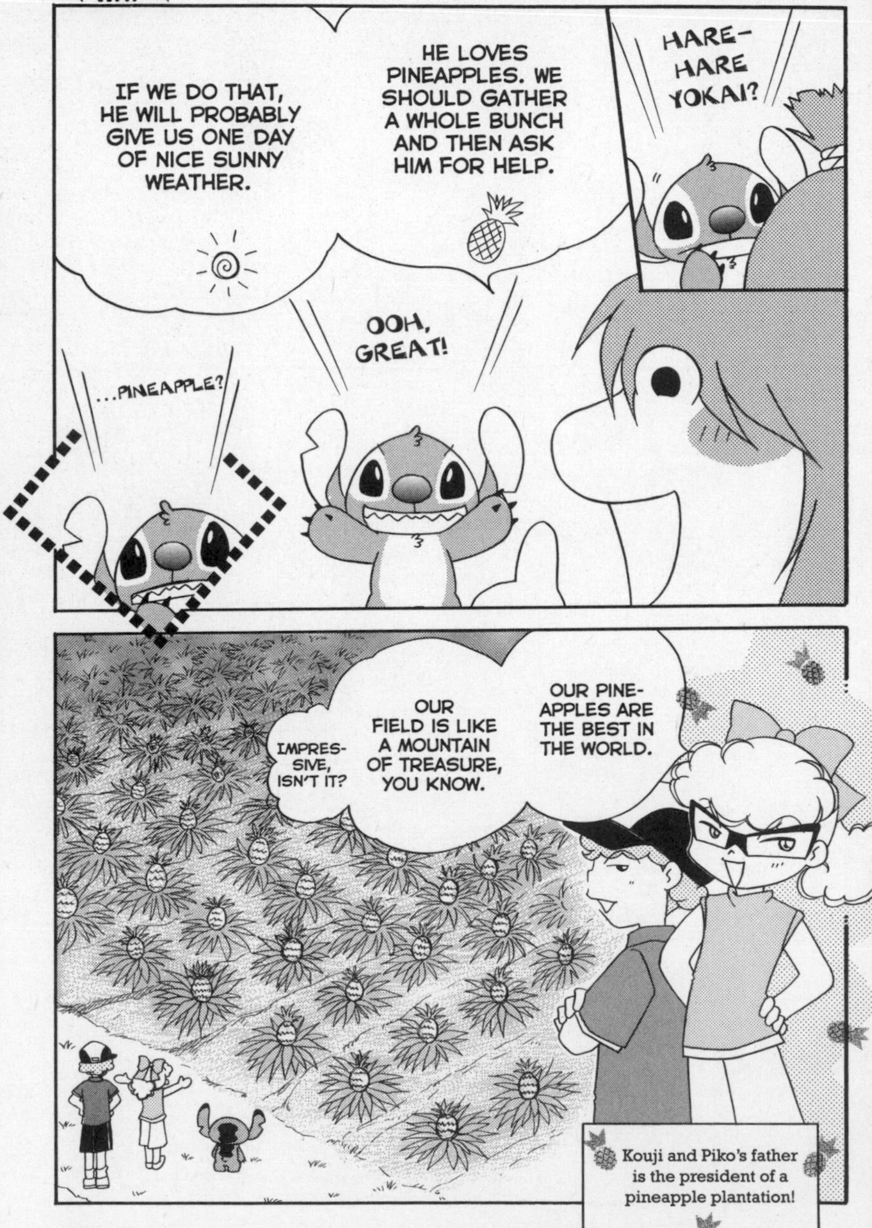
HARE-HARE YOKAI?
HE LOVES PINEAPPLES. WE SHOULD GATHER A WHOLE BUNCH AND THEN ASK HIM FOR HELP.
IF WE DO THAT, HE WILL PROBABLY GIVE US ONE DAY OF NICE SUNNY WEATHER.
OOH, GREAT!
...PINEAPPLE?
OUR PINE-APPLES ARE THE BEST IN THE WORLD.
OUR FIELD IS LIKE A MOUNTAIN OF TREASURE, YOU KNOW.
IMPRES-SIVE, ISN'T IT?
Kouji and Piko's father is the president of a pineapple plantation!

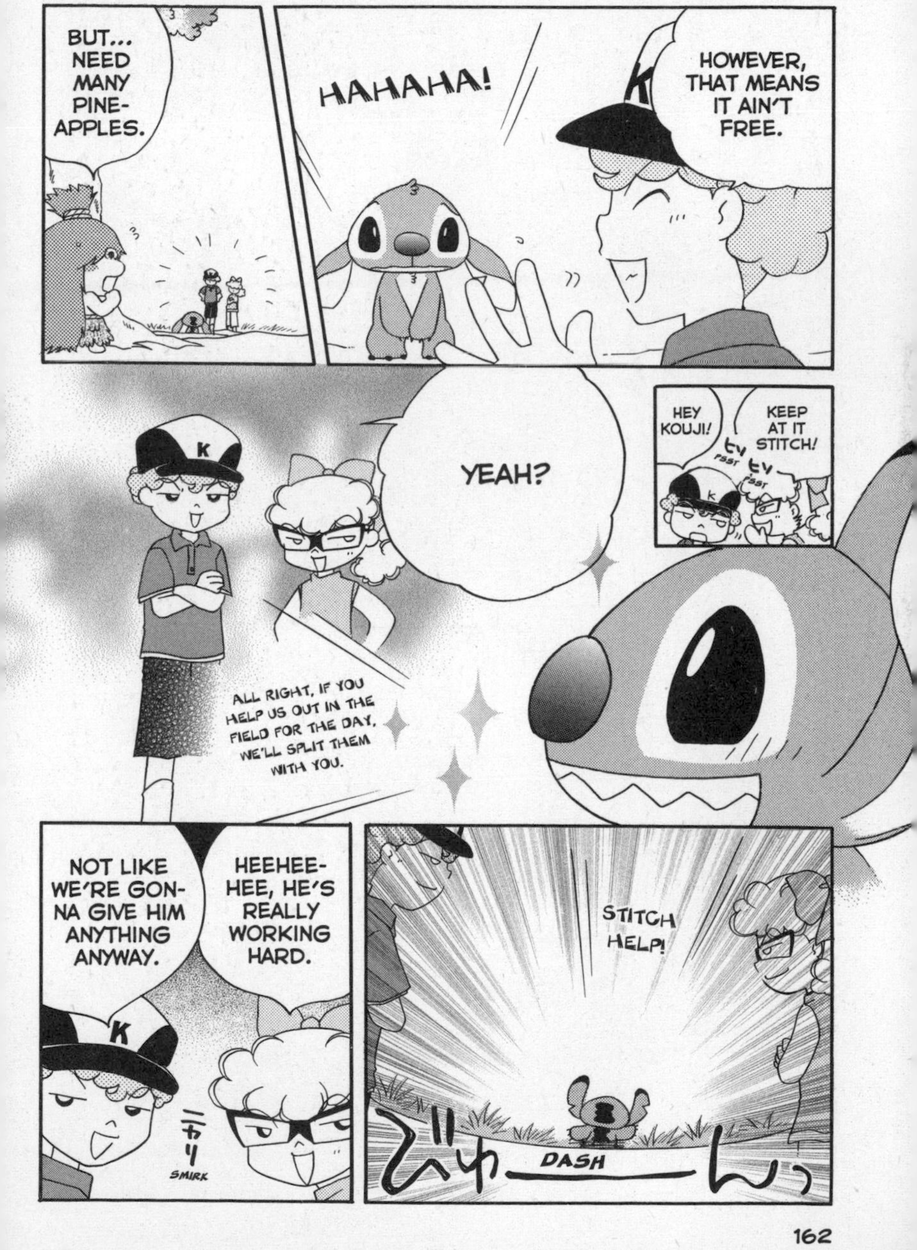
HOWEVER, THAT MEANS IT AIN'T FREE.
HAHAHA!
BUT... NEED MANY PINE-APPLES.
KEEP AT IT STITCH!
HEY KOUJI!
PSST
PSST
YEAH?
ALL RIGHT, IF YOU HELP US OUT IN THE FIELD FOR THE DAY, WE'LL SPLIT THEM WITH YOU.
STITCH HELP!
DASH
HEEHEE-HEE, HE'S REALLY WORKING HARD.
NOT LIKE WE'RE GON-NA GIVE HIM ANYTHING ANYWAY.
ニヤリ
SMIRK

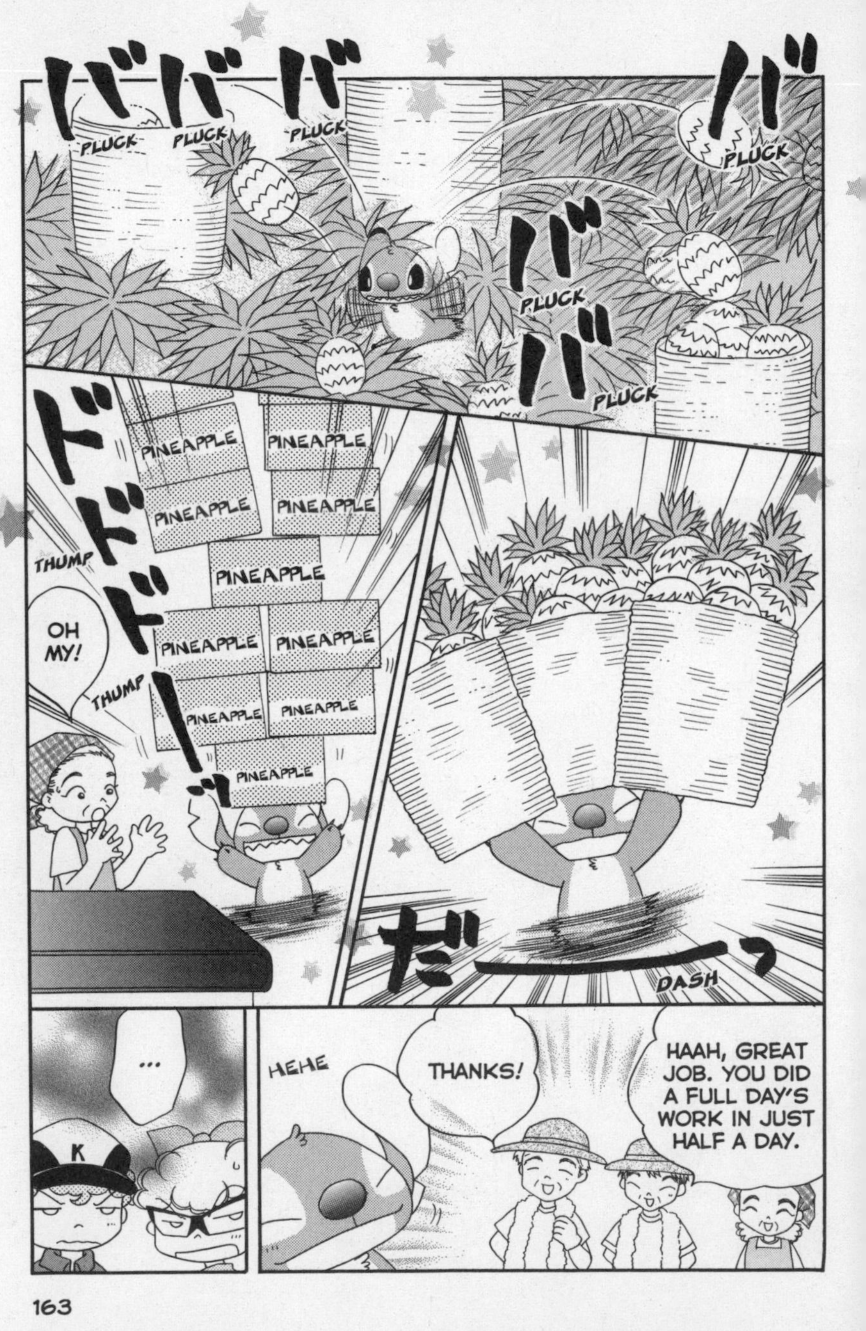
バ
PLUCK
バババ
PLUCK
PLUCK
PLUCK
バ
PLUCK
バ
PLUCK
だーっ
DASH
ドドド！
THUMP
THUMP
OH MY!
HAAH, GREAT JOB. YOU DID A FULL DAY'S WORK IN JUST HALF A DAY.
THANKS!
HEHE
...

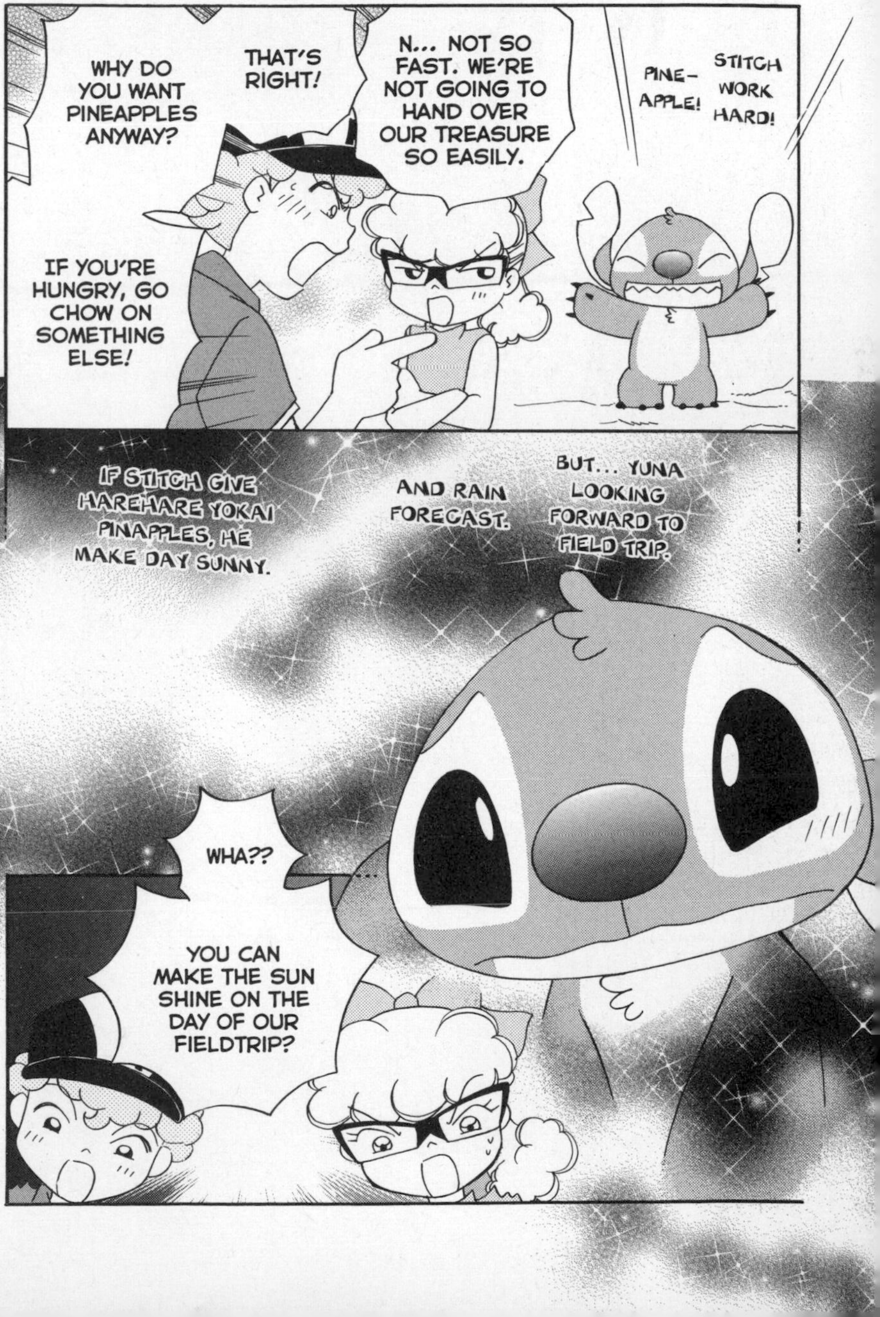
STITCH WORK HARD!
PINE-APPLE!
N... NOT SO FAST. WE'RE NOT GOING TO HAND OVER OUR TREASURE SO EASILY.
THAT'S RIGHT!
WHY DO YOU WANT PINEAPPLES ANYWAY?
IF YOU'RE HUNGRY, GO CHOW ON SOMETHING ELSE!
BUT... YUNA LOOKING FORWARD TO FIELD TRIP.
AND RAIN FORECAST.
IF STITCH GIVE HAREHARE YOKAI PINAPPLES, HE MAKE DAY SUNNY.
WHA??
YOU CAN MAKE THE SUN SHINE ON THE DAY OF OUR FIELDTRIP?

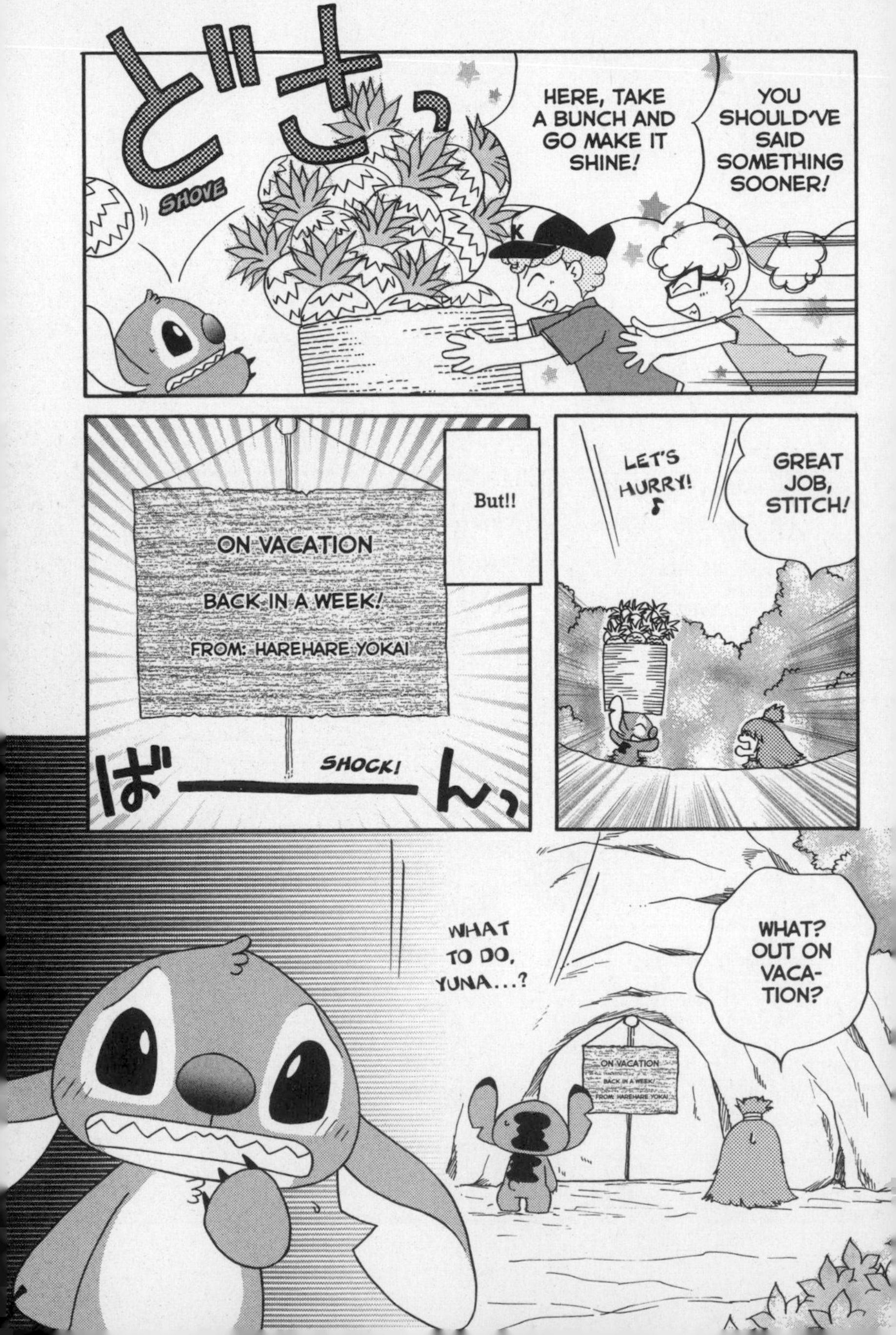
YOU SHOULD'VE SAID SOMETHING SOONER!
HERE, TAKE A BUNCH AND GO MAKE IT SHINE!
どさっ
SHOVE
GREAT JOB, STITCH!
LET'S HURRY! ♪
But!!
ON VACATION
BACK IN A WEEK!
FROM: HAREHARE YOKAI
ばーーーんっ
SHOCK!
WHAT? OUT ON VACA-TION?
WHAT TO DO, YUNA...?

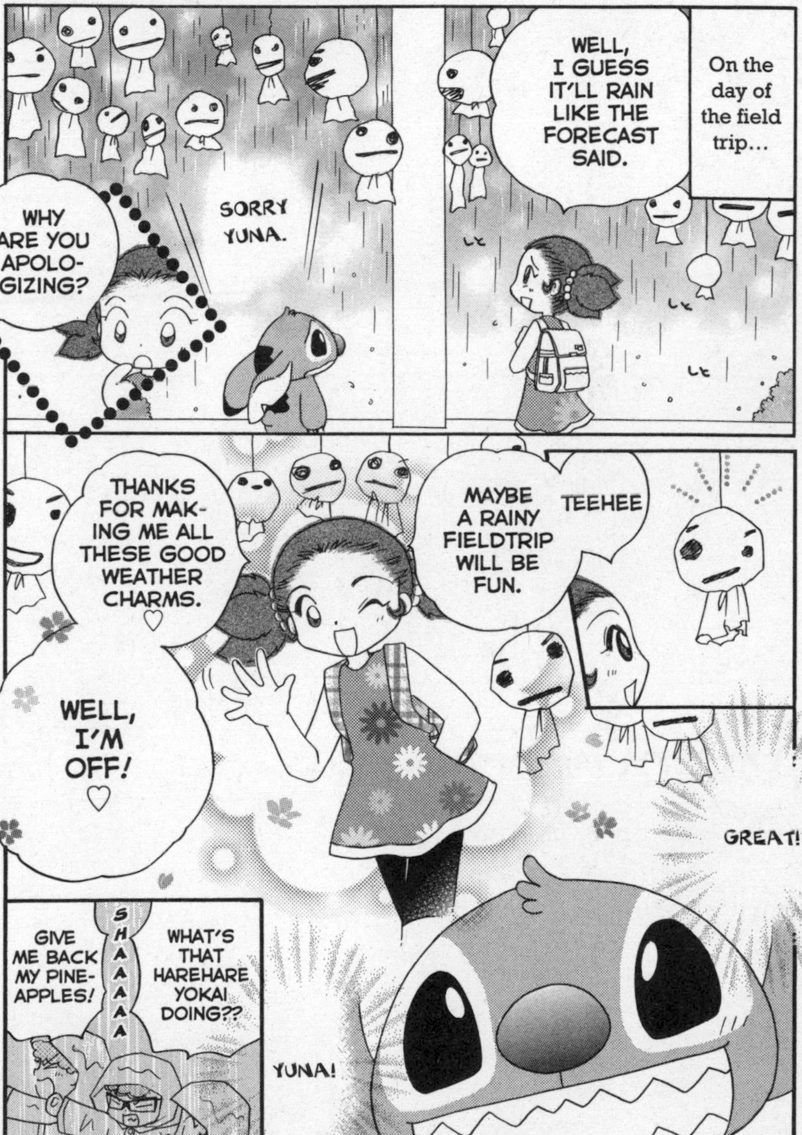
On the day of the field trip…
WELL, I GUESS IT'LL RAIN LIKE THE FORECAST SAID.
SORRY YUNA.
WHY ARE YOU APOLO-GIZING?
MAYBE A RAINY FIELDTRIP WILL BE FUN.
TEEHEE
THANKS FOR MAK-ING ME ALL THESE GOOD WEATHER CHARMS. ♡
WELL, I'M OFF! ♡
GREAT!
YUNA!
WHAT'S THAT HAREHARE YOKAI DOING??
SHAAAAAA
GIVE ME BACK MY PINE-APPLES!

ORIHIME ANGEL ☆

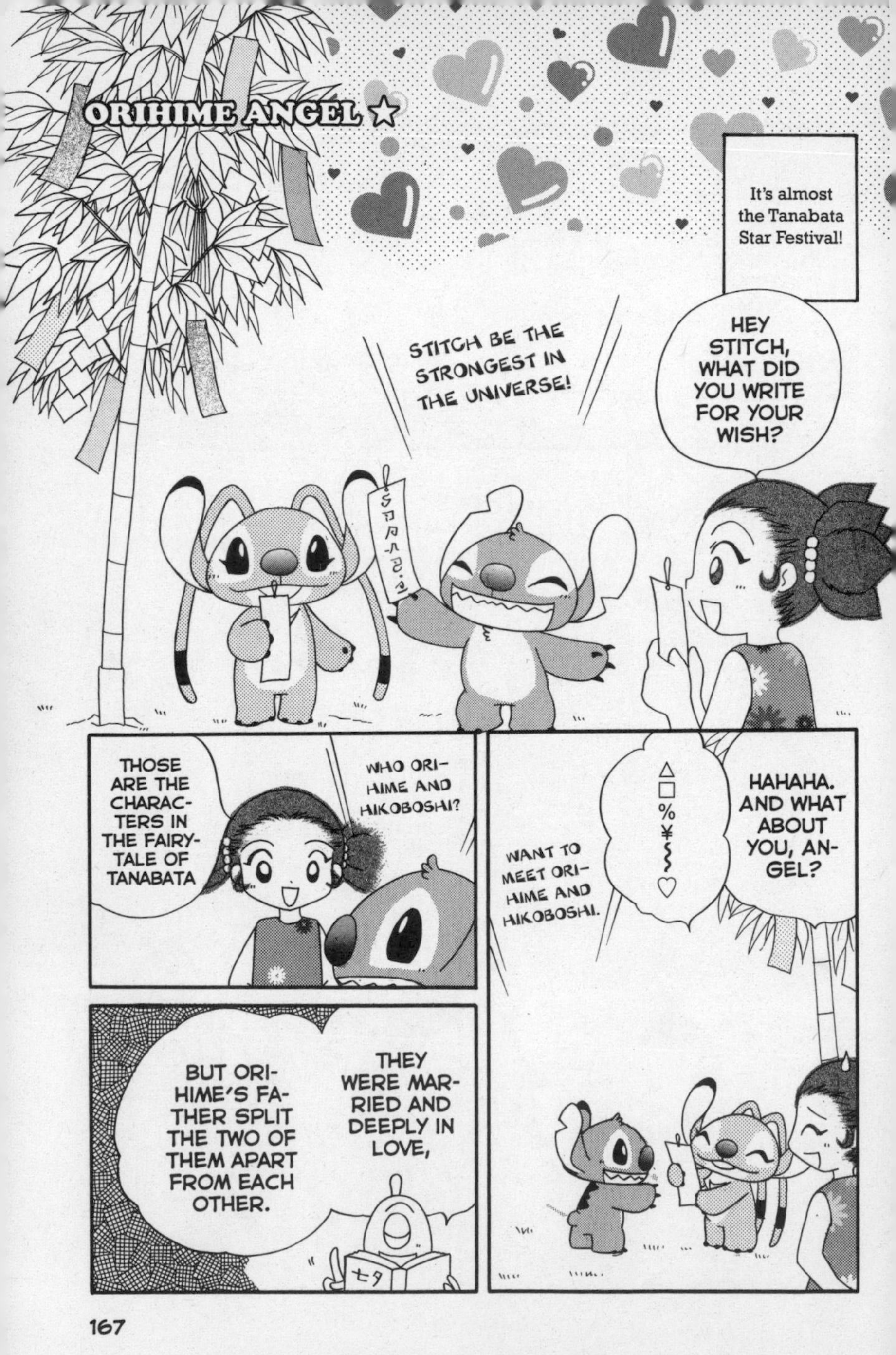

It's almost the Tanabata Star Festival!
HEY STITCH, WHAT DID YOU WRITE FOR YOUR WISH?
STITCH BE THE STRONGEST IN THE UNIVERSE!
HAHAHA. AND WHAT ABOUT YOU, ANGEL?
△□%¥~♡
WANT TO MEET ORI-HIME AND HIKOBOSHI.
WHO ORI-HIME AND HIKOBOSHI?
THOSE ARE THE CHARAC-TERS IN THE FAIRY-TALE OF TANABATA
THEY WERE MAR-RIED AND DEEPLY IN LOVE,
BUT ORI-HIME'S FA-THER SPLIT THE TWO OF THEM APART FROM EACH OTHER.

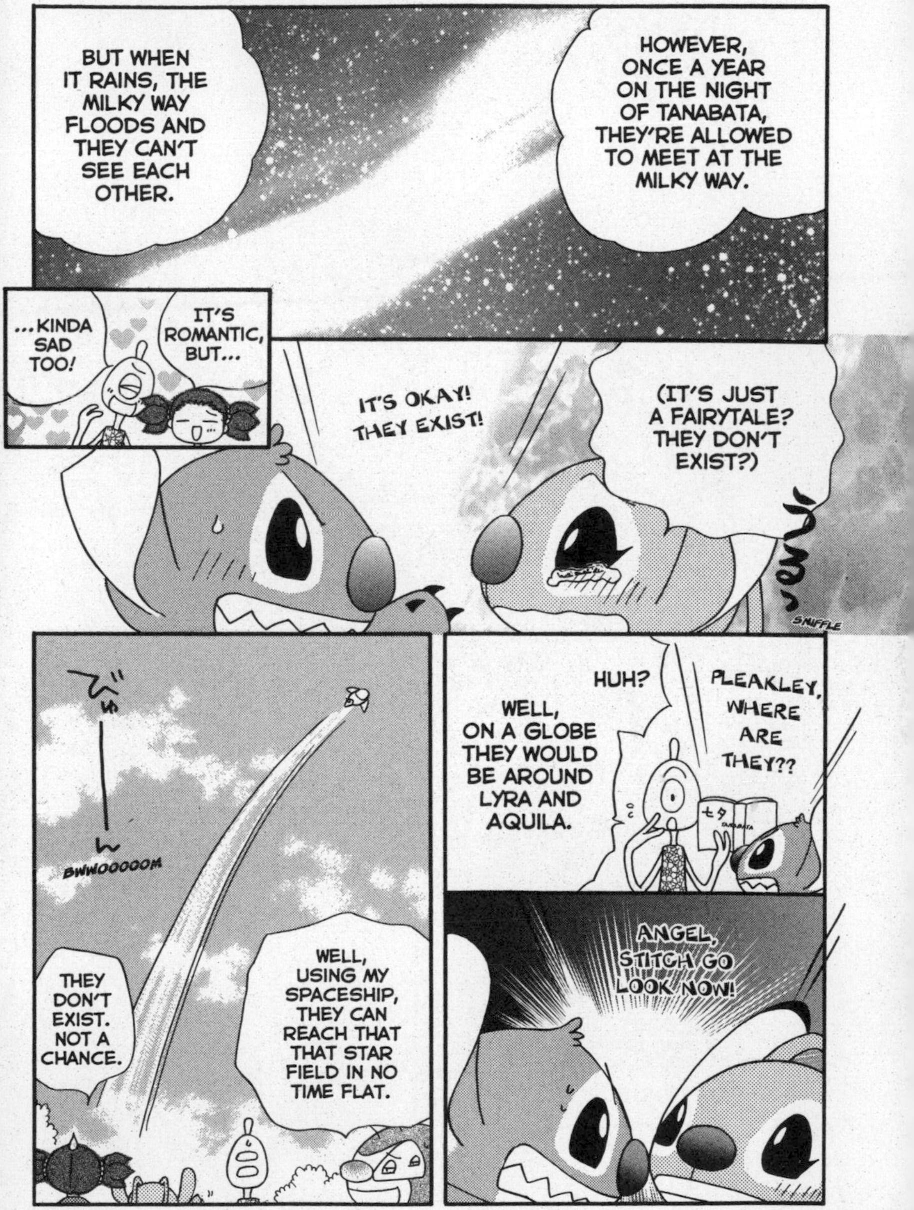
HOWEVER, ONCE A YEAR ON THE NIGHT OF TANABATA, THEY'RE ALLOWED TO MEET AT THE MILKY WAY.
BUT WHEN IT RAINS, THE MILKY WAY FLOODS AND THEY CAN'T SEE EACH OTHER.
IT'S ROMANTIC, BUT...
...KINDA SAD TOO!
(IT'S JUST A FAIRYTALE? THEY DON'T EXIST?)
SNIFFLE
IT'S OKAY! THEY EXIST!
PLEAKLEY, WHERE ARE THEY??
HUH?
WELL, ON A GLOBE THEY WOULD BE AROUND LYRA AND AQUILA.
ANGEL, STITCH GO LOOK NOW!
BWWOOOOOM
WELL, USING MY SPACESHIP, THEY CAN REACH THAT THAT STAR FIELD IN NO TIME FLAT.
THEY DON'T EXIST. NOT A CHANCE.

READ THIS WAY

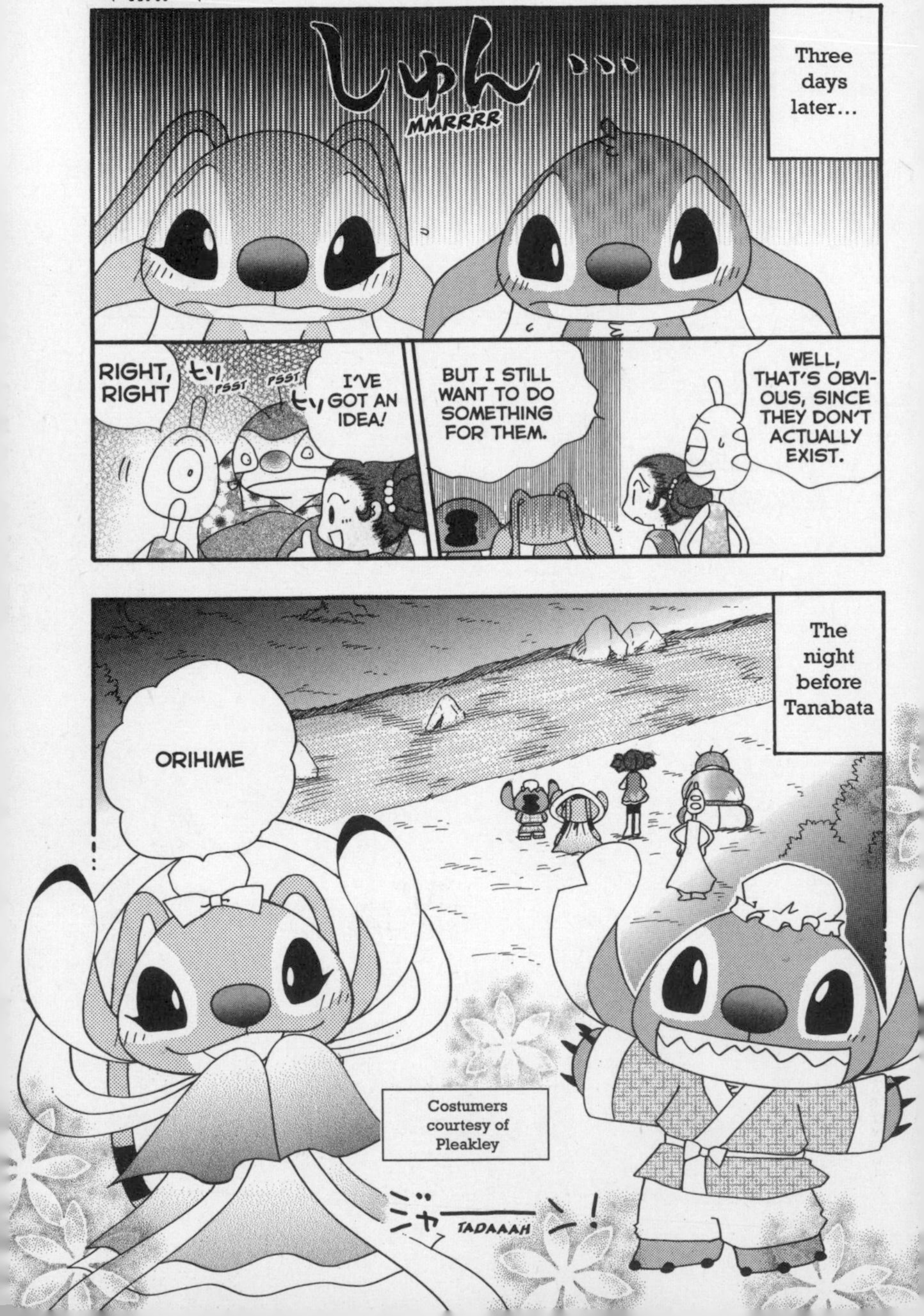
Three days later…
しゅん…
MMRRRR
WELL, THAT'S OBVIOUS, SINCE THEY DON'T ACTUALLY EXIST.
BUT I STILL WANT TO DO SOMETHING FOR THEM.
I'VE GOT AN IDEA!
ヒソ
PSST
PSST
ヒソ
RIGHT, RIGHT
The night before Tanabata
ORIHIME
Costumers courtesy of Pleakley
ジャーン!
TADAAAH

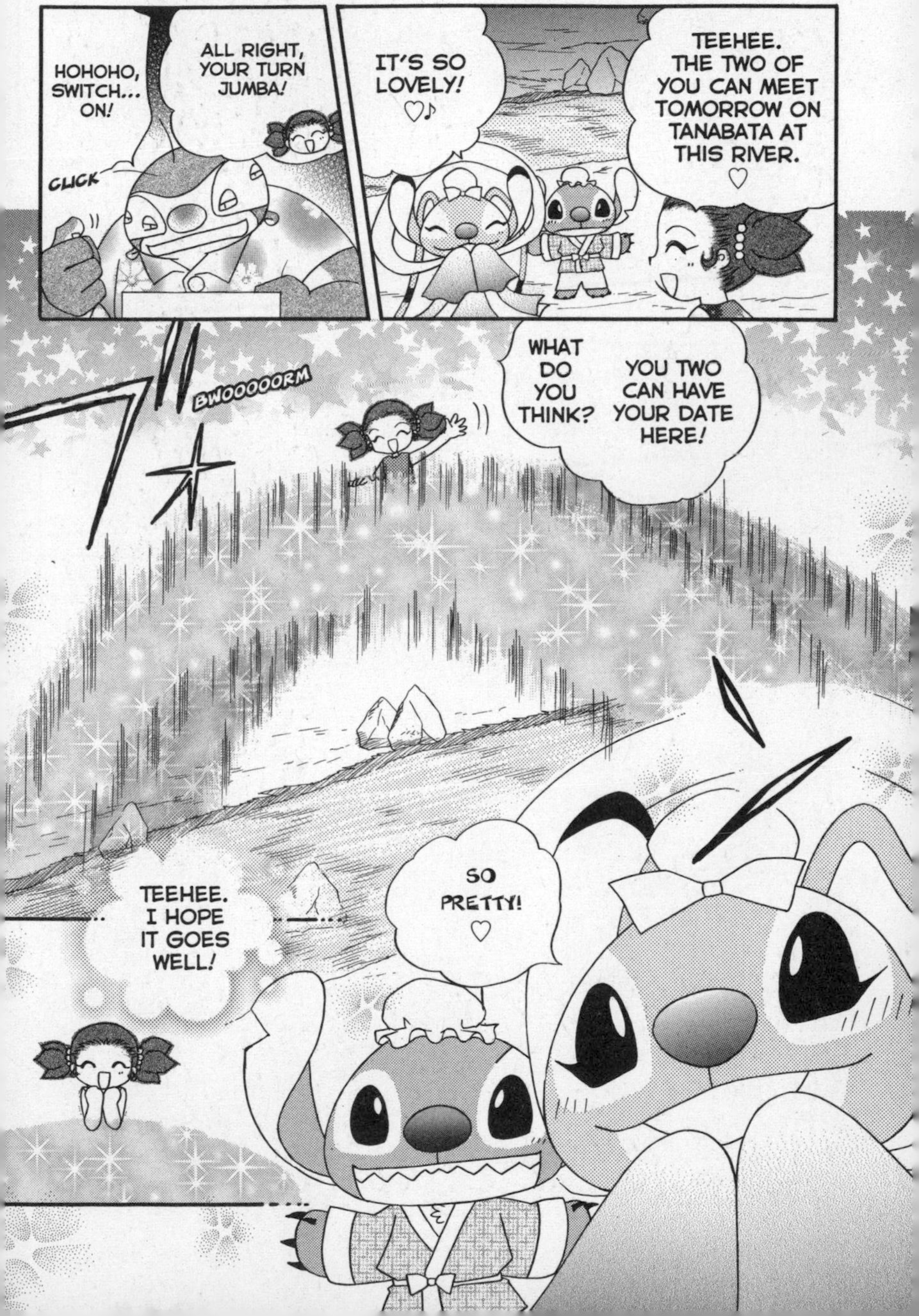
TEEHEE. THE TWO OF YOU CAN MEET TOMORROW ON TANABATA AT THIS RIVER. ♡
IT'S SO LOVELY! ♡♪
ALL RIGHT, YOUR TURN JUMBA!
HOHOHO, SWITCH... ON!
CLICK
BWOOOOORM
YOU TWO CAN HAVE YOUR DATE HERE!
WHAT DO YOU THINK?
SO PRETTY! ♡
TEEHEE. I HOPE IT GOES WELL!

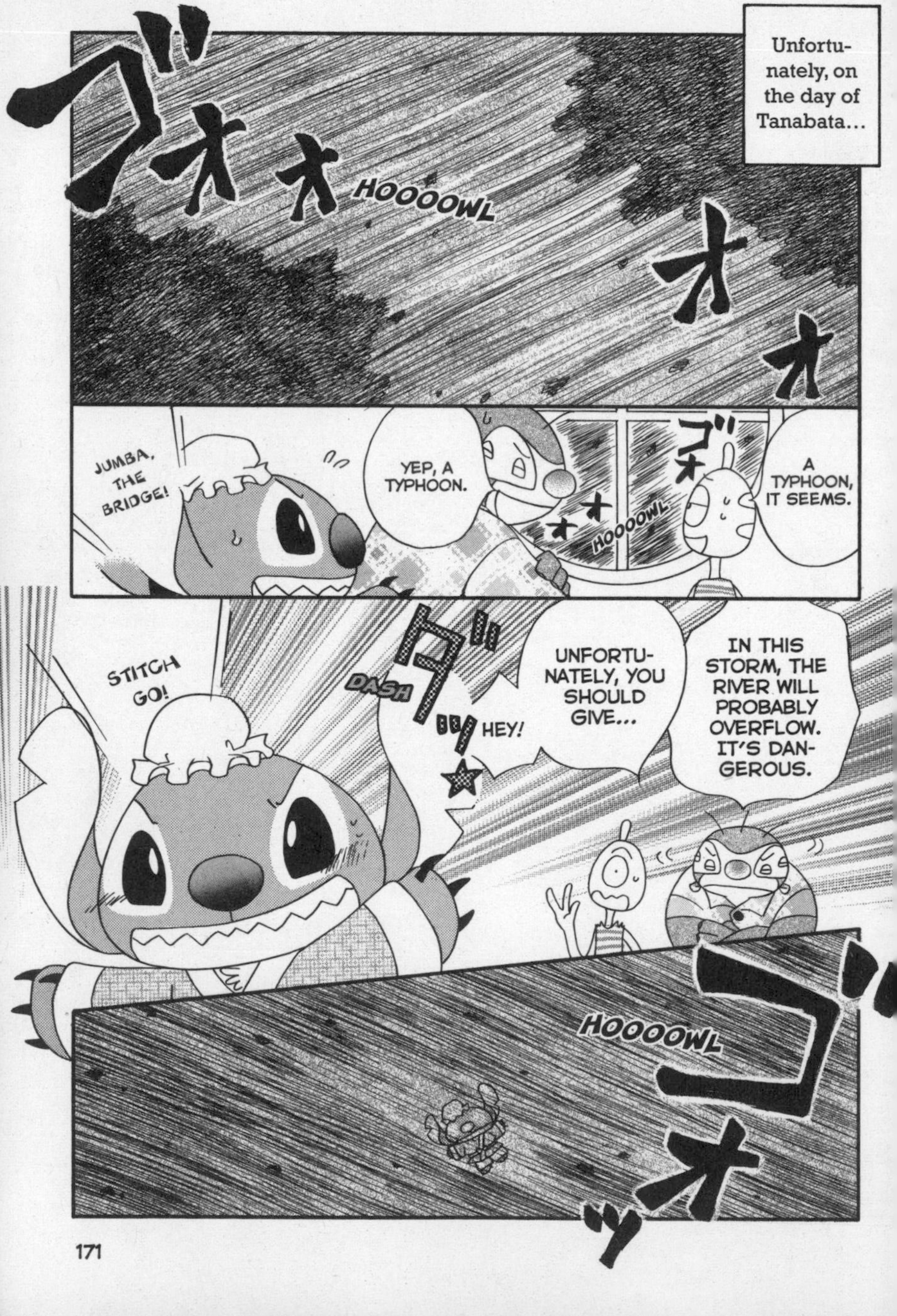
Unfortunately, on the day of Tanabata…
HOOOOWL
A TYPHOON, IT SEEMS.
HOOOOWL
YEP, A TYPHOON.
JUMBA, THE BRIDGE!
IN THIS STORM, THE RIVER WILL PROBABLY OVERFLOW. IT'S DANGEROUS.
UNFORTUNATELY, YOU SHOULD GIVE…
HEY!
DASH
STITCH GO!
HOOOOWL

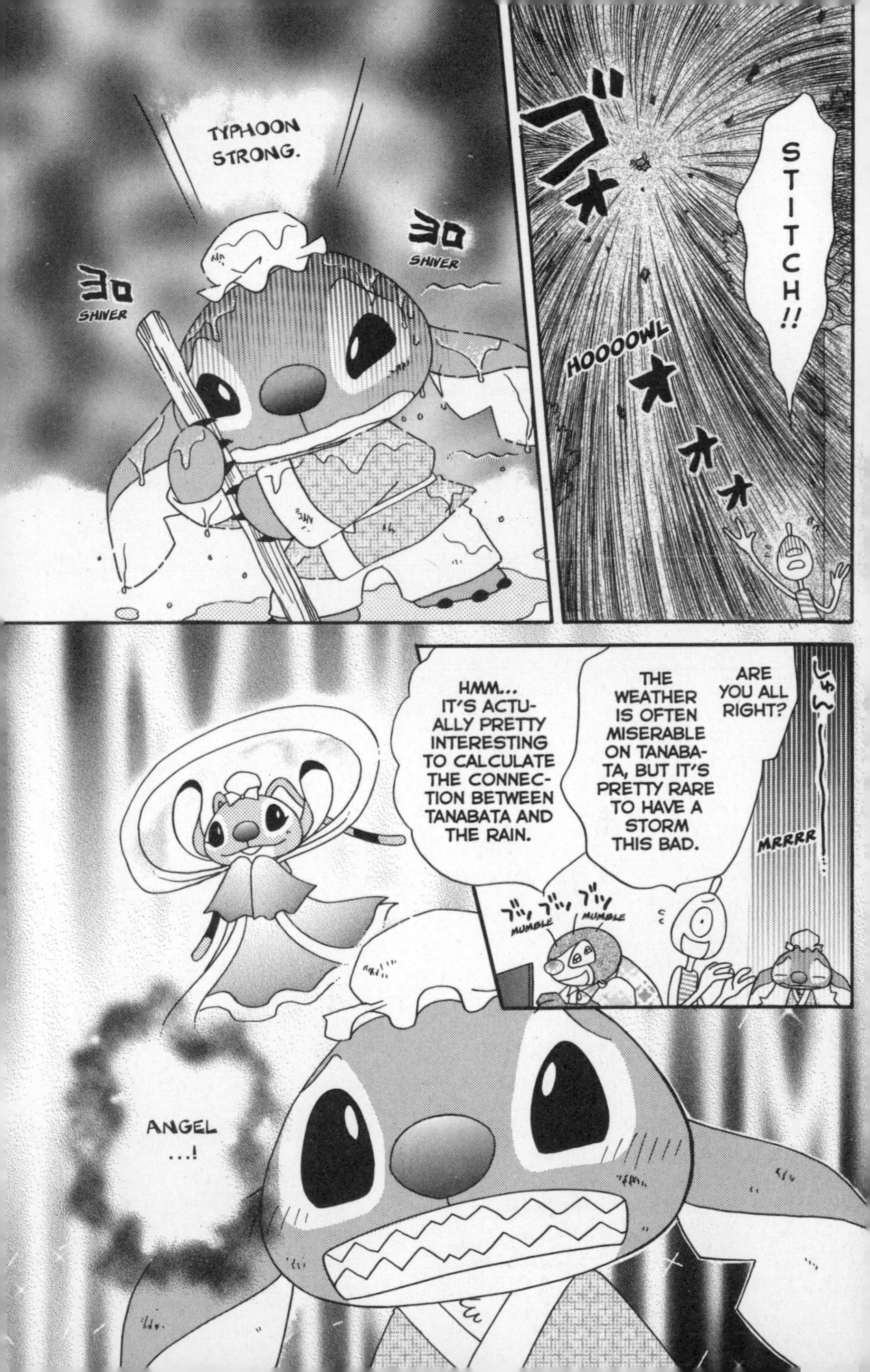
STITCH!!
HOOOOWL
TYPHOON STRONG.
SHIVER
SHIVER
MRRRR
ARE YOU ALL RIGHT?
THE WEATHER IS OFTEN MISERABLE ON TANABATA, BUT IT'S PRETTY RARE TO HAVE A STORM THIS BAD.
HMM... IT'S ACTUALLY PRETTY INTERESTING TO CALCULATE THE CONNECTION BETWEEN TANABATA AND THE RAIN.
MUMBLE
MUMBLE
ANGEL ...!

READ THIS WAY

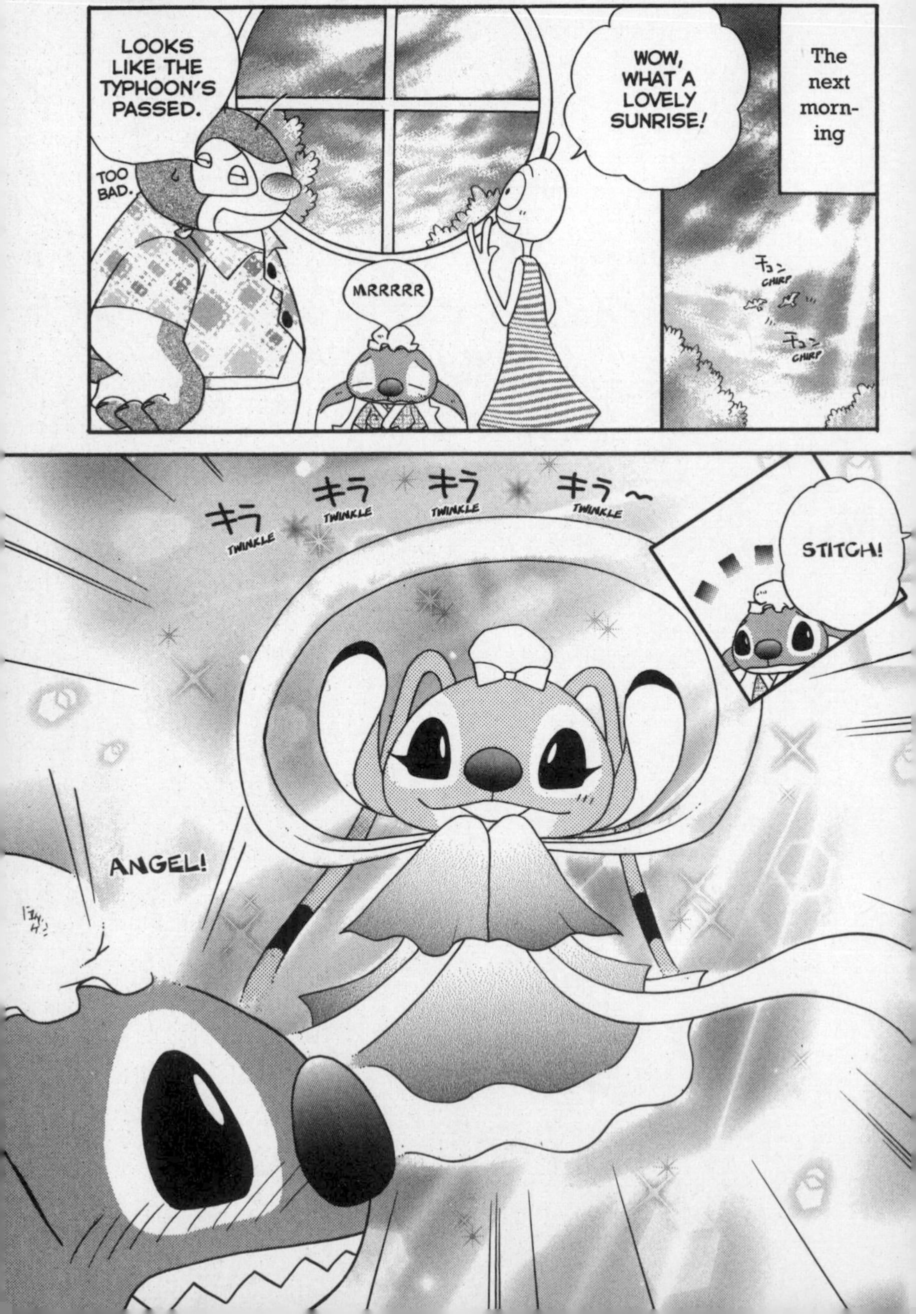
The next morn-ing
チュン CHIRP
チュン CHIRP
WOW, WHAT A LOVELY SUNRISE!
MRRRRR
LOOKS LIKE THE TYPHOON'S PASSED.
TOO BAD.
STITCH!
キラ～ TWINKLE
キラ TWINKLE
キラ TWINKLE
キラ TWINKLE
ANGEL!

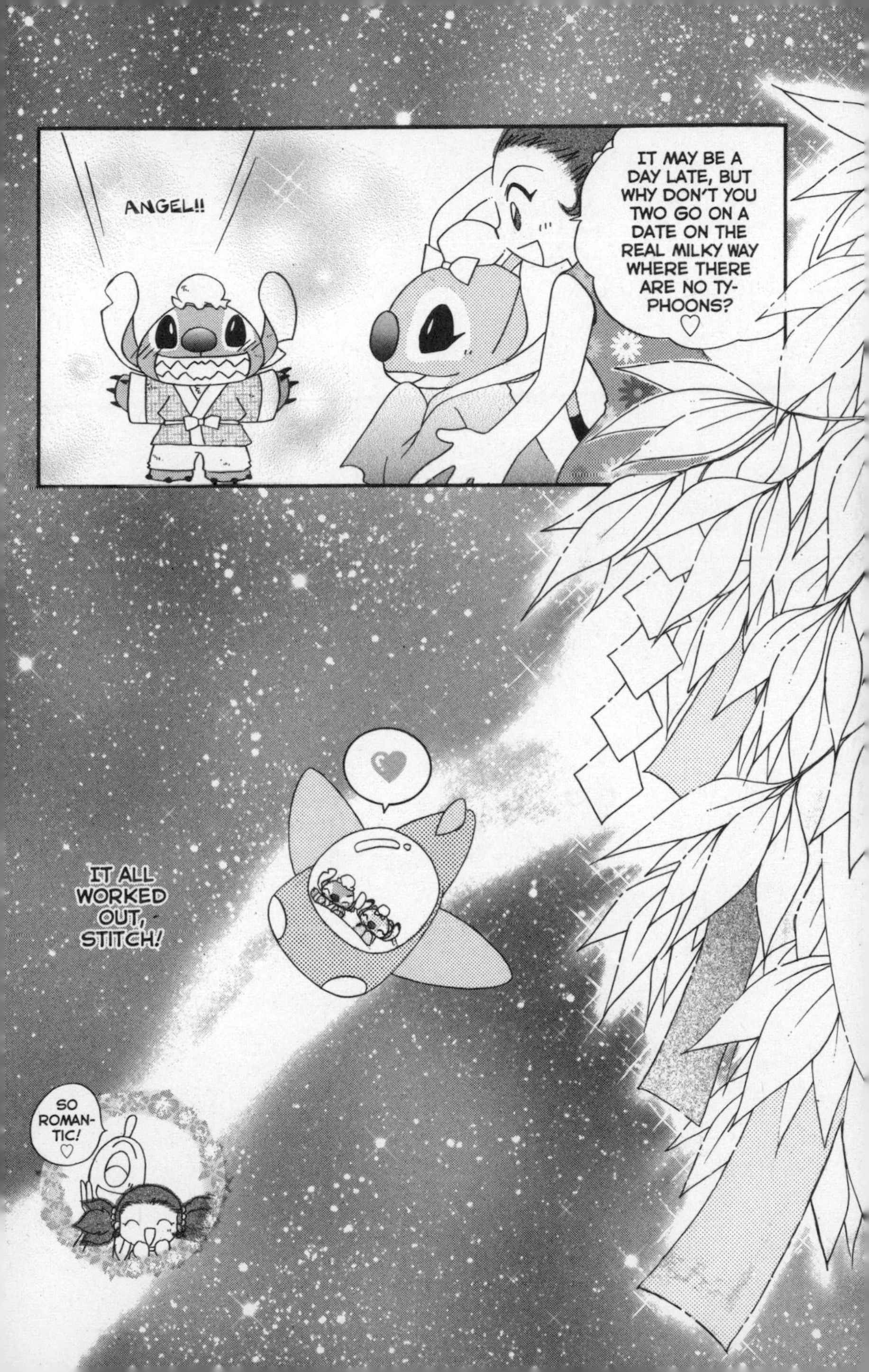
IT MAY BE A DAY LATE, BUT WHY DON'T YOU TWO GO ON A DATE ON THE REAL MILKY WAY WHERE THERE ARE NO TY-PHOONS? ♡
ANGEL!!
IT ALL WORKED OUT, STITCH!
SO ROMAN-TIC! ♡

Disney Stitch! Volume 2
Story and Art by: Yumi Tsukirino

Publishing Assistant - Janae Young
Marketing Assistant - Kae Winters
Technology and Digital Media Assistant - Phillip Hong
Retouching and Lettering - Vibrraant Publishing Studio
Translator - Jason Muell
Graphic Designer - Al-insan Lashley
Editor - Julie Taylor
Editor-in-Chief & Publisher - Stu Levy

A 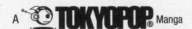 Manga

TOKYOPOP and ⊙ are trademarks or registered trademarks of TOKYOPOP Inc.

TOKYOPOP inc.
5200 W Century Blvd
Suite 705
Los Angeles, CA 90045 USA

E-mail: info@TOKYOPOP.com
Come visit us online at www.TOKYOPOP.com

f www.facebook.com/TOKYOPOP
y www.twitter.com/TOKYOPOP
▶ www.youtube.com/TOKYOPOPTV
p www.pinterest.com/TOKYOPOP
▣ www.instagram.com/TOKYOPOP
t. TOKYOPOP.tumblr.com

ISBN: 978-1-4278-5675-3
First TOKYOPOP printing: December 2016
10 9 8 7 6 5 4 3 2 1
Printed in the USA

STOP!

**This is the last page of the book!
You don't want to spoil the fun
and start with the end, do you?**

In Japan, *manga* is created in accordance with the native
language, which reads right-to-left when vertical. So, in
order to stay true to the original, pretend you're in Japan
-- just flip this book over and you're good to go!

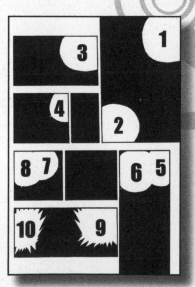

Here's how:

If you're new to *manga*, don't
worry, it's easy! Just start at
the top right panel and read
down and to the left, like in
the picture here. Have fun and
enjoy authentic *manga* from
TOKYOPOP®!!